Norah was an experienced Nurse Tutor, being responsible for Student Nurses within three major hospitals in Northern Ireland. She has just recently turned her skills to writing. This novel is her first and she is currently writing her second. She is married with two children and six grandchildren.

I would like to dedicate this book to my dear brother, Derek. A true historian, this book would never have been written without his devotion to me and his knowledge of events in Northern Ireland in the last sixty years.

Norah Humphreys

NO GREATER LOVE

AUSTIN MACAULEY
PUBLISHERS LTD.

A CIP catalogue record for this title is available from the British Library.

ISBN 978 184963 545 5

www.austinmacauley.com

First Published (2014)
Austin Macauley Publishers Ltd.
25 Canada Square
Canary Wharf
London
E14 5LB

Printed and bound in Great Britain

Acknowledgments

I wish to thank my granddaughter, Sasha for all her hard work in typing this manuscript. A big thank you to my daughter Jayne for having such patience with me regarding my lack of computer skills. A special thank you to my son Malcolm and his wife Susan for their enthusiasm and encouragement while reading my work.

Chapter 1

1917

Rob wakened suddenly in the darkened room. Some noise had disturbed him; he was sure of it. Not a loud noise, little more than a low rustling whisper, but enough to alarm him. If he kept his eyes closed he would not have to face the dreaded shadows in the bedroom. He had never been frightened of the dark; he had after all, his sisters for company and comfort in the bedroom. Just recently, however, it had started to hold awful terrors for him. It was Dorrie, slinking out of their bedroom during the night, who had created this fear in him. She probably meant well, and was trying not to disturb them, but it just seemed to give him this awful feeling of panic.

The calm, undisturbed nights he had shared with his sisters, in the security of their bedroom, had gone, but when he thought about it, he realised how much everything had changed. Since his mum had taken sick, it was all so different. No one had any time for him, his father didn't seem to even notice him, and his sisters never spoke to him, much less play with him. Everyone was acting as if he was a two-year-old and him nine years old last November. Dorrie, who had always spent hours with him in the evenings, scarcely seemed to notice he was there. Well, at least Maggie and Eve appeared to be their usual carefree selves and even though they mostly ignored him, he had started to tag along with them. But he really had to talk to Dorrie, if she would hurry and come back to bed soon, he would tell her he was going in to see Mum first thing in the morning.

His eyes were getting accustomed to the dark, and he could just make out the outline of the tall dresser which held all their clothes. He could see the double bed in the corner where Maggie and Eve slept. Dorrie's small bed lay alongside his own and now he realised her coverlet was smooth and unruffled. She had never been to bed. Where was she? She certainly had been in the room; she must have come in to check on them all. What was wrong? He began to shiver uncontrollably, and he could feel beads of sweat forming on his forehead and chest. Trying to ease his trembling, he put his arms round his body and held himself tightly. Forcing himself to sit up and peering through the darkness, he could see Maggie and Eve sleeping quietly and peacefully. Not wakeful and worried like he was. The relaxed way they were lying, curled up side by side, Eve's arm flung across Maggie's body, reassured him. Holding himself still, and keeping as quiet as he could, he crept from his bed, crossed the room and climbed in beside Maggie. He knew if he disturbed her, she would be very cross and make him go back to his own bed. But she only stirred a little, then rolled over and continued to breathe easily and deeply.

He lay back, straining his ears for any movement from his parents' bedroom across the landing, but he could only hear the steady drip of water from the roof into the rain barrel at the rear of the house. It was a comforting sound and the warmth radiating from Maggie's body seemed to envelop him. Gradually he stopped trembling and his body became heavy with sleep.

"Rob, you'd need to get up this minute. You're going to be late for school. I'm not calling you again ... I've called you twice already."

Maggie's voice penetrated his dream. He thought he was in a railway carriage at the station, but his father was telling him to get off. He and his father couldn't go to Newry today, they didn't have any tickets.

He struggled awake, his dream disintegrating, and saw his sister at the side of the bed, dressed and ready for school.

"Oh, right, I never heard you ... I'm coming now." He swung his legs out of bed and reached for his clothes.

"Will I have time for breakfast?"

He was expecting a ticking off from Maggie for being in her bed, but strangely, she never mentioned it.

"You'll need to hurry, you've only got about five minutes." She did sound really annoyed with him.

"Do you think I would be able to see Mum before I go to school?"

"You'd need to talk to Dad. He's in the kitchen ... but I wouldn't." Maggie sounded definite about it. "You know what the doctor said about spreading the infection round the family."

It was four days since he had seen or spoken to Mum, and he missed her so much. He missed her words of encouragement over his schoolwork, and although he had always objected to her fussing over his appearance, he found he missed all the attention she gave to his hair and clothes. She always made sure he and the girls were spotless before leaving for school. Above all, he missed her warm hugs and cuddles and at the end of the school day, seeing her comforting, familiar figure waiting for him outside the school gates.

He was quite determined to see her this morning. He knew the doctor had said they must be patient, but surely speaking to her, even from the bedroom door could do no harm. She would want to see him as much as he wanted to see her and to hear all about school. Besides, if Dorrie was allowed into the bedroom at any time, why shouldn't he? Just thinking about it spurred him on and he raced down the stairs to the kitchen where a bright fire was burning in the range. His father sat at the table, his hands clasped round a steaming mug of tea, his shoulders hunched, and his dark brown hair unkempt round his head. His bright, blue eyes, which always seemed to twinkle in his face, now seemed shrivelled in their sockets. Somehow Rob's question about his mother died in his chest.

He sat down at the table, pulled out a chair and sat down. He reached for a porridge bowl – all the time watching his father, who seemed miles away.

"Dad..." Rob poured some gruel from a pot in the middle of the table and reached for the milk jug "Dad." ...His father looked up, and suddenly seemed to realise his son was sitting facing him. "Sorry, lad. Are you all ready then?"

"Yes. Dad..." Rob's voice held a note of desperation. "Aren't you going to work? ...You're not ready."

"Not just yet, son." He looked vaguely across at his son. "One of the other men is coming to take over the station for a little while. The doctor said he would call this morning, you see."

Rob wanted to ask him about his mother, but something in his father's face, a look of torment, caused real fear to grip him and he was unable to voice the words. The look of his father distressed him so much that he felt compelled to go to him, and putting his arms round him, kissed the rough skin on his cheek. "I'm off to school now, Dad. ...Are you alright?" His father held him fiercely for a moment, and then put him from him, patting his shoulder in an absentminded way.

"Everything will be fine, you mustn't worry your young head about anything." He gave a fierce sort of smile and led him out of the kitchen, his arm tightly gripping his shoulders.

"Dorrie's not going into the shop today, so I'll have company, son. Off you go with Maggie and Eve."

Eve and Maggie were waiting for him in the front hall and though secretly he just wanted to stay at home with Dorrie and Dad, he didn't say anything. He knew it would be pointless, he would never be allowed to miss school. Picking up his schoolbag he reluctantly joined his sisters on the short walk down the street, across the square to the building adjoining the local church. A building which served as their school during the week, their Sunday school on Sundays and the church hall for year round festivities.

Poyntzpass School coached twenty-five pupils, their ages ranging from five to fourteen years of age. They all lived within a four mile radius of the village and when they reached the age of fourteen the majority of them would go to work in the local mill in Banbridge and a few others might be lucky enough to obtain employment in the shops there. Some others would be glad to help out in the neighbouring farms. It was only the "well-to-do" who had any hope of going to university. Although none of the Hamptons had aspirations to go to any university they knew they were fortunate enough. They weren't rich but they had security. Their father had a steady job and he lived right beside his work and because he was stationmaster, they had a fine house supplied by the Great Northern Railway.

This morning a strong March wind was blowing, but the sun shone and helped give everywhere the first inkling that spring was in the air. Winter was almost gone and people hoped that all the ailments the severe weather had brought would soon pass. The worst epidemic had been the influenza which had swept Europe, and many people had lost their lives as a result of it. However, by the time it had reached Ireland it had lost much of its aggression and virulence and people seemed to recover reasonably quickly from it. Even so, the attendance level at school had fallen during the past week, with several of the pupils being quite poorly.

Rob knew his first subject this morning would be English, probably essay writing, which he didn't mind. Then they would have arithmetic later, and that was his favourite subject of all. He knew he outshone everyone in the class and could do the most complicated subtractions in his head faster than anyone. His exercise book showed page after page of "Excellent" in Miss Quigley's neat handwriting. Yes, most of the time he enjoyed school, except for the woodwork lessons they had once a week. He dreaded those sessions; he hated all that hammering and chiselling. He just didn't seem to have the hands for any of it. To make matters worse, the carpenter who came to the school every Tuesday seemed to take great pleasure in drawing the class's attention to Rob's efforts, even declaring him useless in front of everyone. Well, today was Monday, and he didn't have to think much about any joinery until tomorrow and he would make an effort when he went into school to concentrate on his lessons. He loved Miss Quigley and more than anything, he always liked to please her.

Mary Quigley had been teaching in Poyntzpass School for fifteen years. She was forty-five years old and lived alone in one of the small terrace houses just along the street from the school. She had given up any idea of marriage since coming here, it wasn't exactly the sort of place one was likely to meet a handsome stranger. So instead, she had devoted her time to teaching the young children of the village, taking responsibility for their tender years. She delighted in observing their young minds developing, soaking up the knowledge she imparted to the best of her ability. She had grown to love this area, there was a real community spirit here, and everyone helped each other, sharing what they had; those who were better off always eager to help those less fortunate. Yes, she could have done a lot worse than come to Poyntzpass all those years ago.

This morning she had just nineteen pupils, five were still off sick with influenza and by the look of a couple of others they were sickening for it too. She had actually asked Rob Hampton twice if he was feeling alright, but each time he had simply nodded and said, "Yes, Miss, I'm fine, thank you." Although she wasn't convinced, she let it go, perhaps he was just tired.

At one o'clock every day Mary organised the children round the big table at the window for lunch and was just placing the chairs when she noticed two people approaching the school. She recognised Dorrie Hampton immediately and a terrible dread and unease washed over her as she looked at her. Dorrie was not a very tall girl but now she looked shrunken, holding on to the older woman as if she might fall at any moment. Her face was colourless and her fair hair, usually gleaming and thick, clung lankly to her head. The heavy, grey haired woman accompanying her was a stranger to Mary. Something was terribly wrong; relatives were not encouraged during school hours, unless it was important.

With an awful foreboding, she slipped out of the classroom, and was waiting in the outer hall when they entered the school. Before the older woman introduced herself as Matt Hampton's sister and told her the sad news, she knew by Dorrie, who was on the verge of collapse, that she and her three siblings were now motherless.

She had known Evelyn Hampton had not been well but it was only the flu, for goodness' sake, and Evelyn only thirty-six. She should have had the chance of seeing her children grow up. Why, it was only last week she had been speaking to her, trying to encourage her to think of university for them, because she believed they were all clever enough to succeed.

Evelyn had listened carefully to all Mary was saying but had stressed Matt and she would never be able to afford to do that.

What was to become of them all now? What of Matt Hampton, how on earth would he cope? Everyone knew they had been devoted to one other. It was so very cruel. She had heard of people dying during this epidemic, but surely they had been elderly, that was the natural order of things, but not young people. Not a young mother of thirty-six with four children.

The next minutes were a blur to Mary. She knew she hugged Dorrie closely and exchanged condolences with Olive Anderson. She knew she had gone into the classroom and quietly led Maggie, Eve and Rob out to the hall. But she did it all so mechanically that afterwards she could never remember what she had actually said or how she had behaved towards them. She did remember watching miserably as realisation dawned on Dorrie's siblings. She remembered vividly afterwards how a white-faced Rob clung to Dorrie's arm in despair as their aunt took Eve and Maggie's hand. And then they left her to watch broken-heartedly as they left the school, back to a home which was now changed forever.

Olive Anderson stayed at the station house for another week after her sister-in-law's death. It was a long, harrowing week for her, having no experience of young children who were so bewildered and whose father was in such anguish. But she knew she must try to bring some normality back into their shattered lives, so she insisted the children return to school and Matt go back to work immediately after the funeral. She kept Dorrie at home for a further two days to help her sort out Evelyn's possessions, insisting Dorrie pack them into suitcases she found in the attic. Even though her niece was in tears and begged her aunt to leave some of her mum's photographs on display, Olive felt they were better hidden away, well out of sight. To Olive's way of thinking, it was better for everyone if there were no reminders – nothing that might keep the wound raw. The children and their father had their whole lives ahead and Matt had a responsible job and his family to think about. Time would soon pass and children were very resilient. Someone had to be practical about everything. It wasn't as if the children were babies. Rob was nine, Eve, eleven, and Maggie and Dorrie must be in their teens.

Chapter 2

1918

Matt Hampton never knew how he continued to work day in, day out, so instinctively, but he carried on getting up every morning, made tea, and then walked the few yards from his house to the station. But it was as if he was watching someone else perform the duties of stationmaster, noting the times the next train was due, checking with the signalman and the signal box, organising the relief guard and the porters onto the platform. Watching the continual round of passengers as the trains shunted in and out of the station. He was only thirty-eight but he felt so old and so apathetic. He had been stationmaster here for the last ten years and a signal man before that. He had loved his work, loved stations and anything to do with trains. It was all he had ever wanted to work at. During that time he had become used to the noise and bustle of the stations and had never noticed the rattle of the trains as they chugged into the halt. But now they seemed to echo "Evelyn... Evelyn..." or sometimes his sister-in-law's words... "You need to mind your job, Matt... If you had no job, what then? What about the children? You have to mind your job. What about the children?"

So he had "watched" his job for the last year since Evelyn had died, but he had lost heart in it. Life was now something to be endured and the days stretched endlessly in front of him. He had taken Olive's advice not to rake up memories of Evelyn, so he had done what she said and distanced himself from his children, from their suffering. He could not take on their anguish; he had his own pain to deal with. At least they had each other. They still all shared the same bedroom, and he knew Rob spent most of the night in Dorrie's bed, but he never intervened. He, on the other hand, went into an empty bedroom night after night, into a cold, comfortless bed. He had no one, no one to talk to, to share his troubles with, and to put out an understanding hand to. Many times he had been sorely tempted to ask Rob to come and sleep with him, but he knew he was being totally selfish. Dorrie was the one Rob wanted to be with, she was able to comfort him, better than Matt ever could. So he just had his memories; memories which he must make a continual effort to keep buried. His heartbreak could not be shared with anyone.

He owed so much to Dorrie. It was Dorrie who had kept the family together during the past year, who cared for the others, did the shopping, cooked the meals and looked after the house. She did all this, and still managed to go to work for a few hours every day. After her mother's death she had gone to Mrs Carson and renegotiated her hours in the shop, so that she was home when the others came from school, and there to see them off in the mornings.

The end of the Great War had come a few months ago, and people were trying to look forward to better times and better prospects. But it was hard, so many had suffered so much during those four years, and the loss of so many young men had left dreadful, permanent scars on the whole nation.

Then too, it had been a long, hard winter with plenty of snow and frost, which did nothing for anyone's spirits, but only seemed to pull them even lower. But now it was April and with its arrival had come glorious weather. The morning sun was already trying to break through the clouds as Matt made his way along the path to the station. But apart from the remarkable change in the weather, there was nothing to indicate that the day would be anything other than the routine one, with people coming and going the day long, exchanging the most casual greetings as they commuted.

The first train of the day was due into Poyntzpass from Newry at 7 a.m. It carried passengers returning from night work in the mill. It would then pick up passengers at Poyntzpass, who would travel on to various destinations between Poyntzpass and Belfast. A number of local people now worked in Harland and Wolf's shipyard and the train was their only means of commuting.

This morning the usual group of passengers were milling about, their footsteps echoing off the platform and their voices resounding through the metal supports and roof of the station. The train was a bit late, as it sometimes was, but Matt could already see the stiffening of people's shoulders, their impatience mounting. Getting to work on time was of paramount importance because others were always waiting, eager to take someone's workplace. Losing employment because of bad time-keeping was a constant threat.

The train was now thirty minutes late, but even so Matt was totally unprepared for the Telegraph Message when it came. The news he had always dreaded, which every stationmaster feared, had happened. They had had a derailment. There had been an accident, just a short distance down the line, between Scarva and Poyntzpass.

Nothing in his experience had ever prepared Matt for the hours that lay ahead. By eleven o'clock that morning it had been established that four men returning from night shift in Banbridge mill had lost their lives and many more had been injured. One of the carriages had become derailed and had gone down an embankment.

Perhaps all the training he had had around accidents helped him that morning as he gave orders to the signal men, to porters and guards. He gave information to passengers and relatives as sensitively as he knew how, but no training could help him with the feeling of nausea and distress he had to fight off constantly as he worked. At times his despair threatened to overwhelm him. During that long day he witnessed a scale of human emotions in the people gathered at the station. Some of them agitated at the prospect of losing their job, because of the delays, others so demanding and uncaring in the face of tragedy, insisting on alternative transport being provided. He observed raw terror, hysteria and grief, and tried to give individual support under horrendous circumstances, until he felt all his reserves of energy and judgement had been exhausted.

Now he had just told this woman sitting across the desk from him, that her husband was among the dead. The hope he had seen in others during that morning was mirrored in her eyes, when she had first entered his office, but that hope had been extinguished by his words, to be replaced by a look of such desolation he could not bear it. She had been watching his face the whole time he spoke, and now she dropped her head on to her chest and clasped her hands viciously together in her lap. The silence in his office began to be oppressive, and the atmosphere felt totally airless. Why did he have to be the harbinger of such bad news to this woman? He could take no more of this today. He needed to get away, right away from this awful place. But when he looked at the young woman seated before him, he knew he had to see it through, no matter what. He had to try and contend with her grief, and help her when she broke down altogether. He wished someone else could have been the bearer of such news to her – not him. He had no strength left to cope with anyone else's pain and despair. He had done more than enough to people this morning, and he felt a real sense of injustice that he, who was so ill-equipped, was left to deal with it all.

But when the woman facing him eventually raised her head, and looked at him again – although tears glistened in her dark eyes, he saw an inner strength burning in her. He felt strangely awed and humbled in the face of such courage. He instinctively put out his hand to touch hers, still clasped together at her chest. He desperately wanted to help her, but how could he comfort anyone, he who had been so little comfort to his own family? He had nothing to offer in the way of solace. His hand fell limply to his side. He was, after all, a total stranger to her.

But long after she had left him, making her way out of the station with such dignity, he sat alone in his office, his head in his hands. And his mind began to run on to so many things, the loneliness of his life, the grief he had witnessed here today, the horror which had visited this place and its people.

It was long past midnight when Matt left the station, but before leaving he established that the young woman lived in the country about eight miles from the station. She had two sons, so at least she wasn't entirely alone, but like him, had a family to think about. He would call someday soon, as he would with the other families who had suffered a loss today. It was part of his role as stationmaster to pay his respects.

Chapter 3

Carson's shop was well positioned in the village, occupying a prominent site in the square. A grey, two storey building, with a large glass window to the front displayed the range of fare available. The ground floor consisted of the shop with its stock room, and a small room to the back of the building containing a small kitchen area with a range. The Carsons lived above the shop, and over the years Emily had made an attractive home for herself and her husband. An airy living room, two bedrooms, a washroom and a kitchen ensured their privacy and comfort. A wide entry ran down the side of the building to a flat green area with numerous shrubs and outhouses. One of these outhouses had been converted about ten years previously into a bar. It measured about fifteen feet square, with one small latrine lying to the side of the building. Custom in the bar was excellent, and well able to accommodate the men who came from miles around, either walking or on bicycles, for their evening tipple. In the summer, chairs were placed outside on the green, where everyone was able to enjoy either their beer or whiskey.

It was Monday morning and after seeing the children off to school, Dorrie walked the few yards from the station house to the shop. Mrs Carson would already have opened up, and she would be waiting for her, cheerful and smiling, her small round figure encased in one of her many floral pinafores, her grey hair neatly tied up in a bun. She would have the usual cup of tea and biscuit ready for her, as she had every morning. It was a routine they had shared since Dorrie first started work three years ago. Afterwards they must begin stacking shelves, sorting cheese and bacon, making out price lists for the coming week. Dorrie hadn't minded the work at first, it was, after all a new experience for her, but now it just bored her, and the monotony of it all did little to inspire her. But Mrs Carson was so good to her, and so generous and thoughtful to all her family, that recently she felt more and more trapped. It seemed she was stuck here, here in this grocer's shop, in this tiny village. To think when she had been at school, she had had such hopes for her future. Her teacher had supported her in her aspirations, had often told her she could go far. Her mother, too, had always emphasized the wonderful opportunities there seemed to be for young people in Belfast. She had always viewed Mrs Carson's shop as a stop-gap.

Now everything was so changed. Their mother had been taken from them almost two years ago so suddenly and so cruelly, leaving Dorrie heartbroken and with a deepening sense of commitment to her siblings. Why, by the time Maggie, Eve and Rob were of an age to fend for themselves, no one would want to employ her anywhere.

Dorrie gave an audible sigh as she pushed open the heavy door of the shop. It would be quiet here this morning, it always was on Mondays, and that never helped her lack of motivation. She had decided last night that the time had come to tell Mrs Carson how she felt. She could not go on like this. She was getting a real feeling of resentment about the place, but with that emotion, there always came, on its heels, a real sense of guilt.

She had tried talking to her father several times, but he had just told her she should content herself, be glad she had a job, lots of young people had none. He always reminded her that she must appreciate everything Mrs Carson had done for them. When he said that, it just had the effect of increasing her resentment. She did acknowledge how good Emily Carson had been. She didn't think they would have survived the awful days after their mother's death, if she had not been there for them. But even so, she felt she must tell her how she was feeling.

She could hear the whistle of the kettle and Mrs Carson bustling about in the back of the shop. "I'm here, Dorrie, tea's just ready ... come and tell me how everyone is." Her boss's voice seemed more cheery than ever, which made Dorrie feel more dejected.

"They're fine, Mrs Carson." She tried to keep the note of resentment out of her voice. Did no one think of anything else;

only her sisters and brother? Just for once couldn't someone ask how she was? "They've gone to school..." She tried to sound a bit cheerier, she felt mean and selfish... "They're fine, really." She knew she was being unreasonable, Mrs Carson had always been concerned for them all, and deep down Dorrie knew that.

"I'll have tea... but nothing to eat." Her throat and stomach felt so tight, she doubted if she would be able to swallow the biscuit sitting on the plate in front of her. "I must go and start packing shelves." Faced anew with Mrs Carson's kindness, Dorrie felt her courage desert her. Maybe she wouldn't say anything yet, maybe later, or maybe even tomorrow.

Half heartedly she left the kitchen and began stacking tins of soup and spam onto their shelves in an effort to disguise her feelings. But Emily followed her, and well attuned to her young worker's frame of mind, looked at her quizzically as she worked.

"There's something bothering you this morning, Dorrie. Am I right?" She just hoped Dorrie hadn't heard any of the rumours that were circulating about her father. Her heart sank as she regarded her. It would be such a shame if she got wind of any of the gossip.

"I told you, everything's fine." But suddenly, Mrs Carson's obvious concern was too much for Dorrie and self-pity washed over her. She broke down completely and covering her face with her hands, burst into tears – tears which coursed down her cheeks, into her hands and onto her blouse. Struggling to get a handkerchief out of her skirt pocket, she tried to apologise through her sobs. "I'm so sorry; I don't know what has come over me... I'll be alright, really I will."

In answer Emily put an arm round her shoulders and led Dorrie back into the kitchen, pulled out a chair and gently but firmly guided her into it.

"Come on, Dorrie, let's have it, what's the matter? ...You have so much to carry on those young shoulders ... and you have been so brave." She knelt down beside the chair. "Is it just a bad day for you?"

Dorrie made a conscious effort to stop crying, and the kindness in Mrs Carson's voice, the warmth and cosiness of her plump body was so comforting, that she found her courage returning. Haltingly, she began to speak between sobs. "There was so much I wanted to do when I was at school," she hesitated, "I wanted to be a secretary... I didn't always want to be serving in a shop." The words sounded all wrong, now that she'd said them. Did she sound conceited, or worse, ungrateful?

"I don't mean that I haven't enjoyed being here." She went on apologetically, "I hope you're not offended ... I wouldn't want to offend you." She tried to smile. "You have been so good ... but with the children and everything, I feel I will be here always. So you'll be stuck with me." Her words sounded insincere. "You see, I always wanted to work in an office... I don't know why it always appealed to me." Dorrie looked up at her employer, and she was surprised to see she was smiling. "You're not offended?"

"Offended?" Emily held her closer. "You haven't the ability to offend anyone, child. Offend me? Well, I never." She seemed quite taken with the suggestion.

"I'm just annoyed at myself, my selfishness, keeping you here." She nodded her head vigorously. "Of course, you must try to do something more." Secretly Emily was very annoyed at herself. It had never entered her head that Dorrie might want to better herself, and why not? She was annoyed too, at the girl's father, he had never once encouraged her to do anything more than come here day after day. It disturbed her to think that everyone had just assumed this was her life here. That she must take on the responsibilities of her siblings, and the running of the home. And simply because she had shown a willingness to do it all, her whole future had been shelved.

"Right, let's think about this. There'll be no customers for a while – I should think," and practical as ever, Emily proceeded to put the kettle on for yet another cup of tea.

"Let's see what can be done to help." She seemed to have almost forgotten Dorrie sitting watching her, her eyes red and swollen. The kettle whistled again and absentmindedly she poured water into the teapot, her mind racing on as to what could be done in practical terms to help. "Now I believe the children will be able to manage fine." When she spoke her tone was light, reassuring. "Maggie's over fourteen now ... isn't she? Time she was working, isn't it? She can step in to your shoes. No problem there."

"Maggie...?" Dorrie was taken aback by the suggestion, "Maggie do it? But she's so young."

"Isn't she at home now, doesn't she do some cooking? And she's the same age as you were when you were left with everything. I know she's not like you, but she can soon learn." Emily's voice was animated, she was warming to the whole idea.

"Yes, Maggie can work here in your place, when you get a clerical job." She began to pour tea into two mugs. "I'll talk to Ernie; he'll know someone who'll know someone who needs a clerk."

Dorrie was astounded. "Mrs Carson... I didn't mean you to help," she protested. "You've been good enough. I just wanted to let you know how I feel. I thought it only fair, that's all." Dorrie reached for one of the biscuits as she thought about what Mrs Carson had suggested; she felt hungry suddenly. "I don't know where to start looking. It's so kind of you. I would really appreciate it... I don't know where to start, and that's the truth."

Emily smiled and nodded, at the same time she was thinking she must talk to Ernie tonight about Dorrie and Maggie. Mentally she was also comparing the two sisters. Dorrie might not have the stunning good looks of her younger sister, but she was still an attractive girl with her quiet manner, fair hair and blue eyes. Maggie, on the other hand, was tall and slender, with the same dark hair and blue eyes as her father. But Maggie was the scatterbrain of the family, at least that's what she thought. Not like Dorrie at all. But no doubt she would manage, and Emily herself would guide her in the shop as best she could.

Dorrie's voice broke in on her thoughts. "I better go and do some work – get started out here. I feel so much better, I really do." Dorrie rose from her seat with renewed vigour and impulsively hugged Emily. "I'll finish the stacking ... and thank you so much for your kindness."

"Dorrie, I'm so glad you told me. You did the right thing." Emily nodded understandingly. "I'll talk to Ernie; he knows lots of business men in Banbridge. He might get you something there. If so, you would be able to travel and still see your family at night." She sounded so enthusiastic. Dorrie was overcome, and had to struggle anew with her emotions. She had never expected such support.

"You have been wonderful to me today, I can never repay you for all your help."

"I haven't done anything yet." Emily dismissed the praise. "Time enough when you get something."

Dorrie got through the shelf stacking in double quick time, more enthusiastic than she had been for weeks. Mrs Carson hadn't thought her selfish or uncaring towards her family. Nor had she scoffed at the idea she could better herself. She seemed to understand.

Chapter 4

"I hope Dorrie didn't sound too ungrateful when she told you she wanted another job, after all you've done for us." Matt Hampton seemed in a right state as he spoke to Emily across his desk.

"Matt, we both know Dorrie's more than appreciative for anything that has been done for her." Emily was determined to defend her young employee as best she could, and to encourage Matt to give her an opportunity to better herself.

Ernest and she had decided the previous evening that Emily herself should tell Matt Ernest had managed to get Dorrie an office position in Banbridge mill, even if Matt did accuse Emily of being an interfering so and so.

So here she was, sitting facing him across the station desk, and by the cheerless look on his face he wasn't very impressed with her.

"Dorrie has worked hard for me, Matt. She never shirked her duties, far from it," Emily smiled in an attempt to lighten the atmosphere, "but I'm no charity ... I needed her as much as she needed me."

"Dorrie is a worker and always has been." Matt's voice held a note of pride. "It's just... well... we really need her at home. I don't know what we'll do."

"Yes, you will all miss her, I know that, Matt." She knew very well that Matt felt the family's whole stability was about to be threatened. She went on, "We have to remember about Dorrie too." She had to make him see how important Dorrie's future might be. "Look, Matt, you and I both know Dorrie's capable of so much."

Then suddenly – feeling braver – Emily went on... "Working in a corner shop, that's what she's doing. Is that all you want for her, Matt? She is intelligent and capable of doing so much in her life."

Matt was silent for a moment then added, "I the was happy enough, doing what she was doing, and ' home."

"Of course she was, but she wants more, and we mustn't blame her for that. And she will still be coming home every evening. A bit later, granted, but you still have Maggie and Eve, and even Rob is capable of helping around the house."

"Actually, Emily, I'm more worried about Rob than anything else. He depends on Dorrie so much. The both of them are stuck in the parlour every evening... What is he going to do now?"

"He'll soon be grown up, Matt. Then he too, will go to work." Emily responded promptly. "What of Dorrie then? Do you really want to see her regretting any opportunity?"

"I know you're right, Emily." Matt pushed back his chair and rose to his feet. "It wouldn't be fair to Dorrie, but I am worried about the others," smiling quite affectionately at her, he went on, "and myself, of course."

When Emily spoke again, her voice was softer. She had to get across to Matt that she did understand. "We will all miss her. I'll miss her too, but please let her try this ... and keep in mind you will still see her every evening." Adding as an afterthought, "It would be worse if she was going far and unable to get home regularly."

"You are absolutely right, Emily, and," Matt added graciously, "I have to thank you. And Ernie of course, for all you've done to help my daughter." He extended his hand. "Tell her she has my blessing."

"I certainly will, but you must do so too, you know."

"Tell her I'll see her this evening and I'll do my best to be happy for her."

Matt seemed to struggle with his emotions and Emily tried to think of something to say to ease the desolate look on his face. She could think of nothing, so feeling strangely guilty now, quietly said her goodbyes and took her leave of him. As she made her way back to the shop she had to make a conscious effort to forget about Matt's sad appearance, and concentrate on Dorrie and what this meant for her.

It was a dark, dank afternoon and rain was threatening again. But it was, after all, almost the end of October and winter would soon be here again, with all its frost and cold, northerly winds. No doubt they would have snow sometime in the next two or three months – they rarely escaped it. With it would come the inevitable train delays and people fretting about getting to their place of work. As Emily thought about this aspect of their community's lives, her thoughts returned to her commitment to taking on Maggie Hampton when Dorrie left her. She had some reservations about Maggie; she was such a deep girl, not open and frank like her elder sister. But no doubt it would all work out somehow, and Matt seemed delighted with that aspect of things, which meant a lot to Emily.

As she thought again about Matt, her mind ran on to the gossip that had been circulating about him and the widow Brankin. According to some people he could be seen cycling to her farmhouse on at least two evenings a week. Emily had never any time for gossip, even though she had had to listen to a fair amount over the counter in the last number of years. Well, whatever the truth was, she sincerely hoped it would never reflect on any of his children. And no doubt, Matt and Jane Brankin were able to sort out their own affairs.

Later that evening Dorrie waited anxiously in the kitchen while her father sat idly at the table, a cup of tea in his hand. Her sisters had gone upstairs and Rob was waiting for her in the parlour. She busied herself at the sink, wondering when her father intended bringing up the subject of leaving Carson's. Emily had told her everything was alright, but maybe he was having second thoughts about everything. She was just thinking the suspense was too much, and she would have to ask him, when he spoke.

"Well, Dorrie, you're bringing some changes. Going to spread your wings a little."

She turned sharply to look at him, and saw he was smiling broadly at her and his voice held a note of pride. It was a wonderful sound, and she felt such relief, that she went to him, threw her arms round him and kissed him fervently on the cheek. "You really don't mind." Dorrie could scarcely believe it, and it was all thanks to Emily Carson. "You really don't ... I can see that."

"When Emily first told me, I did get a bit of a shock, but I am happy for you, Dorrie, and I really hope you like it." He hugged her tightly. "We'll be fine and we'll have something to look forward to every evening, hearing all about your new job. Now, go and tell the others all about it, and go easy on Rob. Tell him you'll still see him every evening, in case he thinks he's going to miss out on some of your precious time together." He proceeded towards the back door. "I'm just going out for a bit of a cycle, I'll see you all later."

As Dorrie went off to tell Rob and her sisters her news, she reckoned this was the happiest she had felt since her mother's death two years before.

Matt was later than usual when he set off for Jane's farm. As he cycled through the village to head down the Scarva Road, the town clock told him it was ten minutes past eight. Still, there was no fixed time for him to call, Jane more or less expected him when she saw him. As he sped along he thought about Dorrie and her new job, and he felt really proud of his daughter, it must have taken some courage to approach Mrs Carson in the first place. He knew she would do well in an office, and it was better than being stuck in a corner shop for the rest of her life. And Finlay's mill, well, it was renowned over all of Northern Ireland.

This evening he was really looking forward to visiting Jane, to tell her all about Dorrie, help her with the farmyard chores, and have supper with her in her huge kitchen with its polished range and scrubbed table. It was all so relaxing and soothing, after the noise and bustle of the station. Jane and he had found they could confide in one another about their loneliness and how they had loved and missed their partners. For Matt, who had buried his sorrow for the past two years, it was a wonderful release to be with someone who understood.

He had been cycling this narrow road once or twice a week for the past year. Initially he had felt it his duty to visit the widow and her two sons, who had been bereaved so tragically. But now he had to admit he just loved going to see Jane, her reassuring ways and strength of character seemed to soothe him as nothing had ever done during the dark days following Evelyn's death. He didn't expect anyone to understand how two people who had suffered loss were simply glad of one another's company from time to time.

The farm was approached by a long country lane just off the Scarva Road . It contained a low, detached dwelling with a few outhouses scattered to both sides of it and a large cement yard to the front. Although the rain had stopped, it was quite dark, and as he parked his bicycle along the wall of the house, he could see a lantern swinging in one of the outhouses. Obviously Jane hadn't finished clearing up yet, he would be able to give her some help.

Someone was out in the shed with her. He could hear the low rumble of voices. It must be one of the boys, although they rarely helped her, being so busy with their lessons. He went on into the barn, but stopped dead in his tracks. A man he had never seen before in his life, was scooping swill into a bucket, and even with the dim light, he could see he was a very handsome man. Involuntarily, he took a step back, and was shocked at the strong wave of jealousy which rose in his throat and threatened to choke him.

"Oh hello." The stranger approached him, hand outstretched. "I'm giving Jane a helping hand here." He turned his head towards the darkest corner of the barn. "Jane... a visitor for you." At that Jane came forward to both men.

"Oh, hello, Matt, I must say I thought you weren't coming ... you aren't usually this late." She indicated the man beside her. "This is Dan – he called to see how we were managing." She smiled warmly at both men. "He soon got a job, there's always plenty to do around here."

At that Dan went over to her, and holding the lantern close, proceeded to relieve her of the bucket she was carrying. "Look, I'll do that..." He put an arm round her shoulder in a familiar way. "You go and make supper, I'll finish off here."

Jane turned to Matt with a smile. "Coming in for some supper? The boys will be glad to see you."

"No, no." Matt spoke more sharply than he had intended, but he couldn't bear to stay a minute longer. He couldn't watch this cosy scene; Jane and this man seemed so comfortable and familiar together. How well this Dan must know her, to embrace her in front of him. He, himself had never dared put an arm near her, not ever. Even as he thought about that, he knew, more than anything, he had always wanted to, ever since he had first seen her, sitting in his office, her eyes full of tears. He had wanted to wrap her body in his, to feel her total compliance when he touched her. To kiss her soft lips and neck, feel her cheek against his and hold her care worn hands against his body. Now it was too late for any of that. He was just an outsider in this happy scene of domesticity. He must get away. He stepped back and nodded briefly to her. "I thought I could give a hand, but you have it all done. I have to get back, to the children, you see."

With a puzzled look on her face Jane asked him again. "Are you sure, Matt, just a cup of tea?" She smiled so invitingly to him, that for a moment he wavered. Shaking his head and mumbling, "No, thanks," he proceeded out of the barn over to his bicycle. There was no way he was staying here any longer.

As he cycled down the lane he imagined he heard her calling something to him, but he couldn't hear what it was. He was just so thankful he had never let her know how he felt about her. He would have made such a fool of himself, when all the time, she had someone else she cared about.

Chapter 5

There was no snow at all that winter of 1920 in Poyntzpass, just a strong north wind which blew incessantly from November to the middle of February, bringing with it heavy downpours of rain which pelted and lashed against everyone's hands and face, and felt colder than any snow. It flowed down footpaths, gushed into gullies and drains and the leaves – which had fallen during the previous months, became brown, sodden, slippery masses, so treacherous underfoot. But at least the railway lines had remained open, and that was always uppermost in everyone's mind, getting to work on time and home again at a reasonable hour. More and more of the young people who lived in the village and surrounding countryside, now travelled to Belfast to work in Harland and Wolf's shipyard or in one of the more productive linen centres in the province.

Today when Rob came out of school, he was delighted to see the rain had stopped and the sun was shining. The footpaths looked drier and safer than they had done in weeks. He would just love to go straight home and get out into the garden to play with Eve, but there was probably little chance of that happening. No doubt he would have to hang around Carson's as usual while Eve went in to see if Maggie was ready. He hated that part of the day, dallying around waiting for the two of them, but no matter what he said Maggie never let Eve go home with him. And he never, ever wanted to go home on his own. And even though Maggie knew how much he hated it, she thought nothing of leaving him alone in the house after tea in the evenings, while she dragged Eve back down to the bar for an hour, before their father came home.

"Are you calling for Maggie? ...I thought maybe we could go on home and play outside"

"I have to call for her, Rob. You know we can't get into the house without the key and Maggie keeps charge of it."

"Well, today I'm going over to the station to see Dad. I'm not hanging around... what keeps you and Maggie anyway?" When Dorrie had worked for Mrs Carson, she had been ready for home always when he called – always.

"Maggie isn't waiting for us when we call. She always seems to have something to do." Eve sounded exasperated about something. But then, she always seemed tense when she was going in to Maggie. Rob never could understand it, but he often wondered when he peered through the shop window, what Maggie started to whisper to Eve about, when she got Mrs Carson out of earshot. She certainly never had much to say to Eve while Mrs Carson was there, but waited until her employer went round to the back of the shop.

Today he was determined to go to the station, no matter about them. So in gloomy silence he continued up the street beside Eve, and when they reached the shop, she pushed the door open sharply without enquiring further what Rob intended to do. He hung about for about a minute, uncertain, he hated getting into Maggie's bad books, and it wouldn't be worth it. But he hesitated only briefly, before resolutely starting to walk the short distance down the incline, past the terrace houses with their brightly painted doors, which opened directly onto the pavement. The small, bright windows with the winter sun shining on them sparkled and seemed to wink at him as he headed towards the station.

He still missed Dorrie so much since she went to work in Banbridge, she had always involved him in anything she was doing and enquired about his school. Now it was so different; Maggie and Eve mostly ignored him, either whispering in the kitchen while Maggie made the tea, or going to their bedroom. Or worst of all, leaving him alone, while they went back to the bar. Maggie always insisted Mrs Carson needed her help, but Rob didn't really believe that, he knew a bar man was employed in the evenings. The Carsons themselves didn't even work after six o'clock. He never talked to anyone about why his sisters went there. Some instinct told him it might cause trouble at home and he didn't want to make trouble for anybody.

As he turned into the platform at the station he spotted his father talking to one of the porters, and when he spied his son his face broke into a welcoming smile, and he waved him over. And Rob forgot all about Eve and Maggie, he was so glad to be here. He loved being with his father in the station, he loved the whole atmosphere of the place, the noise and bustle of the trains and their passengers, the smell of the fuel and smoke. He loved the opportunity of sitting at his father's desk in his office, with its worn leather chairs and books and papers lining the walls. His father put an arm round his shoulder and led him in there now, at the same time talking animatedly to him.

"How was school today, Rob?" Not waiting for an answer he hurried on, "Are the girls still at the shop? Good, I got a bar of chocolate given to me this morning, so you can have it. I've only one, so you should eat it up." His father proceeded to open a drawer in his desk, and produced a long, thick bar of chocolate. "Are the girls calling for you?"

Rob couldn't answer, his mouth was so full, so he just nodded and smiled at his father. Besides he didn't know what they were going to do. His father wasn't expecting any answer, because he just smiled back at him. Then he disappeared into the back of the waiting area and returned with a grubby looking flannel, which he ordered Rob to wipe his mouth and hands with. "We don't want you going home with a face covered in chocolate," he tilted his son's face to consider it, "Maggie and Eve might think we should have shared it."

"Dad, I hope I'm not keeping you back, am I?"

"Look, Rob you come here anytime you want." Matt was emphatic. "Even if I am busy you can occupy yourself. I'm only too glad to see you."

"Thanks, Dad." Rob seized his opportunity. "Can I come back down at seven o'clock to meet Dorrie off the train? You'll still be here, won't you?"

"Well maybe." Matt nodded but looked a little uncertain. "If I say 'yes' will you make sure you've all your lessons finished and the girls have the place tidied? Is that a deal? Dorrie seems tired in the evening."

"Yes, Dad... I do my homework straight after school most days. Dorrie just likes to check everything over for me." Secretly Rob felt peeved at his dad's reaction, but he knew his father didn't really understand that Dorrie and he loved that hour in the parlour in the evening. It was true she did look over his homework, but she always told him all about her day at work, and he was really interested to hear it all. Although Dorrie always discussed how well Maggie and Eve seemed to be coping with the housework and cooking, he never told her anything about them going to the bar before their father came home. Somehow he knew it would upset her, and besides, he didn't want to get into trouble with Maggie.

The rumble of an approaching train put paid to any further talk with his father as Matt left the office to organise porters, passengers and luggage. Rob looked at the mahogany clock above the fireplace – it showed a quarter to four. He was just thinking his sisters had gone home without him when they appeared in the doorway, swinging Eve's schoolbag between them.

Their happy faces told him they were in good form and that usually meant they would cook tea without any grumbling. He would do his usual job of relighting the fire before doing his homework. He certainly wanted to have finished before Dorrie came home.

The fire still glimmered in the range when they entered the house. Even though Maggie came home at lunchtime to check it, sometimes if they were lucky it would still be lit, other times it would be out altogether. Now Rob simply put a few small pieces of coal on and then placed the long poker underneath to allow air to circulate and encourage the flames. While he was waiting to make sure it was going to light he sat down at the table and retrieving his arithmetic book from his schoolbag, he finished his lesson in double quick time. After checking the range once more, he went into the parlour to light the fire in there for Dorrie later. This room was where the two of them spent much of their evening.

He could hear Maggie and Eve busy in the kitchen, then the clatter of their footsteps on the stairs. Maggie always insisted Eve and she go and tidy the bedrooms, but Rob knew she just wanted to gossip about something or other. What they talked about he had no idea, but he could always hear the drone of Maggie's voice overhead, Eve just seemed to do the listening. As he was leaving the parlour, they were coming back downstairs, and Maggie casually told him Eve and she were going back down to Carson's.

"The table's set and the stew is cooking on the range," she remarked to Rob as she opened the front door. "We'll be back before Dad and Dorrie come."

Rob hated being left alone in the house because he was very likely to take one of his panic attacks. Now, as he felt one coming on, he sat down and hugging himself tightly and taking deep breaths he tried to reassure himself that his father and Dorrie would soon be here, and the attack would soon pass.

Chapter 6

Dorrie's time in Finlay's Mill was very different from what she had known in Carson's. For one thing, her hours were much longer, commencing at eight o'clock in the morning and finishing at six in the evening. But she loved the work, even though she was only concerned with the filing system and a bit of book keeping, but she hoped she would soon be given more responsibility in the future. She worked with three other girls in an airy office on the top floor of the building. She had been here just three months but had learnt quickly, was a methodical worker, and got on well with the other girls.

Now today, Mr Finlay had called into the office and asked to speak to her. He told her they needed help in their main office in Belfast, and wondered if she would be interested in a transfer there. She had been recommended by Mr Wilson, the manager of Banbridge mill who was impressed with her dedication and disposition. He told her she need not decide there and then, but if she would let him know within the next two weeks what her decision was.

As Dorrie waited for the 6.30 train coming into Banbridge station, she could think of nothing else only this opportunity of going to work in Belfast, but if she did accept this offer, what would her family do? It always came down to that. Dorrie knew they were all managing well, but if she transferred to Finlay's main mill, she would probably only get home at weekends. She knew Maggie and Eve wouldn't mind, but she was unsure as to how Rob might feel – he still seemed to depend on her so much, and he had such a nervous disposition that she worried a lot about him. More so, since he had told her about the shivering attacks he took, when he was left alone. She had tried to reassure him as best she could. But sometimes, she felt that Mrs Carson was right, and they all, including Rob, needed to become more independent.

Since her mother's death Dorrie hadn't cared much for any train journey, especially the one from Banbridge to Poyntzpass. It brought back such vivid memories of the happy times they had all shared. Her mother had made any journey interesting, with her enthusiasm for everything around her. She delighted in identifying the different animals, as they grazed in the fields, or lay sheltering under trees. As the train wound its way through the countryside, she would tell them the names of all the farmers who lived in the quaint cottages, and the more well-to-do who resided in their fine stately homes.

The memories of those idyllic days were as painful to Dorrie now, as three years ago when her mother had died. When did the heartbreak and sense of desolation ease? Well meaning friends always reassured her that time would heal her loss. But Dorrie knew she would never forget the nightmare of her mother's illness and how quickly she had changed from being vaguely unwell to becoming so gravely ill. The initial hopes they had had of her recovering, only to be followed by torment and despair as her father and she watched her fading. Her own sense of shock and bewilderment and how aware she was of her father's withdrawal from them all, how he locked his grief away and never spoke of it. She had always wondered how much Aunt Olive had discouraged him from talking. She would never know but she had been shocked how quickly Olive had cleared their mother's possessions into the roof space. Then one day, about six months after Olive had gone home, Dorrie had determinedly retrieved her parents' wedding photograph from the suitcase, and now kept it on her dressing table.

Above all, she would never forget Rob during that awful time, he was inconsolable. He clung to Dorrie, craved solace in her bed, and cried brokenly and incessantly for weeks on end. Yes, the only thing time had done for Dorrie was to help her realise the transience of life and everything in it. Her mother's death had given her such a sense of vulnerability and insecurity that she felt the world and her place in it was shifting beneath her. Perhaps that explained why she was so anxious to carve a niche for herself and establish some sense of security and safety.

The train had pulled out of Scarva junction and started its descent to Poyntzpass before Dorrie realised that, after all, she had thought very little about Finlay's mill, even though it had been uppermost in her mind. It was just as well she had a couple of weeks to make a decision. She was so tired now, her emotions spent, that she couldn't possibly think of anything else this evening. She just wanted home to see the family, to have a warm dinner made by Maggie, and then to sit a while before crawling into bed.

When she alighted from the train, she felt a return of energy when she spotted Rob waiting with her father on the platform. She was always delighted when Rob was there, but tonight their father's and his presence seemed particularly welcoming. It put a stamp of approval on what she was doing. As she stepped down to meet them, sidestepping the people who mingled about, she felt a wave of emotion and tears came to her eyes. Their very presence was so comforting, Rob, in the long trousers he insisted on wearing now he was over twelve. He looked so tall for his age, and so attractive with thick brown hair and steel grey eyes. As for her father, she reckoned he must be one of the most handsome men around. He was tall and lean with dark hair and an angular face. His dark blue eyes with that haunted sad look seemed to add to his attractiveness. She took a deep breath in order to hide her emotion.

"I'm so glad to see you both." She linked her arm through Rob's and then her father's.

"Have you finished for the night, Dad?" She looked over towards the station, and was glad to see it looked fairly quiet.

"I'll just be another half hour, Dorrie, and then I'll be along. Will you wait and have dinner with me?"

"Of course... Rob and me have plenty to talk about till then." Dorrie disengaged her arm from her father's. "We'll go on, see you shortly."

Matt began to make his way over to the office.

"Rob tells me he has his lessons all done ... haven't you, Rob?" In answer Rob nodded and waved over to him, and still linking Dorrie's arm, they made their way towards the station house.

The station house was a fine red brick two storey house, set back from the station, surrounded by small gardens at front, sides and rear with neat shrubbery and low hedges. Secure gates and a paved path led directly to the station. It had started to rain and a low mist encircled the grounds and their home seemed more secure than it had been for some time and suddenly, indecision washed over Dorrie, and Belfast seemed such a long way off.

She was surprised when they entered the hall at the silence enveloping the place. The oil lamp burned brightly in the kitchen and a saucepan bubbled gently on the range, but there was no sign of either Maggie or Eve. She slipped off her coat, calling upstairs as she did so. "Maggie? Eve?" There was no answer, and she was about to ask Rob if he knew where they were, when they burst in the back door.

"Easy... easy, Maggie." Half playfully Dorrie backed away, as if to ward them off. "What on earth's the matter?"

"Nothing." Both girls slowed down, though it was Maggie who spoke. "Nothing... we didn't know you were back ... that's all," and Maggie smiled benignly at her sister, Eve stood silently beside her.

"Where've you been?" Dorrie looked at the clock in the kitchen. "It's going to be dark soon out there."

"We called down to see Mrs Carson, that's all," Maggie appealed to Eve, "didn't we, Eve?" Eve nodded quietly.

"Maggie ... you're only fifteen, Eve's not even fourteen, so come off it." Dorrie was firm. "Mrs Carson wouldn't want you there ... at the bar, I mean, I know that."

"Honest, Dorrie, she didn't mind... I swear," and Maggie appealed again to her younger sister, but Eve remained silent. And Maggie, anxious to change the conversation, moved towards the range.

"I've your dinner ready, Dorrie... and Dad's... will he be long?"

"Thanks, Maggie, he'll be here shortly, I'll wait for him."

Maggie was relieved she had avoided any further questioning and thoughtfully checked the saucepan, and proceeded to set knives and forks on the table. She had just finished, when they heard their father's key in the door, and Dorrie and he soon sat down to the warm meal of mutton, carrots and potatoes.

Later, Dorrie and Rob retired to the parlour, Eve and Maggie cleared up and Matt sat quietly in the kitchen, his pipe in his hand. The sense of contentment pervading the house convinced Dorrie that they all worked well together and if what Maggie and Eve, said about going to Carson's was true, she must be very popular with her boss. Before she fell asleep that night, Dorrie was convinced she must grasp the opportunity of this position.

Chapter 7

1921

It was four months before Dorrie transferred to the mill in Belfast, and on a beautiful sunny Monday morning in late May 1921, Matt helped pack her luggage and kissed her goodbye as she boarded the 7 a.m. train to Belfast. Mr Finlay himself was to meet her there, take her to his home to unpack and from there he would take her to the York Road mill where she would start her new employment.

Now as Matt sat at his desk in the station with the bright sunshine gleaming brightly through the windows and glass roof of the station, he could only marvel at the kindness and generosity of this man who had given Dorrie such a start in life. And to top it all, she would stay with the Finlays during the week. He had even arranged for Dorrie to attend commercial courses in one of the colleges in the city, on two evenings a week. Matt had found the man's kindness a very humbling experience, and had felt compelled to travel to meet Dorrie's benefactor and to thank him personally for his grace and hospitality.

He felt so inadequate that day, if only he could have provided more for his family. Struggling with emotions, and trying to find suitable words, he began, "I will never be able to repay you for all your kindness..."

Mrs Finlay was quick to reply. "You must never think like that." She smiled in an understanding way. "It will be such a pleasure to have a girl here. We have four sons – two at home and two at university." She went on, "We have been so fortunate, my husband was left the mill by his father. We like to share our good fortune."

"Don't think we intend to spoil your daughter, far from it. Everyone must work hard in the mill," Mr Finlay added. "And her weekly pay will be geared around the cost of her accommodation. She needs to catch the bus every morning and evening and attend the night classes, so no – she will not be spoiled by us." As Matt listened and watched their kind faces, he felt humbled by their generosity. When he left them that evening to catch the train back to Poyntzpass, he felt more confident about Dorrie and her happiness than he had done since Evelyn's death.

Still thinking of Dorrie and the Finlays, he tried to settle down to his own work and sort through some paperwork. He felt it was a godsend that he had had to occupy his mind with Dorrie. It had distracted him from dwelling on Jane Brankin and the last, miserable evening he had gone to visit her. He had never gone back since, maybe he was being petty, but he couldn't face the place. Besides, she probably didn't need him around, if she had Dan. The experience that night had left him with such a sense of loss and hurt that at times it bewildered him, and at others totally shamed him. She had never given him any reason to think it was anything more than friendship between them. Well, he was glad he hadn't let himself down – never once had he betrayed how he really felt about her. But then, he himself had never realised his feelings for her until that night, when the presence of another man at the farm had devastated him. But at least he still had his pride, he had escaped with that. Besides, he had his family to think about, they occupied his spare time and stopped him from dwelling on what might have been. His children were so dear to him, but even their presence, didn't seem to appease the longing he had for her company, to see her smile and hear her low, lilting voice.

"Matt, the three o'clock's due in five minutes... will I organise the other porter?" It was Fred, the head porter, who had entered his office and stood beside him.

"Sure, Fred ... I'm coming now, just finishing off here." He hadn't realised the time, and mentally composing himself he went out to the platform to supervise the arrival of the train.

He had just finished overseeing staff and passengers, when he spied Rob coming up the platform, accompanied by a tall, gangly boy, with a thin face and a mop of thick blond hair. "Rob, how nice to see you." He studied the other boy. "Who have we here?"

"Dad, this is Tom Greenlees." Rob indicated his friend. "Tom and his family have just moved into the old manse on the hill ... you know, the one that was being fixed up." Rob looked impatiently at his father. "Remember, I told you, they've come up from Monaghan."

"Oh, yes... of course." Matt vaguely remembered something about the Greenlees coming from Monaghan. It was reputed the man owned canneries all over the place, and now he fancied doing a bit of farming, so had moved here. "How nice to meet you... Tom, did you say?"

"Yes." The boy had the most attractive, southern brogue. "I'm in Rob's class now."

"Well it's really nice to meet you, I hope you'll be happy here ... and Rob certainly needs company."

"Dad we came to ask you if I could go to Tom's house for tea, and to play in his fields." Rob sounded anxious. "Would that be alright?"

"Of course, Rob," patting his son's head, "have you told Eve, so they won't make tea for you?"

"I said I would ask you first, Dad."

"Well, call in the shop and let Maggie know before you go."

"I'll do that, Dad," and the two boys ran out of the station, anxious to escape into the brilliant sunshine and enjoy the rest of the day.

Matt was relieved to see Rob had taken to this boy Tom. He usually didn't bother with other boys of his age, preferring to cling to his family, especially Dorrie. It was such a godsend, because he had been dreading how Rob would be, now that Dorrie would no longer be home during the week. Now he had something else to occupy him, exactly what he needed.

Later, he was walking over to advise the signalman of the next train to Newcastle, when he saw her coming towards him with her sons on either side of her, hands clasped tightly. His breath caught in his throat and his heart began to race as he drank in her whole appearance. She had tied her dark hair back with a black velvet ribbon, and wore a cream, flowing skirt and flowered blouse, cut low at the neck, revealing creamy tanned skin. He thought she had never looked so beautiful. He was so overcome with a mixture of emotions – of longing for her, of shame for his past behaviour and his avoidance of her. He longed to escape into his office, but it was already too late – she had spotted him, and was smiling and waving to him.

"Oh, Matt, how nice to see you." She seemed so at ease with herself, and really pleased to see him. "It has been so long." Privately Jane was glad of the opportunity to find out why he had been avoiding her. He hadn't been to see them for months and it was so unlike him. Many times, she had considered trying to get in touch with him, but had had no occasion to come to the station until today. "You never call now to see us. Is anything wrong?" She turned towards her sons. "The boys miss you too. Don't you, Jim? Harry?" She pulled them towards him. "Say hello to Mr Hampton"

He was glad of the diversion of the boys, he was afraid she might read his innermost feelings, so he concentrated his gaze on Jim and Harry. "Hello, boys, going somewhere nice?"

They both answered at once, hopping from one foot to the other. "Newcastle, to stay with Dan."

"Oh." There it was again, that jealousy and resentment. He took a step back. "Have a good time then. How long are you going for?"

"A whole week..." Harry's voice was full of excitement. "We're going to the beach with Mamie and Davy, our cousins."

"Your cousins." Matt was nonplussed. "Where will they be?"

Jane intervened. "Let me explain, Matt." Her eyes were riveted on him, searching his face. "Dan, whom you met at my house, is my brother. They used to live in Enniskillen but we never had much contact until recently, as he lived so far away. Recently they moved to Newcastle. They had just moved there a couple of days before you met him and now my boys are going to stay for a holiday."

"Oh, I see." Relief floated through Matt, and suddenly he felt as if he was floating, he felt so liberated. Dan was her brother. As he stood there an overwhelming sense of shame at his behaviour on that evening at her farm washed over him. He hadn't even waited to be introduced properly, but pigheadedly had cycled off.

Jane interrupted his thoughts. "Maybe, you'll call some of these evenings." She tried to sound casual. "It's nice at the farm at present." She indicated the train which was pulling into the station. "We must hurry now – the boys are travelling alone, will they be alright?"

"Of course they will." Matt was at his most reassuring. "Is someone meeting them at Newcastle?"

"Dan and Sara will meet them. They'll be there for a whole week. Matt..." she hesitated, then went on, "I'll be on my own, so I'll be glad of some company, and some help in the evenings."

She moved off towards the train, and Matt watched her go, her sons skipping excitedly beside her. His emotions were in turmoil, relief mixed with a longing he had not experienced for a long time. And the acute embarrassment he felt now at jumping to the wrong conclusion; he cringed when he thought of how he had cycled away without even stopping. What had Jane thought of his churlish behaviour? He had been so childish. He hadn't behaved like that since his teenage years, and he certainly never intended to behave like that again.

Over dinner that evening, Maggie thought her father was in sparkling form, she hadn't seen him so animated in months. She had expected him to be really down in the mouth, what with Dorrie going to be away all week, and herself having taken more hours with Mrs Carson. But he had enquired if Rob had remembered to tell them about Tom Greenlees, and had complemented her highly on her cooking skills.

"There's some apple pie, Dad, I baked it earlier." Maggie was quite proud of her cooking skills. It was about the only thing she was any good at.

"Oh, I'll have some of that ... then I must be off." Reaching for his portion of pie, he added, "I'm going for a bit of a cycle, haven't been in a long time, it's a lovely evening for it."

"That's fine ... we'll be here when Rob comes home, Dad," Maggie turned to Eve, "won't we, Eve? He said he'd be back around nine."

"Yes he did." Eve's quiet voice confirmed to Matt all was organised, and he made preparations to set off for Jane's.

Thirty minutes later he was cycling along the road to Brook farm. He had changed into light trousers and a short sleeved shirt before setting out, but he still felt warm. The evening sun seemed to shine as brightly as it had done all day, the hedgerows and gardens were a riot of colour and a tractor and baler wound their way lazily up a field alongside him as he rode past. The whole evening seemed in tune with his frame of mind, and yet as he turned into the lane which would take him to the farmyard, self doubt assailed him. Would Jane appreciate him coming so soon, that very evening, would he seem too keen? Would she think the worst? That he had come straight away because he knew she was on her own. He was horrified at the thought, he would have been coming straight away anyway, even if her boys were at home, he had missed her company so much.

But when he saw her coming to meet him as he placed his bicycle against the wall, all his doubts disappeared and nothing mattered only that he was there. And her face, glowing with pleasure, told him she was just as glad to see him as he was to be there.

Chapter 8

"Tom will go with you part of the way home, Rob." Mr Greenlees was gathering up Rob's schoolbag and sweater as he spoke. "It's a good mile and a half back to your house; with a bit of company it won't seem long. It's the least I can do after the help you have given him with his homework. You're a wizard with figures, Rob," he added, and putting an arm around Rob's shoulders went on, "You have the ability to go far."

"Thank you, Mr Greenlees, I was glad to help." Was he really that good? He just liked to help Tom when they did their homework together, and after such a wonderful time in the Greenlees' home, felt he had contributed something in return for their kindness. "Thank you for having me and thank Mrs Greenlees too, for a lovely tea."

"You must come back soon, Tom could do with the company and," indicating the rolling fields stretching away from the manse, "there's plenty of scope for your energy here."

"I'd love to come, and thank you again, but I best go on now, I told my sister I'd be home by nine o'clock."

"I'll show you out, Rob," and with that Mr Greenlees accompanied the two boys out of the door, and across the expansive patio with its ornate fountain, flowering tubs and lions' heads decorating low pillars. He watched them for a time as they made their way down the avenue away from the house, and felt glad that Tom had found a playmate so quickly. He missed his brother since he had gone to university, and Rob Hampton seemed a good boy, quiet and decent. And there was something about him that was so very appealing. He seemed lost and vulnerable, no doubt losing his mother at such a young age had been hard for him and was bound to have left its scars.

Rob and Tom continued down the avenue and out on to the Castlewellan Road in a comfortable silence. Rob was thinking about the great time he had had, and that he had never seen a house like the Greenlees'. There were rooms everywhere, the hall itself with its sweeping staircase must be as big as the whole ground floor of their house, and the height of the ceilings made him wonder how anyone could have reached up to paint them. But it was the bathroom that had impressed him the most. It was a vast room, with a huge bath with its clawed feet and gold taps. It sat in the middle of the room, dominating the area. Pale turquoise marble tiles stretched from floor to ceiling, and the floor too, was paved with marble. He couldn't wait to tell Dorrie all about it. Then suddenly he remembered Dorrie wouldn't be home tonight, wasn't that why he had been so anxious to go to Tom's house today? Suddenly a long, dark shadow seemed to fall across the evening as he thought of their home without her tonight.

"What do you want to work at when you leave school, Rob?" Tom's question broke in on his thoughts. Tom had been thinking about his father's enthusiasm regarding Rob's aptitude for figures.

"I don't know." Rob struggled with his thoughts. "I haven't really thought about it."

"Well, it'll have to be something to do with figures and accounting ... you're so good. You heard what Dad said and he means it, Rob." Tom's voice was full of admiration. "I just wish I was half as good as you. I have to struggle with it all, but it just comes naturally to you. And to think Dad wants me to study medicine. Can you imagine? Me? Can you see me passing those exams?"

"Oh, Tom. How wonderful would that be?" Rob's voice held respect. "Now that would be something, and of course you could. Besides, you could afford it, I couldn't."

"Oh it's not the money, Rob," Tom sounded quite dejected, "it's my brains, but I mean to try my best anyway. I know my dad would be proud of me."

Rob thought for a moment or two, before answering. He was reflecting on how easily he could confide in his friend, and Tom never passed comment while Rob talked but just listened quietly. Earlier today he had told him how much he was going to miss Dorrie when she was away, how much he depended on her.

"Well, I for one know you can succeed, Tom... and you're so kind, you would make an excellent doctor... and... you listen to people, and that's important."

"I do like people, you know, Rob. Look, I'll walk as far as this next junction; you'll manage from there, won't you?"

"Of course I will, and I'll be home in good time."

After bidding each other goodbye and acknowledging they would be at school as usual the next day, they separated, Tom to make his way back home and Rob proceeded along the road leading towards the humpback bridge which preceded the entrance to Poyntzpass. He trudged past the main gates of the station knowing his father would have stopped work by now and be at home. He went through the side gate and up the path leading to the back door. He entered the kitchen but the house was so quiet he knew immediately that Maggie and Eve weren't there. But his father must be here, his uniform coat was hanging in the hall – he must be in the parlour.

The evening sun shone through the front window reflecting in the mirror above the fireplace and casting its rays on Dorrie's chair, but in spite of the sun Rob suddenly felt cold. There was no sign of his father. He raced upstairs and went through into the bedroom he shared with Maggie and Eve, but it too was empty. He hesitated outside his father's bedroom, but he did not go in. He had never been in there since the day Dorrie had come to school to tell him their mother was dead. His mum had lay in that room and no one had allowed him to see her, and he knew so well that she would have longed to see him, as much as he wanted to see her. But they had been kept apart. Since that awful time he had always felt convinced that if he had seen her it would have helped her, and maybe she would not have died.

Panic stricken, his heart thumping, he raced downstairs and went out to the shed, but his father's bicycle had gone. He was alone in the house, it was getting late and he was afraid. A terrible feeling that something was wrong washed over him and the familiar tightness in his chest gripped him. He began to tremble and beads of perspiration gathered on his forehead and neck.

He went back into the house and sitting down in the kitchen, consciously tried to ease his panic by holding his arms tightly round his chest. He tried to reason with himself, but he knew he couldn't stay here; he would have to find Maggie and Eve. More than likely they were down at Carson's.

He would have to go down there, they mightn't be too pleased to see him, but that didn't matter, anything would be better than staying here feeling like this. He made his way out of the house and ran up the incline towards the shop. As he neared Carson's he couldn't see any sign of either of his sisters. Just a few men, obviously from the bar, hung around the entrance to the alley. He edged round past them, but they didn't seem to even notice him, they were so engrossed in conversation. He was a little way down the alley which led to the bar, when he spotted Eve – she was standing watching up the alley. Then, for some reason, his eyes were drawn away from her to the outside wall of the bar where a familiar figure, with long black hair, was being embraced by a tall angular man with a head of bushy, unkempt hair. It was Maggie. For a moment he stood transfixed, as if hypnotized, then he turned and began to race back up towards the street, but not before he knew Eve had spotted him. He never hesitated, but raced on past the men on the corner and down the hill towards home. When he entered the house he went straight up to Dorrie's bed, and flung himself, fully dressed onto her familiar quilt and buried his head in her pillow, in an effort to block out his vision of Maggie.

"Maggie, I told you we were late ... I knew we should have gone home long ago." Eve's voice sounded more firm than usual. She knew Rob had seen them, and she was anxious to follow him. Did he realise she was keeping a lookout for Maggie? This was terrible; she was mortified at the thought of it. Why did she continue to do it for her sister? She didn't know, but somehow, she didn't have the courage to say no to her. Besides, she felt if she always tried to stay around Maggie she would come to no harm. But now she could only think of Rob and the panic he seemed to have been in.

"Maggie ... I'm away home ... you please yourself."

"Oh, right ... I'm coming now." Maggie disengaged herself from the man's arms. "I have to go. Eve's going."

"What's the hurry, precious, it's only after nine o'clock – no one can see us here. Not where we are standing."

"Look, I'll see you tomorrow." Maggie pushed him away as he made to detain her, and turned to follow Eve. "Eve what's the hurry all of a sudden?"

"Didn't you see? For goodness' sake, didn't you see Rob? But of course you wouldn't have." Eve sounded agitated. "Rob was here in the alley. I'm sure he saw you, he went running home." Eve began to quicken her pace as she spoke and now Maggie had to run. "He'll likely tell Dad."

"Rob here? He never comes here." Maggie was taken aback.

"Well he was just now, that's for sure." Eve sounded accusing now. "I think he saw you hugging your man."

Maggie shrugged her shoulders, attempting to make light of the situation and putting an arm around Eve's shoulders added, "Cheer up, Eve ... Rob will never tell Dad, I do know that." Her tone was convincing. "Anyway, Dad's out, and we'll all be in bed when he gets back. And listen, Eve..." Maggie tightened her grip on Eve's shoulders, "if Rob doesn't mention anything about it to you, don't you mention anything about it to him?"

"OK, I won't, but please, Maggie, let's run and make sure he's home safely, and he's alright." Eve was pleading now.

In reply Maggie took her sister's hand and they raced down the incline, through the back garden, into the kitchen and then tiptoed upstairs, where they found Rob fast asleep in Dorrie's bed.

"There, I told you he'd be fine – he's missing Dorrie, you know," Maggie explained on the way downstairs. "You know what he's like about her. It's a pity he came looking for us, but maybe he never saw me at all."

Long after the two sisters had gone to bed, Maggie lay thinking about that evening. They should have gone home earlier, but it had proved difficult getting away from Phil. But she had managed to get a florin from him, just for a few kisses, and he had told her there was more where that came from. Some men were very liberal with their money, no doubt about that. She had the florin safety under her pillow, and tomorrow she would put it with the others she was gathering in a small cupboard off the bedroom. But she wouldn't go back to the bar for a night or two, just to be sure, she was determined no one would catch her out.

Eve, meantime, was thinking of Maggie and the man who had approached her tonight. He was really filthy and ugly. There was no other way to describe him. What was Maggie thinking of? What was she getting herself into? Sometimes she did warn her, but Maggie always reassured her that she knew what she was doing.

Meanwhile Rob had feigned sleep when his sisters had come into the bedroom. When they had gone back downstairs, he had undressed quickly and was in his pyjamas. But would he ever get to sleep tonight, with those images of Maggie in the company of that awful man? When he thought of what he had seen earlier, he cringed with shame and embarrassment. How could she? He must be far older than their father was, and so rough and dirty looking. He just hoped no one he knew would find out what she had been doing. Certainly, he would never tell anyone, not even Tom, what he had seen. He thought back to all the times Maggie had huddled up to Eve in the shop, whispering in her ear. And the worried look Eve constantly wore. He knew now she must be covering up for Maggie, there was no doubt about that. And what was worse, he sensed Eve did not like what she had to do for her older sister. Eventually he fell into a troubled sleep, where he dreamt a gaunt man with a huge nose was trying to carry him off.

Chapter 9

As Matt prepared for bed, and organised his uniform for the following morning, his mind was filled with thoughts of Jane and the evening that had flown by so swiftly. He had never meant anything to happen between them. In fact, he had been determined on his way to her that nothing would. But when she had led the way into the house and turned to him in the hall, they had come together so naturally, their bodies blending so perfectly, his resolve had weakened. He had kissed her, a gentle kiss at first, but her answering response was so full of passion and longing, that it wakened feelings in him he had suppressed for so long. After Evelyn's death he had thought that that part of his life was over and he would be alone for the rest of it. He had never expected to meet another woman he could love and cherish. Now was he really being given a second chance at happiness? And when Jane had gently taken his hand, and led him to the bedroom, he followed her willingly, his heart full.

Afterwards he had lain beside her, and the feeling of having found an inner peace and contentment, at the end of a long, dark tunnel, overwhelmed him. He wanted to thank Jane for her very existence. They lay together, arms entwined, in the quietness of the room and watched the red glow of the evening gradually fade until darkness fell. Later Matt tried to talk about their future together, it seemed a natural progression but Jane was adamant they must leave things as they were for the present.

"We'll see one another any time we can, Matt." Her arms tightened round him as she spoke. "Let's be happy together, just for now, but we shouldn't bring any more changes to our families, they've had so much to deal with in the last three years."

"Do you think they might object then?"

"Let's not even think of anything like that, not just yet, please, Matt." Jane knew she was deeply in love with this man beside her. She loved him more than she had ever loved Stan. She had cared deeply for her husband, he had been so good to her and their sons, and she had been devastated at his death. But Matt had awakened feelings in her she never knew she had; he had brought a whole new meaning of love to her, of total compatibility. But their situation was a complex one, what with her having the farm, him with the station house, and the effect any change of circumstances might have on them all. Something in her voice persuaded Matt not to pursue the subject, and when she reassured him of her love and commitment to him, he had to be content with that.

Later they went into the kitchen, and had supper of tea and hot buttered toast, with the oil lamp casting shadows on the dresser. Suddenly Jane realised the lateness of the hour and insisted Matt set off home at once. "The children will wonder where on earth you are. I mustn't be selfish – just because mine aren't here." She sounded anxious.

"I didn't realise it was so late." Matt hastened to reassure Jane. "They go to bed reasonably early – they should be fast asleep by now. You mustn't start fretting about my ones. They are pretty independent." And he smiled lovingly at her. Then together they made their way to the door, where reluctantly Matt parted from her. He retrieved his bicycle from the wall, but reached towards her again, and kissed her gently before mounting his bicycle and heading towards home.

When he entered the house later, all was quiet. He tiptoed up the stairs, silently opened the children's bedroom door, and saw that all three were fast asleep with Rob snuggled into Dorrie's bed. That was more or less what he had expected to see, he knew his son would miss Dorrie more than any of them. But hopefully, her absence from home during the week would help him stand on his own two feet.

"Where's Rob this morning, Maggie, is he not up yet?" Matt was just about to leave for the station.

"He must be tired, Dad ... maybe walking to the Greenlees and back." Maggie sounded concerned. "It must be a good three mile walk there and back to that manse." Maggie purposely had not wakened her brother – she wanted to leave it as late as possible, in case there were any awkward questions asked by anyone.

"I'll call him in a minute ... don't worry, he won't be late for school," she nodded reassuringly, "I'll see to that."

When Rob did appear in the kitchen he was disappointed he had missed his father, but Maggie was particularly nice to him, and had his breakfast sitting ready. She was so loving to him he found he just couldn't bear a grudge with her. Surely last night was just a trivial incident, because he knew Maggie was a really good girl. And later, after Maggie hugged and kissed him goodbye, he set off with Eve in a much happier frame of mind. Dorrie would be home on Friday, and he might talk to her about it.

Dorrie hadn't expected to feel homesick in Belfast. After all, hadn't she longed for the opportunity to see the place and this way of life? But the weather during her first week there was so glorious, that she had overpowering images of Poyntzpass and the effect sunshine always had on it. Their village was always homely and welcoming, and when the housewives brought their chairs out onto the pavement, to chat to one another with a cup of tea, it emphasized the relaxed and cosy atmosphere. She could visualize the green fields so vividly, and thought of the summers when she, her sisters and Rob had spent hours playing in them, listening to the birds, and trying to identify the different species. They could spend hours out there, just swinging on gates or watching the farmers busy with their haymaking, and watching to see if their wives would soon appear with baskets laden with food for the hungry men.

Belfast was so very different. It smelt of fuel and smoke, and the constant hum of traffic contrasted sharply with the drone of bees, or the clip clop of horses along the roads at home. There were no green fields either, at least not that she had seen. But then, she had been so busy since she arrived here, that there was no time or means to visit the suburbs. Monday and Wednesday were taken up with night classes. She went straight there from work and caught the last bus to Stranmillis Road at 10 p.m. The other nights were spent mostly in her bedroom studying bookkeeping notes, which the teacher in night class had assured her were elementary. Mr and Mrs Finlay had been kindness itself, but that only seemed to have the effect of making her more homesick. Mrs Finlay insisted she dine with them on the evenings she came straight home from work. And she really loved the bedroom they had given her – it was so calm and peaceful. In it her yearning for home subsided, yet nothing could really compensate for Rob's company, and Maggie and Eve's light-hearted chatter, never mind her father's dependable figure always in the background.

Now it was Thursday evening and she had come straight up to her room after dinner, in order to pack her case in readiness to go home on Friday. The good weather looked set to stay, and the first thing she intended to do when she got home was organise a picnic for Saturday. She was really looking forward to that.

She was delighted to see her family waiting to meet her when she alighted from the train the following evening. They gave her such a welcome, with hugs and kisses all round that she felt it was nearly worth it to be a bit homesick during the week. Later on, after dinner, they retired to the parlour and exchanged one another's news and Dorrie was relieved they all seemed to have survived well without her overseeing them, and had even managed to establish a bit of a routine.

Saturday turned out to be one of the hottest days of the year, the sun shone high in a blue, cloudless sky. They all helped pack the family hamper with Maggie's homemade bread and currant buns and different cheeses from Carson's. Before they set off over the fields, Dorrie insisted on calling on Emily Carson. Even though she had written to her earlier this week, she had to let her know how much she was enjoying the type of work she was doing, but she didn't say anything about being homesick.

The fields they had always played in since childhood stretched along the side of the railway line, but today they intended to cross these fields to go to their most favourite pasture. Here the hills levelled out round the whole area, creating a flat secluded, verdant green meadow where bushes of hawthorn grew abundantly, undisturbed by wind or rain.

As they walked across, baby rabbits scuttled away from them, their tails bobbing as they ran terrified, back to their burrows. Rob and Eve had spread the rug they had brought and they all declared that Maggie's bread and buns were the best ever, and of course, Mrs Carson's cheese. Afterwards, they scattered the crumbs for the birds and other wildlife, and Dorrie thought it was idyllic, just what she needed after her busy, strange week. Meanwhile, Rob fleetingly contemplated telling Dorrie about Maggie, but then decided he should say nothing. They were having such a wonderful time – it would be a shame to spoil it. He might confide in her some other time, but he wanted this weekend to be perfect.

Maggie on the other hand, had been determined, even before Dorrie came home, that she would stay around this weekend. She would stay away from Carson's, and stick with Dorrie. She didn't want to give Rob a chance of any time alone with her, in case he told her about Phil and her.

Chapter 10

The mail to Poyntzpass always arrived on the 8 a.m. train, but it was eleven o'clock before Matt had any opportunity to begin to sort it. As he did, he recognised Dorrie's handwriting on a blue envelope postmarked Belfast. It was a Wednesday morning in September 1922, Dorrie had been working for eighteen months now in Belfast, and although he knew she corresponded regularly with Emily Carson, this was the first time she had written to him, preferring to keep all her news for the weekend. Feeling uneasy, Matt slit the envelope open – was anything wrong? But as he read through the letter his anxiety evaporated when he realised she was writing to let them know she wouldn't be home this weekend. This was the first time she had done this and he read eagerly.

Dear Dad,

Mr Finlay has booked tickets for the Grand Opera House on Saturday evening, and has invited me to join his family. You will remember me telling you about his sons, and that John had recently returned home after obtaining his degree at university and had joined his father's business.

She went on to say she hoped no one would mind her not coming this Friday, but she would be with them the following weekend as usual. Then she added, *John, Mr Finlay's son, would love to visit Poyntzpass. I suppose I have painted glowing pictures of the place. Would you mind if he travelled up with me the following Weekend? I know we can't put him up, but Mrs Carson has always said if any of my friends wished to come, she would welcome them to her spare room. So, if you think it would be alright, perhaps you would mention to her. Meantime, I'll write to her as well.*

Hoping to hear from you soon, and please give all my love to Rob, Eve and Maggie.

Love you
Dorrie.

As Matt sat at his desk, his daughter's letter in his hand, he tried to grasp what was really going on in his daughter's life. Although Dorrie talked about her friends in work and the Finlay boys, this was the first time she had wanted anyone to visit Poyntzpass. Was John Finlay just a friend, and only anxious to see their village? He doubted it, but Dorrie was over nineteen and he supposed it was inevitable she would meet someone soon. She was so attractive, and with her calm, gentle manner was bound to have men noticing her and eager for her company. He intended to call with Emily Carson to see if she was agreeable to having a house guest, and he would try to find out if she knew anything about John Finlay. Maybe she knew something he didn't. He would answer the letter today and assure his daughter he had no objection whatsoever to her bringing any of her friends home. He was just disappointed they didn't have a spare room.

Later, as he thought about Dorrie and John Finlay coming the next weekend he realised that he would have to entertain them. It was the least he could do, the Finlays had been so good to Dorrie. That being so, he would not be in a position to visit Jane, so he must make sure he spent time with her this weekend. If only Jane would agree to them telling their families about their feelings for each other. It would please him so much if he were in a position to have her and her children at his home to meet everyone. It was a year now since they had realised how they felt about one another. And he was tired of snatched evenings, hurried kisses and lovemaking any time her boys were away. But she had remained resolute; the children needed a little more time. She still thought Rob and her youngest boy, Jim, too young to understand. Rather reluctantly he had to go along with her wishes.

Maggie never seemed to object to looking after the place but seemed content to work at Carson's, then come home and prepare food, and always seemed in the best of spirits. As for Eve, she never wanted to go anywhere since starting work in Banbridge Mill; she seemed so tired when she came home in the evenings. Rob on the other hand, would not need much encouragement to spend Friday evening at Greenlees manse, especially when he heard Dorrie wasn't going to be home. He would be disappointed when he heard that, he always looked forward to seeing her. But at least he had Tom Greenlees, they got on well and spent a lot of time together.

Later, on his way home, he called with Emily, but she couldn't throw any light on the fact that John Finlay was coming visiting. But she said he was very welcome to a bed in her house. Later over dinner he told Rob and the girls Dorrie's plans and showed Rob the letter from her. "Read it out to us, Rob, will you?" Maggie was dishing out dessert, which was a plate of rice and stewed apple. "Imagine one of the Finlay's coming here." She was really looking forward to that.

There was a silence for a moment as Rob finished reading.

"Oh, he's staying with Mrs Carson then." Maggie was disappointed.

"Well, there's no room here, Maggie, is there, Dad?" Rob was relieved Dorrie would still be here, that much hadn't changed.

"We have no room to put him up, which is a pity. I can't very well ask him to share my room, can I?" Matt was thinking about the home the Finlay's lived in and the number of people they would be able to accommodate, if they needed to.

"I wonder why John's coming to visit Poyntzpass?" Eve had been silent until now, but she was curious. "Is she going out with him, do you think, Dad?"

"She certainly hasn't said anything about that to me ... we'll have to wait and see". It was interesting that Eve's thoughts were similar to his on the subject of John Finlay. "If there's anything between them, we'll all hear in good time, I suppose."

"Would you mind if there was, Dad?" Rob was anxious to know how his father was feeling. "Didn't she say he was just a friend."

"Of course, Rob, of course ... as I've said, we have to wait and see."

"By the way, Tom has asked me to stay with him some night soon, and I wonder if I might stay on Friday night." Rob had decided that being at Tom's would be the next best thing to seeing Dorrie.

"Good idea, Rob." Matt was relieved he hadn't even had to suggest it. "I'll go over on my bicycle to his dad later on, and ask him and Mrs Greenlees myself – that's the proper thing to do."

He turned to Maggie and Eve. "We'll need to spend time with John Finlay when he comes – make him more than welcome – I was thinking I would work at the station this Friday evening. Would you be alright?" He always felt guilty about lying to his children, but there was nothing else for it, just at present.

"We'll be fine ... Dad." Maggie sounded impatient. "I'm seventeen now." She looked at him steadily, a frown on her face. "I think everyone forgets that sometimes."

"Ok." He turned to his youngest daughter. "What about you, Eve? You're very quiet."

"I'll just be glad of the rest. We sit up late when Dorrie's at home, and usually go somewhere or other on Sunday. That mill's very hard work and I'm always tired."

"You do look weary." Matt studied her now, she was the smallest of the three girls, with a neat waist and fine wrists and ankles, but it struck him that she had lost weight. She was bordering on skinny, only her bright blue eyes and olive skin redeemed her thin face.

"You'll have to try to eat more, Eve, and get more rest."

"Eve eats well," this was Maggie, "don't you, Eve?"

"Glad to hear it. Is it working at the mill? Are you not happy there?" Matt was still concerned. Maggie seemed content enough in Carson's but he did wonder about Eve and her choice of work. But what else was there for her? She wasn't as bright as the others, not by a long chalk.

"I like my work, Dad." Eve was emphatic. She longed to tell him what really tired her. Accompanying Maggie, and keeping lookout for her, tired her more than any day's work. But she could never tell her father that.

Rob had a great night at Tom's home. He went straight from school on Friday, having taken a small holdall with a change of clothes, his toothbrush and pyjamas with him.

Matt and Jane had a wonderful few hours together. Dan had earlier taken her two boys to Newcastle for a drive in his new car. He was the only one Matt and Jane confided in. When Matt left Jane late on Friday night, he was a very contented man. He had told her all about Dorrie, and what he really thought was behind her bringing John Finlay home. They had both reached an agreement that after Dorrie's visit the following weekend, they would be more open with their families.

Meantime Maggie, after watching her father go off on his bicycle, had gleefully told Eve that the coast was clear, and she intended to bring a couple of men back to the house after they visited the bar. She reassured Eve that no one could see them, as the evenings were getting dark. Eve had a miserable time that evening. She was fraught with anxiety in case anyone came to visit them or their father returned early. But the last thing she wanted was a confrontation with Maggie so had gone along with her idea. She was horrified when Maggie suggested she could entertain one of the men in their father's bedroom, because she was going to entertain her man in their bedroom. This latest barbaric idea of Maggie's she flatly refused to do. Her only alternative was to sit the whole evening, miserable and overwrought, in the parlour, making small talk with a man who seemed to be as embarrassed as she was by Maggie's behaviour and Eve's obvious discomfort.

Chapter 11

Dorrie had mixed feelings about taking John to meet her family. Perhaps she should have been more open in her letter, and told her father she was bringing home the man she intended to marry. She had been reluctant to do this, believing it would be better to tell everyone when they would all be together. Anyway, it was too late now, her letter had already been posted, but she knew her father well enough to know that he would wonder about it all. He would probably even suspect there was more to it than she had said. She felt guilty too. She, who had intended to make something of herself in Belfast and had ambitions to become a private secretary, here she was, just eighteen months later, thinking of giving it all up to get married. When she did tell her father, would he feel her leaving Poyntzpass and her family had all been futile. Would he feel she was too young to even think of getting married? She had tortured herself so much since she had written to him, that she dreaded his reply in case he discouraged the visit. What then? And even if he did agree to the visit, would he like John? Dorrie knew if her father gave John an opportunity to be himself he would soon approve of her choice, because everyone who knew him respected him highly. Even as she thought of him now, her eyes softened and her face flushed with pleasure. She had been so aware of him since their very first meeting when he had returned from university, but she had never imagined he could possibly have any interest in her. After all, she was a simple country girl, unsophisticated and ordinary, who spent most of her spare time with her commerce books. When he had started to join her at the table in the works canteen she had thought he was merely being mannerly because she was a guest in his home. But one evening, as she came down the steps of the college, she saw him waiting on the footpath, stretching his tall frame above the other students who spilled down the steps in front of her. When she spotted him he waved and moved across to meet her. Taking her bag of books from her he explained he had been working late and thought she might like a lift rather than waiting for the last bus. After that, he always made a point of being there to take her home after her evening classes. A few weeks later one evening after dinner – as she made to go to her room to study – he asked if she would like to see the countryside around Bangor and Helen's Bay.

During the following three months, meeting after work and going for long drives together became routine for them. He showed her a side to Belfast she had never known existed, with quiet parks, small sandy coves, and houses which could only belong to the very rich. They spent hours wandering through the wooded glens, talking about work in the mill and their aspirations for the future. John told her how glad he was to be done with university, he had disliked the life there immensely, and was just thankful to be home and established in the family business. For her part, she felt content and totally at ease in his company. He was such a good listener and so undemanding, interested in her college work and keen to hear all about her family. And gradually she was able to talk about her devastation over her mother's death, the immense loss to her family and the sense of responsibility she had towards them.

That same evening as she opened her heart, he stopped the car and turning towards her, had taken her hands in his and kissing her gently, told her he loved her deeply and wanted to protect her for the rest of her life. She was so overcome, that the tears, which had been close to the surface as she talked, coursed down her cheeks, and her mouth trembled beneath his. Sensing her emotion, he put his arms around her, and drew her towards him, until she felt more composed. She had no experience of the feelings that swamped her, but she knew she felt secure and cared for when she was with him, and the world that had seemed to be shifting beneath her since her mother's death, now felt a settled and comfortable place to be. She knew she wanted to spend the rest of her life with him.

Since that evening everything had moved on quickly, John had told his parents how they felt about each other. They were delighted and had given their total approval and blessing. Then they had suggested that, after they were married, they could make their home with them until they found a suitable place. Dorrie could only hope her own family would be as accepting of their relationship. In the meantime, she had to wait for her father's reply and see if he even approved of John coming to visit.

The letter arrived on the Monday after Dorrie's weekend with the Finlays, when, as arranged, they had gone to the Grand Opera House on the Saturday. On Sunday, even though it was still a secret, they had celebrated their engagement by going to a small, select restaurant they had discovered on one of their outings at their favourite cove.

Dorrie opened the letter anxiously; aware John was hovering beside her in expectation. As she scanned it, she saw the words, "Wonderful... delighted," and breathed a sigh of relief. Whether or not her father suspected anything between John and she, he had said nothing, just extended a warm welcome to her "Friend" and more especially a Finlay.

"Dad says he is looking forward to meeting you..." Dorrie relaxed visibly.

"I'm glad to hear it ... you had me worried, you know."

"Well, I've never brought anyone home before..."

"I'm glad to hear that, I can tell you." He smiled in an amusing but loving way. "It's heartening to be the very first."

"We still have to tell him that we hope to get married next year," Dorrie reminded him... "He still doesn't know that yet."

"Well he soon will... but you must stop worrying..." He kissed her tenderly. "In a few days he'll know, and everything's going to be fine. I'm really looking forward to it, and to seeing your home village."

"John, it's only a small, old-fashioned place you know." Dorrie was wondering now, had she been over enthusiastic about Poyntzpass when she had spoken of it to John? Would he see the place as she did, or would he be disappointed?

"That's exactly what appeals to me. Initially I thought of driving up there, but the train journey sounds more attractive, what do you think?"

"Yes, it has to be the train, because knowing Dad he'll be waiting to greet us in his stationmaster's uniform ... he'll love to do that. In the meantime," Dorrie looked at her watch, "I have to get down the road to go to work."

Dorrie and John caught the afternoon train to Poyntzpass the following Friday. John's father had insisted they must go early to make the most of their weekend together, adding he would send a message with one of the Banbridge workers to Matt, to let him know their time of arrival.

As Dorrie stepped off the train with John beside her, she saw her father immediately, looking very smart, as she had known he would. Any anxieties she had about their reception, dissipated when she saw the welcoming smile on his face. John saw a tall, distinguished looking man with the most remarkable blue eyes, so expressive yet so haunted looking. His warmth seemed to embrace John, and his earlier resolve not to mention anything about Dorrie and himself until later, was all forgotten about. He put out his hand saying, "I'm delighted to meet you Mr Hampton, and I think you should know I wish to marry your daughter – with your permission, of course."

Chapter 12

Dorrie was married on a beautiful, sunny May day in 1923 in the church in Poyntzpass where her mother's funeral had been held six years before. She had wanted to marry John here, where she always felt her mother's presence so strongly.

For her wedding she had chosen a cream, silk fitted dress with long, narrow sleeves and a simple spray of flowers for her hair. Maggie and Eve were bridesmaids and wore simple, sleeveless, coffee coloured dresses with simple rosebudded headbands in their hair. One of John's brothers, Ian, was best man and Rob had felt really honoured to be asked to be groomsman. After the church service guests strolled across the street to Emily and Joe's place.

In the months leading up to the wedding Matt had organised everything for the young couple. He booked the church, ordered flowers – and because Dorrie was adamant she wished to have the reception at Carson's, had given up any thoughts of reserving any hotel. He had then inveigled Maggie into helping Emily with all the food.

Earlier in the morning, tables had been placed out on the green lawn at the side of the bar. The best cutlery, china and napkins that Emily possessed had been brought out, and thanks to her and Maggie the whole setting for the occasion was flawless. After the speeches were over, Maggie changed into a simple, blue cotton dress which she felt would be more comfortable for carrying the cooked chicken, pork, beef and a variety of potatoes and vegetables to the tables.

It was a small, exclusive group who attended the celebration. All the Hamptons were part of the bridal party, and the only other relatives present were Aunt Olive, as Uncle Joe had had a stroke and was unable to attend. John's parents, his two other brothers, and an aunt and uncle represented the Finlays. Of course the Carsons were both present, as was Miss Quigley, the children's teacher, accompanied by the farmer who had been wooing her for the last couple of years. As far as Matt was concerned though, the most important guests there were Jane and her two boys. He had quietly insisted to Dorrie that he would like her to be present, but had not divulged the true nature of their relationship. Jane had been anxious to say nothing at this stage, she didn't want anything to hijack the young couple's day.

Matt felt so proud today of all his family, and how they had survived the dreadful time of Evelyn's death. How beautiful they had grown, – Dorrie, radiant in her wedding dress, Maggie still looking as pretty in her simple, blue dress as she had in her coffee coloured bridesmaid dress. Eve too, seemed transformed, her thin face bright and smiling, as she talked animatedly to Ian Hampton seated beside her. As for Rob, he had never seen his son more relaxed looking, he seemed to be finding the whole occasion fun, and was waving heartily to Tom Greenlees seated with his parents at a table a little way from theirs.

The whole day flew past, and then it was time for the happy couple to depart for their honeymoon. Ian Hampton had driven from Belfast by car, and John and Dorrie were using it to visit Portrush, and from there would go across to Donegal for a week before returning to take up residence with the Finlays. After many goodbyes, a few tears and all good wishes for the future, the couple managed to steal away, driving through the village to the accompaniment of yet more cheering. After they had gone and people began to disperse, Matt made the most of a lull in the festivities to seek Jane out. He seated himself beside her where she sat quietly watching everyone enjoying themselves, and as she smiled up at him, he relaxed visibly and returned her smile.

"Matt, this has been such a wonderful day... a great success, thanks to you."

Matt nodded and his face was animated. "I think everything has gone well... we have managed to give them a good send off." He was pleased how smoothly everything had gone. It had been worth all the effort of planning and organising, not to mention the expense.

"Unfortunately etiquette dictates I must stay to the end of the night. I have to wait until everyone else has gone. But I know you understand, Jane."

"Of course, Matt, that's no problem... I'll wait with you." She indicated her sons sitting talking to Eve and Maggie at another table.

"My boys are having too good a time to think about home. Besides..." she added, almost wistfully, "the bride and groom have gone... we have given them their day... maybe it's our turn now. I think we have waited long enough. Anyway," she looked round the guests who still lingered over their drinks, "I don't believe it's news to anyone here about us. I think most people in Poyntzpass are well aware of our relationship, don't you agree?"

Matt was quite surprised.

"Do you think so? I hadn't really thought much about it." He had been too absorbed with her, to think or worry about any gossip. He might have been vaguely aware of it in the early days, but he had supposed it had all died down. Turning to her, he put his arms round her and kissed her full on the mouth, and then whispered in her ear, "Let's put paid to any gossip then, shall we?"

In reply Jane promptly returned his kiss and leaned her head down on his shoulder in such a loving gesture, that anyone watching could not possibly misinterpret. Then they sat quietly together, hands entwined, enjoying the late evening and one another's company.

Rob had been sitting with Tom discussing the amount of food they had consumed, and wondering how they had managed it all, when he noticed his father make his way across the green to Mrs Brankin. He had noticed her earlier and vaguely wondered who had invited her. She was a really beautiful woman, quiet, graceful and elegant in a hyacinth blue flowing dress. Now as he watched his father approaching her, his senses were alerted, and he became more and more uneasy. There was something about the eagerness of his father's walk, and the way Mrs Brankin looked at him as he neared her, that stuck a note of fear in his chest. But he was totally unprepared to see his father embrace and kiss her, then sit with her, their arms entwined so lovingly. There was no mistaking the message in their whole conduct. Rob turned his head away, reluctant to witness anything else. He looked over towards Maggie and Eve to see if they had noticed anything, but they were so engrossed with the Brankin boys, they could not have seen any of it. Then Tom's voice interrupted his mood.

"My parents seem to be getting ready for home, Rob. I've had a super day, old chap." He looked quizzically at his friend. "Are you alright? You look a bit shook up."

"Sorry, Tom," Rob made a conscious effort to pull himself together, "I suddenly feel very tired." So he did – he felt totally drained – but his senses were still alerted to his father sitting across from him.

"Call over tomorrow, Rob, will you? Come for your lunch. Will you?"

"Sure thing, Tom... I'll do that." Rob rose from his seat as he spoke. If Tom was going, he would go and join Maggie and Eve, maybe quietly mention what he had seen. Perhaps, everything would be fine tomorrow, it was just the spirit of celebration had made his father behave so foolishly.

He walked down the alley with the Greenlees, and after bidding them goodnight and making final arrangements for the following day, he made his way over to Maggie and Eve. Eve was still talking to Harry Brankin, but Jim had gone over to speak to his mother, and Maggie sat quietly on her own. Rob quickly made the most of the opportunity, and drawing up a chair, whispered in a conspiratorial tone what he had just witnessed.

Maggie looked briefly over at her father and Jane then turned to Rob. "Yes, he's with the widow Brankin," she smiled knowingly at her brother, "I've known for some time something was going on." She looked at Rob in surprise. "Where did you think he was going to all those evenings, when he went out on his bicycle? You must have known he was going somewhere important."

Rob looked at her in amazement, his face drained of colour. "He always goes cycling to get fresh air and exercise, after being in the smoky station all day." He sounded adamant.

"Well if that's what you want to believe," Maggie looked at him with something like pity in her expression, "that's fair enough." Had Rob been so gullible and so naive? Now in order to take his mind of his father, she could see it was distressing him, she went on, "Look, help me clear up here, and then Eve, you and I, we'll head home and don't worry, Rob," in a reassuring tone, "Dad will soon follow I'm sure. First of all, though we have to tear Eve away from Harry."

Although Rob felt inclined to go straight to his father and confront him for telling lies, he knew it would spoil the day for everyone. So instead he busied himself helping his sisters and Emily Carson clear up the mess, all the time aware he was on the verge of one of his panic attacks. He had come to dread these feelings, and now he had to concentrate on what he was doing, to try and keep another one at bay. When the whole place looked as if nothing had ever taken place, the rubbish was emptied, the bar was gleaming and every dish had been washed, the three of them headed back over to the station house. As they left, Rob stole a glance over at his father, and was relieved to see they were both on their feet. Good, his Dad would soon be home, and they would all enjoy talking about the wonderful day they had had.

When they entered the house everything seemed particularly quiet and still after the noise and bustle of the wedding, and the house felt very comforting. Maggie departed into the kitchen while Eve and Rob flopped down in the comfortable chairs in the parlour, to await their father's return. For a while, they sat and chatted about the guests, Eve and Maggie discussing outfits and Miss Quigley's new boyfriend. But Rob kept looking at the clock, and when over an hour had past he realised his father had gone somewhere else, and was not coming home directly. He told his sisters in quite an aggressive manner that the whole day was ruined because of his father's absence.

"Oh, come on, Rob," Maggie encouraged him, "it's not the end of the world, you know... Dad needs to lead his own life too." She got up from her seat and went into the kitchen.

"I've just the thing to relax you, Rob... everything will seem better when you have some." She came back from the kitchen with a tray containing three glasses of light amber liquid. "Here – try this ... it's just a light whiskey." She handed each of them a glass. "I got this given to me as a present."

Rob hesitated, shaking his head reluctantly but Maggie insisted. "It's really light – and we should celebrate Dorrie's wedding in our own privacy." Maggie had just reminded Rob that Dorrie was gone from their home for good, and although he knew she was very happy, already he missed her desperately. She, more than anyone, would have reassured him about Dad. But God knows what would happen now, between his father and Mrs Brankin. He suddenly made the decision to try the drink; it might ease the pressure in his chest. He knew he had to do something to prevent these horrible attacks he was so prone to. He took a mouthful, and it tasted so foul and burned the back of his throat, that he began to splutter.

"For goodness' sake... you're supposed to sip it, not gulp it like a glass of water. Look – sip it ... like this." Maggie proceeded to put the glass to her lips. After that Rob took the drink slowly, and after the first glass he realised that Maggie had been right, it did relax him and he could feel himself unwinding as he took it. Between them they finished off the first bottle and Maggie fetched another one, although Eve insisted she did not want any more, could not drink another drop.

The next day Rob was late going to visit Tom. He had felt so ill when he had wakened earlier. His head was pounding, his mouth and throat were parched and the very thought of food nauseated him. He vowed that would do him drinking whiskey – never again. Enough was enough. When he told Maggie how he felt and that he couldn't remember going to bed, she thought it was very funny.

Chapter 13

1925

Jane had set her alarm clock for 6 a.m. but she was up and dressed long before it went off. She had so much to do before she went to catch the nine o'clock train to Newry. She had made arrangements for Dan to call for her at 8.30 a.m. He would leave her at the station, before taking Jim on to school. Although Harry had left school and helped with a lot of the farm work, it was still all pretty new to him. Before she left she must give him careful instructions about separating the new litters of pigs, and transferring the cattle to a different field.

It was Dan who insisted she must make a doctor's appointment, after noticing how tired and listless she seemed to be. When he first mentioned her lack of energy she had been tempted to confide in him, but decided to tell no one until she had told Matt about her suspicions that she was pregnant. How Matt would react when he heard it, she didn't know – she had such conflicting emotions about it herself. If it hadn't been for the children she would have been delighted, but the thought of their possible reactions cast a huge cloud over her happiness. How would they all feel about it when they heard, children could be so unkind. Would they feel disgust at the idea that Matt and she had a sexual relationship? She really didn't mind for herself that people might gossip, but was fearful at the sense of shame the young ones might experience.

Since Dorrie's wedding a few weeks ago, Matt and she had discussed the possibility of marrying soon. They had never got around to making definite plans and now it looked as if their wedding would have to be sooner rather than later. But so many issues were still unresolved. For one thing, where was everyone to live? She couldn't visualise either Maggie or Eve coming here, they were so independent, and they thought the farm very remote. If Matt came to live on the farm, what would they do about the station house? If she went to the station house what about the farm? Selling up didn't seem to be an option, because Stan had left the place to Harry. As was always expected, the first born would inherit, and he did seem to be taking a keen interest in it all. As for Rob, he would be fifteen years of age in November. Would he like to live out of the village?

She had asked herself these questions over and over again until her head ached and her body felt weary, but had yet to come up with a satisfactory answer. When she tried to discuss it with Matt, he always said he had every confidence they would work something out. She supposed he meant his words to be reassuring, but she felt in practical terms it solved nothing.

Later, after Dan had left her at the station, she was thankful Matt was busy organising his workforce and the goods which had just arrived. She had told him the previous evening that she was going shopping in Newry, but she knew if he had had time to spare this morning, she would have been tempted to blurt out all her worries to him. As it was they simply exchanged endearments with each other, and Matt promised to be over to the farm in the evening.

"Dad, did you know Rob's going to start work as a porter in the station at the beginning of September?" Tom Greenlees sat across the dinner table from his father, a concerned look on his face. "He says he's no interest in going to college." It was the last week in August and Tom was beginning to panic about his friend. He himself was going to college, and hopefully then go to university. He intended to work really hard, and at least try to achieve good grades. But Rob had such a natural ability, how could he even think of going to work as a station porter? He – who would fly through university.

"Would you talk to him, Dad? I know he likes you a lot, maybe he would listen to you?"

"I did try, you know, Tom." Will Greenlees would have liked to see the two boys going off to college together, and he knew Rob had real talent.

"There's little more we can do... I've spoken to his father – he's disappointed too – then I spoke to Rob, but he's adamant about being a porter." He did not add that he had offered to pay for Rob's education. He understood from Matt Hampton that father and son had had words several times, and Matt had only relented when Rob had dissolved in tears over it all.

"I believe Rob's wasting himself, that's what I think." Tom sounded reasonable, but there was impatience in his voice,

"He's got more brains than I'll ever have. I thought that with his father getting married next week, he would have jumped at the chance to get away from it all. I know he's not too happy about it. I think he's really insecure. Does he simply want to work alongside his father, or is he really keen on railway stations and trains?" Tom appealed to his father.

"You're very astute, Tom." Will Greenlees agreed with his son, he did think Rob was very insecure, but surely that was to be expected? He had lost his mother at such a young age, then his sister – who had replaced his mother in Rob's eyes – had left home, was now married, and to cap it all here was his father getting married again and under a cloud. Obviously the boy still needed an anchor in his life and no doubt the prospect of working with his father was just that.

"I promise you this, Tom," with a comforting tone in his voice, "I'll keep in touch with Rob, and I'll keep an eye on him. It's all we can do."

"Thanks, Dad." It wasn't much, but he knew his father would keep his word, he always did, and that was reassuring to him. "By the way, where are the Hampton's going to live after the wedding?"

Will Greenlees admitted he wasn't sure, it was all a bit vague, but understood from Matt that he intended to divide his time between the farm and the station house. Rob, Eve and Maggie would stay on in the home they had always known. Will thought the terms of the station house very strict – surely the railway company could rent out the station house – it shouldn't matter where Matt lived. But it seemed if you were stationmaster, you must reside in the house provided by the Railway Company. So naturally Matt wasn't prepared to take any risks over it, and so the children would stay there and he would come two or three nights each week to check everything was in order. To Will, it sounded most unsatisfactory, but then Matt's children were growing up fast. Maggie was eighteen now, and Rob practically fifteen. They should be able to manage, and at least they were closer to their work than they would be out at the farm. He wondered how they all felt about Matt and Jane Brankin's forthcoming marriage, never mind all the gossip about Jane's condition.

Rob sat in the front pew of the church with Maggie and Eve on one side of him and Dorrie and John on the other. Across the aisle Harry and Jim Brankin were seated beside their Uncle Dan and Aunt Barbara, and as he stole a glance in their direction, Rob envied their happy-go-lucky expressions. They didn't seem to mind their mum getting married again. As he listened to the minister's voice droning on – he was an awfully boring speaker – he just wished, more than anything, he was home in the station house with his own mother and Dorrie, and that nothing had ever changed.

He had tried to talk to Dorrie two weeks ago, when John and she had come over to Poyntzpass but she said she was more concerned about his future and the lack of prospects he had joining the Railway Company.

"You know, Rob, promotion is most unlikely for years – becoming a stationmaster, I mean. Dad happened to be lucky, but men do stay in these posts until they retire. Why are you doing this?" she had asked him directly then, in her quiet, composed way. "The whole school always knew you were capable of so much more... do you like trains that much, Rob?"

He had to reassure her that he just loved the whole atmosphere, and besides, he might be as fortunate as his father had been, and become a stationmaster. After that Dorrie had closed the subject, by saying she hoped he was right. He was left with a strong feeling that she was disappointed in him, and that bothered him more than anything. Her praise had always been important to him, but this was what he wanted to do. The very idea of leaving Poyntzpass and going to a strange college with strange people was nearly enough to bring on one of his panic attacks. He knew he would be more able to cope here, and he would see his father every day.

Now the organ was starting to play, and Rob brought his mind back to the moment, and as he watched his father and Jane proceed down the aisle, smiling at them all as they went, he felt a sudden lift to his mood. His father looked so happy and Jane Brankin was so beautiful that he was able to reassure himself that everything was going to be alright.

Chapter 14

1926

Rob had been feeling unwell all morning, and the fumes and noise of the station made him feel worse. He had wakened around four in the morning feeling terrible and, for the first time since starting work, dreaded going to the station. Since he had been on duty he knew his father had been looking at him anxiously a few times, but so far had passed no comment, and Rob tried to struggle on organising letters and parcels as best he could. But he was relieved when his father called him and announced it was time for their morning break. Cups and saucers were laid out for Fred, his father and himself and at first Rob didn't notice the sandwiches on the plate, but when he did his stomach heaved, he tasted bitter bile at the back of his throat and the colour drained from his face. Weakly he sat down in the chair across from his father.

"What's wrong? You look all in, Rob." His father was concerned.

"I don't feel so good – I won't eat anything – just a cup of tea for me." Rob made an attempt to reach for his cup but his hand was shaking so much the liquid spilt over his trousers and onto the tiled floor.

"You're not well." As he spoke his father crossed over to him and put his hand on his forehead. "You're in a real sweat, I think you must be sickening for something." He turned to Fred. "Get Rob over home and help him back into bed." And as he reached for his son's coat hanging on the rack behind him, he went on, "You'll need this, Rob, it's one miserable November day out there." He placed the jacket round his son's shoulders. "I'll call over later to see you, meantime stay in bed. It's a good job it's Saturday and Maggie's home – she'll see to you." He kept his arm around him as he helped him out of the office. "I want you recovered by tomorrow ... we've a big celebration, remember, Catherine's christening and your sixteenth birthday. Let's hope we don't have to postpone anything."

"No way, Dad... I'll be fine... I'll go to bed for a while, I think that's all I need." There was no way Rob could say it was drink that had affected him, he would never want his father to know that. That had to be his secret. Besides, he knew from previous Sunday mornings he had always recovered if he lay on in bed. Why did he drink so much last night instead of Saturday when he knew he needed to be fit for work on Saturday morning? He'd have to make sure he never drank on Friday night again.

Fred held him firmly as he was escorted across to the station house. When they entered the kitchen there was no sign of Maggie but as they were going up the stairs she appeared from the parlour.

"What on earth's the matter, what's wrong?" She was shocked at her brother's appearance. He looked a right mess.

"Rob's not feeling the best, Maggie... your dad sent him home." Fred continued upstairs. "Matt says to keep him warm, he thinks he is sickening for something."

"Just put him in the bedroom on the left there." Maggie, having quickly assessed the situation, showed Fred Rob's bedroom. Fred helped Rob into the room he now occupied on his own and helped him onto his bed. Since Catherine's birth his father stayed at the farm all the time, only calling in on his way home to check all was well. Maggie and Eve had claimed their father's bedroom, with Eve using Dorrie's old single bed which occupied a corner adjacent to their father's. Maggie had insisted on having their father's double bed. Now she ushered Fred out of the room, thanking and reassuring him as she did so. When she heard the front door close behind him she approached Rob where he lay curled up in bed.

"That'll do me for giving you drink." Her voice was scathing. "How much did you have anyway?"

Rob made no answer, there was no need to, she probably knew better than he did, she was the one who bought it.

"Maggie, please don't say anything to anyone." He held his head in his hands. "Father thinks I've caught a chill." He would never want anyone to know he had been so drunk he had to leave his work. To make matters worse there was a party tomorrow, and Dorrie and John were coming from Belfast to join them all. But he would probably be fine if he could sleep it off, providing Maggie kept quiet about it.

"What do you take me for?" Maggie's voice cut in on his thoughts. "Who would I be saying to, would you tell me?" Sarcastically she went on, "You needn't worry on that score. I don't intend to say to anyone, especially Dorrie if that's what's concerning you? I'm well aware you wouldn't want her to know you were so drunk."

Rob buried his head in the quilt in an effort to block out the cutting edge to her voice, and with a wave of his hand dismissed her from the room. It really didn't matter to him what Maggie thought. She didn't care what he thought when she brought men home in the evenings and at weekends. And the most surprising thing about that was he just didn't care anymore. He had suffered so much secret shame and humiliation over her in the past and then, more recently, the stigma and disgrace surrounding his father's marriage and birth of his stepsister. The whole village were preoccupied with that, and he sensed, rather than heard, all the gossip. The knowing, pitying looks levelled at him both in the station and in the street were hard to bear. The way people stopped talking when they saw him made him feel like running away. He had felt compelled to block it all out, and thanks to Maggie, her whiskey had helped him do just that.

Sometimes he wondered how Eve felt about everything – about his father and Maggie's behaviour. But if she felt perturbed by it all, she certainly never showed it. She just sat quietly in the parlour in the evenings after work, while Maggie entertained men upstairs in the bedroom. Certainly nothing was ever discussed between them – for himself, he couldn't bear to and probably Eve felt the same. The three of them always acted as if nothing untoward ever happened, it seemed an unspoken agreement between them.

Dan arrived at the station house at 2 p.m. on the Sunday afternoon to take them to the farm. The christening had been held in the church that morning, but only the parents attended. Jane and Matt had felt the family would enjoy the party, with no great interest in going to church, so they had left Harry and Jim at the station house on the way.

Matt and Jane were standing at the door of the farmhouse as Dan pulled up in the courtyard. Dorrie and John were already there and Dorrie was holding baby Catherine in her arms, who gurgled happily at all the attention. As they all climbed out of the car, Rob stood back to allow Maggie and Eve to go ahead and he fell into step behind them, with Jane's boys bringing up the rear. Matt kissed his daughters warmly, turned and hugged Rob fiercely and putting his hands on his shoulders he studied him closely. "Thank God you seem so much better, Rob – the look of you yesterday – I was worried."

"I'm fine, Dad. Totally recovered." Rob was rather proud of how he looked today. He had gone to considerable lengths with his appearance. He had scrubbed his hair and body until his skin tingled, he had blackened his shoes and spit polished them. He had ironed his grey trousers and jacket carefully, and when he looked in the mirror he was well rewarded for his hard work. He knew he had never looked better, and he felt as fit as a fiddle. Yesterday, and how he had felt, all had a feeling of unreality to him.

By way of reassurance he remarked to his father, "Thanks for letting me go home yesterday, getting straight to bed was the answer. It nipped the infection, or whatever it was, in the bud." His father had probably been right about it being a chill. It had nothing to do with alcohol. He was probably just very vulnerable because of the early hours he kept at the station.

After everyone had made much of Catherine and Rob, Jane led the way into the dining room, where she had gone to considerable measures to provide a hearty meal. A cake with sixteen candles celebrating Rob's birthday took pride of place on the table. Later as everyone looked on, Rob opened his presents; Eve and Maggie bought him thick, heavy socks to wear with his boots during the winter months. His father and Jane had presented him with a ten shilling note, which overwhelmed him, considering he didn't even earn that much in a whole week. But secretly the book about the history of trains and stations in Ireland from John and Dorrie was his favourite. Jim and Harry gave him two packets of Woodbine cigarettes. Later that evening, Matt and Jane congratulated themselves on how the day had gone, and how settled and complete their family were.

Chapter 15

1925

Rob loved his work in the station, he enjoyed the atmosphere and after being there for almost a year knew most of the daily passengers by name and felt comfortable dealing with them as they travelled to and from their employment. Most of all he loved being with his father, as they worked side by side. Seeing him every day meant he didn't miss him so much at home, though Matt still did his best to call in the station house on his way home to the farm. Rob wanted to make his father proud of him, and worked hard to establish himself as a dependable, hardworking porter. Since the Saturday morning his father had sent him home believing he had a chill, Rob had never touched the whiskey on a Friday night again.

It was September and the holiday season was over, schools and colleges had reopened and Tom Greenlees had gone back to medical school and Rob found he missed his friend more than anyone. They had had a great couple of months together, catching up on all their news. Tom was happy to be going to study medicine, even though he knew it would be difficult, but he had given up trying to talk to Rob, realising he seemed happy at his work. While Tom was at home the two of them had spent most of their spare time together, and he hadn't seen much of his sisters, so mostly he managed to ignore the men who still visited Maggie at the weekends. He had noticed that Eve took nothing to do with the situation either now but instead slipped out of the house most evenings, claiming to be going for a walk. Rob knew she went off to meet Harry Brankin, he had spotted them together a few times. He kept that knowledge to himself, however, whether anyone else in the family knew, he had no idea. After all, Eve was almost nineteen now, and he supposed it was up to her what she told anyone.

Now as Rob walked across to the station, he was thinking how much he had enjoyed the summer evenings with Tom, driving along the coast roads in his father's car, stopping at harbours or quaint teashops along their route.

As soon as he saw Dan pacing up and down the platform he knew something was wrong. Why else would Dan be here at this time of the morning? It was only 6.30 a.m. He looked around for his father but there was no sign of him. Even before Dan spoke, Rob felt panic rising in his chest, and his heart began to race uncontrollably. He raced over to Dan. "What is it... what's wrong?" His voice sounded little more than a whisper.

"Take it easy, Rob... there has been a bit of an accident, late last night." Dan's voice was very calm. "Your dad's in Banbridge Hospital, but he's going to be alright."

Rob cut in sharply. "What happened? Just tell me!"

"Matt fell from some hay bales – he has broken his leg, that's all." Looking at Rob's white face Dan felt the need to reassure him. "He could have been much worse."

"Can I get to see him?"

"Absolutely, but leave it until later this evening. He wants you to take care of everything here for him. He says you know what to do, he has shown you many times." He put a friendly hand on Rob's shoulder. "You can do it, can't you? He's depending on you this time."

Rob suddenly felt quite calm. "Of course, of course I can do it." He had an immediate sense of responsibility. "But will you take me to see him this evening?"

"Yes, that's the arrangement. I'll be back around seven. I'll call with Maggie and Eve – I'll have to ask them to look after Catherine for Jane, as she'll be going too."

With the help of Fred, Rob worked all morning, concentrating on his father's duties, organising the signal man, the ticket collection. During the break he sorted the mail as his father always did. As he carried out his duties he thought of little else only the hospital – impatient for the evening to come – so he could see for himself how his father was. In spite of his anxieties, the day flew past, far quicker than he could have anticipated. Six o'clock seemed to arrive very quickly, and after sorting out the details for the evening trains with Fred, he made his way across home to have dinner and wait for Dan.

When the family visited Matt later, they were surprised to find him so cheerful. The doctor spoke to them, explaining that, due to the severity of the fracture, compounded by a laceration, it would be several days before they could immobilise the leg. When that was done he might even be allowed home on crutches. Meantime, he was being sedated for the pain.

Matt had his plaster on within a week of the accident, and initially, when he began to complain of feeling unwell, the doctors explained that the effect of drugs would most likely be the cause of his sickness. But the nausea persisted, he began to lose weight, and all the family voiced their concern about his condition. Their worst fears were realised when they were told he had developed diabetes. Gangrene had set in to the broken limb, and the surgeon must amputate as a matter of urgency, in order to save his life.

For his own and his father's sake Rob tried to be optimistic, and reassured him, that with the aid of an artificial limb, he would soon be fit to return to his post. But it soon became clear that the railway company had no intention of waiting any longer, and meant to replace him with a new stationmaster. Matt was discharged from the hospital a few days before Christmas, and on the same day the family were informed they had a month to vacate the station house and find other accommodation.

It was Maggie who, in the end, approached Mr Greenlees about the possibility of renting a small terrace house she knew he had recently purchased. She did it because there was no way she intended to go and live at the farm house – she knew her whole life would change if that were to happen. Rob felt he had no option only to go with them to the terrace house. He had such an early start in the mornings he needed to be close to his work, and the farm certainly was not.

Three weeks later, they left the only home they had ever known, and with what little furniture was theirs, they moved into the two bedroom house. Mr Greenlees had had it all painted for them, had even installed a cooker, oil lamps, a couple of comfortable chairs and a kitchen table.

"I've told you before, Hampton, keep to the platform." The stationmaster's voice held a deeply, sarcastic note – a tone Rob was becoming all too familiar with.

"This is my office – sort out the mail in that one." Kevin Todd pointed a thick, grubby nail bitten finger in the direction of a room at the bottom of the platform. He gave Rob a vitriolic look. "I'll collect anything for the stationmaster when I'm good and ready."

Quietly Rob retrieved the mail from the desk he still thought of as his father's, turned on his heel and made his way down to the dark, dank windowless room which, until Kevin's appointment, had been used as a store. He opened the door, and a putrid smell, so nauseating, filled his mouth and nose. If only he could find the time to clear out the room, and give it a good spring clean, but his new boss kept him attending him and keeping his own office spick and span, that he never had a minute. Now he stood in the doorway, the only means of light he had, and began to sort through the day's post, putting it into bundles ready for the pigeon holes in the waiting room. As he worked he thought about how one person had been able to change the station so much. Certainly, it seemed no matter how hard he tried, his work just wasn't good enough for Mr Todd. How much he missed his father. He had learned something new from him every day. Now it all seemed so wasted, the new stationmaster kept him at the most menial tasks in the place. If only the railway company had waited just a little bit longer, his father was now doing so well. In the last three months he had mastered his artificial limb so adeptly he was able to help Jane around the farm. His father should be back here, in his old post.

"Right, Hampton, are you ready for the 10.45 yet?" The voice, belligerent as always, boomed down the length of the platform – it didn't seem to matter to him that commuters were gathered there. "You can't dawdle all day you know ... get those trolleys ready."

Rob made his way to the waiting room, where he placed the mail in their appropriate boxes, leaving Mr Todd's on the table as instructed. Trying to keep calm, he went over to the trolley bay to prepare for the next train. He did try his best not to provoke his boss, because Kevin Todd's anger always managed to bring him to the edge of a panic attack. Why, the man seemed to enjoy being unpleasant to everyone, but Rob, in particular, seemed to be in the firing line of his vile temper. Well at least it was Saturday, he could look forward to a few drinks this evening and a lie in bed tomorrow morning. It was about all he had to look forward to, he certainly no longer enjoyed coming to work – work he had previously loved so much.

He was still preoccupied with Kevin Todd as he entered his home and didn't, at first, notice how quiet everything was. It was only when he saw his sisters sitting engrossed with a sheaf of papers spread out before them, he realised Maggie had no man with her this evening. And he felt some of the tension he had grown used to, drain from him, and he relaxed somewhat.

"Rob you look all in." Maggie rose from the table, went over to the cooker and began to stir the stew she had prepared earlier. "Go and get out of that uniform – I've your dinner ready." She smiled affectionately at her brother. "Eve and I have something to tell you."

As he hung his uniform in his bedroom, Rob wondered idly what the girls were up to now, but nothing prepared him for the news they related to him as he sat with his plate of dinner. "Eve and I are going to Canada, Rob." Maggie started to sift through the papers she and Eve had been studying earlier.

"You're what, Maggie?" He was astonished. "Going where?" Rob had heard of lots of people immigrating to Canada to try to better themselves, but he had never dreamt that anyone in his family would ever think of it. Obviously they had been planning this for some time. A thought stuck him. "Does Dad know about this?" His mind was in turmoil.

"No one else knows yet, Rob, but because you live with us, we thought it only fair to tell you first."

At least that much was reassuring – no one had tried to keep it from him. But so many questions flooded through him.

"What about you, Eve?" He spoke quietly. "Do you really want to go? I thought Harry and you were serious about each other."

"We are serious, Rob." Eve's face was unreadable. "Maggie and myself are going first – then Harry says he will join me out there. He thinks his mother and Matt, now that Matt is no longer working at the station, are glad to have the farm and well able to manage it. Besides," Eve continued, "we intend to come back home at some stage."

"But what will you do for money? How will you survive? Have you jobs to go to?"

"Of course not, Rob." Maggie sounded irritated. "You can't get a job until you're there, but there's plenty of work. Besides I've been saving money for quite some time." There was a note of pride in her voice as she went on, "You didn't think I was serious about any of those men who came to visit me, did you?" She looked steadily at Rob. This was the very first time she had referred to her behaviour. "I never intended to spend the rest of my life here... I made sure I was well paid for my favours. I deserved any money I got I can tell you, putting up with those animals."

Rob sat quietly, studying his sister across the table. She had no regrets whatsoever about her behaviour. That was obvious. She had no sense of shame at all, she couldn't have, or she wouldn't be sitting here explaining her reasons to him. There must be something wrong with him – he had felt her stigma and disgrace so deeply. He had always gone to the ends of the earth to keep her behaviour a secret. And all the time, she hadn't really cared about Eve and him, or what anyone might think. It had all been for money, and instead of the fact appeasing him, Rob felt the disgrace even more. It degraded her and the family so much – God knows how many people knew what had been going on. What about the men themselves? Did they talk about her? Or had they been anxious to keep it furtive and underhand. He would never know now.

"When do you go?"

"Not for another three months."

He would be alone then, but Maggie hadn't considered that. Of course, she didn't know how much loneliness affected him. He would come in to an empty house after work, have to cook his own food, pay the rent and keep the place clean. He would have to go to bed knowing no one else was in the house. But now suddenly, much as he dreaded the awful feeling of isolation he knew he would experience, the relief that he would no longer have to cover up for Maggie, was overwhelming. He felt a real sense of freedom, and thought it would all be for the best if she did leave Poyntzpass. Somehow he would manage, he knew that. He knew how to clean and he could soon learn how to cook. As for any panic attacks he might experience, he knew he was able to control them very well. If he felt one coming on, he could just have a whiskey or two, and that would be enough to relax him.

Chapter 16

1926

"Dad, I was wondering if I might borrow your car tomorrow evening. I think, I hope, I've managed to persuade Rob to come to the dance in Banbridge with me." Tom addressed his father across the dinner table. It was July, 1926 and once more he was back for his summer vacation. He had his first year done in medical school, and although he found it tough going, at the same time he was enjoying it all.

"I've been asking Rob to come to this dance every time I come home but he always comes up with some excuse or other, but..." Tom sounded adamant, "this time, I'm not taking no for an answer. Anyway, I'm concerned what he does with himself at the weekends. He tells me he has a drink or two on a Saturday night, but I know when I've been here and gone over on a Sunday I never get an answer when I knock on his door. Is he drinking much, Dad?"

"I don't think you've anything to worry about, Tom. He's at his work every day, then he goes home and makes his own dinner. He calls to see your mum and I once a week and I call with him as often as I can. I did promise I would keep an eye out for him, and I do, Tom." Tom's father was reassuring.

"He always tries to give me rent money, but I simply couldn't take it. It was different when his sisters were contributing but I'm sure his pay as railway porter is not a lot, so I don't really need the rent money and I've told him so."

"That's good of you, Dad and so typical. Talking of Eve and Maggie, he's bound to be lonely since they went abroad." Tom couldn't understand why he worried so much about Rob. But he knew he would be happier if he would come out with him some of these Saturday nights or open the door to him on a Sunday morning. "I still think it's terrible the way those two girls took off like that, leaving their younger brother to fend for himself. I suppose they thought he might move to the farm, but how could he when he has such an early start at the station? Have they written to him much, do you happen to know?"

"Eve writes all the time, but Maggie hasn't put pen to paper since she left here." Will Greenlees was able to tell Tom that Rob had had a letter from Eve just recently, but no news of Maggie.

Tom was tempted to tell his father it was unlikely Maggie would ever be back. Just recently Rob had told him something of Maggie's behaviour over the years and he knew Rob had buried his feelings about it all, he felt the disgrace so keenly. But he could never betray Rob's confidence, even to his own father. There was no doubt Rob had had a lot to cope with in the past and more recently, he had to put up with a rogue of a boss.

"Perhaps he's getting used to living on his own, just so long as he doesn't drink too much I think he should be alright. Another thing, I don't know how he sticks that ignoramus of a stationmaster – Kevin Todd would turn anyone to drink." Tom's normally calm voice sounded harsh. "Where the railway company got him from I don't know."

"Kevin Todd was head porter at Newry, and it seems he had his name down for the next stationmaster's post for a long time. It isn't a job that comes up too often, Tom." Will Greenlees hesitated, then went on, "Rumour has it someone told the authorities Matt was no longer living at the station house, but was out on the farm, but," he stressed, "you must never repeat that to anyone, least of all to Rob, it is only hearsay after all."

"It wouldn't surprise me one bit if Kevin Todd was the one who reported it." Then Tom, anxious to reassure his father went on, "I wouldn't dream of saying anything, I think anything like that might make matters worse between them."

Will nodded in agreement.

"Organise yourself and Rob to go to this dance, enjoy yourselves and see what you think of Rob's form. He seems pretty settled to me, but you know him better."

Rob wasn't looking forward to the dance but Tom seemed so set on him going that he had finally agreed. For one thing, he couldn't dance, for another he hated crowds, and most of all, he would miss sitting in the privacy of his own home enjoying a few whiskies. But he had turned down Tom's invitation so many times he felt compelled to accompany him on this occasion. Besides, it was a lovely evening and he always enjoyed a drive in Mr Greenlees' car. So that was something to look forward to, and he could still have a drink or two before Tom called for him. It would help steady him up enough to face the crowd that would be there.

By the time Tom arrived at 7.30 p.m. Rob had got quite used to the idea and was quite looking forward to the evening.

When they entered the dance hall they were surprised to see the place was not so packed after all. It was, after all, the middle of summer and lots of people were probably away to the seaside, which would explain the drop in numbers here tonight. Tom soon spotted a quiet table in the corner of the dance floor and they weaved their way through the dancers and sat down to enjoy a cigarette, listen to the band and watch everyone on the dance floor.

Tom rose from his seat immediately the next dance was called, made his way over to a slight, blonde, curly haired girl and was soon quickstepping around the hall. Rob was happy to just sit and watch it all. Two or three more dances were called and Tom never missed a chance to participate fully, asking several different girls onto the floor. Each time he returned to his seat, he tried to encourage Rob to get up and request a dance from some of the girls milling around. But although Rob admired Tom's lack of self consciousness and his dancing skills, he knew he himself lacked the courage to venture across the room to any of them.

Ellen Graham had arrived early with her sister Ethel, who had arranged to meet her boyfriend in the place. She too, had been contentedly watching all the activity and differing styles as the girls were whirled around the floor. She had seen the two young men when they had entered the hall, and watched them as they made their way over to the corner table. The lean, dark haired one had yet to make any attempt to get up and ask anyone for a dance, and she began to wonder if he intended to just sit there all evening. He looked such a vulnerable young man, his face wearing an almost haunted expression as he smoked his cigarette, and she found herself more and more intrigued by him. She began to pass the time trying to imagine where he might live and what he worked at. Two more dances were called, his friend returned to talk to him during each interval, he looked as if he were trying to encourage him to involve himself in the atmosphere. But each time the young man just smiled and shook his head, and lit up another cigarette.

Suddenly the band announced the next dance would be a "ladies choice" and before Ellen thought too much about what she was doing, she crossed the floor and asked him if he would like to dance. Rob had been quite comfortably watching the dancers on the floor, at the same time avoiding looking at the young women who sat round the edges of the room. Now at the sound of a girl's voice beside him he looked up sharply and saw the most beautiful girl in the place standing in front of him. She was tall, probably taller than he was, long legged and slender. But it was her eyes and hair which made her so striking looking, and accounted for her whole presence among so many pretty females. Her eyes seemed almost black to him, and they shone brightly from a perfectly chiselled face. Her hair, thick and glossy, tumbled down to her shoulders and framed her whole beauty. He stood up as she spoke.

"I would like to dance, if you will dance with me. It is the 'ladies choice'." She spoke in a soft, persuasive voice and added, "My name is Ellen."

Chapter 17

1929

As Ellen made her way along the footpath leading to her mother's house, she was preoccupied with thoughts of this latest piece of news she had for her. Surely her mother would be delighted to hear of Rob's promotion and that they would soon be moving to the South of Ireland to live, to a property which would be totally rent free, and where her parents and sisters might come for a holiday. But the truth was, Ellen had no idea how her mother would react to this news. Since her marriage to Rob two years before, her relationship with her mother had been, to say the least, strained and uncomfortable. Even the birth of their beautiful son, Matthew Robert, over a year ago, didn't seem to have thawed her mother's coldness towards Rob and her.

From the very first evening after their meeting at the dance, when Rob had called at her home, her mother had made it clear that she felt Ellen was marrying beneath her and had told her so in no uncertain terms "A railway porter, that's what he is." Her mother had spat the words at her when Ellen told her of her intention of marrying him.

Thankfully her mother's attitude had done nothing to dampen Rob's ardour for her, who faithfully cycled the four miles from Poyntzpass two or three evenings each week. He rarely discussed Ellen's mother with her, and any time Ellen tried to make excuses for her behaviour Rob just hugged and kissed her, telling her it wasn't her mother he intended "to marry". Now as Ellen bent down to release young Matthew from his pram, she was confident Rob's promotion to stationmaster would sit a bit better with her mother, no matter where that station might be. She was about to raise the knocker, when the front door was opened by her mother who seemed pleased enough to see her.

"I saw you passing the window, Ellen." She reached for Matthew's hand and led the way into the small living room which lay to the back of the large terrace house where Ellen's parents, her brother and sister lived.

"I don't often see you so early in the day and in the middle of the week too." It was more a question than anything else.

"Shall I put the kettle on the range? I'd love some tea and Matthew here would love a drink, wouldn't you, darling?" As she spoke Ellen busied herself lifting down cups and saucers from the dresser and proceeded into the kitchen to fill the kettle.

"Where are your toys, Matthew? In this bag of your mother's I suppose." As Ellen looked on her mother arranged her grandson's toys on the floor and watched Matthew toddle over to them. When he was settled with a drink and his playthings and they were enjoying their cups of tea, Ellen related her news to her mother.

Her mother listened intently as Ellen told her Rob had applied for this promotion and although it might seem some distance away, he was delighted to get it.

"If he hadn't tried for this, Mother, he might have been stuck in Poyntzpass for years, and even you must know the sort of stationmaster he has to work with."

"Yes, I'm glad for you both, Ellen. You will be better off and more secure, I hope."

Ellen was so relieved at her mother's unusual warmth towards her she impulsively reached across and hugged her. She need not have been so worried after all, everything would be alright.

Dromin Junction lies to the south of Dundalk, on the Great Northern Railway line between Belfast and Dublin. The village, if it could be called that, comprised the station with its station house, a small corner shop which sold little more than newspapers, cigarettes and sweets. An ancient looking rather run down public house occupied a corner site. A beautiful parish church with its own cemetery lay imposingly on a hillside overlooking the junction.

Ellen and Rob had already paid a visit a few weeks before, to what was to be their new home, and they had been delighted with everything. The station house was so grand and spacious that Ellen was totally enthralled with it. The grounds too, were beautiful, well enclosed with secure fencing all around them, so necessary to ensure young Matthew's safety. And Rob would only have to walk a few steps every day in order to fulfil his new role as stationmaster.

But today, as they began their journey to their new life together, Ellen couldn't understand why she felt such insecurity and an utter sense of loneliness. Even the thought of their beautiful new home or the train journey itself, something she usually loved, failed to cheer her. Instead she could only think longingly of her sisters and brother, Ethel and Hugh both happily married now, and Sara, her youngest sister, and knew she was going to miss all their support and their kindnesses to her and her baby son.

Thankfully Matthew had fallen asleep on the seat beside her, curled up with his favourite blue blanket. She looked across at Rob and knew instinctively, she could not share any of her misgivings with him because he was so looking forward to his new position. He had talked of nothing else for the past three months. But he had few family ties, apart from his father, whom he worshipped, and Dorrie and John who had been infrequent visitors to Poyntzpass in the last two years. They still lived in Belfast but they had two sons and a daughter who took up all their time and attention. Eve did write regularly from Canada and Ellen had made sure she had their new address, because even though she had never met her sister-in-law she looked forward to her letters. Maggie they never heard from but they understood that Eve kept regular contact with her and always reassured Rob that Maggie was well.

Now making an effort to overcome her melancholy she spoke softly to Rob. "How long until we reach Dromin, love? Was that Dundalk we just passed through?"

"We should be there in less than an hour, Ellen." Glancing at his watch Rob added, "Round about four thirty, I hope. I have the stew still safely in this basket here." Indicating the basket stowed beside him on the seat. "I don't know what we would do without Ethel, I never thought of food, I was so excited about Dromin." At the mention of her sister, Ellen felt a lump rise in her throat, but taking a deep breath, and looking down at her sleeping son, went on. "Let's hope Matthew sleeps until we arrive, he'll be starving, and he'll enjoy Ethel's stew."

"You look exhausted yourself. Working so hard packing boxes and cleaning out cupboards must have wearied you. You need to rest, Ellen." And with that Rob moved from the seat facing her to the seat beside her, and placing the basket at his feet, put his arm around her and laid her head on his shoulder. Ellen, reassured by his warmth and comfort, nodded off, only waking as their train pulled in at Dromin Junction.

Chapter 18

1930

After eight months in her new surroundings Ellen was happy and contented. They had been made so welcome by the villagers who were so kind to them, bringing vegetables, potatoes and even chickens from time to time. Above all Ellen loved her home, with its spacious rooms, the rich mahogany furniture and the black range in her kitchen which radiated continuous heat. Rob too was always talking about how much he loved the place. He loved his work and had befriended his colleagues from the very beginning. They all met up in the one and only public house in Dromin every Saturday night, a fact which made Rob so sleepy on Sunday mornings he rarely rose before lunch time. But Ellen didn't mind, it was the only break he had every week.

Now to complete her happiness, her second baby was due in two weeks time, and Ethel and Sara were coming today to stay until after her confinement. She was so looking forward to their visit and in spite of her bulk and awkwardness, had made the bedroom with its twin beds, as inviting as she possibly could. She had gone by train to Ardee with two-year-old Matthew, and shopped for what delicacies she could find. Then she had filled her tins with her favourite cakes and tarts, just to be sure there were plenty of provisions when she went into labour. Now glancing at the clock on the mantel, and at Matthew sleeping soundly in his pram, she realised her visitors were not due for another hour, she settled down in her favourite chair for her afternoon nap.

Always alert to Matthew and his boundless energy, she wakened with a start to discover he was trying to undo his harness and get out of his pram. Then she realised that the sound of voices and a trolley coming up the path, must have wakened her son. Quickly she released him and taking his chubby hand, proceeded down the hall and opened the door to meet her sisters, who were accompanied by Rob pushing a trolley laden with their luggage. And their happy smiles and hugs and kisses for Matthew, and their obvious enthusiasm for being in Dromin seemed to give Ellen much needed energy.

"What date exactly did the doctor give you for the baby's arrival, Ellen?" The girls had been here for four days already and today was the coldest day in February so far. Ethel had lit a fire in the Victorian grate in the sitting room, and the flares from the logs seemed to light up the room. All three were enjoying afternoon tea, while Matthew played happily with the wooden blocks Sara had brought for him. Ethel was trying to write a letter to their mother who was looking after four-year-old Colin and two-year-old Gladys.

"Are you getting impatient, Sara?" Ellen smiled at her sister. "Let's see... the new arrival is expected on the 20th, that's not this Saturday but next. But that doesn't mean it will happen then, Sara, some babies arrive a bit late."

"Well officially that's only another nine days, I'm just thinking of you, you'll be glad when it's over."

"I certainly will, I'm like a beached whale, and I don't know how I would have managed without you and Ethel."

Ethel paused in her letter writing. "Rob's very good too when he comes in the evening – and his draughts and playing cards have been a great pastime, especially these dark evenings."

"Well he won't be here tomorrow evening; he usually meets his colleagues from the station and goes for a drink with them."

"That means one of us will win for a change, he's unbeatable, especially at draughts."

"Quite simply," Ellen answered, "his father taught him well."

Somehow they never got round to playing any games the following evening. After dinner, when Rob had gone out to join his friends and Matthew was safely tucked up in bed, they just sat and talked. Ellen was brought up to date about young Colin and Gladys, Sara talked about Jim Seymour – his father owned a butchers shop in Banbridge – and how pleased their mother seemed to be about that. Ethel and Sara exclaimed again about the grand house Ellen was so fortunate to live in, and they hoped she would be here for years, because it was such a grand spot for holidays.

"Are you tired, Ellen? You have been watching that clock a lot; do you want to go to bed? Or do you wait for Rob?"

"I'll wait a little while. If he isn't back soon, I'll leave the back door open for him."

"Would you like me to wait with you?" Ethel was more than happy to keep Ellen company.

"Oh no." Ellen was horrified – she didn't want her sisters to see Rob when he came home, he was usually quite drunk. "We'll leave the back door unlatched; he always comes in that way."

"Right, let's do that, and leave the oil lamp low for him," Ethel was already on her way to the kitchen as she spoke, "and then we shall head upstairs."

After the final check on Matthew in his bedroom, Ellen made her way into her own room and undressed slowly and laboriously, at the same time listening for Rob's familiar footsteps in the kitchen. She felt very tired but even so sleep eluded her. She knew Rob was later than usual; did that mean it would be really obvious to everyone tomorrow that he was the worse for drink? Suddenly she was alerted by the sound of the back door opening, and of something being dragged into the kitchen and strange voices talking to one another in muffled tones. Then she heard the back door closing again. Ellen lay silently for a few moments, then putting on her dressing gown and her slippers and carrying the oil lamp from her bedside table, made her way downstairs and into the kitchen. A strangled cry rose in her throat when she saw her husband. He was lying on the red quarry tiles where, she thought bitterly, someone had just dumped him. His face was white, his eyes closed, and he was breathing with great difficulty. She went over to him and felt his hands and face, both icy cold to her touch, but she thanked God when he moved and tried to speak to her. He really was just dead drunk. But she knew she couldn't help move him tonight, he would have to stay where he was. Slowly she made her way back upstairs, and taking two thick blankets and a pillow from the box in their bedroom, returned to make him as comfortable as she could. After placing the pillow under his head and wrapping him in blankets, she made her way back up to bed.

Bone weary, Ellen fell into a fitful sleep, checking the oil lamp was still alight, looking at the clock on the bedside table from time to time. Finally at 7 a.m. she rose and gathering Rob's pyjamas and slippers, made her way downstairs into the kitchen. Rob lay in the same position she had left him in, but she noticed his colour had improved. Bending down, she spoke softly. "Rob."

He opened his eyes and looked at her. "What on earth? Where am I?"

"Someone brought you here and left you here. I couldn't move you but I made sure you were warm, at least."

Rob struggled to sit up, then his eyes fastened on something behind her. Looking round, Ellen saw Ethel quietly watching them both.

"Can I help you, Ellen?" Ethel crossed the room to her brother-in-law. "You certainly can't do it. Let's get him moved before Matthew needs to come down for breakfast." Gently Ethel began undoing Rob's jacket, shirt and tie. "Rob, you need to go to bed and sleep this off," she remarked as she worked and reaching for his pyjama jacket from Ellen she began to put it on.

Shaken and humiliated at her sister being witness to Rob in such a state, Ellen stood silently for a moment. Then realising that Ethel was actually undressing him she moved quickly to remove his trousers and long johns, covering him with the blanket as she did so. With help from Rob she managed to put on his pyjama bottoms, then quickly gathered up his discarded clothes and put them in the wash tub, only too aware they were sodden with urine. The two women were just finished and were encouraging Rob to stand up when Sara appeared in the kitchen. She looked questioningly at her two sisters, and then at Rob, before turning on her heel and walking out into the hall. "Sara," Ethel called her back, "would you mind giving me a hand to get Rob upstairs, he's not feeling the best." Ethel's voice was firm and authoritative. "Obviously Ellen should not be doing it."

"Oh, right, sorry I didn't realise." Sara moved over and took Rob's arm, and herself and Ethel supported him upstairs, guided him on to the top of the bed and covered him with a blanket.

Before heading back downstairs, Ethel gripped Sara's arm firmly. "Not a word of this to mother when we get back, she thinks little enough of Rob as it is." By way of explanation, Ethel added, "He just had a drop too much to drink last night... it could happen to anyone, but please, not a word, Sara."

"Right of course I won't," Sara reassured her.

Ellen went into labour at 4 a.m. the following morning and Rob alerted her sisters before cycling the two miles to inform the midwife. Ellen was safely delivered of a baby son at 9 a.m. the same morning. He weighed 8lbs 4oz and Rob and she decided to call him Thomas, after Tom Greenlees, Rob's old friend.

Ethel and Sara both stayed at Dromin for another fortnight. During that time no one ever mentioned the incident with Rob, and Rob never once crossed the door to go to the pub. He never wanted anyone to see him like that again. He had never been so humiliated in his life. He still didn't know how it could have happened, but he'd make sure it would never happen again.

On the day of her sisters' departure, Ellen had great difficulty keeping her tears at bay. "I don't know how I would ever have managed without you both." Her voice was shaking as she hugged them. "Thank you both for everything, and thank you, Ethel for writing and letting mother know about Thomas. Tell her I'll write soon."

"You are going to manage fine, Ellen." Ethel was confident. "You're lucky he is such a good baby." She looked over at Thomas lying sleeping peacefully in the cot.

"He just seems to eat and sleep, Ellen," Sara added, "and I hope it lasts."

As they made their way down the path with Rob faithfully pushing their luggage trolley, Ethel hesitated for a moment then returned to Ellen. Putting her arms around her, she said in a low voice, "If you ever need me at any time, don't hesitate to ask, promise me that," and Ethel's grip tightened on her sister.

"Everything will be fine, I'll manage fine, but if I do need you I'll let you know." Ellen was overwhelmed by her sister's kindness. With one last farewell, Ellen, taking Matthew firmly by the hand, as he attempted to follow his aunts, went into the house and reflected on the last few weeks, and how the time had simply flown.

Chapter 19

"We have to go and find out what's wrong with Harry." Rob held the letter they had just received from Eve.

"She seems worried about him, he hasn't answered her last two letters and she wonders if they have been lost in the post." He hesitated.

"It's possible, I suppose. We were thinking of going up North soon to see everyone, anyway. Now we have a good reason to organise ourselves to go, Rob." Ellen had been feeling guilty that they hadn't been to see either Rob's parents or her own since Thomas's birth, they always seemed to keep putting it off. "Thomas is three months old now, and our parents have never seen him yet. If we do go this weekend we'll find out what the problem is with Harry, then we can write back to Eve and let her know. Maybe Harry hasn't been well."

"This weekend it is then, love." Rob set the letter on the table. "I'll get back to the station and organise the details with my colleagues. I'll let Jane and Dad know and your ones as well."

Rob seemed anxious about Eve, and Ellen hastened to reassure him. "I'm sure there's nothing to worry about. She told me in her last letter that Harry hoped to join her out there in about four months, and I'm sure that still stands."

Ellen enjoyed the regular correspondence she had with Eve, it was always interesting and Eve seemed interested in their lives too, and she felt she knew her well.

Rob nodded as he listened to his wife, but he said nothing. He was worried, it was very odd, and he just hoped Harry Brankin would never let Eve down. He was the only boyfriend she had ever had and they had been devoted to one another, and only for Maggie insisting on immigrating to Canada, Harry and Eve would have been happily married now and living in

Poyntzpass. Instead of which she was thousands of miles away and probably worried sick about everything. Well, he was worried too, and the weekend couldn't come quick enough. The sooner they spoke to Harry the sooner they could reassure Eve.

Ellen was occupied for the rest of the week, washing and ironing Matthew and Thomas's best clothes, so they might look their smartest when they met their relatives. She baked an assortment of buns and two moist fruit cakes – wrapped them well and put them in airtight tins, before placing them in the coolest part of her dining room.

It was a beautiful day in May when they boarded the train the following Friday. The sun shone continuously in a cloudless blue sky and the hedges and fields were a riot of colour as they travelled through the countryside and Ellen was so happy and optimistic that she believed nothing could possibly go wrong.

Later, when the train pulled into Poyntzpass the first people Rob saw were his father leaning on his walking stick; Jane standing beside him, and a young, blonde girl. Suddenly he realised it must be Catherine, his half sister.

"Ellen, there's Catherine, I do believe I would have passed her in the street without recognising her."

"She must be six, Rob." Ellen had done a quick calculation. "She looks much more, she's so tall and she is really lovely." Automatically Ellen smoothed Mathew's blond hair and adjusted Thomas's blue jacket, anxious they too would look handsome and well cared for. Then they were on the platform and were hugging one another and talking at once.

"Let's get to the car ... this leg of mine gives me jip if I stand around too long," and Rob's father began to lead the way out of the station. When they were all safely seated with Jane behind the driving wheel, Rob turned to his father.

"How have you been, Dad? ...We meant to get up to see you before this, but it is difficult to get a full weekend off, and it never seemed worthwhile to come for an afternoon."

"I've been fine, Rob, you need never worry about me. Jane looks after me well, spoils me, in fact, and I'm able to help round the farm, as long as I'm careful."

Soon they were driving up the lane leading to the farmhouse and when Rob looked round him, time seemed to stand still. Nothing had changed here, the doors of the barns were propped open just as he always remembered them and he could see the buckets used for meal and water for the livestock still in their usual place just inside the door. And there, propped up against the wall of the house, he could hardly believe it, was a bicycle, so like the one his father had always used.

"Don't tell me that's your bike, Father? Do you still have it?"

"Indeed I do." Matt was smiling broadly... "Even though my days of cycling are long gone, I couldn't bear to part with it. Too many memories," he added.

"It looks in good condition, Dad."

"Aye, Harry's glad of it many a time, if the car's in use and he has someplace to go. He keeps it well oiled and clean."

"Is Harry here this afternoon?" Ellen asked, from her seat in the back of the car.

"He's just walked across the fields to help one of the farmers with their sheep. He said he would see you later."

As they entered the farmhouse, Ellen began to relax, it didn't seem to her that Harry was trying to avoid them. They would know what was wrong, sooner or later. She accompanied Jane into the kitchen, depositing her fruit cake on the large table, which Jane had already set for their evening meal. Then her mother-in-law led the way to the room at the end of the long hall where everything, apart from a cot erected in the corner for Thomas, was just as Ellen remembered it.

Later, after a delicious meal cooked by Jane they put the children to bed and then retired to the sitting room, where Matt had lit a roaring fire.

"This is our favourite room in the house. We come in here after all has been finished outside. We usually just have our dinner on our lap, to be honest... but with the children here, we thought it best to serve it in the kitchen," Jane remarked as they all made themselves comfortable in the easy chairs round the fire. They played draughts for most of the evening, with Matt and Rob fighting for supremacy in every game, while discussing the joys of railway stations and trains.

Later, as Ellen and Rob were preparing for bed, as quietly as they could because of the children, Ellen suddenly remembered about Harry and his non-appearance. Hopefully, they would meet him in the morning. Just now she didn't want to think about anything anymore, she was so tired.

The next morning both parents and children overslept, and by the time everyone was washed and dressed and made their way to the kitchen for breakfast, Matt informed them that they had just missed Harry.

"He said he couldn't wait any longer, he really had to go. He'll meet us in Carson's pub at 7.30 this evening, if that suits."

Matt looked across at his daughter-in-law. "What are your plans for today, Ellen? I'm sure you'd like to see your own folks, after coming this distance."

"Actually, Dad," Rob interjected, "we were wondering, if you and Jane don't need it, might we borrow the car?"

"We don't intend to go anywhere today," Jane assured them... "Matt doesn't go out every day, or anything like it. He gets tired, you know. So the car is certainly available."

"Rob and I think he's great the way he manages so well."

"Absolutely," Jane agreed, "but we are anxious for everything to stay that way."

"Would you mind if we go for a drink later, Ellen?" Rob looked across at his wife.

Ellen only hesitated for a moment. "Of course not. I'll have the children in bed when you come back." Rob couldn't come to much harm having a drink with his father and stepbrother, she assured herself, as she ladled bowls of porridge from the pot on the range for herself and Matthew, before making preparations for their day to Banbridge.

They had an enjoyable but tiring afternoon visiting Ellen's parents and sister Sara in Reilly street. Sara had invited James, her boyfriend, to meet them. Hugh arrived too with Anna – the girl he had confided in Ellen about. She was beautiful, Ellen thought, with her slim figure, ash blond hair and deep violet blue eyes, and Ellen could see they were very much in love. They all crowded round the table in the living room and had tea of cold chicken and ham. But Thomas became very fractious before the meal was over, so as soon as they could – and without appearing rude – Rob and she packed up the children's belongings and with several goodbyes, hugs and kisses, began their drive back to Poyntzpass.

Thankfully, both boys fell fast asleep in the car and were still sleeping when they reached the farmhouse around seven o'clock. Rob carried Matthew straight down the hall to his bed, with Ellen following with the sleeping Thomas. Then Rob, catching sight of himself in the hall mirror, tidied his hair and straightened his tie, before joining his father and offering him his arm to support him to the car to go to Carson's, where they would meet Harry.

After young Catherine had gone to bed, most reluctantly, and only when Ellen promised she must visit Dromin and stay with them, the two women settled down for a couple of hours in front of the fire. Ellen enquired after Jim, Jane's youngest son, and learned that he was staying with Dan and helping in the newsagent shop in Newcastle.

"He isn't interested in farming, never has been. I don't really know what will happen to this place in later years," but Jane smiled quite happily as she spoke, and Ellen doubted it was a big concern for either Matthew or her at this stage of their lives.

"I'll make a cup of tea. I'm going to fall asleep if I don't make a move." Ellen got up from the easy chair.

"I'll get a few more logs for the fire – we might have to wait a while for the men."

"Oh, surely not." The very thought of Rob spending a lengthy time in any bar filled Ellen with unease. "They did say they wouldn't be late."

It was after eleven before the three men returned, and Ellen was mortified to see that Rob seemed to be supported by Harry, with Matt following behind.

"I think Rob needs to go to bed, Ellen." Harry indicated Rob's condition to Ellen with that one brief sentence.

"Of course, Harry." Ellen moved towards her husband

"I'll help, Ellen... we don't want to waken the children, and two of us might be quieter." Harry began to make his way down the hall towards the bedroom.

With the help of Harry, Ellen made sure Rob was safely tucked up in bed, before returning to join Matt and Jane.

"Is Rob often like this, Ellen?" was Matt's first question to her. "Incapable because of alcohol?"

As honestly as she knew how and yet conscious she did not want to distress Rob's father, she began.

"Sometimes, Matt, but I can never decide if he drinks too much or has no tolerance for it." She appealed to Harry. "Did he drink much tonight?"

It was Matt who answered. "Harry and I both suspect he had nearly twice as much as either of us." He hesitated then went on. "Harry had a lot to tell him, and from then on he kept going up to the bar and buying extra whiskies in between our rounds – just for himself. But still, if it only happens once a week, Ellen, he must be able to cope. It doesn't interfere with his work in any way, does it?"

"No, definitely not ... Matt," Ellen was adamant, "he loves his job too much to jeopardise it, I'm sure of that."

"Then we'll talk no more about it. We have more important things to think about, unfortunately," and Matt proceeded to tell Ellen the truth of the situation between Eve and Harry. And all Ellen could think on hearing the awful news, was that it was no wonder Rob felt the need for a few extra drinks.

Chapter 20

It was Ellen who wrote to Eve and as compassionately as she knew how, told her that Harry Brankin would not be going to Canada to join her. Nor could she come to Poyntzpass, if her intention in doing so was to marry him. He was going to wed another girl because the other girl had become pregnant by him and to quote Harry's words, "He must do the honourable thing and marry her."

In her letter Ellen begged her sister-in-law to come to Dromin to stay with Rob and her. She stressed that her father longed to see her, to comfort and support her. He had explained that Jane and he would travel to Dromin, no one would ever expect her to come to Poyntzpass.

Ellen knew Matt was very distressed about Eve. He had confided in Ellen that he felt guilty now that he had not discouraged Eve from ever going to Canada in the first place. He had always known it was really Maggie's idea and she had more or less insisted Eve must go too. He had no doubt if Eve had remained here, Harry and she would have been married by now. Ellen knew that Matt was echoing Rob's thoughts about Eve going so far away and leaving the man she was so in love with. He too, had told Ellen he never understood it, but believed somehow that Eve felt a huge responsibility towards Maggie and so had felt bound to go.

Now glancing out of the window, as she sealed the envelope, Ellen saw Rob coming up the path for lunch. She could give him the letter to take with him to put in the mailbag. She watched him now and thought how unchanged he was since she had first met him in the dance hall some time ago. He was so handsome, with his thick mop of brown hair, deep grey eyes and sensual mouth and she loved him dearly. His behaviour on the previous Saturday evening had never been mentioned between them, and, Ellen thought wryly, probably never would. For his part, Rob was always very defensive, and for herself, she felt it was important that she tried to be more accepting and dignified about Rob's occasional fall from grace.

Rob was later than usual coming from the station that same evening and Ellen was beginning to fret that he had gone to the pub with his colleagues, when he appeared through the back door. She was so relieved to see him that she didn't question him about the cause of his delay. It was Rob himself who enlightened her.

"I stopped off just for one drink on the way here, Ellen... I'm just so annoyed about Eve, all those miles away from any of us." Certainly looking at him Ellen could see he was annoyed, but before she spoke he went on. "How will she cope? Why on earth did she go in the first place?"

He seemed very anxious to talk, Ellen could see that, and as he seemed to be getting more agitated by the minute, she remained silent while she set their plates of dinner on the table.

Pulling his chair towards the table Rob continued to talk in an anxious manner. "Did she think she could look after Maggie all her life? Or was Maggie just so persuasive, convincing Eve they would make their fortune out there? Even as he pulled the plate of dinner towards him he carried on in the same tone.

"I should have begged her to stay. I know I should. I'm sure too, had Dad known about Maggie's behaviour he would not have allowed Eve to go with her." He appealed to Ellen. "I should have told Dad, or even told Dorrie about Maggie, but how could I? You do agree, love, I couldn't have done?"

"Of course you could never have told your father such a thing, Rob. It would have destroyed him and he would have blamed himself. No," Ellen was adamant, "you absolutely did the right thing. Whatever else has happened your father must never know any of that."

Ellen was surprised she and Rob were even having this conversation. There had only been one occasion before their marriage when he had confided in her that Maggie had taken money from men for her favours. Even then Ellen had felt Rob's shame and sense of disgust about Maggie's conduct, and the subject had never been broached again. Obviously his feelings still ran very deep. She persisted in a firm voice.

"Please try not to think about it too much. Just pray Eve will decide to come to us for a time. Then we can see for ourselves how she is coping. But, Rob, don't make a habit of going to the pub – please don't."

Rob seemed to brighten up considerably after listening to Ellen and after assuring her that his pub visit was "a one off" they enjoyed their dinner in companionable silence.

Afterwards when Ellen remarked she must go and check on the children, Rob said he would take a walk round the garden to cool off a bit. He did this a couple of times during the evening, which made Ellen realise he was not himself; he rarely left the sitting room any evening. It was only when they were snuggled up in bed together and Ellen leaned over for her usual goodnight kiss that she smelt a really strong smell of whiskey from him. She couldn't understand why she hadn't noticed it sooner; he must have had more than one drink on his way home.

Two months passed before the long awaited letter arrived from Eve. During that time Ethel and William and their two children had visited for a weekend, so too had her brother Hugh and the beautiful Anna. They were such a welcome respite for Ellen, who had been so worried about Rob and his obsession about Eve. No matter how much she tried to reassure him he still insisted he could have done something to help his sister while he had the chance. He even, it seemed to Ellen, held himself responsible for how Maggie had turned out. He still insisted from time to time, that he really ought to have told someone about her. He told Ellen many times in the last few weeks that he had no courage – never had had – to deal with such a dilemma. All too often Ellen had become exasperated about the whole situation. Then she would feel so guilty for her impatience and she would hug Rob closely assuring him, time after time, that he was only a young boy when it was all going on. To make matters worse, just recently she had discovered Rob was carrying drink home and hiding it in the garden shed. She thought it ironic that she felt better able to cope with that rather than watch and listen to Rob's obvious emotional struggle.

So she really enjoyed her sister's and brother's visit bringing with them all the news from Banbridge. She was genuinely delighted when Hugh and Anna informed her that they had just become engaged and were marrying in three months' time. Ethel's children, Colin and Gladys, were a delight and kept Matthew and young Thomas entertained throughout their stay. In fact, young Colin was very upset when the time came to head for the train, demanding that he be allowed to stay on his own with his aunt and uncle. His mother had to gently but firmly explain that he must come home as he had school the following day. After much weeping and promises of a return visit in the near future they all headed home.

On a wet afternoon in late October Rob brought the letter straight up to the station house and when Ellen saw his smiling face, she knew immediately it must be from Canada.

"Oh, Rob... news at last... it is from Eve, isn't it?"

"Yes, love... let's hope she's going to come home." Rob pulled a chair towards the table, and indicating Ellen should sit beside him, went on. "You read it out to me, would you mind?"

Taking the seat beside him and the letter from him, Ellen opened it and began to read.

Dearest Ellen,

First of all I want to say how much I appreciate the kind, sensitive way you let me know the devastating news about Harry. You must have found it very difficult to write such a letter. As you can well imagine, it has not been easy for me to accept that Harry is lost to me forever, but accept it I must.

Now I find myself to be so very lonely over here, even though Maggie is here. She keeps telling me I will get over it, and that there are plenty of men in Canada, if I would just look for them. But for me there really isn't anyone else, and now I really would just like to get out of here for a time, and come back to Ireland. So I do hope it is alright if I take you up on your very generous offer. Indeed I have already booked my *passage on the liner which will dock in Belfast on the morning of the 30th November. Then I hope to catch the midday train to Dromin and will be with you all by late afternoon. This means I would be able to spend Christmas with you all. I dread the thought of Christmas here – whereas I can look forward to meeting you and the children at last, Ellen – and to seeing dear Rob again. I am grateful Father and Jane realise I would find it impossible to visit them in Poyntzpass. I am writing to let them know my plans and hopefully see them in the near future.*

I am looking forward to seeing you all.

Love,

Eve.

"We can't even begin to imagine what Eve has been through in the last couple of months." Ellen set the letter on the table and spoke to Rob. "She must have some strength of character to make the decision to come back to see us all."

"Yes, Eve might be petite and fragile looking, Ellen, but mentally she is very strong and stoical." Rob sounded very proud of his sister as he spoke... "And by the sound of things, Maggie hasn't been of much support to her. But then, I didn't really expect anything else."

"Well, at least she'll have us for a time, and your father and Jane of course. " Ellen went on "Wouldn't it be nice if your father and Jane could spend Christmas with us. Maybe you should try to encourage them, Rob"

"Good idea, but I'll wait until I think they have had the letter from Eve, then I'll contact them to make some arrangement for the holiday time. Now I must go, I must get back to the station."

"I'll try to have Matthew and Thomas in bed, so we can talk. Now the darker evenings are coming they are starting to settle a little bit earlier." Ellen didn't add that she had news of her own for Rob. But he had shown such relief about Eve she was sure he would be as happy about her third pregnancy as she was, even though she thought of Thomas as little more than a baby himself. Her new baby was due the following April, and

119

Thomas would be fifteen months by then – out of diapers and well weaned.

On a dreary, cold Wednesday afternoon in November the train from Belfast, with Eve on board, shunted into Dromin station. Ellen had wrapped the two boys in their woolly caps, scarves and gloves, before putting on her own, and making her way the short distance to the station. She joined Rob on the platform where he was waiting anxiously for his sister and together they watched for her alighting.

Although Ellen had never met her sister-in-law, she recognised her immediately from family photographs. She hardly knew how Eve would be, but it was a bright-eyed, slim, well-dressed girl with her head held high who came along the platform to them.

"Oh, Ellen, it's so good to meet you at last," as she hugged and kissed her. She hugged Rob closely and then knelt down to her two nephews. It was only when she stood up Ellen realised her eyes were bright with unshed tears. Anxious to avoid any embarrassment and in order to create a distraction, Ellen asked, "Is your luggage in the guards van, Eve?"

"Yes," and Eve smiled, "it's a trunk actually ... I hope you don't mind. I just brought everything. I thought,. I mean, I need to sort myself out. I felt that maybe this is the place to do it."

In answer Ellen hugged her sister-in-law warmly. "It certainly is... it is so peaceful... even though the winter can be pretty rough... but you'll find our home is warm all the time." Ellen turned Thomas's pram towards home and taking Matthew's hand added, "Let's get you up there, Eve, then you can see the place for yourself. We can leave your luggage here in the meantime. Rob will have someone bring your trunk across later."

Chapter 21

The Saturday after Eve's arrival, Matt and Jane travelled down to Dromin. Matt was very anxious to see his youngest daughter and offer her his support. At the same time he was aware of Jane's predicament and acute embarrassment in the whole situation. After all Harry was her son, and although she accepted he had brought Eve dreadful unhappiness and despair, she still loved him unconditionally.

They were both relieved to find Eve dry eyed and totally accepting of the situation she now found herself in. There were no floods of tears and wringing of her hands. It was much later, after tea had been served and the washing up done, that Eve asked Jane quietly if Harry was now married. Jane – sensing a note of despair creeping into Eve's voice – rose and crossed the room to her stepdaughter. Taking her hands in her own, "I'm afraid he is, Eve. I'm so sorry – he knew he had to do his duty and make the best of things. I am so sorry."

"I do hope he will be happy, I really do." Eve made a conscious effort to keep her voice steady. "Otherwise it is all so futile."

"I wish I could believe he is, Eve, but I think he is truly miserable."

On hearing this Eve made no answer but sat in silence for some time, her thoughts in turmoil. Then looking round the room at everyone,

"I know how important it is for me to move on – to forget about Harry. So, I don't intend bringing the subject up again, and I know all of you will respect my wishes." And quickly she changed the subject.

"What do you think of the latest news Ellen and Rob had for you today? Isn't it wonderful? Although I'm not sure what my long term plans are, I'd like to stay here until April, when this baby's due. After all, I missed the birth of both Matthew and Thomas, so here I'm staying." She turned to Ellen. "We have it all arranged, haven't we, Ellen?"

"We have indeed. Rob and I wanted Eve to be here when we told you. It is something to look forward to and of course, we're delighted." Looking across at Matthew and Thomas playing with their wooden trains she added, "Matthew and Thomas will be delighted that Eve is staying. She's only been here three days but they look for her all the time, wanting her to play, to go for walks with her. I've never had it so easy and I know we will all enjoy Christmas so much with you all being here."

"Jane and I mean to travel down on Christmas Eve, and probably travel back up north after Boxing Day – that will give us three full days here and we'll hear all about Canada and Maggie and how she is enjoying married life. You did tell me, Eve, she's married to someone about thirty years older who seems to have plenty of money." Matt spoke wistfully about his elder daughter. "Not what I envisaged for Maggie when she was growing up, but if it's what she wants out of life, you can't influence people, can you? And then of course she never writes, not like you, Eve keeping us up to date. No, all we get from Maggie is a Christmas card, that's it." ...Matt went on quickly, "I'm not being critical you know, Eve. I'm just stating a few facts ... everybody's different."

Rob, looking across at his father now, with his artificial limb and his walking cane, was glad that he had never let him know anything about Maggie and her conduct with men. It was far better if their father never learned anything about that sordid side to Maggie's life.

A week before Christmas, when the two women had most of their shopping done, the house decorated with streamers and holly picked from the surrounding bushes, and the Christmas cake and puddings safely stowed in the larder, Rob informed Eve that the girl in the office was leaving after Christmas. If she would like to help him two or three hours a day, the job was there for her.

"Oh, Rob," Eve clapped her hands in delight, "that's the best Christmas present you could have given me," she could scarcely believe it, "and two or three hours would be perfect. It still leaves me plenty of time to spend with Ellen and the boys."

"I'll sort it all out before Christmas and if you started in the first week of the New Year would that suit?"

"Oh, perfect, Rob," and she hugged her brother fiercely.

Ellen, who had been listening intently, was delighted. This probably meant Eve would stay here permanently, if the job was to her liking. Well, at least it would be a great help at the present time. She was very glad for her – and also very glad because she seemed to be having a good influence on Rob. He hadn't been near the pub or touched a drink since Eve's arrival. Ellen reckoned that was simply because he could see Eve was fine and seemed to be coping well. Ellen knew he had been worried about his sister, and he was always able to fool himself into believing the whiskey helped lessen that worry. While she had little tolerance for this excuse of Rob's, she overlooked it. They really had so much to be thankful for – Rob had a secure job and they had a beautiful home. She was now five months pregnant and feeling very well and both their sons were obviously thriving and alert, intelligent children. Eve seemed to bring out the very best in them and she was really appreciative of that. She intended to make Christmas as happy a time as she knew how for all their sakes, but most especially for Eve.

Eve had a much more contented, happy Christmas than she had ever thought possible. Ellen had gone to so much trouble to make it a magical time for the children, so that that same magic seemed to rub off on all of them. Her parents were wonderful, participating in helping with the cooking and making much excitement over present opening on Christmas morning. To Eve, their three days' stay seemed to fly past and then they were packing up and heading down to the station with promises to return in the near future. After they had gone Eve felt their absence deeply – their understanding towards her had been a real life line for her. And something she realised she really needed. She was thankful that she now had a job to look forward to; it would be a new challenge for her. Besides Rob had promised to give her all the support he could. She hoped it would keep her from dwelling on the past, and what might have been, had she stayed in Poyntzpass in the first place.

Rob was delighted how well Eve and he worked together. He discovered his sister learned very quickly; was far more methodical than his previous office girl had been. When Martha Jennings had been there, the desk and filing cabinet had always looked chaotic and she always had difficulty finding the necessary document, whereas Eve just seemed to have everything to hand. Now, because everything was better organised, Rob found he was so much more relaxed at work and at home. No doubt, Eve's help in the house was invaluable to Ellen too. Recently he felt relaxed enough to go to the pub on a Saturday night again, but made sure he never drank too much. He couldn't let himself down ever again in front of his family.

One very cold wintry morning in March, as he stood on the platform organising the porter and guardsman in time for the next train due in from Belfast, he decided he would send Eve home early. She should be enjoying the heat of their home on such a morning, not be stuck in a draughty office.

As he entered the office to chase her from her work, she looked up at him with a puzzled frown on her face.

"Oh, Rob, good to see you." Rob noticed she was rather worried looking. "I need to talk to you ... I hope you don't mind?"

"Talk away, Eve." Rob felt panic rising in him – was she thinking after all, of going back to Canada.

"It's about the amount of coal we always seem to need. I've just have to order another supply. And I've been looking at our bills for the last few months, they do seem very high."

Rob sat down on a seat on the opposite side of the desk, relief running through him. "Oh, Eve, I thought for a minute you were going to pack your bags and leave us."

"Rob, of course not. What made you think that? No, but I am worried about this."

"Eve, you mustn't worry, you aren't here to worry about anything." Rob hesitated for a moment, uncertain how much to tell his sister. "The truth is, I give the odd bag of coal to some of the villagers when they need it." By way of explanation, he added, "It has been a hard winter for them and some of them simply cannot afford to buy it. Most of them have small children too." He added firmly, "No one will ever know the difference, Eve, everything will be fine, I know it will."

"Oh, Rob, please," Eve was distraught, "you must stop doing this at once. Why, the Great Northern Railway has only to check our fuel consumption with other stations to notice the discrepancy," she looked at him sternly, "what then?"

"I never thought of that, how stupid of me." Rob shook his head, amazed that he himself had never thought of any consequences of his actions. "Look, its March now anyway, Eve," he sounded confident, "That's it, no more handouts." He leaned over impulsively and kissed her. "Thanks, sis, for forewarning me. By the way, I actually came in to tell you to go home early today and enjoy a warm, snug afternoon in our kitchen, instead of freezing here behind the desk."

"I would love to do just that. Give me five minutes to clear up here."

As Eve made her way up the path to the station house, she was glad to get away from all the bills she had spent the morning poring over. She had wearied herself worrying about the coal bills for Dromin, but she had never, in her wildest dreams, expected to hear Rob confess to having handed it round the neighbours. What had he been thinking of? Distributing buckets of GNR coal out to people. She was appalled, but obviously Rob had never considered the consequences of his action. Still – she was sure he had no intention of doing anything like it again. As for herself, she didn't intend broaching the subject again unless she saw any further discrepancies. One thing she was quite sure of, Ellen must never know anything about it, how Rob had so foolishly jeopardised his position and indeed, his home.

Chapter 22

1931

In the early hours of the 15th of April, Ellen was safely delivered of a healthy baby boy whom she promptly decided to call Charles. During this pregnancy she had been reading David Copperfield and a Tale of Two Cities and she decided to call him after Charles Dickens. Rob was delighted to have a third son, and had taken a few hours off work. As for Eve, she had scarcely left Ellen's bedroom all morning, tending to both the new baby and to Ellen. Thomas and Matthew had been consigned to the kitchen, under Rob's supervision and seemed singularly unperturbed by the new arrival. Indeed they seemed more enthralled by the fact that their daddy was home from work and looking after them.

Eve had just brought up a tray with tea and biscuits to the bedroom, where Rob had joined them, when from the window Rob saw the figure of the head porter approach their front door. Instinctively Rob's senses were heightened, something was wrong, none of the rail men ever left the station without permission. Had there been an accident? Puzzled, he went downstairs and opened the door. Eric, the head porter stood there with a cable in his hand and something about the man's pallor and stillness froze Rob to the spot. From a great distance away he heard Eric speak.

"I'm so sorry, sir ...it's bad news, I'm afraid." Tentatively he passed the cable to Rob.

"It's your father, sir ... a massive heart attack ... I'm so sorry." Eric Leathem stood, the cable still in his hand, uncertain what to do. His boss's colour and whole stance was truly alarming and Eric feared he might faint.

Suddenly, Rob, realisation dawning, reached over and put his hand on his arm. "Thank you, Eric," reaching for the cable, "I'll take this."

"Will you be alright, sir? ...If there's anything you need..." His voice tailed off and he began to make his way back to the station, away from his boss who seemed to have aged visibly in the few moments he had spoken to him.

As Rob climbed the stairs to break the awful news to his wife and sister, he felt numb and bewildered. How could this be? They had all been so happy not five minutes before, and now he was about to shatter that happiness. Had his son only been born a few hours ago? It was as if that happy state had never been. With the loss of his father, he didn't think he could ever be happy again. His father was dead. His anchor throughout his whole childhood and working life was gone forever.

It was Ethel who arrived in Dromin the next day to look after Ellen and the children, to enable Eve and Rob to travel to Poyntzpass to help Jane prepare for Matt's funeral. Rob had cabled Ellen's mother, asking for assistance now when they needed it most, but she must have enlisted Ethel to do it. Eve was so thankful Ethel had arrived to take over everything. She was determined she would be accompanying Rob to their father's funeral.

"Are you sure you can face going to the farmhouse?" Rob was concerned for his sister. "You'll have to meet Harry Brankin, you know. I don't see how you can avoid it, but you know that of course." More than anything Rob wanted Eve to accompany him – he didn't know how he would face it alone.

"Rob, I've done nothing wrong," Eve answered quietly. "I am going to my father's funeral. Nothing or no one is going to stop me."

Rob reached towards Eve where she stood, a look of immeasurable sadness on her face but still with a determined gleam in her eyes. They threw their arms around one another and gave vent to their grief with loud, anguished sobs which seemed to echo throughout the house.

Ellen was heartbroken when Eve and Rob left the next afternoon for their journey to Poyntzpass. It was only the thought of her new baby and the arrival of Ethel earlier which sustained her. She had loved and respected Matt Hampton, and knew he had felt the same about her and now he was gone. At fifty-one years of age and on the very day of their son's birth. What a cruel twist of fate for them all, her third son's birthday would always be a reminder of their terrible loss. As her new born son lay at her breast, and Ethel was downstairs organising Matthew and Thomas, she gave way to her grief and her tears flowed onto her son and the blanket enclosing him.

When brother and sister arrived at Poyntzpass Station, Eve was relieved to see it was James, Harry's brother, who was waiting to meet them. In spite of her grief she had thought about Harry a great deal. She knew she would meet him sometime during her stay. After all Matt had been like a father to the two boys and they too, must feel his loss very sorely. But she had come through so much because of him, she had no idea how she might react on seeing him. But at least in the meantime, she had been spared such a meeting, simply because Jane had thought to organise her younger son to meet them.

Although Eve had only been to the farmhouse on a few occasions with Harry, she had always thought of it as a bleak looking place with its huge barns and long cement frontage. Now today, with the knowledge that her father would not be coming to the door to greet her, the place looked even more desolate and exposed than ever. And she, who had tried to remain dry eyed and strong for Rob's sake, broke down completely.

It was Jane who was the calm, composed one now and led Eve and Rob quietly into the sitting room and comforted them both while James went, on his mother's orders to bring tea and scones from the kitchen. As the three of them sat with their tea cups in their hand Jane explained how the arrangements stood for the next day. After explaining quietly where Matt would be buried and the format for the service, she went on to say Dorrie and John would be travelling up from Belfast tomorrow morning.

"So you will see them before the service." Jane addressed this piece of information directly to Rob.

"I'll be glad to," Rob answered. "We haven't heard from Dorrie for about three months. She did tell Ellen in her last letter she was expecting another baby. So we weren't sure if she could make it or not ... I'm really glad to hear it." Although Ellen and he only saw Dorrie and John occasionally now, he would never forget the unwavering support she had given him during his childhood.

"Harry will be going directly to the service from his mother-in-law's house – that's where he and his wife are living. But he comes here at 6.30 each morning until 7.30 each evening and does most of the farm work for us." She spoke to Eve. "I thought it best to let you know that." Eve nodded quietly in response, she was thankful Harry wouldn't be here before the service. She felt she might be able to cope if she only saw him at the church.

Harry Brankin made a conscious decision the next day to be at the service just immediately before its commencement. He wished to sit at the back of the church, not in the front pew with his mother and family. Because of his shameful behaviour which he knew had scandalised the whole neighbourhood, he had jeopardised the right to sit there with them all, as they paid their last respects to a loving father and husband. But although he felt the burden of what he had done weighing heavily on him, how one mad, impulsive night had affected so many lives, he too, wanted to pay homage to Matt. He had loved his stepfather, a quiet, unassuming man who had treated James and him as his own, simply giving them his love and encouragement. He had borne his disability with patience and fortitude and since that awful night with Rob and him when he had to confess the situation he found himself in, not once had Matt uttered one word of condemnation towards him. Something he had marvelled at many times, because his own mother had reproved him many times. Reproof she was quite justified in airing.

Every time he thought of Rob's insistence that he would be the one to let Eve know the worst, he had tried to say that the news must come from him. But Rob had been adamant, if Eve saw a letter from Harry she would think all was well, and Rob didn't want her hopes raised and then dashed. Harry knew it should have come from him directly and if he had a chance to speak to her today he would try to explain.

After the service, Matt Hampton was buried beside his wife Evelyn in the small cemetery adjacent to the church. The rain had started in the early morning and at the graveside it began to come down in torrents and was somehow in keeping with the family's feelings. After they had all placed soil on the coffin before it was lowered into the ground, and the minister had said his final prayer, Eve noticed Harry Brankin make his way over to her.

"Eve..." He extended his hand to her, but she stood resolutely, her hands clasped in front of her. In response Harry placed both his hands over hers. "I'm truly sorry about your father, Eve." She regarded him, his fine, chiselled face with its deep, brown eyes, as he hurried on.

"I need to say I'm so very sorry about everything – about us. I was so lonely for you, and I was so drunk that night." His grip tightened on her wrist. "I did want to let you know myself but Rob thought it best if I didn't communicate at all with you."

He went on passionately. "I think about you day and night and I want you to know that I love you and always will. I'll pay for my mistake for the rest of my life," and with that, he turned on his heel and left her alone.

Eve watched him go across the cemetery to join his mother. His words had chilled her to the core. What was to become of them all? What chance had his marriage? What of his wife who must surely love him as much as she did? With a heavy heart she made her way across to join her brother, who was standing with Tom Greenlees. Tom had flown over from England where he was now practising, to attend Matt's funeral. Tom offered his condolences to her in such a heartfelt way that Eve had difficulty maintaining her composure, but she managed to give him a return kiss on the cheek, before going over to join Dorrie and John who were starting their walk back to the station house.

Eve's mind was a whirlwind of mixed emotions as she travelled back home with Rob the following day. Tortured by her grief for her father, she also found herself agonising over the last words Harry had said to her. She knew she must try and forget the hopeless, lost look of him. She must think of herself and her own future, but she was finding it impossible at the moment. If only she could talk to Rob about it. But she knew at the present time she couldn't, because Rob had more or less ignored Harry at the funeral and obviously felt very strongly about him. Besides, Rob himself seemed agitated and impatient to get back to Dromin. So the journey was a silent one, only broken when Rob announced the name of every station as they passed through them.

They were both glad to see Dromin Junction in the gathering dusk, with its familiar platform and kind faces of the porters as they waited for the train to pull to a stop. When they entered the station house later, the warmth and welcoming lights seemed to soothe and envelop Eve and probably because she was spent both emotionally and physically, it felt like coming home. So she was really surprised to hear Rob say that he was going to go down to the station to check on everything – he would have dinner later – and with a kiss for Ellen, he raced down the stairs and out through the door.

Chapter 23

Charles was now three months old, and since his father's death Rob had been drinking every evening and Ellen was having increasing difficulty getting him up in the mornings to go to the station and she was getting concerned about the security of his job. What if the officials in the Great Northern Railway became aware that Rob was invariably late for his work and when he was there he must be scarcely able to function?

Eve was fully aware of what was happening. She had tried talking to her brother, but he always reassured her that everything would be alright. That the drinking he was doing was only temporary, and was helping him to cope with the loss of his father. He would pull himself together, he always told her, but so far, there was no sign of that happening. The truth was, that more and more, she noticed when she was at the station the two porters and guardsman seemed to be taking on the stationmaster's responsibilities. She herself worked as hard as she possibly could, handling orders for fuel, the mail and any cables that arrived at the station. Rob still seemed to engage well with the commuters, issuing their tickets for them, and generally being very sociable. Of course, he had come to know so much about the people who travelled by train on a daily basis that he must feel totally at ease with them. This was of some comfort – at least he was still popular. She said very little to Ellen about how things really were at the station. She knew Ellen was frantic about Rob, but seemed powerless to do anything to change the situation.

Today, everything had changed and she knew she was going to have to let Ellen know the true situation. Officials from The Railway Company had informed Rob they would be travelling down to Dromin the next day. That afternoon she told Ellen that she was very worried about this impending visit. She watched her sister-in-law as she pulled up a chair to the table in the kitchen, placed her arms on the table and put her head in her hands with such a pitiful, weary gesture that Eve's heart ached for her.

"Ellen... it may not be so bad. Maybe I'm thinking the worst, but I thought it best to be prepared." Her voiced tailed off – she was at a loss as to how to console her.

Then Ellen raised her head, and with some new resolve, spoke.

"I am expecting the worst. I have been for some time – I just didn't want to face it. Now it seems to me that it is outside our control. I have tried everything." She gave a deep sigh. "We have to accept the consequences and try to do the best for the three boys and for each other." Resolutely Ellen rose from the table. "Well, we just have to wait until tomorrow comes and see what happens."

After interviewing Rob the following afternoon and upon learning Eve was Rob's sister, Denis Reid, a director with the Great Northern Railway, asked her to accompany him to the station house where he would like to speak to Mrs Hampton. This was the side to his job he hated most; it was one thing when a man lost his job, but when his family were about to be told they were to lose the roof over their heads, he found it all very distressing and nerve-wracking.

When Ellen Hampton opened the door in answer to his knock, he was stunned by her beauty and bearing. She was tall and willowy, with vivid dark eyes, which shone brightly in a perfect chiselled face. This was going to be even more difficult than he could possibly have imagined.

After introducing himself, she politely asked him to follow her into the sitting room. As she did so she asserted that she wished her sister-in-law to be present. Ellen had prepared herself for this and had made sure the two older boys were occupied in the kitchen with their brushes and paints, and that Charles was in his cot, fast asleep. She wanted Eve to be there, she was so much a part of their lives she had every right to know what was happening. Now she offered him a seat and Eve and she sat down facing him.

Both women listened intently as he informed them that Rob's contract would be terminated in a month's time and that, he was very sorry to say, meant that they must vacate the station house. Then in a much stronger tone, he went on to tell them the reason for Rob's dismissal. Quite simply, he had been distributing GNR coal to the villagers, something Rob had freely admitted to upon being questioned. Coal which, Denis Reid stressed, belonged to the GNR. It was theft, pure and simple, which automatically led to dismissal. No mention was made of Rob's timekeeping or inefficiency during the last three months.

Ellen was utterly stunned as she listened. Her husband was being sacked because he had been handing out coal to their friends. How ironic it all was. She had thought it must be his drunkenness, drunkenness that had worried her for the past three months. Instead it was something entirely different, something she had been totally in the dark about. As he rose to leave them, Denis Reid turned to Ellen. "I understand you have three very young children?"

Ellen drew herself up straight. "Yes, we have three boys," she answered proudly.

"I intend to arrange for your husband's dismissal to be in two month's time, not one. That will give you some time to think and plan your future," and he smiled gently at Ellen as he spoke. "I shall inform Mr Hampton of this change on my return to the station."

After Ellen had politely shown him to the door, and he had apologised once more, she turned to Eve. "That was some change of heart he had – it will give us time to plan what to do for the best."

Not wishing to cause Eve any more distress, Ellen was determined to appear practical and optimistic, in the face of this awful news. Eve simply nodded, too overcome to trust herself to speak. She had been watching Denis Reid as he spoke to Ellen, and she doubted if his change of plan had much to do with the children. She could see clearly that he had been totally bowled over by Ellen's looks and charm. That was why they had got an extension of time. But now was not an appropriate time to say anything to Ellen about that, she didn't think she would be very impressed.

That evening, much to Ellen's surprise, Rob came straight home from work, and totally sober as well. She had feared that perhaps he would feel, because no reference had been made to his drunkenness, he had some sort of a licence to continue as he had been for the last three months. After the children had gone to bed and dinner was over, the three of them adjourned to the sitting room in an effort to try to come to terms with the enormity of what was happening to them. It was Rob who spoke first, breaking the uneasy silence.

"I think, Ellen we must go back up North, I've a better chance of getting work there. In fact I know I have." He was still stunned at how well Ellen seemed to be coping with the whole sorry business. There had been no recriminations from her, no tears, just a total acceptance of their fate, and he felt he had never loved her so much as he did now. How stupid and thoughtless he had been, never giving a thought towards her and the children, just simply thinking of the neighbour's children and how cold they all might be.

"I think we must, Rob, I've given a lot of thought to where you might get work and there is little down here. But you know that still doesn't solve the problem of where we are to live, and we must be residing in the North to have any chance of actually getting a house there." She went on, "I intend to write to my mother tonight and ask her to accommodate us – only as a very temporary measure of course."

"Well now, you and I both know how she feels about me, do you really think she's going to see me in any more favourable light now?"

"I know it won't be ideal, but she won't see us stuck – not when she has three grandsons to consider." Ellen was confident her mother was bound to help them. "I'll write straight away, and you can put it in the mail in the morning."

Eve had been sitting quietly, listening intently to their conversation, and now when she spoke, her voice was trembling.

"I need to let you both know, at this stage, that I plan to return to Canada." She hurried on, aware Ellen was about to interrupt her, "My boss over there did say he would always have a job for me, and as you know, I have my apartment rented, so I have it to return to."

Ellen was horrified. "Oh please no, Eve. You can't do that. You are part of our family now. We want you with us. You'll soon get a job." She appealed to Rob. "There is plenty of work up there, isn't there, Rob?"

Before Rob could answer, Eve hurried on. "I don't feel I could go back, at least, not at present."

To Ellen, this was the worst aspect of the whole sorry business, Eve going to go abroad again, but somehow it had inevitability about it and just something else Ellen must come to terms with. Obviously Eve still felt the further away she was from Harry the better.

Five days later Ellen had a reply to her letter to her mother. In the letter she said, that if the worst came to the worst, she and the children could come to her in the short term. However, she could only have them to stay on one condition, and that was that Ellen must leave Rob. Ellen showed Eve the letter that afternoon.

"Leave Rob, imagine," she sounded desperate, "I could never, ever do that." What would become of him? She appealed to her sister-in-law. "How could I? Leave him, I mean? Where would he go? What would become of him?" She flung the letter on the table. "What am I to do, Eve? My marriage vows are sacred to me."

While Eve had been listening to all Ellen had been saying, her mind had been running over how best to help. Then she remembered Ethel – plump, kind, generous Ethel. And now she was smiling at Ellen. "But of course, you must write to Ethel immediately. She's the one who'll help you, you know that."

Then Ellen recalled her sister's words to her that evening after Rob had been so drunk when Ethel had so quietly and efficiently helped her with him. "If you ever need me, Ellen, you only have to ask." How prophetic those words had been.

Later that evening when Rob read his mother-in-law's letter he turned to Ellen. "She's right you know, if you never wanted anything more to do with me, I would understand why."

Shocked and surprised at such a statement, Ellen impulsively threw her arms round her husband and hugged and kissed him. "Rob, we're family, we're in this together, I'm confident you'll soon find work but you'll have to look after your next job better than you have this one."

"I'll make it up to you, darling, I promise." Rob held her tightly. "What would I do without you?"

"There's one thing I want you to do, Rob. I want you to apologise to Eve for messing up her life the way you have. That's something you must do." Ellen busied herself at the range. "She is in the sitting room with the boys – go and see her."

Chapter 24

It was a subdued family of Hamptons who travelled on a bright day in September to Banbridge. Leaving Dromin was a traumatic and harrowing experience for Ellen and she knew Rob was suffering too. They were leaving behind caring friends, their beautiful home, and worst of all, their whole security, Rob's wonderful job and their dreams of a bright future.

She was grateful the children were too young to understand what was happening, Matthew and Thomas were just looking forward to the train ride with their Aunt Eve who was travelling up North with them, although she would only spend three days there, before setting sail for Canada. So Ethel must initially try to accommodate six of them, a fact which distressed Ellen further. Ethel only had three bedrooms in her neat terrace house and Ellen was anxious her sister was inconvenienced as little as possible. But Ethel had insisted, when she heard Eve needed somewhere for a couple of days, that there was plenty of room for them all. Besides, it was clear to everyone that Eve could not go to Jane at the farmhouse, even on a temporary basis.

Ellen's heart lifted when she saw Billy Wilson, Ethel's husband waiting on the station platform. He was such a cheery, placid man, who looked unperturbed by the tribe of bodies bearing down on him, as if he accommodated people in his home every day of the week.

"Oh, Billy, it's so good of you to be here." Impulsively Ellen hugged and kissed her brother-in-law, and then suddenly burst into tears. "There, there, Ellen." Billy patted her shoulder awkwardly. "You've had a long, hard day."

"It's not that, Billy, Ethel and you have been so kind," she gulped back her tears, "that's why I'm crying."

Billy, embarrassed now, turned to Rob. "Let's get everyone to the car. Not my car, you know, a neighbour kindly lent me his." Overwhelmed at yet another kindness being shown them by someone who was an absolute stranger, they quietly strapped their suitcases and pram onto the roof rack, then settled themselves to begin the last leg of their journey into an uncertain future.

No sooner had Billy parked the car outside the house than the front door was opened wide and young Colin appeared in an obvious state of excitement. He was such a beautiful boy, Ellen thought – as she began organising the children out of the car – with his blond hair and blue eyes. "Matthew and Thomas are going to sleep in my room – and Gladys too of course." Crossing the path to take Matthew's hand, Colin rushed on, "I'll be able to look after them for you, Aunt Ellen – I'm ten now, you know."

Just then Ethel appeared. "Let's get everyone into the house, Colin, then they can see for themselves where they'll be sleeping." Her voice was gentle as she spoke to her son, then turning to kiss Ellen, "Just to please Colin, he's been waiting rather impatiently all afternoon. I'll show you and Rob the arrangements before we have anything to eat," and with that Ethel led the way in and upstairs.

"This is just perfect for us, you have gone to so much trouble." Ellen felt very humbled when she saw the arrangements. She and Rob had a room of their own, with Charles sleeping there too, in his pram until his cot would come from the station. Matthew was to share a bed with Colin, and Ethel had thoughtfully placed Gladys' old cot in a corner of the bedroom for Thomas. Gladys' single bed occupied the other corner. Billy had even organised the small box room for Eve with a camp bed in it and hooks on the back of the door. Eve was delighted with it but quickly told Ethel she would have been quite prepared to sleep on the sofa.

"I thought you might like some privacy before boarding that liner for Canada," was Ethel's thoughtful response. "You're sailing in three days time, isn't that right?"

"Yes, I am," Eve answered quietly. "I have a job to go to there and I have my own apartment, so it is all for the best."

She was anxious not to remind Ellen, whom she knew was taking her departure very badly. "My trunk's at the station, so I just collect it on my way through, but I do need to get a few basic essentials tomorrow before I leave."

The next morning promised to be a glorious one. There wasn't a cloud in the sky and the sun shone brightly as Eve made her way to purchase the few toiletries she would need for her journey. She had intended to buy them in Dromin, but everything had been so hectic that she had had no opportunity. She bought a tin of toothpaste, a new toothbrush, carbolic soap and a flannel in the local store. Then on impulse, although she had already bought going away presents for everyone, she made her way over to the sweetshop to buy sweets for them all and some chocolate for herself for the journey. She had just stepped out on to the pavement when she saw him. It was the pram she noticed first, then the familiar figure with its broad shoulders, and the head of thick, brown hair, bending over the baby lying there. It was Harry, and Eve's world seemed to stand still as she looked at him. There was something so final, so horribly decisive in what she saw, that her heart seemed to shatter in her chest, and physical pain engulfed her. Breathless now, she somehow managed to walk purposely along the pavement. She had to escape from the scene she had witnessed. She was incapable of taking in such a tableau. Yet out of all her confusion and unhappiness she now knew with certainty, that she was doing the right thing by leaving all this behind.

Chapter 25

It was April 1932 before Rob and Ellen were told by the Housing Association that a house would be available for them in a month's time. They had now been with Ethel and Billy nineteen months and during that time Rob had been frustrated by the Association's apparent indifference to their plight. Certainly they had visited them on occasions, had taken plenty of notes and nodded encouragingly when Ellen and he had tried to stress the urgency of their need. But it wasn't until Rob went into the offices one day and informed them Mrs Wilson was expecting twins they seemed to take any heed. The following week they were told they were being allocated a three bedroom house on the edge of town.

Rob was thankful he had managed to get a job soon after their arrival in Banbridge. He was out of the women's way all day, and since their arrival at Ethel's house, he had been able to pay his family's share of expenses. He enjoyed selling the books he did and although they were expensive and his area was just local, he had done well. He had managed to stay away from alcohol and he hated to admit to himself how difficult he had found this. But the memory of the humiliation he had suffered on the occasion in Dromin when Ethel had helped undress him was a big deterrent. He didn't want to face that again. Besides, he had come to realize that he wasn't capable of going into a pub and having one or two drinks, as other men did. No, he must drink himself into oblivion. So it was better all round if he just stayed away from pubs altogether.

On the same day they heard about their new home Rob's boss told him he wanted to broaden the area he was working in, and for that reason he would provide him with a car. Rob would however, have to pay something each month for this and it would be deducted out of his commission.

They had only moved into their home a month and Ellen had made the whole house comfortable and homely, and was beginning to feel secure again, when Rob disappeared for two days. He had set out on the Thursday morning in his car, the back seat bulging with books his customers had ordered and he was going to deliver. He told her before leaving he might be late because of the bigger area he had to cover. So Ellen was not unduly anxious when the evening wore on, all three boys were in bed fast asleep, the dinner was ready and there was no sign of him. But when the hands of the clock in the kitchen crept round to 11 p.m., instinct told her that Rob was drinking again and he would probably drink until he was quite incapacitated. If he got himself in a state surely he would not attempt to drive? But past experience of his drunken episodes told her he would be beyond even that, so at least the car ought to be alright. But who would support him and help him in the door tonight? Nobody, she thought miserably, nobody at all. He didn't know these people he sold books to like he had known his colleagues in Dromin. He would have to lie somewhere strange and unfamiliar to him. There would be nobody to care where he lay or how he was.

With a sore heart Ellen undressed and climbed into bed to watch and listen until morning for his return. The following morning Rob still hadn't appeared and Ellen was becoming more and more concerned about as to what to do about him. Since Matthew had started school she passed the police station every morning with the children. Should she call and report him missing? But what if he turned up safe and well? Or what if the police found him lying drunk somewhere? She felt she could not face any further humiliation. She had left Banbridge a happy bride and had returned two years later under a cloud of shame and disgrace, with a husband who had lost a thoroughly important job under suspicious circumstances, and she and her family had had to rely on the goodwill of her sister. She knew by the pitying looks she got from people that there had been plenty of gossip, but throughout it all she had to try and maintain her dignity and ignore it all. But she always wondered if her mother, by practically shunning her, had actually fuelled the gossip in the town.

So, in the meantime, she must do nothing. In fact she couldn't face going out at all in case Rob returned. So she made a snap decision to keep Matthew at home this morning. Far better if they didn't go out at all, just simply wait here in the sanctuary of her home.

Somehow the morning wore on, she kept the children occupied, she fed them an early lunch and put Charles down for his afternoon nap, but all the time she was close to despair. Her thoughts alternated between letting the authorities know and just lying low at home. She was just making herself yet another cup of tea, when there was a knock at the door. In a daze Ellen made her way down the hall, was this the news she had been dreading? Had someone found Rob? Had he been injured? But it was her brother Hugh and Anna who stood there, smiling happily.

"Ellen, we were in town doing some shopping and thought we'd call and see how you are settling in. We've been to see Ethel already this morning and she seems to be blooming."

Hugh was ushering Anna in as Ellen held the door wide for them. "Oh, Anna, it's so lovely to see you. Come through to the kitchen and I'll make tea – I think I have some cake in some of the tins." Ellen was so relieved that there was no bad news and so glad to see and talk to another adult. Eagerly she made a pot of tea, found some fruit cake and set her best china on the table. "Yes, Ethel's very well, and the twins are due in two months' time and Colin will be over as usual after school today for the weekend."

"Does he come every weekend?" Anna was intrigued by Colin's devotion to his two young cousins. "He just loves those boys, doesn't he?"

"And they him." Ellen went on. "I kept Matthew at home today," as the two boys burst in the back door, "he wasn't feeling very well."

"He looks a big strong healthy lad," Hugh remarked as he studied his nephews. "They're both tall lads for their age, aren't they?"

Ellen answered in a noncommittal way, it must be obvious that there was very little wrong with Matthew, but the moment passed, much to her relief, as Anna went on to admire the home they had eventually got from the Housing Association. Then Anna very shyly said, "We've some important news of our own, Ellen – I'm expecting a baby – in seven months' time."

"Oh, Anna ... and Hugh, that's wonderful," and Ellen hugged and kissed them both passionately. "You must take care of yourself. No riding pillion on that bike of Hugh's."

"Hugh only uses that thing for his work, that's all. I would never dream of getting on it."

Later, as Hugh and Anna were waiting for the bus back to Castlewellan, Hugh remarked he was worried about his sister. "I hope Rob's behaving himself, Ellen never mentioned his name or how he was doing and something told me not to ask."

He regarded Anna. "What do you think, darling?"

"I thought she was fine, just glad to see us."

"I thought her very edgy, and Matthew not at school. That wasn't right, there didn't seem much wrong with him."

"I know we all worry about Ellen and the boys, but I wouldn't read anything in to how things looked this morning. Ellen was fine." Anna squeezed her husband's arm. "Please try not to worry."

Somewhat reassured, Hugh concentrated on helping Anna through the bus doors and to finding a seat, he knew he did worry about his sister and the trauma she had been through. He had tried talking to his mother, about her attitude to Ellen, but he had met with such coldness from her it made him shudder. As for Sara, he knew that since she got married to THE butcher in Banbridge, she too, was not nearly as supportive of Ellen as she had been. Indeed, he strongly suspected she carried tales to their mother about Rob. On challenging her on this Sara claimed that it would be better if Ellen would take their mother's advice and leave Rob Hampton. Well, he for one would always be a staunch supporter of his sister. No matter what.

Rob arrived home in time for tea that same evening, about an hour after Colin came from school. Ellen was so relieved to see him safe and sound, that she said very little. She did note his dishevelled appearance and how sheepish he looked and his whole manner told her all she needed to know. He admitted openly enough to having had a few drinks and had decided to spend the night in the car rather than drive home. She listened quietly while he made his excuses, then let him know, in no uncertain manner, how worried she had been and how close she had been to reporting his disappearance. But then, anxious to avoid any heated discussions, for the sake of Colin and their own children, she let the matter drop. She did cherish the hope that because she had told him she had considered going to the police, he would have learnt his lesson. However, she was well aware that Rob had now an addiction to alcohol. Whereas at the start of this nightmare he had only drunk after a very unhappy occurrence, such as his father's death and Harry's behaviour towards Eve, now he needed no valid reason to take him back to the pub.

Chapter 26

1934

During the last two years life had taken on a certain pattern for Ellen and Rob. Matthew and Thomas were both now at school, so every morning Ellen put Charles in his pram, and walked with her sons to see them safely there. Rob continued with his drunken sprees and sporadic spells of sobriety. He did manage to sell books, albeit on an irregular basis, and Ellen marvelled that, somehow or other, he had managed to keep his job. But then he was only paid a commission on what he sold, and in between his periods of drunkenness, he still managed to sell quite a few.

During his spells of sobriety he was still the kind, thoughtful Rob she had married, taking the children for a drive on Sunday afternoons, insisting they would have their tea out. He came home promptly in the evenings, helping with the children as best he knew how. But then, sooner or later, he would make his way home on foot, obvious to anyone who met him that he was incapable. Or else he did not come home at all, staying away one night, or perhaps two. Ellen dreaded these times more and more, and felt such a mixture of sympathy and loathing for him, she could not understand herself.

In the last four months, during which Ellen discovered she was pregnant again, Rob had remained totally sober. He had been coming home directly from work, had not been near a pub and there was no sign of any bottles hidden about the house. She was so relieved that, once again, Rob had been able to straighten himself out and forget about alcohol for a time. She had been feeling quite unwell for the past two or three weeks and had found the added stress of Rob's erratic behaviour difficult to deal with. Now she felt she could relax and rest in the evenings when Rob came home, instead of watching and wondering if he would make it home at all.

Here she was, expecting her fourth child, while her dear sister-in-law, Anna, was still childless, having had two miscarriages in the last two years. Life was strange, Ellen thought, as she wheeled Charles along the pavement, after leaving the boys to school. While Anna had the most dependable, hard working husband and could offer a child so much security. Ellen would be bringing another child into the world, who would have an uncertain future, and a father who was far from dependable. Still, she was just glad Rob was dependable enough at the minute and he had been delighted when she had told him about the baby. Then he had always been thrilled when their children were born.

So far, they hadn't told anyone in the family their latest news, but now instead of going straight home, as she normally did, she was going to see her mother to tell her. She wasn't looking forward to the visit. She knew only too well how her mother felt about Rob, but tell her she must, because it would only make matters worse, if her mother heard it from someone else. She must keep contact with her and show respect for her. Her mother, after all, probably had her best interests at heart, even though she didn't understand why Ellen stayed with Rob.

"Oh, it's you, Ellen," were her mother's words when she answered the door. "You'd better come in." Without waiting for an answer, she led the way up the hall and into the kitchen. In silence, Ellen followed her, Charles still in his buggy, into the room. This was not going to be easy and she almost straightaway said, "Mum, I called this morning on my way back from school ... I wanted to let you know I'm pregnant."

"You are what? I don't believe this." Her mother shot her a look of almost contempt. "You do realise you are making it more difficult to leave that man? That drunk."

"Please, Mother... we've been through all this... I don't want to leave Rob, besides," she added earnestly, "he's doing well now."

"Aye, how long will it last this time, I ask? He'll be back on his whiskey in no time. Just wait and see." Ellen had no answer to that, sadly her mother was probably right. Hastily she changed the subject.

"I would rather you didn't say anything to Hugh or Anna at the minute. It might upset them, I think... or Sara either, in case she tells them."

"Don't worry, dear. I wouldn't be telling anyone about this – that's for sure."

While her mother had been speaking she had been making tea at the same time, and Ellen knew she must stay and take it, even though the coldness from her mother enveloped her from across the room. As soon as she possibly could, she finished her tea and by way of an excuse, said she must get Charles home. Telling her mother she would call again soon, Ellen said goodbye and made her way out of the house and along the street towards home, all the time reflecting on her mother's attitude. Many times she had had to listen to her mother complaining about Rob, but this time she was really furious with her. She didn't really mind how her mother spoke to her, but she had totally ignored her beautiful Charles, who had sat in his buggy the whole time, quietly watching them.

Later that evening when Rob arrived home Ellen was tempted to tell him about her mother, but she knew he would tell her to stop going there, something she would prefer not to do. But just the same, her mother's words were still ringing in her ears and she decided to confront Rob, something she rarely did. "You do know it is vital you keep this job you have. Don't you? We're hearing so much about the depression, about men hanging about the streets in Belfast, no work, no food. Why, they are even known by the street corners they are to be found at, if anyone enquires as to their whereabouts. We're lucky really, we've this house and we have some money. Not a lot I know but we manage. You must keep straight, Rob, you really must."

Ellen was sounding desperate simply because she had been reading the newspapers earlier that day. If Rob found himself in the same boat, the children would be taken into care, into some awful home and she knew that if that were to happen, her own life would not be worth living.

Rob was all concern now for Ellen, she seemed anxious and agitated, not her usual calm self. He too, had been alarmed by the news, day and daily, of the ever increasing numbers of people out of work in Belfast. Belfast, which had been such a prosperous industrial city, its Linen Mills and Harland and Wolff Shipbuilding flourishing for years, now if all were to be believed, both industries were in rapid decline and the city was in the grip of a deep recession.

"I am doing my best to keep going, darling. I still manage to sell some books, not as many, mind you but I'm still earning. There's still money around Banbridge – unlike Belfast. I do know that thousands are out of work there. There are reports of rioting in the streets at night, and between Catholic and Protestant. Imagine! Whatever that's all about. As if things aren't bad enough, without bringing religion into it all. That'll solve nothing. I do intend to hold onto this job, if possible – I know I have to. At least Dorrie and John seem alright, they do say the tobacco factory is thriving. People are probably smoking now more than ever, to keep their mind off things. It's a good job John got the chance of that manager's position in Gallagher's, with his father's business going down the way it did. Who would ever have believed it could ever happen to the linen mills." Rob stressed, "Yes, Dorrie will be alright, and we will be too."

Rob, anxious Ellen would not bring up the subject of alcohol, it always made him feel so guilty and useless, purposely channelled the conversation towards his sister and her husband. Why did he keep going back to it, bringing shame and disgrace on himself and his family? But he was resolved that this time he wouldn't touch it again, there was no way he could afford to.

Rob did manage to remain sober throughout the remaining months of Ellen's pregnancy, resolutely refusing to go near a pub, and handing his money over to her every week. Ellen had a trouble free time, apart from being uncomfortable in bed at night and being plagued by dreams, dreams which were mostly about Anna. She did realise she was preoccupied with her sister-in-law because of her childlessness and continued miscarriages. She had the greatest admiration for Anna, who, no matter what her own circumstances were, had seemed genuinely delighted when Ellen had told her about the baby due in February. Anna had simply hugged and kissed Ellen happily. So Ellen felt it was important to remain optimistic that Hugh and she would soon have a family of their own. Yet her dreams persisted, with Anna sometimes begging Ellen to help her, she so wanted a baby too.

It was a snowy January night and Ellen, Rob and the boys had gone to bed early it was so cold, and they were all so tired they had fallen asleep almost immediately. Suddenly Ellen was wide awake. Someone was knocking at the door. Who on earth could it be? It was twelve o'clock at night. She looked over at Rob fast asleep beside her, obviously he had heard nothing. Quietly Ellen slipped downstairs and opened the front door, but the pavement was deserted. There was no one there. She must have had another one of her dreams, but one that was more vivid than ever. She slipped back into bed beside Rob, glad of the heat emanating from his body, and soon fell asleep.

But again she was wakened by the same rapping noise, more insistent than ever and now the clock showed 2 a.m. Reluctantly Ellen went downstairs and opened the door. But again the street was deserted, the snow falling steadily in thick flakes now. Shivering, she went back up to bed the second time. How she wished this pregnancy was over, she was sure these dreams of hers would stop then.

"Rob, surely you aren't giving Matthew money for sweets for Thomas and him again this morning?" Ellen had been watching Rob count out some coins from his pocket. The boys were ready for school and were standing watching their father, an expectant look on their faces. "It's only a penny each, dear," as he put the two pennies into Matthew's hand.

"But you'd need to hurry up if you want to call with Mr Thompson in the sweetshop before school." Rob spoke directly to the boys, handing them their satchels as they headed out the door. Then giving Ellen a sheepish smile he headed up the stairs to get ready to go out. Ellen, shaking her head in exasperation, began clearing the breakfast table before going upstairs herself to waken Charles. Suddenly the back door opened and Matthew and Thomas stood there, white faced and trembling. It was Matthew who spoke first. "Mum, mum, Mr Thompson says we can't go to school today because Uncle Hugh was killed last night," and he threw himself into his mother's arms sobbing bitterly, while Thomas stood motionless in the kitchen. Even as her son spoke the words, Ellen saw, through the window, her sister, Sara, coming to the door to tell them the awful news. Her darling brother, her champion, her friend was dead, and Ellen immediately thought of her dreams about Anna, poor, desolate Anna, who would never now have a child of Hugh's. A fortnight after Hugh's death, Ellen gave birth to a baby daughter, whom she decided to call Lucie.

Chapter 27

Since Hugh's death four years ago, Rob had worked hard for them all and had never touched alcohol in all of that time. For a year after his brother-in-law's death he had continued with his bookselling with moderate success, but then he had an innovative idea for a venture he wanted to patent.

"The farmers round the country are in desperation for a disinfectant and it's all because of these new health regulations that are coming in. It seems they must all disinfect their byres and their outhouses." Rob had just sat down at the dinner table with the children while Ellen ladled out bowls of steaming stew to them all. "I'm thinking seriously of making my own and selling it to them and I was speaking to a man today, by the name of Murray, he says he'll tell me the ingredients and where to buy them." He turned to Ellen and then to Matthew, Thomas and Charles. "Well... what do you think? Does it sound a good idea?"

"Where would you make the disinfectant, Rob? We have nowhere suitable here." Ellen sounded dubious.

"I'd have to use the range but it doesn't take the solution long to boil ... and I understand all you need is a good bucket to put all the ingredients into." He sounded so enthusiastic about his project and the idea had certainly caught the boys' attention. They were all listening carefully.

"Could we help? After school I mean." This from Matthew.

"Sure you could, it's perfectly safe when it's boiled, you use specially designed cards, dip them in the mix, and put them somewhere to dry. I tell you there's plenty of money in it. I know there is."

"Is anyone else doing it?" Matthew asked.

"Not that I know of, son... we'll be the first."

Although Ellen remained doubtful about the venture Rob went ahead. He drove to the gas works and obtained quantities of the ingredients he needed. He bought two large buckets in the local hardware store and had cards printed with the word "Disinfectant" along the top.

That had been three years ago and since then the entire kitchen seemed to be taken over by the process and, strangely enough, Matthew and Thomas were still enthusiastically making the cards of disinfectant. These were then taken upstairs where they were laid singly along the iron springs of one of the beds until dry. The house seemed to Ellen to always reek of disinfectant. Every night before bedtime, the cards must be removed and the mattress and bedding replaced. It was such hard work but Rob had been right about it being a good venture. He soon became very busy and began to make a lot of money and at night he did all his own accounts and bookkeeping. These were kept in apple pie order at all times. Rob's natural aptitude for mathematics was now being well utilised.

The only ones in the family who showed little interest were Charles and Lucie. At four years of age, Lucie was too young, and as for Charles, he was more interested in reading about how these disinfectants worked to destroy the germs that caused so much disease. But then Charles was the bookworm in the family, reading anything he could get his hands on, should it be the daily newspaper or one of his mother's classics.

Ellen knew her sisters and parents were happy for her and her new found security. Her mother had even taken to calling in to see her from time to time, and Ellen was eager to forget her mother's contempt and coldness in the past. She knew her mother was impressed with Rob's new business and how they were now so much better off than they had been for a long time. Ellen realised that Hugh's death had had a profound effect on her mother – she seemed more accepting of Rob and for that Ellen was very grateful. She also felt great empathy towards her mother; she was frail now and had developed a marked tremor in her head and neck shortly after his death. The doctor had told the family it was shock which had brought it on.

Now today Ellen was expecting them to call later, Sara had looked in early that morning to say she and her mother would be along later. So today would be as good a day as any to tell them what Rob was proposing to do to expand his business.

When Sara and her mother arrived in the afternoon, Ellen had tea and apple tart ready. Her mother hugged and kissed Lucie and presented her with a bag of sweets, and remarked, looking at Ellen, "She's getting more and more like you every time I see her with her beautiful dark hair and those dark eyes."

"Everyone says so, Mother." Ellen knew it pleased her mother that Lucie looked like her and bore little resemblance to her father.

"Sara has something important to tell you, Ellen. Haven't you, Sara?"

"Yes... it's about Anna. She's getting married again in September." Sara and Anna had forged a very strong relationship in the aftermath of Hugh's tragic death and they were very close.

"Oh, Sara, is she really going to marry Mr Dixon, the headmaster in the academy? You did tell me she had been out with him a couple of times, but..." Ellen's voice tailed off. Mr Dixon was, to Ellen's mind, so plain and dour. Not like beautiful Anna, who had been so full of life before the tragedy of losing Hugh had taken its toll. Obviously Anna felt she needed security. Ellen suspected that would now be priority for Anna, she would never again be looking for the love she had experienced with Hugh.

Now as she studied her mother, she saw again that deep grief for her lost son. Yes Anna could move on because she must, but his mother, Ellen knew could not and would grieve for Hugh for the rest of her life.

"I know... I know," Sara answered, "but she seems keen enough I think. If it's what she wants we have to be happy for her."

"I have some news today myself." Ellen didn't know how the two women facing her would react to what she was about to tell them. Looking now at their faces she hurried on, "No I'm not pregnant." She smiled at them. "No, we're going to move to Portstewart for a time. Rob knows there is so much business up there that he ought to be targeting. We're going to rent a furnished house, so we won't be giving this one up. We intend to continue to pay the rent here of course. It's only a temporary move in the meantime, maybe about six months, Rob estimates. I needed to let you know."

Ellen didn't add that Ethel had known about the move for some time. Ellen usually confided in her about any important matter, knowing Ethel was the soul of discretion. At least now that Colin was working he was a less frequent visitor at the weekends than he had been, and she knew he would not mind the separation from his cousins so much.

It was a wintry day in early December 1938 when they locked up the house in Banbridge and started out on their journey to Portstewart. Rob had had to take their clothes, bed linen, towels and food the day before when he had received the key from the landlord.

Ellen had serious misgivings about this move they were making, even though it was only temporary, but Rob was so excited about his plans for extending the business, that she had kept her thoughts to herself.

But her sense of foreboding increased as they drove through the blinding rain which lashed against walls and roofs of houses and battered against the windscreen. Their four children didn't seem to mind the weather or the fact that they would be changing school, they were so buoyed up with the thought of going to live at the seaside, and it was a real, new adventure to them all. At least they would be back living in Banbridge by the time Lucie was school age.

The family lived in Portstewart for several months and for most of that time, to Ellen's mind, the weather was horrendous. The rain, sleet and snow seemed to be never ending and the wind was relentless in its fury. It howled through the windows and down the chimney all night. During the day it whipped up the waves in the sea, which were huge and so very frightening that trips along the seafront were out of the question. And in order to get to school the three boys must face all this every morning then return home through it and Rob must go and try to sell disinfectant to people who only longed for the warmth and comfort of their homes.

It was late April the following year before any sign of Spring appeared. At least the heavy torrential rain which had been a constant companion to them, eased into a steady drizzle and the high winds abated considerably. There were even glimpses of sunshine some afternoons during which Ellen made sure she took the children after school, along the seafront where they might at last dig in the sand and paddle in the sea.

Eventually summer arrived, June was a glorious month, and Portstewart was transformed into a place of beauty and tranquillity. The sea was calm and peaceful, the sand appeared white and the sky overhead was a constant blue from early morning until late evening. But Rob was by now quite desperate. He knew it had come all too late for him, this venture to the North had been a failure. The floods, the snow and ice and people's apathy towards disinfecting their outhouses had all contributed towards it. But why had he never once considered the weather? He knew now, when it was all too late, that it stood to reason that a seaside town on the edge of the Atlantic Ocean would suffer all the elements of a severe winter. He had been a fool. He realised he should have been content with his thriving business in Banbridge, instead of branching out into unknown territory. Worst of all his desperation had brought with it his craving for alcohol. A craving he had managed to control until last week. But at least he managed to keep his whiskies to two, on the couple of evenings he had gone into a bar. He was confident now he could do as other men did and just have a couple. He was confident too, that his business in Banbridge still held good and he knew they must return there as soon as they possibly could. The rent on their home was a bit in arrears, but he could soon sort that out. Now this evening he would have to tell his family they must return home and forget about Portstewart, just when Ellen was beginning to enjoy everything here. He knew that, like himself, she had loathed the winter with all its storms and freezing conditions, but now she was enjoying the school holidays with the children and the exceptional summer they were having.

After dinner that same evening Rob told Ellen of his plans to return home. Nine-year-old Charles and four-year-old Lucie were in bed, but Matthew and Thomas were present when he broached the subject.

"Business isn't good here, Ellen." He launched straight in. "In fact it's very poor. We need to go back home. Folks here don't seem very interested in my product. The bad winter..." his voice tailed off. "I'm sorry, darling, I know you and the children are enjoying it here now. I'm so sorry."

"Rob, I want to go home." Ellen was emphatic. "I couldn't face another winter here. The last few weeks have just been an interlude, that's all, like being on holiday."

When Rob looked at his wife smiling happily, relief etched on her face, he felt part of the burden had been lifted from his shoulders. He looked at his older boys who had been listening to what he was saying. "How do you feel, Matthew? Thomas?"

Matthew answered firmly. "Thomas and I have talked about it a lot, Dad. We feel like Mum does. This place isn't really for us. We'll be glad to go back to Banbridge."

"That's good, son. We'll start tomorrow and fold things up. You help your mum pack up. At least on the return journey I have a roof rack for the cases, so one run will do us."

The family left Portstewart on a glorious summer day at the end of July, so unlike the one they remembered when they were first starting out those few months ago. As they drove along the roads Ellen thought back to that journey and her misgivings about Rob's new venture. How she regretted she had not had the courage to voice her thoughts and ask Rob to reconsider what he was doing.

It was almost dark when they arrived back in Banbridge and afterwards Rob and Ellen were grateful for the privacy the night offered them.

"All of you wait until I go and open the house." Rob parked the car alongside the pavement. "I've the key to the front door right here, then everyone can carry something in and we'll soon get the car emptied."

At first Rob was not concerned when the key seemed to be sticking in the lock, it was some time since it had been used. He took it out, gave it a good clean and reinserted it. Then realisation dawned on him. "Oh my God," he thought, "the locks have been changed!" Slowly he made his way back down the path to the car and got back in the driver's seat.

"The Association have changed the locks," he whispered to Ellen. "I know we owe rent to them but not that much." He laid his head on the steering wheel in despair.

"What are we to do?" Ellen sounded desperate.

"I have to go round the back and break a window. We've no choice at this time of night. We're not going anywhere else at the minute, we can't."

Ellen nodded dumbly in the darkness. She turned to Matthew and Thomas. "Go and help your dad to get in, and be quiet, we don't want to wake half the street." No use in trying to bluff the two older boys, they must have heard what Rob had said.

"Right, boys," Rob got out of the car, "this won't go down too well with the association. They'll probably do us for trespassing when they find out we're back here and gaining entry illegally. But I'll go and talk to them tomorrow, I need to pay some rent I owe anyway."

The following morning before Rob had an opportunity to go to the Housing Association office, an official from there called with them, and gave Rob a month's notice of eviction.

Rob had wasted no time in combing the countryside to find alternative accommodation before he and his family found they were homeless. He was fortunate he had good contacts with farmers and land owners simply because of his disinfectant business. After rejecting a large, beautiful house situated in beautiful grounds and only requiring a reasonable rent – he felt it was too isolated for Ellen – Rob opted for a long low cottage with plenty of outhouses, situated two miles from Lisburn.

Chapter 28

On the first day of September 1939 Hitler invaded Poland, and two days later, Britain declared war on Germany. Ellen, Rob and the four children were so absorbed in packing up their belongings and leaving the house they had known and loved for the past eight years, they scarcely took heed of such a catastrophic event.

Ellen hadn't seen the house they were going to, but Rob had been quite enthusiastic about it, so she was depending on him that it was alright. He had told her the school was situated just across a field and over a stile, so that meant a lot to her. As for the town of Lisburn, she had heard of it but had no idea what it was like. Today she had insisted they arrive at their new home as early as possible, they needed to get beds erected and the kitchen up and running before dark. Mr Murray – Rob's friend – had kindly offered his van and his services for the day, free of charge. A gesture much appreciated by them all.

Rob seemed to take his time driving along roads which Ellen was fairly familiar with then on to unfamiliar ones, before they eventually turned up a long lane and Rob turned to Ellen. "This is it. We're here, dear." The car slowed down as the lane widened out into a large, open, cobble stoned yard with several quaint outbuildings surrounding it.

"This is different." Ellen's response sounded quite neutral but as she looked round the place, she knew she liked what she saw. Before she could say anything more, the children were spilling out of the car and racing across the yard, shouting at one another as they ran.

"Right, boys, that's enough. We'll have plenty of time for all that later." Rob's tone was commanding. "There's a lot of work to do here first, so let's get started."

He turned to Ellen. "This is the front of the house, it may seem back to front, but the back door is on the other side and opens onto a bank and green fields. Let's go in, we can start unpacking when you've been round the place. Hopefully the van will be here shortly." Together they entered a small hall with doors leading off it, Ellen was pleased to see that the living room and kitchen were more than adequate and they had three good sized bedrooms. In a few hours she would soon have the place in some sort of order. The hardest thing would be getting used to oil lamps again after the luxury of having light at the touch of a switch. But as far as she knew, no one in the countryside had yet acquired electricity.

This was Sunday, but Rob had already arranged with the headmistress of the local school, that the children would not start until Tuesday the 5th of September, that meant they had two days to settle in. It would be Lucie's first day at school and Ellen intended to take her and introduce herself to the teacher.

That evening, Ellen managed, with some difficulty, to cook some mutton and potatoes in a large black pot which hung from a crook above the fire. Ellen soon discovered that the open fire appeared to be the only means of cooking. Later they sat down to listen to the wireless Rob had managed to acquire a few weeks ago. Now, they could hear the chilling details of Neville Chamberlain's address to the nation, which had been relayed at 11.15 that morning, reiterating that Britain was indeed, at war with Germany.

Two weeks after war broke out, Colin Wilson, having enlisted with the Irish fusiliers, was sent to Aldershot for army training. From here his unit was despatched to France early in 1940, where he and his comrades found themselves in the thick of battle, fighting for their lives and their country.

"Ethel, we might have known Colin would do something like this." Ellen was buttering scones for her sister, who had made her way from Banbridge this morning to visit her.

"Look how he was with my boys, so mindful of them." She was upset by Ethel's news of Colin enlisting, but somehow she must comfort her sister, who was inconsolable. "There was no way Colin could have listened to pleas for men in the country's hour of need, and not join up. We should be so proud of him – his spirit and his loyalty."

Colin hadn't stood idly by, as so many from Northern Ireland seemed to be doing. Why, the streets of Belfast were full of men idling away their time, as if the war was nothing to do with them. On the few occasions Rob and she had driven through the city streets, she had been appalled to see them, lurking about alley ways, playing shove halfpenny or the likes. Ethel's voice broke in on her thoughts.

"I know I am proud of him, but then I always was. If only he'd told me sooner of his plans, maybe I could have talked him out of it."

"I doubt it very much, Ethel. That's why he didn't say. He knew how much it would upset you and was afraid you might persuade him to change his mind. All we can do is pray every single night for his safe return and that this wretched war will be over soon."

"Oh, Ellen," Ethel hugged her sister, "I'm so glad I came today. It has helped enormously just talking about it."

"Now, come on, Ethel, eat something." Pushing the plate of scones over to her, "After that walk from the train in Lisburn, you must be hungry."

"Well, it certainly seemed much longer than Colin always maintained it was, he was forever telling me it was a mere dawdle from the station."

"I'll certainly miss his visits here at the weekends. I am so thankful that there was no question of Rob being accepted because of his work with farmers and agriculture. Besides no one expects this war to last. God will not let such evil go on and then Colin will come back home, safe and sound." Ellen was doing her best to reassure Ethel who must be heartbroken that it was her son who was there. A mere slip of a boy now thrown into an alien world. Ellen could not even begin to contemplate how she would feel if it were one of her boys.

Chapter 29

Winston Churchill was appointed Prime Minister on the 10th of May 1940, and on that same day the German army invaded Belgium and the Netherlands, having just the previous month occupied Denmark and Norway. The British and French troops were immobilised to defend the Belgians, but the Germans advanced to the mouth of the Seine, effectively splitting the Allied Forces in two. The British troops, together with some French, were forced to retreat back to the channel coast, and when Belgium was forced to surrender on May 28th, the British found themselves in circumstances fraught with danger.

As a result of that humiliating defeat and in the confusion and chaos that followed, innumerable British troops became isolated from their battalions. The Enniskillen Fusiliers were one such battalion who found themselves in a strange country and separated from other troops, with no firm orders of where to go or what to do. All any of them had been told was to head for the coast.

Dejected and caught up in a war they were relentlessly losing to the Nazis, the men did their best to keep one another's morale up. But as they trekked through the forests, climbed hills and walked through the narrow streets and alleys of France it became more and more an uphill struggle to keep spirits high. Gloom and despair and the threat of death filled their minds and the whole air around them, yet they must remain alert and on the lookout for the German sniper who might be lurking in an outbuilding or behind shrubbery, ready to shoot on sight. And all the time the drone of enemy aircrafts overhead and the merciless echoes of gunfire, accompanied them every step of the way.

Colin and most of the battalion had somehow or other managed to stick together as they tried to make their way safely to the coast. Colin had been thinking of his parents and siblings, of his cousins and wondering if he would ever see them again, when disaster struck. They were negotiating a particularly rocky steep hill. He did not see the pothole until it was too late and he just felt the searing pain in his ankle. He fell awkwardly, his gun on his shoulder thrust against his neck in another agonising jerk.

"Colin, are you alright?" Jack, his buddy whom he had enlisted with, was beside him immediately, helping him to his feet. "Can you stand, Colin?"

In response Colin plunged the hull of his rifle into the ground and managed to stand up. "Yes, thank goodness. It's my ankle I seem to have hurt. It's bloody sore." He tried to take a step forward. "Whether I can walk or not is a different matter."

"Right, lean on me." Jack lent his friend his whole support and placed his arm firmly round his waist. By now, the rest of the battalion were nowhere to be seen.

"Jack you must go on without me. You'll soon catch up on the others. I'll lean on this," indicating his rifle, "And go as best I can, but you must go on, please, Jack."

"You must be joking, mate. I'm not going anywhere without you. We're in this bloody war together. That is, if you could call it a war. Seems mighty one sided to me. But we joined together and we are going to stay together. So, no more of that talk." And Jack began to step up the hill, supporting Colin as best he could.

It had started to rain, a slight drizzle at first which soon became heavier and heavier, until their uniforms were sodden, their boots heavy with wet and the fields around them were now boggy.

Jack could see Colin was weary now and pain was etched on his face.

"Look out for a good clump of trees, Colin and we'll take a rest. Somewhere that will give some shelter from those Nazis. I don't think we have much further to go. But, by the sound of the Luftwaffe, we should be in no great hurry to get there."

The noise of the enemy aircraft and shelling was now deafening and Jack knew they must be close to the coast. But what awaited them there? The idea that the Royal Navy would simply be waiting to take them to safety was just a dream. Colin and himself would soon be walking into some sort of hell, he reckoned. But he had to keep his thoughts to himself, because they must continue on, they really had no choice.

They trudged on quietly until Colin spotted a ditch, almost completely surrounded by foliage. It looked the ideal spot to hide and rest. They both seemed to get a burst of energy to climb into it, and Colin promptly bent down and removed his boot to try to ease the agonising pain in his ankle.

Jack looked at his pal's grotesquely swollen ankle.

"Right, I'll take my vest off, you need something round that. Then we'll have a short rest, but it can only be a short one, mind."

Jack hadn't meant to fall asleep, he had just been anxious that Colin should rest. He was getting concerned about how his friend would manage the last leg of their journey, he was in so much pain. But he too had nodded off, cocooned with Colin in that small ditch, a haven before they must face whatever lay ahead.

"Colin, we must get on, there seems to be a bit of a lull in the shelling at the minute. But from here on I think we have to crawl. It would be too dangerous to stand. Can you manage that?"

Colin seemed to have got a new burst of energy. He had had a very vivid dream whilst he slept, his mother and Aunt Ellen were talking to him, telling him to keep going and they would see him soon. By concentrating on his dream and how they had smiled so encouragingly at him,. he seemed to make much better progress. Besides, crawling along took the weight off his ankle, much easier than trying to walk. He just dragged his injured leg behind him. As they reached the top of the incline, the enemy shelling started again. It seemed much nearer and much more intense than before. But the harrowing scene of devastation they witnessed as they crawled over the top, was one which would haunt them for the rest of their lives.

The English Channel lay before them, stretching away to what seemed like infinity and it was awash with troops wading knee high through the water. A few ships were dotted here and there, tiny fishing boats lurched and swayed as men, able bodied, injured and dying, were being helped aboard. The beaches too were thronged with soldiers, some kneeling and others prostrate in the sand. And always, overhead, the constant drone of aircraft and the whirr of their shells as they fell from the sky. Then suddenly, the frightening sound of an explosion as a doomed ship fell foul to the Nazi regime.

"Is there any point in heading down there, Colin? Should we lie low for a while?"

"Well, Jack, our uniforms are the same colour as the sand. We can slide along, bit by bit. We've come this far so we aren't giving up now." Colin felt more optimistic than he had ever felt in spite of the devastating scene before them. If they got safely back to England, he intended to make it his business to recommend Jack for his bravery. He knew, with certainty, he would never have made it to Dunkirk beach without his dear friend.

Rob followed the events unfolding on the beaches at Dunkirk avidly, well, as much as his wireless with the batteries would allow him, and such as news coverage was permitted. And all the time he listened he thought of his nephew Colin, who had been like a son to them, helping with the children, helping him with his disinfectant project. And Colin and all those young men became one in his mind, all so inexperienced and so selfless. And his anxiety was all encompassing for each and every one of them. He was just so thankful he had been exempt from such unbelievable horror such as they were all facing.

On the morning he turned on his wireless and heard Winston Churchill announce that the Royal Navy along with all the help from the civilians with their small fishing boats had successfully rescued a total of 332,816 men from the beaches of Dunkirk , he thanked God for all those lives saved.

Jack Collins and Colin Wilson were among those 332 thousand men rescued. They had been in the water for three days and nights.

For a time Colin and Jack had lain huddled low in the sand dunes, watchful and fully alert until there seemed another lull in the bombardment on humanity. Then with a brief nod to each other, they began to crawl along to face the horror that lay ahead of them.

The two men soon found that the military precision was as much in evidence here as it had been on the first day of their training, despite their exposed and highly dangerous situation. When organising able bodied and injured men into some sort of order Colin's sergeant immediately noticed his swollen foot and leg. He informed him that because of it, he would be considered a priority and placed with the other injured men. This Colin adamantly refused to do, telling his superior he must stay with Jack and besides, there were so many more severely injured than he was. The sergeant relented but stressed they might have to wait some time before they could get a place on a boat.

Colin and Jack were three days and nights in the water, mostly up to their necks. When their turn finally came to scramble aboard a small fishing boat, Colin was beyond feeling anything in his lower limbs, and his lips and tongue were so dry and cracked he was unable to speak. Kind careful arms reached out for him. Someone took the weight of his legs and then, miraculously, a mug of warm tea was put to his lips and with instructions to sit up he had his first fluids for three days.

Someone whispered in his ear, "They're away again, Colin, to reload, no doubt. When they come back, we'll be well out of here." He recognised Jack's voice and in spite of his lethargy he thanked God aloud for bringing them into the arms of friends. Soon, several soldiers on that small boat were taking up his prayers, and someone began singing "Rock of ages, cleft for me." And the sound echoed across the English Channel and lulled by the sound, Colin fell fast asleep.

Chapter 30

May 1941

During the evacuation of the troops from Dunkirk, Ellen had been troubled by dreams of Colin and seas and water but she knew anxiety for her young nephew had contributed to them. Her mind had been preoccupied with thoughts of him; his whereabouts, and what he must be coming through. When Ethel was informed by the War Office that her son was in a military hospital in England and they had been assured his injuries were not life threatening, the whole family thanked God for bringing so many young men safely home.

Now, someone was shaking her urgently, she thought at first she was dreaming again. Then she head Rob's voice, "Ellen you must get up." She was instantly awake.

"What is it, Rob? What's wrong?"

"It's the Germans, don't you hear them? They're flying very low and dropping hundreds of flares over Belfast. It's like daylight outside. I'm away to get the children up. They must see it. They're starting to bomb Belfast, after all the government's assurances that it would never happen."

He was heading out of the bedroom, towards the children's rooms to waken them. The three boys were up and out of the bedroom instantly but Rob hesitated about bringing Lucie out to witness such unfolding horror, then decided she must be with them. She may not remember much about it afterwards, or understand what was going on. But some day he knew, they would read about this in their history books.

This would surely bring it home to them that their country was at war. The whole country had believed this fighting was removed from them all, it could never possibly affect them. The whole government, the whole country had been lulled into a false sense of security.

Rob, Ellen and the children stood huddled together in silence as they watched the awesome spectacle going on in the sky. The whole sky was ablaze with stark, white lights, glowing over the city of Belfast. Lights which appeared suspended from small white silk parachutes. The whole of the sky was clearer and brighter than a summer's day.

"They're dropping flares first," Rob explained, "in order to see where to drop their bombs and explosives." As they stood there the steady drone of aircraft went on and on as more and more flares glided down to earth.

Then the raid began. First the crackling sounds which seemed to be made by small devices, followed by much more sinister, rumbling moans and then the overpowering, shattering sound of the blasts.

Ellen had not spoken a word since coming outside but stood watching in horror, her arms around the children, while Matthew stood resolutely beside his father.

"Ellen I think they must be targeting the docks area." Rob's voice was very subdued.

Ellen did not answer for a moment. She knew only too well, if Rob was right, what that meant. It meant the Shore Road would not escape the bombardment and John and Dorrie and their family were in peril.

"Let's get everyone inside, please. We've seen enough." Ellen's voice shook but she indicated to them all to get back into the house. Quietly she persuaded the children to get back to bed. At least they were all safe here, out in the country.

But Rob and she sat in the kitchen listening to the thundering and whistling of the bombs, of the monstrous drones of the planes, and talked of Dorrie and John and prayed they would be safe.

The siren announcing the "All Clear" sounded several hours later and it was only then Ellen and Rob decided to go to bed. They both knew the next day would be a harrowing one and some rest would be essential if they were to cope with finding out what they could of Dorrie and John. They both were up and about by six thirty the following morning, neither of them having been able to sleep. Rob hadn't closed his eyes when he went to bed; he was so close to despair about Dorrie. Why hadn't she and John listened to him when he suggested they come to his house? But their answer was always the same. They were unlikely targets, why would the Nazis want to bomb Belfast? Besides they were so close to Eire, they were all one island. And Eire was decidedly neutral.

But to Rob a blitz on Belfast seemed inevitable. He had closely followed the news about the blitz in England, London, Coventry and Portsmouth, all of whom had suffered so much, and he had felt it was downright lunacy for everyone here to be so complacent. To him, Harland and Wolff with their shipbuilding, and Short and Harlands, with their aeroplanes, were such obvious targets and tonight was the reality of it all. The Nazis must have found their job so easy, the whole landscape so easy to identify. He knew people thought his mind was befuddled with drink sometimes, but on the contrary, he felt the whiskey alerted his senses, and had got him out of many a predicament in the past.

"Thomas, you need to get up now, Dad says you've to go with him to Belfast."

Matthew was already up and about, keen to get to work on the neighbouring farm, work which Winston Churchill had stated quite categorically was essential to the War Effort and that anyone who worked as labourers on farms were contributing so much. If only he had been of age, he would have enlisted the way his cousin Colin had. He would have been fighting those bastard Nazis. But at least, after listening to Churchill, he felt he was doing something worthwhile.

"Right, Thomas, waken up. Dad's going to try to find out about Aunt Dorrie. I heard Mum and him talking last night. He wants you to go with him."

Thomas was awake instantly. "He wants me with him? Oh God, Matthew – I don't know if I can. What will we see? It'll be horrible, I know it will."

"Well I can't go, I've to go to work. You'll be alright with Dad with you. Let's hope Aunt Dorrie's safe and they'll all be back here with us."

Matthew proceeded to put on his jacket. "By the way, Mum's doing boiled eggs for us as a wee treat before we go."

When they entered the kitchen they could hear the drone of the wireless and the solemn voice of the newscaster relating the events of the previous night. They all listened intently as they had breakfast. The raid had lasted some three to four hours, high explosives and hundreds of incendiary devices had fallen on the York Road, the Shore Road and the Docks. Shipyards had suffered appalling damage and, according to the newscaster, fires were still raging through the city.

"Right, Thomas, are you up to this?" Rob turned the wireless off. "I need someone, that's for sure. We have to find out. We need to know about Dorrie, what has happened to them, anything would be better than this uncertainty."

Ellen had been watching Thomas as he listened to the awful news. He had an anxiety about him which disturbed her. She wondered at the wisdom of letting a mere thirteen-year-old go on such a journey. Then she thought of John and Dorrie and their children whose ages ranged from thirteen to two. There was no knowing what their plight was, or whether they were alive or dead. The least she could do was to agree with Rob.

She hugged Thomas tightly as she reached him his coat. "Be brave, son, and try not to look at what's around you and may God go with you." Thomas simply nodded and attempted a smile before following his father out to the car. He only knew when his father needed him he would follow him to the ends of the earth, even though he was terrified.

The only time Rob spoke was as he was starting up the car. "We don't know what we're in for in Belfast, Thomas – but we have to do this."

"I know, Dad. We'll be fine."

As they drove along, initially they saw nothing to account for the noise and mayhem of the previous night. Only the crimson flames still leaping into the air gave an indication of what had gone on. As they drove along, those same flames always seemed to be quite far ahead of them. Then suddenly they were in the middle of it all, the burning, crackling sound of ruined buildings and the gush of cascades of water flowing everywhere from burst pipes. Mere shells of buildings and houses on either side of the roads loomed menacingly towards them as Rob determinedly drove on, expecting at any moment for someone to try to stop him. The whole place was crawling with people, some trying to quench fires, or digging frantically through rubble, others struggling to try to make buildings safe from eminent collapse. Blackened, breathless and weary with fires and smoke, they worked relentlessly on, quiet and sombre, in the face of the horrors they had witnessed last night and still had to face. The pavements were strewn with bundles covered in blackened, burned clothing, and the whole scene was so unnerving that for a brief moment, Rob only wanted to turn back. He knew, with an awful certainty that those same bundles, lying discarded on the pavement, were bodies, bodies of innocent people, who until last evening had been alive and well.

As they drove along the Shore Road, Rob's breathing was laboured and he wondered how Dorrie's family could have survived such a blitz as this. Thankfully Thomas hadn't remarked on the bodies lying there, he seemed more intent on watching the work that seemed endless and so hopeless for everyone involved.

When they turned into the drive where Dorrie lived they could not believe their eyes, every one of the neat houses was intact, unscathed by any of the violence of the previous night.

Later that day when they were all safely back with Ellen, Dorrie explained to everyone that although tons of explosives had fallen on the playing fields at the back of their house, the huge green which stretched the length of the playing field had acted as a barrier between the houses and the bomb. Dorrie maintained it was an absolute miracle and God had been taking care of them. Thomas, frozen to the core, was given a prime seat at the fire and hot fluids to help thaw his icy limbs. On the return journey he had had to sit on the running board of the car, holding on to the headlamp, the whole way home. The warmth from the fire soon penetrated his body and his frozen limbs and fingers but he knew that the memory of the scenes he had witnessed and the iciness in his heart would not be erased so readily.

Chapter 31

1941

"Is Rob often like this, Ellen? With drink I mean?" Dorrie was peeling potatoes to make a pot of stew, enough for two hungry families, while Ellen was baking bread.

"I'm afraid so, Dorrie, I never did tell you much about it. Rob has serious spells of drunkenness, then somehow or other, he manages to sober himself up, starts to work hard and is his usual self. His binges are never referred to. But any trauma at all, either real or imagined, is enough to set him off again."

"He was so awful last night, not my brother at all, just some drunken stranger, that's how I felt when I saw him."

"I know it was a big shock to you, Dorrie, but over the years I have got used to seeing him like this. I never let myself forget he's my husband, he's my responsibility and," Ellen added quietly, "I guess he always will be. This time it was the sights and trauma of the blitz which set him off. It's only three days ago he drove to Belfast for you all but he more or less turned to alcohol straight away. I have to admit that when he's like this it is an effort to remember the good times."

She turned to Dorrie. "I've never told anyone this before, but you're his sister and you will be living here for a while. You'll probably see him like this again. Will you be able to tolerate it do you think?"

Dorrie, drying her hands on the towel at the sink, went to Ellen and putting her arms around her, said in a matter of fact manner, "Ellen if you have put up with this behaviour of Rob's for most of your married life, I can't see how it could possibly be a chore to me."

"As for Matthew and Thomas last night..." Ellen felt compelled to explain her sons' behaviour towards their father, when he had arrived home. It amazed them all how he managed to drive home, but he always did and as yet had never had an accident.

"I know they didn't seem to show much respect for him. That is simply because when their father's drunk they are very intolerant of him. You could see that for yourself, but they always get him to bed for me now and I am very glad of their help. I know it looks as if they are manhandling him, but I don't have to do it anymore. They also check his pockets to see if he has any money, money I really need. At least he comes home at night now. He used to stay away for perhaps three nights at a time. No doubt he's afraid of being caught up in another blitz." Ellen paused and looked at her sister-in-law rather sadly. "Now you know all there is to know, Dorrie."

"I'm glad, Ellen that your boys are such support to you. You don't have to explain their behaviour to me. It must be very hard for you all."

"When he's sober they're the best of buddies you know; the boys help him with the disinfectant, go with him when he needs more supplies, they play draughts together at night – but unfortunately it isn't like that all the time."

"Ellen, I could see how well they worked together the day they brought us here, getting a bedroom organised for us, borrowing a van from your neighbour to get our beds and bed linen." Dorrie had marvelled at how speedily Rob, Matthew and Thomas and even young Charles, had worked so hard that day. "I do understand, I really do."

Ellen, now starting to feel rather disloyal towards Rob, was anxious to change the subject.

"You must be so cramped in that bedroom, all six of you in one room. When we took our sofa and chairs out I never thought there would be room for three beds, but the sitting room's bigger than I thought. Do you sleep well, Dorrie? Any nightmares about that awful night you all endured?"

"Not really, it must be the country air, I am sleeping quite well."

"I've been having bad dreams, it must be listening to all the stories of the bombing, the destruction of Belfast and those lives lost. I keep having this dream where we're all dressed in black, crying and wondering endlessly up and down some street." Ellen paused. "But then I've always had dreams, of some sort or another."

"I'm sure it's the blitz and Rob out and about the way he is. It must be a real worry."

"I'm always glad to hear his car, no matter what state he's in."

"Ellen, in a few days time it will be Easter, let's hope Rob sobers up before that. I was hoping he might take me back home for a few things we need – maybe Monday or Tuesday – that's if you all think it's safe." Dorrie had only brought the minimum of clothes on the day Rob had come for them. She desperately needed some of baby Leo's belongings. She found it difficult to keep up with the washing because of the limited facilities Ellen had here. There was neither running water nor electricity in the house. The water was carried in buckets from a well, the latrine was outside in the garden and light was by the use of a couple of oil lamps. She marvelled at her sister-in-law, how she coped with everything and never seemed to let it annoy her.

"Must you go, Dorrie? I still think it would be risky going back so soon. According to Rob, rumour has it the Germans will come back again. And very soon he says." Ellen was very dubious about Dorrie's notion to go back to Belfast. "Let's wait a couple of days and see how Rob is."

When Dorrie broached the subject two days later with Rob, who had sobered up once more, he maintained that if they left early in the morning on Easter Monday, there should be little or no risk.

"The Germans only do their bombing at night," was his firm answer when Ellen expressed her anxiety about it.

On Easter Monday morning Rob set off for Belfast with Dorrie and Matthew. Matthew had a day off from his farm work and was interested in seeing the damage done by the blitz and the cleanup operation which was still going on at the docks and surrounding area.

Rob insisted they go directly to Dorrie's house, collect whatever she needed and then drive to the dock area to let

Matthew view the destruction himself. However Matthew's ambition to see firsthand the devastation of Harland and Wolff's and the dockside was to be thwarted. Just as they were packing the last box of clothing into the car, the air raid sirens wailed, followed shortly by the sound of anti aircraft fire, then the noise of a single plane low in the sky. Matthew looked skywards when he heard the unmistakable drone and saw an aircraft swooping above their heads, so close and clearly visible.

"Right, let's get out of here." Rob proceeded to start up the car, as Dorrie and Matthew hopped in. "Now, we'll be alright, as long as we just keep driving."

Rob could see Dorrie was terrified, reliving her experience of the week before. Matthew just sat quietly in the back but alert and watchful as the single plane disappeared into the horizon. Rob drove at top speed along the roads. As they came onto the Lisburn Road the sound of the "All clear" was music to their ears. He would get them safely home again. What they weren't to know was that the plane was a German reconnaissance aircraft and very soon the Germans would return.

Easter Tuesday morning began dreary and very cloudy with drizzling rain. Matthew and Thomas abandoned their earlier plans to go to Belfast Zoo, much to Ellen's relief. Every time anyone mentioned going anywhere near the city her heart sank. Instead they went outside to the barn to play netball with Dorrie's older boy and Charlie in tow. Later, that evening the weather became mild and bright and the rain stopped, and the boys proceeded to erect wickets in the field at the back of the house to play cricket. By around ten o'clock that evening the clouds had dispersed completely and the moon shone brightly.

At 10.40 p.m. the air raid sirens sounded and some twenty minutes later the unmistakable drone of approaching aircraft could be heard: and in some towns people thronged the streets to listen to the convoy passing in huge numbers.

That night 180 German aircrafts were active over Northern Ireland. Some 29000 incendiaries fell on mainly working class districts and 674 bombs fell, tearing down streets, rupturing water mains and entering chimneys. Explosions ripped across houses and tiny streets and in some cases shelters were destroyed.

It was in one of those shelters that Amy Brankin and her grandmother lost their lives. Amy and her parents had become concerned for the old lady's safety after the initial dockside bombing. Amy had volunteered to drive to Belfast on Easter Tuesday to bring her grandmother back to Poyntzpass. But instead she had had to guide her to the nearest shelter, a shelter which was demolished by a direct hit.

The postal services, after the blitz, were almost non-existent with letters either lost forever or taking weeks to be delivered. Ellen hadn't heard from either her own family or Rob's stepmother for quite some time. When the letter arrived from Jane, informing them of Harry's wife's death, a month had already past. Although Ellen had never met Amy she was saddened by her death and the cruel way she had died. From all accounts by Jane, Amy had worked hard to make her marriage work and had earned her mother-in-law's respect. Now Harry was a widower with the responsibility of a young daughter to rear, and Ellen and Rob felt deeply for him at such a time. It was Rob himself who wrote to Harry to express their condolences, all bitterness about his sister and how she had suffered forgotten about in the face of this tragedy.

Chapter 32

The Germans returned to Belfast during the first week in May 1941. Their main objective lay in the north-east where the shipyards, aircraft factory and the harbour were situated. The extensive use of incendiaries, 95992 were dropped in less than four hours, resulted in fires blazing across Belfast, fires which were well beyond the resources of the fire brigade. Two – thirds of the Harland and Wolf's shipbuilding works were decimated, including engine works, workshop plant, repair shops and stores. The attack began at 1.07 a.m. and ended at 4.55 a.m., leaving Belfast a scene of a continuous, blazing inferno, simply a sea of flames.

Matthew Hampton had not gone to bed on the night of the 4th of May, but watched the holocaust of destruction going on relentlessly. He knew, with certainty that the Nazis' target that night was the Shipyard, Short and Harland's and the surrounding area. He had never felt so frustrated, yet what could he do? At fifteen years of age, he felt so useless, it was all very well for his mother to keep on about farm production being essential for the war effort but he needed to do more. When those fires were extinguished he intended to go down there. There must be something he could do to help, something to help in this terrifying, horrible war.

If he was three years older he would have been in the thick of it just like his cousin Colin had been. He had been to Banbridge to see Colin on a few occasions since he was demobbed. He had been anxious to hear about his experiences, what it was really like to be in the middle of it all. But his cousin would not be drawn to talk about it – "some time maybe" he would simply say, or "no one could possibly want to think about it". To think about it would be to relive it, and he could not bear to do that. Matthew had always left Colin feeling oddly disappointed. Maybe if Colin talked to someone about what he had been through he would start to feel better.

According to Aunt Ethel, he complained a lot about pains in his arms and the doctor was treating him for his "nerves". Certainly Colin was a changed man. He had become withdrawn, and not the extrovert, happy cousin they had looked forward to seeing so much.

Four weeks after the devastating attack on Harland and Wolff, Matthew successfully secured night shift employment there, helping with urgent work to ships and engines. He had been taken on immediately when he offered himself for night shift. Current employees had refused to operate shifts between 10 p.m. and 6 a.m., such was their fear and awareness of their vulnerability in the light of further attacks. But Matthew felt no such fear and rationally told himself they would hear the Luftwaffe approach in reasonable time to seek safety.

Six evenings each week Matthew cycled the seven miles to Belfast through the destruction of torn up streets, mere shells of shops and what had once been beautiful buildings. The awesome sights seemed to give him renewed energy to get to his work and toil laboriously side by side with others who felt as he did – get production of all the war machines up and running once more. This unspeakable evil which had invaded Europe and Britain had to be stopped. Every morning he cycled back home through the same harrowing scenes of poverty and destitution. He knew his family were fortunate to be living in the country where food, although not readily available, was sufficient for their needs and they had simply to go to the well to fetch their water whereas several areas in Belfast were still deprived of it.

Gradually, as the raids in England lessened and certainly when the Germans crossed the Russian border at the end of June 1941, everyone seemed to become more optimistic. Many of those who had left the city where gradually returning.

This morning as Matthew cycled home with the warm sun on his back, he felt more buoyant and carefree than he had done for weeks. It was a Monday morning and he always worked until 9 a.m. on his Sunday night shift simply because he was paid extra for working on the Sabbath. Production in both the shipyard and the aircraft factory was improving all the time. Everyone in Belfast seemed to be out in force clearing up rubble, reopening shops, even those still without windows, in order to commence trading once again.

He was looking forward to home this morning, there should be no one, only his mother there. His father was giving Dorrie and John and his younger cousins a lift to the train station before he went to work. They were going onto Poyntzpass to see Jane and give their condolences to Harry Brankin. A significant number of people were now using the trains again to visit relatives, even though signs everywhere were still asking "is your journey really necessary?". His brother, sister and his other two cousins would be at school, so he was looking forward to peace and quiet and a leisurely breakfast, just his mother and him. Then to bed to get a good day's undisturbed sleep. Sometimes the noise and bustle of the two families in the house drove him to distraction. But he never said anything, a lot of families were a lot worse off than they were.

His mother too, seemed in a happier frame of mind.

"Your dad's away, with a good load of those disinfectant cards – and they are all orders he got last week. This is July, Matthew, that means he has been sober for two months." Ellen was putting scrambled eggs on a plate of toast as she spoke. "I know two months isn't much, but it means a lot to me."

"I know. It's always a relief when he sobers up, even if it turns out only to be for a short time. Here's your breakfast, the eggs are thanks to Mr Sloan again. That man is so very kind. I tell him they are much appreciated even though we are better off than we were when we came here first. Thanks to the money you are earning, plus the government paying us for Dorrie and her family, and of course your dad back at work again." Ellen was at her most talkative this morning and Matthew just listened as he ate his breakfast, but before going to his bedroom, which was just a few steps from the kitchen, he insisted on clearing up his breakfast dishes.

A loud, single, strangled scream awakened him. At first he thought he must have been dreaming, but it was so obtrusive he knew it was real. Struggling out of his sleep and out of his bed, he raced through to the kitchen.

His mother was standing at the table, ashen faced and trembling. In her hand she held a buff colour envelope, and Matthew's heart sank as he went to her. Sitting her down in the nearest chair, he gently retrieved the cable from her outstretched hands and the stark words leapt out at him. COLIN DEAD – HEART ATTACK THIS MORNING. ETHEL.

Matthew accompanied his parents that very evening to Banbridge, leaving Thomas to look after Charles and Lucie. After Ellen's initial shock at this latest awful news, she had managed to compose herself and concentrate on her sister and what she must be going through. The need to support her in any way she could was uppermost in her mind. The loss of her beautiful son, who had meant so much to so many people, must be truly unbearable.

Ethel was inconsolable in her grief – Billy her husband, more stoic and accepting of their loss. Ethel had been so worried about Colin all weekend. The pain in his arms, his sweating and clamminess were so terrible she had insisted on calling their doctor out. Doctor Jackson had persisted in his original diagnosis that it was "Colin's nerves", due to his awful experiences, and had strongly recommended he return to work on Monday morning. Colin had calmly accepted his doctor's advice, and had begun his walk to his work. He had only walked a few yards from home when he collapsed and died on the pavement. He had died because he had followed his doctor's orders. But Matthew knew the Germans had killed his cousin. Those days and nights in the English Channel had frozen his circulation and his body and he had never recovered. How many other young men out there would suffer the same fate? That was something they would never know. But watching his aunt now, Matthew thought she epitomised the grief of the whole nation, of all the mothers, wives and families who were being called on to face this nightmare.

"Rob, I must stay here with Ethel, you can see for yourself how she is. I'll be here as long as she needs me." Ellen had had great difficulty setting her own grief aside, when she had seen the broken, tragic figure of her sister. Ethel had alternatively wept and screamed during the time that they had been there, crying out about the injustice of it all, threatening to have their doctor removed from the Medical Register, until Ellen and Billy despaired for her.

"I think we may have to get the doctor to give her some sedation – that's if she will let him back in the house. But Matthew and you go home." Ellen was determined to support her sister however long it took. "Ethel and Billy never let us down, so I'm here for her now."

Rob was eager enough to get away, he found it all so very sad and disturbing. "I'll leave Matthew to work on the way home, it is coming up to the time for his night shift and I'll drive back for him in the morning." He had just thought of something he could do to help.

"I'll call in with Doctor Jackson now, and see if he has anything he could give Ethel. She needs some sedation and I'll bring whatever he subscribes back here before we head home."

"That's a better idea than bringing him here to see Ethel." Ellen felt somewhat relieved. "I think it would be just too much for her at the minute, seeing their doctor again or having to speak to him."

Doctor Jackson had no desire to return to the Wilson home that evening, he was riddled with guilt about Colin Wilson and Ethel Wilson's fury was not something he wanted to witness again. So he readily handed over medication to Rob which he said should settle Mrs Wilson and she would be able to get some sleep.

Chapter 33

"I did my best to keep him occupied while you were away, Ellen, but in the end he turned to drinking again." Dorrie was clearly distressed. "I'm sorry. I don't think I'm much good at that sort of thing – knowing how to deal with it, I mean."

"Oh, Dorrie, none of us know how to deal with Rob when he starts. I've been trying to deal with it for years and it gets me nowhere." After staying for three weeks Ellen arrived back from Banbridge early that morning to discover, as she had strongly suspected during her last week with Ethel, that Rob had not sobered up for the past seven or eight days. He had not been back to see her during that time and her brother-in-law Billy had kindly driven her home. But Billy had been anxious to return to Ethel and had not even stayed for tea, which was a relief to Ellen as she had no wish to add to Ethel's and his distress because of her misery.

"If it's any consolation to you, Ellen, the children have been terrific. Matthew away to work every evening, Thomas and Charles have seen to Rob when he makes it back home, getting him to bed and cleaning him up. When he gets up in the afternoon I've tried talking to him, getting him to eat something but," Dorrie went on, "as soon as he can he makes some excuse or other and out he goes, how he makes it home I just don't know."

"You certainly didn't need this annoyance, Dorrie, but I had to stay with Ethel. She was so incapable and so distraught, but Gladys is taking some leave from work to look after her." Ellen sounded relieved. "I'm glad of that, and I'm really glad you were here, Dorrie, otherwise I could not have stayed with Ethel. I intend to make a good tea for all of us this evening no matter about Rob. Then tonight I have to sit down and write to Eve and let her know about Colin. She is so very fond of Ethel and she loved Colin too." Then Ellen added as an afterthought, "I better mention about Amy Brankin too, I suppose."

"I think you should, Ellen, I never thought of it, to be honest." Dorrie had been so engrossed in the goings on here that she had thought about little else. "The mail is so uncertain, it might be some time before she gets it. When you're writing I'll enclose a note too, just to let her know we are all thinking of her. She's well over Harry Brankin by now, but she needs to know about Amy."

Later that evening, with the help of Dorrie, Ellen composed a letter to Eve letting her know the latest double war tragedies which had impacted on their own family circle. It was late when everyone finally ventured to bed and there was no sign of Rob. He did not come home at all that night, appearing the next morning, briefly spending some time at the kitchen table, then going to bed, only to disappear after tea that evening. This was to be the pattern of his behaviour for the next three months. Obviously he must be sleeping in the car somewhere Ellen reasoned. He must be confident the Luftwaffe did not intend returning to Belfast, being too engrossed in fighting the Russian army, their terrain and weather.

Two months passed before Eve received Ellen and Dorrie's letter but she knew she was fortunate it arrived at all and she was deeply saddened to read of Colin's death. To have come home after the trials of the Dunkirk beaches, only to be cut down so cruelly when everyone had thought he was safe. She wished passionately she could see Ethel in person, to offer what comfort she could. But with the war still raging over the seas and in the air, she had to be content with writing personally to her and Billy to offer her condolences and prayers.

She was shocked, and saddened too, when she read about Amy Brankin's untimely death. The circumstances of it horrified her. To think she had been there to help her grandmother, only to find herself caught up in a Nazi raid, it must have been truly terrifying and now Harry was left on his own with a young child to bring up. On impulse Eve decided she would write to him expressing her regret. She felt it would be the honourable thing to do.

Later that evening she put pen to paper, also writing to Ellen to thank her for letting her know. She thought of Rob, her darling brother, and the fact that Ellen hadn't mentioned him in the letter told Eve all she needed to know. He must be drinking again; usually Ellen told her directly when she wrote to her, but she probably felt she was the bearer of enough bad news without adding to it on this occasion. What was going to become of him? He seemed unable to fight his addiction on any long term basis.

Rightly or wrongly she blamed Maggie for it all, she had encouraged Rob from a very young age to take it, probably never foreseeing what would happen in the future.

Rob wakened to the sun shining through the windscreen of his car. He felt so cramped, chilled and miserable he wanted to scream aloud for someone to come and help him. But there was no one about and he guessed, by the lack of warmth from the sun, it was very early in the morning. He seemed incapable of easing the violent shivering of his whole body and he felt weighted down by some awful malaise. He would have to try to make his way home, but how? He felt incapable of movement, never mind trying to drive a car, but move he must and soon, before this dreadful feeling totally enveloped him.

How long had he been here? He had no idea, he couldn't remember coming to the car, in fact he could remember very little about anything since leaving home. He began to feel very afraid now, as he tried to recall where he might have gone, but his memories eluded him. He made a superhuman effort to get out of the car and stand. He knew he must have had some quantity of drink this time around – he had never felt like this before. He would have to stop, he knew he must. But the memories of the last couple of months, of the devastation in Belfast, his anxiety for Dorrie, the loss of Colin – who had been like a son to them – had been just too much. He had needed whiskey like he had never needed it before. But enough was enough. If he could make it safely home this time he would pull himself together and get back to work. He never wanted to feel like this again, and the last thing he wanted was his family to see him like this, so far through. There was nothing else for him only to try to make it home.

Matthew had just arrived home from work and Thomas, Charles and Lucie were on their way out to school, when suddenly the whole cottage shook, then the noise of the crunch of metal seeming to come from somewhere outside. Ellen, who had been busy at the kitchen sink, was the first to move towards the door, followed quickly by Matthew.

"I think it's Rob." Dorrie was just coming out of her bedroom door. "He seems to have hit our wall." She looked pale and shaken.

Matthew began to run around the gable of the house, and was aghast when he saw his father's car embedded in the thick stone wall.

"Quick, Thomas, let's get Dad out – he looks frightful." Thomas had followed his mother and brother outside.

Between them they managed to extricate their father from the car, where he lay slumped over the steering wheel and then they gently carried him into bed. This time there was no berating him or searching his pockets for money, this time they removed his outer sodden clothes gently and wrapped him in several blankets.

"Mum, do you think we need to fetch the doctor?" Thomas was worried about his father's pallor and stillness – it was quite frightening. "Maybe he was hurt when he hit the wall".

"I don't think so, Thomas." Ellen was bending over Rob, rubbing his face with her warm hands. "He has no marks anywhere and he appears to be coming round." Ellen proceeded to shake her husband. "Rob can you hear me?"

Rob gave a low moan and made an attempt to nod his head. Ellen breathed a sigh of relief. "I'm going to get some hot tea, you'll have to try and drink it."

"Mum, you stay with him and I'll fetch the tea." Matthew left the room as he spoke.

"I'll lie beside him for a while and try to generate some heat into his body. Thomas, you go and check the gable wall for damage. Mr Harper won't be too pleased when he sees it."

Ellen lay down on the bed beside Rob and enveloped him in her arms. Thomas rounded up his brother and sister for school and Matthew brought in the tea before making his way to bed, both reassured their father was in good hands. The colour was already returning to his cheeks and he seemed to settle in closer to Ellen as they left the room.

Rob was in bed for five days before he regained strength enough to make it into the living room to sit at the fire. During this time he seemed fearful of Ellen leaving him alone, would tell her he was having awful nightmares and would begin to shiver as he talked about them. Ellen patiently attended him and saw a gradual improvement every day. She had feared Rob would end up in hospital, something she knew he would find intolerable.

The damage to the wall and car was slight and afterwards Rob told them he remembered vaguely driving up the lane and then feeling incredibly faint. He had made an enormous effort to get home, then his strength had simply drained from him as he realised he had made it back safely.

Chapter 34

1942

1941 had been the grimmest year of the war. On the land, allied forces were defeated on every side – retreating in Africa, Greece and then the Far East, losing both Singapore and Hong Kong. But gradually with the Nazi shift into Russia and air raids becoming more infrequent, a glimmer of hope and optimism seemed to indicate that some of the panic felt by people was beginning to recede.

Since that awful morning Rob had driven home and crashed his car into the cottage, fear and panic seemed to have become embedded in his whole body. The fear he had felt the morning he had driven through the blitz in Belfast to bring Dorrie and his family to safety, paled into insignificance with the terror he had endured during those few days of his illness. That terror seemed to stalk him day and night. He couldn't concentrate – he was easily agitated and felt the desperate need to have someone by his side at all times – the way he remembered feeling as a young boy. He had to admit, alcohol must have got an awful grip on him, something he was totally ashamed of. He felt there was no justification whatsoever for his behaviour. He knew he was very fortunate he had his wife and family. Where people everywhere had lost loved ones, their homes and all their possessions, Ellen and he still had each other and their sons and daughter. During his last illness, when he had been anxious not to make too many demands of Ellen, it was young Lucie who had stayed with him, seeking him out after school and encouraging him to listen to the radio again. Something he had been actually frightened to do during his illness, he could no longer bear to listen to any news. But gradually, with young Lucie's encouragement, he had forced himself to and hope and optimism returned to him as he heard firstly that the Nazis had invaded the Soviet Union and then later declared war on the United States. He had sought Ellen out in the kitchen, where she was scrubbing clothes vigorously on the washboard at the kitchen sink. To Ellen's surprise he hugged her tightly.

"The tide's turning, love, the die is cast. Hitler is going to be beaten."

Ellen returned his hug enthusiastically – she hadn't seen Rob so animated in weeks.

"Oh, Rob you seem so much better. Are you really feeling better?"

"I feel good – Ellen, I'm getting ready to get back to my disinfectant production this very day. Where is Dorrie? In her room I suppose. I'm going to tell her I'm going back to work."

Later Dorrie joined Ellen in the kitchen, clearly pleased at the transformation in Rob. "He's a different man today, Ellen, back to his usual form. I was so worried about him. He says he is going to go for disinfectant today. Do you think he'll be alright?"

"Dorrie if it's drink you're thinking of, I don't think we need to worry for quite some time. I can't see Rob touching it for a while. He was just so ill and he knows that himself."

Dorrie, reassured by Ellen's words, began to help in the preparing of the evening meal. While they worked quietly together, Dorrie remarked that perhaps if the war was indeed on the turn, she and her family might soon be allowed to return to the Shore Road.

"I'm sure it's still early days, Dorrie, there is so much devastation in Belfast – wrecked streets and unsafe structures. You're far better here, you know."

"I know, and I have grown to love it here, but we have to return home some time."

"That will only happen when there is a guarantee of safety for everyone." Ellen changed the subject, reluctant to think of a time when her sister-in-law would not be living with them. She had found her so easy to live with, eager to help both with the housework and with Rob, when he went off the rails.

"Dorrie, I've been meaning to write to Eve. Do you think we could do that this evening?" Ellen felt guilty she hadn't replied to Eve's last short letter acknowledging Colin and Amy's death. But she had been so preoccupied with Rob and his state of health that she had kept putting it off.

"I'll have to let her know Rob has been unwell. I did promise her I would always let her know how he was managing. She'll be shocked to hear how poorly he has been this time, but I need to tell her."

Eve had made several attempts to answer Ellen's last letter, but each time she had sat down to put pen to paper, her courage seemed to fail her. Several sheets of paper had been crumpled up and consigned to the waste paper bin. She felt so guilty – so secretive about everything – especially since Ellen was always so open and honest in her correspondence. She felt particularly bad at the minute, because Ellen had been very direct in letting her know the awful effect alcohol seemed to have had on Rob during his most recent binge. But if she was honest with herself, she knew she was afraid that her sister-in-law – and Dorrie too, for that matter – might try to dissuade her from what she intended to do. She was convinced they would advise her to wait for a time at least, or at worst, would tell her she was making an awful mistake. She had never told them about writing to Harry after his wife's death, never mind that they had been in contact with each other ever since.

"I knew we would do it, I knew it." Rob's excitement as he listened to his still very temperamental wireless was palpable in the room. "Rommel has been pushed back. Montgomery has done it. The Nazis are away, fleeing for their lives." Rob's enthusiasm was infecting Ellen and Dorrie as they prepared breakfast and organised everyone for school and work. In spite of all the hardships, the losses that had been endured, the rationing that would be with them for some time yet, the news raised everyone's spirits and instilled fresh hope in hearts that had been burdened with such sorrow and dread.

Matthew who had just come in from his night shift was the first to speak. "Do you think the war will soon be over, Dad?"

He knew he was coming to an age where he could join up, but there didn't seem to be such urgency any more for recruits.

"Not yet, son, that's only a battle won – it's far from over. It's work and school as usual, I'm afraid, no holidays yet." Rob purposely switched the wireless off and headed outside. As Ellen went to fetch the children's coats from the hall, she said a silent prayer of thanks that Rob was working hard again and alcohol seemed the furthest thing from his mind.

"I'll walk across the field to the stile with the children this morning. You did it yesterday, Dorrie, and Leo hasn't had his breakfast yet."

When Ellen returned after ensuring all five children were safely across to school, she saw Dorrie at the door with two letters in her hand, and the postman disappearing down the lane on his bicycle.

"Two letters for you – one must be from Eve – it's franked Canada." Dorrie handed the mail to Ellen.

"I'll open this one first. It's from Mr Harper our landlord, I'd recognise his writing anywhere." Ellen slit the letter open, and read; as she suspected that the rent was in arrears. So that was where Rob had got the money from for his last binge, he simply hadn't paid the rent. Well, she would walk over later and pay up. Luckily she had savings for such an eventuality, money she had saved from the government's allowance for Dorrie.

She set the letter aside and opened Eve's, and seeing it was addressed to herself and Dorrie started to read aloud.

Dear Ellen and Dorrie,

I am sorry I have been so long in answering your last letter and to hear that Rob has been so very unwell. I hope that this time he realises the untold harm he is doing to himself with his awful bouts of drinking. It would be wonderful if he could learn from it and perhaps this time he will.

I have found it difficult to write this letter, Ellen – which considering our close relationship in the past, will surprise you. But the truth is, I have decided to return to Northern Ireland and hope to marry Harry in the not too distant future –

when a decent interval has passed since Amy's death. I love him as much now as I have always done and would dearly love all of you to be happy for me and to come to my wedding. I do understand if you feel I am taking a risk, but I don't think so and I intend to go through with it.

Both of you are the first to know, but Harry intends to talk to Jane soon and I hope she will be agreeable to me living with her until we marry. Then I will go to the cottage Harry has been living in with his daughter for the last ten years. I did try to forget him, but I would have been marrying someone else for all the wrong reasons. So do please try to understand. I will be arriving back in Northern Ireland in ten weeks time and I hope to be able to visit you all then.

With all my love,
Eve

Ellen regarded Dorrie as she finished reading, waiting for some response. "Well, Dorrie, what do you think? This is some news isn't it?"

"I don't know what to think." Dorrie sounded dubious enough. "I just want Eve to be happy, that's all – I'm sure it's what we all want."

"I know she was never going to be interested in anyone else. So let's be happy for her."

"I do believe you're right," Dorrie conceded. "I'll write back straight away this evening. We need to, if there is any chance of her getting our letter before she leaves Canada."

"Obviously Eve trusts him enough to take him on. And as we've already had one good piece of news today, about the war in North Africa, let's look on this as another reason for celebration. I'll go and fetch Rob and see what his reaction is."

When Ellen read the letter to Rob, he could really only think of one thing, Eve was coming home for good.

"I think, Ellen you should start saying those prayers of yours for her safe passage across those dangerous, war-torn waters," was his closing comment as he followed Ellen into the house to get his usual morning cup of tea, before going on his rounds to the farmers.

Eve and Harry Brankin were married quietly in Poyntzpass church in December 1942. It was a private affair with only immediate family members present. Any doubts anyone had of the union were eradicated when they saw the couple's happiness as they left the church and joined their guests in the hall for a quiet reception afterwards. They had waited twenty months after Amy's death before tying the knot and had shown the utmost respect for the young woman who had been such a victim of a cruel war which still rumbled on and on.

Chapter 35

1945

"Who changed my work here?" Matthew lifted the page from the small table in the living room where he had been toiling over questions of English for the last hour.

"I only left it for two seconds to go and fetch another pen." He pursued his questioning. "Can nobody leave anything alone in this house?" He looked round the room, waiting impatiently.

There was silence for a long moment; Ellen looked round everyone, at Lucie sitting fidgeting, Charles with his head stuck in a book as usual.

"Sorry, Mum, sorry, Matthew, it was me." Lucie admitted in a low voice.

"Why? Might I ask?"

"Because, because..." she was reluctant to say – she held Matthew in awe sometimes – he could be quite short tempered. Her mother always said it was the long night shifts he did.

"I had to change it."

"Come on, what was wrong with it?" He was less angry now, more interested, the word looked right now, where before he had thought it looked wrong.

"Affronted has two 'F's, Matthew – not one."

"Oh, right, I probably knew that – I just forgot that's all." He couldn't admit to Lucie that she might be better at spelling than he was and him nine years older. "Thanks, anyway, I hope I would have noticed. Did you look at the arithmetic?"

"No, Matthew," Lucie shook her head, "I'm hopeless at sums – you'd need to ask Charles."

Charles, on hearing his name mentioned looked up from "The Three Musketeers" his mother had bought him for Christmas, and this was the first opportunity he had had to read it.

"What is it?" he asked.

"Would you check that page of sums? See if they're right?" If Lucie had spotted a spelling mistake, God knows what his arithmetic was like.

Charles took the page from Matthew and considered it at length. "They're fine – very good in fact. What are all these tests you're doing anyway?"

"I missed out on so much when I left school early I want to try and catch up a bit, that's all. According to the government they're going to try and improve the education system – so Lucie and you will benefit – but it's too late for me."

Secretly Matthew felt guilty for not being more open about what he was actually doing. Unknown to any of his family, he had applied to join the Palestine police and this work was part of the entrance examination he was sitting. If he was successful, he would then have to undergo a medical examination to establish his fitness. So he thought it best to say nothing until he knew he had been accepted. Besides, he dreaded telling his mother his plans; he knew that since Uncle Hugh's and Colin's death, she had a horror and apprehension about any potential violence. But he wasn't going to dwell on that at present – he must concentrate on his exams and see how they went. Depending on those results, he would talk to his mother.

He had thought of joining the Palestine Police when rumours first started to circulate around Hitler's treatment of the Jews and how so many wished to return to Palestine. Something the Arabs were totally adverse to. So Britain was there trying to bring some kind of stability and peace to the place. At long last, he would be doing something for Britain, something worthwhile and patriotic. He had missed out during the war, but by joining the Palestine Police he would get the chance to serve his country.

In some ways he wished Aunt Dorrie and Uncle John were still living here, that might have made it easier for him to leave home. But they had gone home before Christmas last year, and Matthew knew his mother missed Dorrie's companionship, even though she knew they must go back. They had only gone when everyone was confident Belfast was safe once again. The

Nazis would not be back, they were in trouble enough elsewhere.

Less than a month later, Matthew received confirmation of his acceptance to the Palestine Police. It was a Saturday morning in February when he received the official letter. He had been able to intercept the postman on his way home from night shift. Now the letter was safely in his pocket, and he only had to find a suitable time to break the news to his parents. How they might react weighed heavily on his mind. When he went to bed that day he found sleep impossible and then during his night shift he was preoccupied with thoughts of them both. As he cycled home on the Sunday morning he was resolved to tell his mother later that day. He would have a few hours sleep and as Sunday night was his only night off in the week, he made a point of rousing himself around lunch time, knowing he would get a good night's sleep later.

He wakened to the sound of voices in the living room – there seemed to be quite a crowd, all talking animatedly to one another.

"Oh, no," he thought irritably as he struggled out of bed, "bloody visitors." But his annoyance quickly evaporated when he entered the living room and saw Aunt Ethel seated at the table, a cup of tea in her hand. Impulsively he hugged her.

"Oh, Aunt Ethel, you are looking well." He had always adored this kind, gentle woman who had been so generous to them all when they had needed help. Then to have lost her son, who had been respected by each and every one of them, had been such a cruel blow to her that all the family had feared for her health. But today she looked so much happier than she had looked for a long time.

"Matthew, I'm so glad you're here, you'll be delighted to know that Jack Collins, who helped Colin so much at Dunkirk, has been awarded a medal for bravery." She sounded so proud as she spoke.

"Colin was determined to let the War Office know what that man did for him. He would be delighted to hear that Jack has been awarded a medal. And somehow or other I feel he does know – I'm certain of that." Her voice held a quiet certainty about it that was more touching and emotional than any strong passionate words.

"I'm delighted, Ethel, I really am. Mind you I think Colin was equally brave, what he came through. Someone should have put his name forward too."

"This is enough for me, Matthew, that Colin's last wish was granted."

"How did you get here?" Matthew had noticed the tears in her eyes and was anxious to change the subject. "You didn't come by train did you?"

"Sara brought me – she's driving now – she was bringing Anna and her little boy to see your mother and she asked me if I would like to come. I jumped at the chance to see you all and I'm enjoying a quiet time and a chat with your mum. The others have gone outside with Charles and Lucie to enjoy the spring sunshine."

Just as Ethel spoke, Sara, Anna and her little boy appeared beside them. As Matthew exchanged greetings with them all, he noticed that Anna was heavily pregnant and she too wore, if not a happy expression – at least a quiet contented one.

Later that evening, when Charles, Thomas and he had gone to bed, and Matthew still had had no opportunity to talk to his mother, he decided he would confide in Thomas. Charles, in a single bed in the far corner of the room, was such a deep sleeper the chance of him overhearing anything was remote.

"Thomas, I need to talk to you, are you awake?"

"What is it? I'm whacked. All I see at the end of the day and first thing in the morning is jam pots, lids and labels, it wearies me, you know." Thomas had obtained employment in one of Mr Greenlees of Poyntzpass canneries. Mr Greenlees had known his father for years and Thomas knew it was why he had immediately given him a job. He also paid him very generously. Even though he was only seventeen his wages were the same as the much older experienced men who worked there. He was grateful to Tom Greenlees for all he had done for him, but he found the work monotonous and gruelling and he was weary when he came home in the evening.

Thomas sounded so disinterested that Matthew felt compelled to nudge him with his elbow.

"I have to talk to someone. I've been accepted for the Palestine Police and I go at the end of May and I still haven't had a chance to say to anyone."

Thomas was instantly alert.

"Matthew, you're not serious, are you? Have you any idea what it's like out there? Are you mad?" He sat upright in bed. "The Jews are killing the Arabs, the Arabs are killing the Jews and as far as I know, they're both killing the British police, it doesn't seem to matter who they shoot."

"Shush... Thomas, keep your voice down, I haven't had a chance to tell Mum yet, but I needed to tell someone."

"Well, you better tell her, because if you don't, I will. She'll soon talk you out of it."

Now Matthew regretted having spoken at all, the last thing he needed to hear was that anyone might dissuade him. Turning on his side, half heartedly he answered, "We'll see, I mean to tell her tomorrow."

He rose early the next morning after a restless night's sleep and was relieved to find his mother alone in the kitchen. Without preamble he approached her. "Mum, I need to talk to you, it's very important." And then he rather bluntly told her of his plans.

His mother sat down quietly at the kitchen table and listened intently to her son as he told her when he would be going to Palestine and why he wanted to go. He told her he wanted to do something for Britain and how Palestine, in a strange way, with its history of Jesus and his disciples, had always appealed to him.

"Oh Matthew, I'm so glad you told me." His mother sounded quite calm. "I knew something was on your mind – I thought maybe you were in some sort of trouble. I'm glad I know the truth."

"Mum. I intend to send you money every month. The pay is very good out there – and I mean to save as much as I can, while I'm there."

"The money doesn't matter, Matthew, it's you I'll miss. I'll pray you will be safe and come back home when your time is over out there."

Matthew, when he thought about it later, was amazed his mother had not raised one word of objection, but simply accepted his decision. But then that was his mother's way – she was very accepting of most things. He was not to know that it was only after his departure, and as Ellen listened to the news from Palestine, that she walked the floors at night, bitterly regretting that she had not tried to stop him. Somehow or another, she should have prevented him from going into such danger.

Chapter 36

A month after Matthew's departure to Palestine, Mr Harper their landlord, appeared on their doorstep. It was a glorious May evening and the intense heat that had pervaded the countryside the entire day, had settled into a comfortable warmth. The magnolia and japonica bushes were a riot of pinks and reds, the sky still a cloudless blue, with only a mere whiff of fluff drifting along the horizon. But none of these delights were reflected in Mr Harper's face that evening when Ellen opened the door to him. He wore his usual dour, sullen expression – his jaw set, his mouth downcast, and his eyes, as always, shifty and unreadable.

"Good evening, Mr Harper." Ellen was surprised to see him. She knew there could be no problems with the rent. She had been, for some time now, giving the money directly to him, herself. Was he here to complain about the children? What had they been up to?

"Come in, Mr Harper, Rob has just finished his dinner." She always made a point of being gracious to him, mindful that this was his house after all. She stepped aside to allow him to enter the hall and with a brief nod of his head, he followed her into the living room, muttering something about "telling the boss himself".

It was a brief exchange between the two men, Rob sitting in his favourite chair beside his radio, Mr Harper just inside the entrance to the room. He proceeded to tell Rob, totally ignoring Ellen's presence, that the cottage and fields had been sold and he was giving them two months' notice to vacate the premises. Then without waiting for Rob to reply, he began to make his way out of the house and almost as an afterthought, he spoke to Ellen. "You'd better start looking for somewhere to live."

Ellen calmly bid him goodnight and closed the door before he had taken many strides away from the cottage. Her first words to Rob on returning to the living room were, "Such an obnoxious man, I don't care if I never see him again." Wearily she sat down beside Rob, realization of their predicament just dawning on her. "What are we going to do, Rob?"

"Do, – I'll do what I have always done – I'll find us somewhere. Don't you worry, love. That will be my mission from tomorrow onwards." Then Rob went on, "It'll be good to get away from that man; if it wasn't our children who were misbehaving it was Dorrie's who were doing something wrong. He hated the thought of Dorrie and her family being here, knowing we were getting money from the government for them. Only there wasn't a darn thing he could do about it." Rob put his arm round his wife's shoulders.

"Please, you mustn't worry, love, I'll soon find something. I would like to get something handy to Thomas's work and, of course, close to a school."

Rob was confident he would soon have everything sorted out. He had excellent contacts, knew the countryside well and the schools, churches and buses for that matter. "Leave it to me, love, and now do you know what I'm going to do? I'm going to get a good strong cup of tea." As he rose from his seat he remarked, "I think Mr Harper really enjoyed coming here and telling us that."

Unfortunately, Ellen had to agree with him, she could just imagine their landlord rubbing his hands with glee at the thought of having told them such troubling news, never mind the added bonus he would be getting from the sale of this place.

Rob had not reckoned on the number of evacuees still occupying the countryside, he had assumed that because Dorrie and John and their family had returned home the majority of the evacuees would have done the same. But of course Dorrie's home had still been intact and liveable, whereas whole streets of houses in some areas had been totally demolished. In fact people were already saying that it was unlikely they would ever be rebuilt there, because those who had been lucky enough to survive would never wish to return. Their memories were too painful to allow it. They had lost loved ones, and they had known and loved entire families who had all been killed in their own homes during those cruel inhumane nights.

Every farmer had the same story for him. "I'm sorry Mr Hampton, I do have a spare cottage but it's filled to capacity with evacuees from Belfast." Or yet another could only offer him a huge barn or an outhouse for him and his family. In the meantime he knew he needed to get inspiration from somewhere, if his family weren't going to end up indeed, sleeping in a barn, or even worse, being taken into care. He knew one of the publicans in Lisburn very well; maybe he would be able to point him in the direction of someone who could help him. He would go and buy one whiskey – just one – before heading home, and he could find out if he had any contacts.

It was the following evening before Rob made it home, to find Ellen in a more despairing frame of mind than he ever remembered and even though he was barely sober, he made a conscious effort to be optimistic. After telling her his usual story of having too much to drink to drive and sleeping in his car, he went on, "I have found somewhere for us to live – just this afternoon." He sounded reluctant to say anything more. Ellen waited patiently for him to describe the place in glowing terms as he had always done in the past. But he sounded quite despondent as he spoke. "It's not much of a place to be honest, but it's better than us all having to split up. The truth is, I had to take it. We only have a few days left before Mr Harper puts us out on the street. It will do in the meantime until I find something better. It's all the evacuees, you see, Ellen. They have lost so much – their homes and their very streets. There are simply not enough houses."

"Where is it, Rob?" Ellen felt uneasy; she sensed Rob wasn't too happy about it.

"About ten minutes drive from here that's all. We'll go tomorrow morning, Lucie and Charles can come too and see what they think of it." At least with schools off for the summer holidays, Ellen and he would have plenty of help to move.

The next morning they set off early. Thomas had gone to work earlier but Charles and Lucie, full of happy anticipation of a new home and a new area to explore were anxious to accompany their parents.

"Now, it isn't much of a place." Rob remarked again as they drove past several beautiful homes with immaculate gardens where May and Cherry blossom bloomed in abundance. In spite of Rob's insistence not to expect much, she didn't think anywhere along here could be too bad – the existing houses had been built with such expertise.

Rob stopped the car at the side of the road, opposite a beautiful driveway which obviously led to some impressive estate. She looked in bewilderment at Rob; he nudged her and pointed to the field immediately beside her. Ellen could see a roof and part of what seemed to be a wooden construction with a makeshift aluminium chimney running up the side of it.

"Is that it, Rob?"

He just nodded dumbly.

"Rob it's only a shack, for goodness' sake and it's tiny."

"Don't say anything until you've seen it. Mr Chambers said he'd leave it open for us today. It's clean and dry – and totally rent free."

Leading the way, Rob opened a small wooden gate which opened on to a narrow path. At the end of this path, there were two steps up to a door at the side of the dwelling. Upon opening this door, they found themselves in a square bright room with a window facing them. A small wood burning stove was centred on the wall – obviously the only means of cooking and heating. One door off this room revealed another average sized room, scarcely big enough for a double bed.

"Is this it, Rob? Where on earth is everyone going to sleep?"

"Take it easy, Ellen. I have given this some thought. We'll sleep in here with Lucie, and Mr Chambers has offered us the use of the hay loft for the two boys. It's the best I could get this time. The country is swarming with evacuees, all needing a roof over their heads. But I'll make sure this is only temporary for us, believe me, I will. Oh and that's Mr Chamber's place over there," indicating the estate across the road. "A proper gentleman he is, I can tell you. Let's go now across to him, let Charles see where he is going to sleep with Thomas and we must thank Mr Chambers for everything."

They were settled in their "cabin" as Thomas and Charles liked to call their new home in a matter of days although a lot of their furniture had to go to the farm in Poyntzpass to be stored. They managed to fit a double bed into the only bedroom, but ten-year-old Lucie had to sleep in her parents' bedroom in a cot with the end removed and a chair at the bottom for her feet. They simply could not fit an extra bed in there, there was so little space.

Although the hayloft had plenty of room, Ellen soon discovered to her dismay, that it was flea infested and she spent every day spraying DDT powder everywhere and washing the boys' bed linen on a daily basis. The daily visits she must make to the hayloft every day meant she had plenty of contact with Mr Chambers and got to know him well. More and more as the weeks went by she began to believe that it was Rob who had managed to talk Mr Chambers into the whole idea of letting them reside there and also letting them have it all rent free. She would never forget this man's kindness to herself and her family. She had him to thank that they were much better off than many of the refugees were, reports of them continuing to camp out in the hills and fields round Belfast still circulated. They were the people who needed help far, far more than she and her family did.

They remained at Ballyronan for eight months before Rob found alternative accommodation for them. During that time she made sure none of her sisters, or Eve and Harry Brankin had visited. For one thing, there was no room and for another she did not want them to see her in such dire surroundings. She still made a point of going to Banbridge on occasion to visit her parents, but she made do by writing to Eve.

Eve and Harry Brankin had taken over Jane's farm. Jane had gone to England to be with Catherine who had gained employment there. Eve had adopted Harry's daughter, and she was engrossed in a whole new way of life. And everyone knew that she was happier now than she had ever been.

Chapter 37

1944

Eight months after they had first set eyes on the wooden cabin in Ballyronan, Rob came home one evening in May in such high spirits that Ellen knew immediately he had some good news for them.

"You'll never guess, Ellen, I've found the most wonderful place for us to live and what's more, it's empty at the moment, so we will be able to move in more or less straight away." Rob immediately had everyone's attention as they sat at the kitchen table where they were having dinner.

Thomas was first to speak. "That is good news. We've managed fine here but we always hoped it was temporary. Where exactly are we going this time? I hope it's handy to work. That's the main thing."

"What about school? Is it close to a school, Pop?" Charles interrupted. "Lucie and I have a fair walk from here and back home every day. It would be a bonus if school was a bit closer to home."

"One question at a time and you haven't asked a thing about the house."

"I haven't had a chance yet, Rob." Ellen spoke now. "I know that work and school are important but after the inconvenience of this," she looked round the room which she had made as comfortable as possible for them all, but there was only so much she could do with their wooden cabin and the boy's bedroom in the hayloft, "I'd like to hear about the house."

"I'll take you all tomorrow. I know that it is Sunday but the person who owns it, Mr Scott, is very agreeable to us coming. But I can tell you this, it's huge, there's an orchard, there's out buildings. It's great. You'll be sure to love it."

Rob was right about the place being wonderful. Ellen was delighted with her home. There was something about its size and structure that reminded her of the station house in Dromin. Its huge kitchen, with its black range, was a joy to work in compared to what she'd had to contend with in Ballyronan. There was a large living room with an open fire and two other rooms – a large drawing room and a breakfast room. Upstairs there were three light spacious bedrooms approached by a beautiful mahogany staircase. A huge orchard, with various fruit trees and shrubs, lay to the east gable of the house and huge outhouses and green, open fields seemed to surround and shelter the entire dwelling.

Although they were eight miles from Lisburn, there was a village within walking distance with a church, a grocers shop, a butchers and of course the usual pub. The bus stop was a mere quarter of a mile from them, so Thomas didn't even have to worry about cycling anymore. The only drawback was the school, Charles and Lucie had a two and a half mile walk there every morning and afternoon. But at least Charles had just another year to do and then Ellen hoped he would go to the technical college to get a better education than Thomas and Matthew had managed to achieve.

On their very first day at school, the road seemed to Charles and Lucie to be never ending, as they trudged up one hill and down another and never a sign of anything that remotely resembled a school. They scarcely noticed the houses set in their own sprawling grounds or the long low cottages on the road's edge, so intent they were on just arriving at school.

They had negotiated the two crossroads their mother had told them to watch out for, when unexpectedly they heard laughter and children's voices raised in merriment. Then turning another corner, suddenly they were there. They opened the gate cautiously, aware all the laughter had stopped and groups of children were now standing still, gazing curiously at them.

"I hate this." Lucie edged closer to Charles.

"Shush – say nothing – it'll be fine." Just then a lady appeared in the doorway with the most warm, welcoming smile either child had seen for a long time.

"Welcome, Lucie and Charles to our school. I will make sure you will be really happy here with us. Come, I'll show you your desks and where to hang your coats." And from that instant Charles and Lucie loved every second of their time in Killultagh School. Suddenly it didn't matter that the gaping children had been looking at her dowdy clothes and the worn wellingtons she was wearing even though it was a dry crisp day. Miss Andrews' caring personality seemed to envelop Lucie and gave her a wonderful sense of security. When the bell rang at 3 o'clock and she joined Charles on their walk back home, she didn't mind the other children with their rough, strange ways.

As they walked back home, Lucie noticed two girls who had been sitting at the next desk to her, seemed to be waiting for them. One of them – a tall, dark haired girl with vivid blue eyes came over and introduced herself.

"My name is Sheila Morrow." She spoke directly to Charles, as they joined them. "Don't mind those boys. They are harmless really. They are farmers' sons and when they go home lessons won't even be mentioned. They'll all be expected to help with the milking and cleaning out the pigsties." She smiled reassuringly at Lucie as she spoke.

"It's my sister here," Charles answered, "she's timid around strangers – but I'm sure she'll soon get used to them." He couldn't admit to this beautiful girl that he too, found their behaviour nerve wracking.

"Nancy and I walk this road every day," Sheila indicated the girl beside her, "so we will be company for one another. I turn off at the second roundabout, but Nancy lives just a few yards from where you do. You are living in Mr Scott's house aren't you?"

"Yes that's us." Charles was amazed that everyone seemed to know so soon who they were exactly. "And we think it's great, don't we, Lucie?"

"Yes and Mum says we can get a dog now and a rabbit."

The walk back home seemed much shorter than the one earlier that morning, and as Sheila turned off at the crossroads with the promise she would wait for them the next morning, they continued on their way home. Shortly before their house came into view, Nancy Wright, who had not spoken much, asked them quite sharply, "Are you Catholic or Protestant then?"

Lucie was confounded by the question. She really had no idea. What did the girl mean? She had never heard the words before. She turned to Charles but he just shook his head slowly and walked on without answering.

Their new found friend sounded exasperated now. "Well, what church do you go to?"

"Oh that's easy." Lucie was relieved. She could answer that. "The Methodist church, we'll be going next week."

"Then you're a Protestant, silly." And while Charles thought the girl sounded so superior. Lucie just felt mortified, fancy her not knowing she was a Protestant.

"Actually," Nancy went on, "I thought you must be Catholics."

"Oh why is that then?" Charles asked shortly.

"I saw you all out playing yesterday, on a Sunday. It's only Catholics do that."

"Well, we do." Charles was so abrupt Lucie was embarrassed. "Here we are, sis, this is our drive – see you..." and proceeded up the short driveway to home.

"I felt so stupid not knowing I was a Protestant," she remarked to her brother, whose face was set in grim lines.

"Stupid! Us! We are the smartest ones in school I can tell you. Who cares whether we're Catholic or Protestant. I don't like her, and whoever Catholics are, she doesn't like them much by the sound of her. She was so scathing about them." Then putting an arm round Lucie's shoulder, "Let's go in and tell Mum what we learned today. We learned we are Protestants. We didn't know that, nobody ever told us and according to Nancy Wright, Catholics aren't up to much because they play on Sundays."

Ellen was appalled when Charles and Lucie related the conversation they had had with this young girl who obviously lived close by.

"What age is this girl?" she asked Lucie.

"She's in my class, so she must be about ten, the same age as I am." Lucie was puzzled. "What has age got to do with it?"

"Because she's far too young to be worrying about who is a Catholic and who is a Protestant and..." Ellen stressed, "I never want to hear either of you asking such questions. We are all the same. Religion doesn't matter and don't forget that."

"Can we still play outside on Sundays, Mum?"

"Of course you can, in God's green fields. Of course you can. Now before you do your homework I've something to show you both. It's an album from Matthew. It arrived last week, but I wanted to wait until we were settled in here, before we had a good look at it."

Since Matthew's departure to Palestine he had written faithfully every month, always enclosing money in the form of postal orders for her. This month he had also enclosed a beautiful photograph album containing images of him in his Palestine police uniform, some of him on horseback with an Arab policeman either side of him. There was one of the Wailing Wall in Jerusalem where the Jews prayed daily, others of the Sea of Galilee, Damascus, his police station and the King David hotel where all the top British Ambassadors stayed.

As she proudly showed the album to Charles and Lucie they were very interested, because of all they had been taught in Sunday school they could identify with some of the scenes.

Later that evening Ellen's thoughts returned to the young girl, and how important it had been to her to establish Charles and Lucie's religion. She must be very aware of the Protestant/Catholic divide that existed in Northern Ireland. She herself had thought the war had eradicated those feelings from everyone's mind. She hoped this young girl's attitude was not a reflection on the countryside they now found themselves in. Rob and herself had always tried to instil a sense of fairness and non-prejudice in their children towards others.

Charles had no difficulty during the summer holidays obtaining work on some of the farms around them. There was always demand for extra labourers to help with the harvest, cleaning out the pigsties or milking cows. He was surprised how much he enjoyed the work, the comradeship of the other farm hands and their light-hearted banter seemed to make the time fly. The only thing he missed was his reading. When he had started the job at first he had intended to read for at least an hour every night. That idea had never materialised because the minute he got into bed, sleep overcame him and he must blow out his candle and snuggle down beside Thomas.

Today he had just set out to begin the walk up the steep hill leading to Philips farm, when he heard the church bells begin to ring – bells which had been so silent for the last four or five years. They began faintly at first, and then others joined in, until the most beautiful sound to his ears, echoed and re-echoed over the whole countryside. He stood silently for a moment, in awe, and he noticed how wonderful the countryside was with its green fields and hedgerows stretching away before him.

Turning on his heel he began to make his way home, he, for one, would not be going to work, he just wanted to go home. The war was over. The church bells were telling him so, and he wanted, more than anything, to share this time with his family.

As he entered the hall, he could hear the drone of his father's radio and, he thought wryly, some things never change. He proceeded through to where the sound came. His father was in his usual seat, his mother and Lucie standing silently listening to Churchill's announcement.

"Oh, Charles, you're back. The war's over, did you know?" Lucie was certainly excited.

"I knew by the bells, Lucie, they told me." His attention was drawn to his mother standing so still in the room. "Mum, are you alright? You are thinking of Matthew, out there in Palestine in the thick of things." He put his arms around her. "We must be thankful Hitler is not ruling us today and Matthew will be alright – I know he will." He went on, "And we will never, ever forget Colin and all those young men who lost their lives so we might live freely in our own country."

Rob had been watching Charles as he spoke to Ellen. Now he switched the wireless off. "Charles is right, Ellen, that's why we must celebrate. Are you up to doing a spot of your baking? We'll ask a few neighbours over. What do you think?" He looked at Charles and Lucie. "Will you help your mother?"

"Of course, Pop." Charles was enthusiastic. His father never ceased to amaze him, that's exactly what his mother needed, a purpose. Something to do, and sharing her wonderful food was exactly the right thing.

Catholic and Protestant alike gathered that evening in September 1945 to celebrate the end of the war and pay homage to those who had made it possible.

Chapter 38

1948

Ellen studied Rob as they drove along the road which would lead them to the docks and a wonderful reunion with Matthew. She could scarcely comprehend that, after all her worry and the sleepless nights she had endured, their son was finally coming home to safety. During the last three years she had felt compelled to listen and read about the atrocities and the mounting death toll in the Holy Land. There seemed no agreeable solution to the problem between the Jews and the Arabs and the British government had decided to withdraw altogether and asked the United Nations to negotiate a solution.

Now watching Rob as he negotiated the traffic, she sensed an anxiety about him. He seemed unable to share her joy. But he had rarely been sober in the past year, disappearing for days at a time or driving home even though he was so drunk he was quite incapable of being in charge of any vehicle. Where he was getting the money from, Ellen had no idea. She only knew, for certain, that in the last six months he had been unable to sell much of his disinfectant. This was simply because a new disinfectant solution in bottles was being sold to farmers. The Health Authorities had stipulated anyone involved in agriculture must use this new, more innovative solution to wash their byre walls and floors. It now seemed that Rob's method of disinfecting the outhouses was no longer acceptable to the same Authorities. Probably he felt a failure, and Ellen, sensitive as always to Rob's moods, could understand that.

"Rob, don't worry that I might say anything to Matthew – I never would. I've spent the last couple of days preparing for his homecoming and I don't want anything to spoil it." Ellen went on reassuringly, "I think you look well and he'll think so too. So let's both welcome him with open arms and look forward to the next few days with him. Then we'll think about what you're going to do."

"I already have a good possibility in mind, Ellen, but we'll talk about it later," and Rob suddenly seemed to brighten and cast off his earlier uneasiness. "And I'm determined to do something about this drinking. I know I'm just lucky this time that I haven't been as ill as when I crashed the car but I might well have been."

Ellen did not reply. She had heard it all so many times before and had, long ago, accepted he could not control his addiction.

Matthew was glad to be safely home; Palestine had become very dangerous for any British man in uniform. No one knew who their enemy was any more, was it the Jew he met in the street? Or was it the Arab who rode beside him on horseback? He had no way of telling. He had had enough conflict for a while, he fancied living the life of a civilian for a time and he had the means to do just that. During his police years he had saved diligently each month and had amassed a substantial sum in the bank in Lisburn. Now he was contemplating starting a small business of his own. He just needed time to do a bit of research to establish what exactly might prosper him. He was rather proud of the fact that he had been able to save the amount he had and still been able to send some home every month.

After their celebration dinner that evening, Matthew insisted both his brothers and Lucie tell him everything that was happening in their lives. As he listened he realised his last three years of absence had brought considerable changes. He reckoned his siblings were now mature adults. Thomas and Charles, with their height, their thick heads of dark hair and their open, kind faces were quite handsome. But it was Lucie who had changed most of all. When he had gone away she had been a gauche eleven-year-old with nondescript features. Now she seemed transformed, with a slender frame which she carried so graciously, and a finely chiselled face and delicate mouth, which always seemed ready to break into a smile. He had forgotten, indeed if he had ever noticed, that she had the most brilliant blue eyes. Now she was telling him proudly she was attending grammar school.

"Mum insisted I sit the entrance examination for Maidshead High School instead of the technical college and I passed it."

"Oh, that is brilliant. Well done, Lucie."

"I did appreciate the chance, Matthew. I do know I've had a better opportunity than any of my brothers have, so I don't intend squandering it."

"No, don't, Lucie. What do you intend doing when you leave school?"

"Well, I would like to go to university, although I don't think that's likely to happen. We simply couldn't afford it. Some really clever students can win a scholarship, but again, that's very unlikely to happen with me." Suddenly Lucie's confidence seemed to desert her and she was once again the shy diffident girl he remembered.

"Don't say that, Lucie, just continue to work hard and you never know."

Matthew turned to Charles. "What about college, Charles? How is it going for you?"

"It's good; I'll be sitting my Senior Certificate soon. I'm thinking of doing Ordnance Surveying."

"Good for you." Matthew was impressed at all their obvious ambitions – at least they were getting better opportunities than Thomas and he had.

"What about the furniture trade? Thomas, Mum told me in her letters you were working for a Jewish firm selling furniture."

"I was made manager just last week with a good decent pay rise. So I'm happy enough. What are your plans, Matthew?" Thomas was interested as to how Matthew would settle down to civilian life after the excitement and danger he had known.

Rob had been quietly listening to his family's interchanges and during a lull in the conversation, remarked to Matthew, "My good Disinfectant project has become a thing of the past, son, but I have another project in mind. I'll tell you about it in a day or so, when I know more about it."

Rob was anxious to let Matthew know something of how his work had been going and he needed to let him know he had been earning very little money. In a couple of days, when Matthew had settled in, he would tell him about his latest project and the good prospects that were there.

Chapter 39

"Pop, do you think you could give me a lift into Lisburn this morning?" Matthew had been home almost a week now and after enjoying a well earned rest and relating his experiences in Palestine to his family in the evenings, he was anxious to set himself up with some employment. His priority must be to speak to the bank manager. He had been asking his father for the last couple of mornings to drive him into Lisburn. For some reason his father seemed anxious to put him off – telling him there was no hurry, he had all the time in the world to think about his future.

"I can always catch the bus at noon, if you like; I just thought you might be going that way."

"There will be no need for that, Matthew. I'll take you certainly. I just thought a couple more days of relaxation would do you good. We could go to Banbridge and Poyntzpass and visit your aunts and uncles before you think of what you want to do. What do you say?"

"Alright, I would love to see Aunt Ethel and my grandparents too. So let's say we go there today and I go to the bank tomorrow, would that suit?"

"Your father's right, Matthew, a day out to see the family. I would love it. I haven't been for a while myself." Ellen was delighted at Rob's suggestion, she hadn't thought of it. Instead she had intended to write and ask her sisters and Eve and Harry to come next Sunday to see Matthew.

Rob's suggestion proved to be an excellent idea for everyone. Matthew was greeted with open arms by his aunts and grandparents. And his mother was glad of the opportunity to catch up with her parents and sisters. She even managed to fit in a visit to the shops with Sara and Ethel while her father, Rob and Matthew went to the pub for a drink. Matthew was delighted when his father declined any alcohol, instead he just had a soda water. Matthew knew it must be difficult for Rob to avoid drinking, particularly when everyone else was in such a celebratory mood. But hopefully, on this occasion, his father did not mind too much.

Matthew was disappointed the next morning when he found his father still seemed reluctant to take him into Lisburn. He seemed to take longer than usual sipping his tea and listening to the radio. It was Ellen who eventually lost patience.

"Come on, Rob, get going, and take Matthew wherever he needs to go – he is waiting patiently for you."

"Right, I'm ready anytime." Resignedly Rob got to his feet and reached for his paddy hat which hung in its usual place on the arm of the kitchen chair.

"Thanks, Pop. It does save hanging about for buses, doesn't it?" Matthew still felt he was putting his father out. "We could have lunch in the corner cafe after, how about that?"

He still felt the need to kowtow to him. What was wrong with the man? He was usually very keen to give people lifts here and there and this was only into Lisburn. Maybe he was beginning to feel his craving for alcohol again, that would explain it. Probably his father would like nothing better than to go and have a quick drink with his son, to celebrate his safe homecoming. But both of them knew that couldn't happen. That was impossible, for that would be Rob started on another drunken binge. Matthew knew he couldn't take the responsibility for that.

Afterwards when Matthew thought about his interview with his bank manager, it all seemed so surreal. It was such a nightmare that, at first, he was unable to grasp any of it. Then his bank manager suggested that it was a criminal offence and he ought to involve the law. Matthew was shocked at the very idea of such a thing. He just shook his head despairingly and emphasised, "No, No never."

During his time in Palestine he had thought his savings were his own personal secret. He had never dreamt anything could happen to them. But the reality was that a substantial amount of his money was gone and it had been stolen from him by his father. Dear God, what had possessed him to do such a thing? What depths had he sunk to? What desperation had driven him to such a thing? And it had all been so easy for him. They had both been christened Robert Matthew, so his father had, to all appearances, been quite entitled to withdraw Matthew's money out from his account. The bank teller, of course, had never – at any stage – questioned the validity of his father's signature. That's where it had all fallen down for Matthew, and in Matthew's eyes, that's when it had fallen down for his father.

His father was waiting for him in the car where he had left him and as Matthew approached him, their eyes met across the people thronging the pavement. As Matthew saw the remorse and regret etched in his father's face, and he realised he was genuinely suffering over this – his heart softened towards him.

It was Rob who spoke first. "I'm so sorry, son, I wanted to tell you, but I just couldn't." His voice faltered as he turned to his son, so still and silent in the passenger seat beside him.

"The disinfectant business is poor. It is more or less finished, in fact. I do mean to pay you back – every penny of it – I just didn't have enough time to gather any before you came home." Now Rob was unable to continue he was so choked up. He just shook his head sadly.

"Don't worry, Pop, I don't intend to say anything to anyone – that's for sure." Matthew was certain no one must know. He could tell no one, not his brothers or sister, for they would tell their mother and this was something she must never know.

"Thanks, son," Rob managed to say, "and somehow or another, I mean to repay you, it will take time, I know that, but I will."

"Pop, let's talk no more about it for the present." He looked at his father, his slim hands manoeuvring the car along the street. "This changes my plans considerably, and I need to think about my future."

Rob had no answer for that but Matthew could sense he was consumed by guilt and thought of the awesome burden his father now carried. There was no further conversation as they made their way home. Going somewhere for lunch was completely forgotten about. Neither of them had any appetite for it.

Six weeks after the awful interview at the bank, Matthew informed the family at dinner of his plans for the future. "That letter that arrived for me this morning, Mum, was to offer me a post as Sergeant in the Royal Ulster Constabulary."

There was a momentary silence, before Rob spoke. "I'm proud of you, Matthew. And to be given a post immediately as a sergeant. Well done, you deserve it. With your experience in the Palestine Police I should think you have earned it."

"Matthew, are you really joining the RUC? I think that's wonderful." Ellen was delighted and was smiling happily. "You'll be here then, in Northern Ireland. You don't have to go away anywhere and I'm so glad. I thought perhaps you might think of joining some other force and go abroad again."

"I'll be based in Middletown, near the border – but I don't imagine there's a lot of fighting going on there. I'll be reasonably close to home, Mum, so you will see plenty of me."

"I think it will suit you well. It's what you want, isn't it?"

Matthew nodded empathetically – he was looking forward to it. This was his future. Not some uncertain business where he would have had no experience or knowledge of anything much.

Thomas, Charles and Lucie congratulated him. Thomas remarking he was a lucky man, he had got himself a good secure job with a future and a pension at the end of it. Not like him – stuck in a furniture shop all day selling tables and sideboards. "You're making me restless, Matthew. I'll have to think about doing something a bit more worthwhile myself. I don't want to be stuck in a furniture store for the rest of my life – that's for sure."

"If you're not happy with what you are doing, you should think about something totally different. You are only twenty –

a young man – and there are plenty of opportunities out there. Depends what you want."

Lucie had been listening carefully to the conversation going on between her brothers. She knew only too well what she wanted to do but if she voiced it at this stage in her life, her family would think her chances of achieving it were highly unlikely.

Chapter 40

1951

Lucie had never expected to come to love Maidshead High School as she did – initially she had found it all so strange and intimidating. Most of the other pupils who attended were from very well-to-do families, oozed with confidence and seemed to participate in all the sports the school recommended. She was aware that being involved in any sport was going to cost her parents money – money they simply didn't have. She considered herself very fortunate to have been given the chance of a good education and from the beginning had excused herself from any hockey or netball team. Instead she concentrated on achieving good grades in all her subjects. Now today as she waited for the letter informing her of her results in her Junior Certificate, she prayed her hard work had been worthwhile.

Her mother and she were alone in the house when the envelope arrived and Lucie found her hands were shaking so much she couldn't open it.

"Mum, would you?" handing the letter to her mother, she knew so much depended on this.

"Lucie, would you not prefer to see your results first yourself?"

Lucie shook her head dumbly and Ellen proceeded to open the letter and scan the contents. Then they were both hugging and kissing one another.

"You've achieved top grades in every subject. How did you do it? Your own hard work, no doubt. What do you intend to do now?"

"I'd like to continue at school and sit my Senior Certificate, if that's alright." Lucie sounded dubious. "That's if you think we can afford it."

"I was hoping you would say that, with results like these you must sit your Senior Certificate. You should be able to get a good job, maybe in the civil service like Charles has."

"Mum, I have to tell you now, while we are on the subject, I really would love to go to university. That's what I really want to do. I want to get my Senior Certificate and then perhaps sit the entrance examination for Queens." There, she'd said it. "I would like to study medicine."

"Medicine!" Ellen was shocked, never once had Lucie expressed any interest in going to university, but had just continued to work and study hard at school. She was ashamed to think she had had no idea what her daughter's aspirations were. She had been engrossed in trying to encourage Rob in his latest venture and trying to keep him from drinking.

"That would be a wonderful career for you. And of course, you must continue with your schooling. We will sort something out regarding paying for it all."

"Mum please, let's not be carried away. It might cost a lot of money – too much in fact. Wait until I do my Senior Certificate, then we'll see."

"We'll manage somehow, Lucie. Your dad's new work in the Jute trade is doing well, and he hasn't touched a drink in three years, actually since Matthew returned from Palestine. Thomas and Charles are both earning good money too and I'll keep saving as much as possible."

"Next summer I mean to get some part-time office work, I have been thinking about it for some time. But please, in the meantime, don't say anything to the boys."

"I have to say to your dad, Lucie, I wouldn't keep such a thing from him and it will encourage him to work harder and stay away from the pubs."

Ellen believed Matthew's firm influence had somehow helped Rob see the futility of alcoholism. Then when Matthew had started to bring a pretty young police constable home to meet them, then announced they would be getting married three months later, Ellen had half expected that Rob might return to his old ways. But Matthew and Julie had been married for two years now – had a home of their own, and a baby boy of nine months, and through all the celebrations Rob had remained sober.

Then again, Tom Greenlees and his family had returned to live in Poyntzpass. Tom's father had died eighteen months before and Tom now lived in the beautiful home his parents had cherished. His elderly mother still resided there, but now with her son, daughter-in-law and two grandsons. Tom had been lucky enough to be given a partnership in the General Practice in the village. He had proved to be a faithful friend to Rob and they visited one another frequently. Ellen felt it helped Rob considerably that Tom was completely teetotal. She knew she was indebted to this astute man and could only hope that Rob's and his renewed friendship would endure.

The first evening Rob had attended the Alcoholics Anonymous meeting had been six months after Matthew's disastrous visit to the bank. That day he had made a silent vow to himself that, no matter what, he would never touch a drink again. Then the old craving had returned and in desperation he decided to find out more about these meetings where reputedly it helped everyone. It was a place – so he had been told – where people were encouraged to be open about their addiction.

Even now, over two years later, that first visit was imprinted on his mind. The sense of shame and humiliation he felt, must be palpable to those who were already seated there, their eyes turned towards him as he walked in and took a seat. He listened earnestly as one by one someone rose to their feet and spoke of their experiences. Some had been business men – with wives and families – and were now reduced to living with some other relative who had been kind enough to take them in. Others were homeless, living with the Salvation Army. And as Rob listened he realised only too well, that if it had not been for Ellen and her steadfastness, he too would be in that position. He had always nonchalantly assumed that anyone who drank as he did just returned to their wives and families. But those same wives had simply had enough of someone who was rarely sober. It came to him as he listened that if Ellen had known what he had done to Matthew, would that have been the end for him? Would she have wiped her hands of him? He fervently believed that she would have finished with him there and then. Thank God he had managed to stick to his promise to Matthew and was trying to pay him back and had replaced almost half of what he had taken.

When he left the meeting on that particular evening, Rob was filled with a new resolve and determination. He would make it up to Ellen for what she had endured for so long. How had she tolerated it all? Why had she? He would never understand now why she had not taken her mother's advice over the years and left him. The full extent of her faithfulness to him had been brought home to him in the most humbling circumstances and he knew – no matter what or how often he succumbed to his addiction, he would be grateful to his wife and family for their tolerance.

He had found it impossible at first to stand up there and say anything about himself and his behaviour. Instead he had sat quietly, trying to draw strength from the other participants who were going through the same trauma he was. Then one evening, he found himself telling them about Ellen, how utterly faithful she had been, throughout his disgraceful times. He even ended up telling them all about Matthews's money, expecting disapproval and signs of disgust from some of them, but there was none. Then he remembered that, of course, some of them had even broken into people's homes for either drink or money or both.

After that first episode of talking openly to the rest of the group he found he began to look forward to the meetings. Yet, for reasons he could not explain, even to himself, he decided that he would keep his attendance at the meetings from his family. He reasoned that this was something he must do himself.

He had even been appointed a buddy; someone he could talk to if he felt he could not go on without a drink. He knew Gerald had been his saviour on many occasions when he just wanted to succumb. When he just longed to go in to a pub and have a drink – just to taste it once more – to ease the awful craving. He had always promised Gerald, if he felt the craving come on he would contact him. And Gerald, true to his word, had always been there when he needed him. He always managed to distract Rob from what would be utter folly.

Then there was Tom Greenlees. When Tom had written and told him he was coming back to live in Poyntzpass and take a position as General Practitioner, Rob was delighted. They had soon renewed their friendship and Rob had found that Tom, with his wisdom and quiet, serene manner had been invaluable to him on many occasions. Invariably it was Rob who drove to Poyntzpass to Tom's home. This was simply because Tom was reluctant to leave his mother. She suffered from dementia and as Norma, his wife, looked after her during the day, he felt the need to be there in the evenings. On one or two occasions Ellen accompanied Rob but instinctively she knew Rob preferred to go on his own when he might have a quiet tête-à-tête with his friend. Ellen was more than happy with this, as she knew he was safe from his addiction for another day.

Chapter 41

1953

"Sheila, I may not be happy about going to live in Lisburn, but Mum and Dad can't wait. Mum says she has loved living here, but maintains we will be even happier living in town."

Lucie could scarcely believe they were on the move again. They had been living in the country for so long she could not envisage living anywhere else.

"Oh, Lucie, I shall miss you so much, but I suppose with you going off to university very soon, we probably wouldn't see as much of each other. But we must keep in touch. And," Sheila was anxious to comfort her friend, "if it's any consolation to you, there is an excellent bus service between Lisburn and Belfast. Not like here – with one in the morning, lunch time and evening. You are going to need a good transport service."

"I know, and Mum keeps telling me that but I just imagined we would always be here. Stupid of me really, when all the time it was the Scott's house, and now they want it for their son and his wife – I still can't believe it. So of course we have no choice and it was Tom Greenlees, Dad's friend, who pulled some strings and got us this council house. It's in an estate, in a terrace of five houses. We'll be surrounded by people, Sheila, instead of animals, green fields and orchards."

"Lucie, you'll need to keep up with your studies. Don't let this move interfere with that, whatever you do. After getting your scholarship it would be a shame if you were unhappy and couldn't concentrate. Anyway, I mean to have you to stay at weekends when you're free. My parents both say you are welcome to come any time."

"Sheila, I'll look forward to that. As for anything interfering with my work, don't worry on that score. I still find it hard to take in that I actually got a scholarship – how I did, I don't know." Lucie's results of her Matriculation had arrived two weeks ago and the news she had achieved a scholarship overwhelmed her. She had, after all, been given a chance to study medicine. Her dream of graduating as a doctor might soon be realised. Her parents had been ecstatic when they heard and her father had proudly told most of the neighbours and anyone else who was prepared to listen.

"Are you sure your mother is agreeable to taking Monty for me? I could not bear if he went to a stranger. Can you imagine, no animals are allowed in this housing estate. I'll always be indebted to your mother, Sheila."

Lucie's father had brought a poor bedraggled animal home one evening about three years ago. It had, according to some farmer he visited, been loitering about his place all day. The dog was obviously so uncared for and so hungry that Lucie's heart melted when she saw him, and his big brown eyes seemed to be begging her to love him. Lucie never could establish what breed he was – his coat was long, coloured black and grey, he was medium size, and with a long white, straggly tail. But Lucie loved him and they had been inseparable since the first evening they saw each other.

"Let's take a walk to my house and I'll let you talk to Mother, she'll soon reassure you. At the same time we can think about what we're going to wear to the social evening, even though it's not for another couple of weeks, it will give us time to plan our outfits.

Later that evening as Lucie prepared for bed, she felt somewhat more content and happy about the fact that, once again, they were moving house. She thought of Sheila, and the constant, loyal friend she had been to her. She had been a true friend since that very first day at school, when she had walked home with Charles and her. She had faithfully waited at the crossroads each school morning so they might walk to school together. When Lucie had gone to Maidshead High School and Sheila had gone to work in a small draper's shop in the town, they had travelled on the same bus and their friendship had endured. And then today, Mrs Morrow had been so kind, insisting she would love and take care of Monty just as Lucie had done. As she climbed into bed, she was determined that no matter what, her friendship and contact with Sheila must remain constant, no matter where they might be or what the future held for them.

Lucie found her first few days at Queens University daunting and intimidating. She had always been reticent about new places and new faces, but the endless corridors and the streams of people scurrying along, intent on getting promptly to their next lecture, was quite nerve wracking. She was relieved they weren't moving house for another three weeks – she would have found the added stress of that just too much.

In the event, Lucie was scarcely aware of any upheaval with the house move. Her mother had thoughtfully packed all her clothes and other belongings, Thomas and Charles had taken leave from work and the whole thing seemed to Lucie, when she saw their new home, to have been so effortlessly and efficiently done she was quite amazed. As she prepared to go to meet Sheila that morning to catch the early bus, her mother had quietly given her instructions of "where to go" when she alighted from the Belfast bus later that day. She had assured her their new home was a few steps from the bus stop.

The front door of the terrace house was open as Lucie approached it. So this was their new home, and her heart sank as she took in the scene. The terrace was a grey blank wall of stone, with doors and windows dotted along the whole facade. Tiny strips of gardens ran down towards a long low wall which bordered the whole building, but there was no wall, plant or shrub of any description separating each house. And, she thought miserably – no wonder animals were not allowed here. She was so thankful again for Mrs Morrow's kindness in taking her beloved Monty in. Suddenly she was glad her beloved pet was still out in the country which he loved. He would have been miserable here. That knowledge was a relief to Lucie and she felt a weight regarding her dog's welfare had been lifted from her.

"Oh, Mum, this is wonderful for you, and you have electricity at the flick of a switch. It is all so spacious too; big bedrooms, a toilet that flushes and a bathroom too. You won't know yourself, no more oil lamps with their temperamental wicks, gas heating in the dining room and sitting room, and above all, not having to empty the outside toilet twice a day."

Her mother had shown her all round the house before Lucie had even had a cup of tea and Lucie was so happy her mother had at last all the modern conveniences she needed. She hugged her tightly. "It's what you deserve, Mum, and I don't know how you have managed for so many years with what we had."

Lucie felt ashamed that she had been so selfish, only thinking of herself and how much she would miss the countryside, when all this was what her mother needed. She had been surprised at the light that flooded in and how gracious it was. There were large windows in all the rooms which captured the evening sun.

"I love that landing window, Mum," Lucie remarked as they made their way downstairs, "it shows the whole back garden and the area at the back is a reasonable size, isn't it?"

The landing window was at the turn of the stairs and reached the whole length of the wall – opening out easily by means of a simple latched handle. It was a beautiful feature and brightened the whole staircase and landing and after the small lattice windows of their previous home, Lucie felt this must be the latest in modern housing.

"There's a lot of work to be done in that garden though," Ellen remarked. "Not a lot I can do with the front but I intend to work hard out there," indicating the expanse of grass at the back.

"I know you, Mum, you'll want your gooseberry and your blackcurrant bushes, and you'll soon be making your jam as usual."

"We'll have to get inside shipshape first, but at least the beds and curtains are up. We have somewhere to sleep tonight and we have an electric oven. I have shepherd's pie in it, ready for everybody. The boys and your dad have been working, moving furniture all day since shortly after you left this morning."

"And here I am, Mum, I haven't done a thing. I feel really guilty."

"We don't want you doing anything, Lucie. You have a hard slog in front of you and we intend to make it as easy as possible. Your dad is so proud of you and what you are trying to achieve he wants to make everything at home as easy as possible."

Secretly Ellen was glad Lucie seemed taken with their new home, she knew only too well her daughter had been heartbroken about leaving her darling dog and the countryside. But now she felt quite light-hearted after seeing Lucie's reaction to the place.

Chapter 42

1955

"I was beginning to wonder where you were, Charles; you're normally here before this. I'm just about to lock up for the night." Thomas was already pulling down the shutter of the window of the Belmont furniture store when Charles appeared at his side. Charles always caught the 5.30 p.m. bus from Belfast then called for Thomas, so they might walk down the street together at the end of their day's work.

"I missed the first bus but there was another fifteen minutes later so I'm not so late. I thought you might have gone on home. I'm glad you waited." Charles sounded different this evening, Thomas thought, excited and breathless, certainly not his usual self. Thomas locked the shutter, carried the key into the office and then rejoined Charles who was waiting on the pavement. He locked the main doors of the shop and putting the keys in his pocket, turned to Charles.

"That's us then, let's go – we don't know ourselves now, a five minute walk and we're home. Not like our country rambles in the evening and having to be sure to catch the one and only bus home."

Charles nodded in agreement as he fell into step beside his brother. "I'm later this evening because one of the top managers in the survey department called in to see me. He has a proposition for me."

"Oh," Thomas responded, "what sort of a proposition?"

"They want someone to transfer to Kenya to do some surveying out there, and someone recommended me."

"Oh boy – they must think a lot of your work, Charles."

Charles didn't comment on that but went on, "What do you think of it, Thomas? Should I go?"

"Do you want to go? Is it safe enough?" Thomas was amazed at this turn of events in his brother's life. He had seemed settled, and everyone had thought he was set up for life working as an ordinance surveyor for the government.

"I think I would like to go. The salary is really tempting and I've been assured that where I'll be working is totally safe. So, what do you think?"

"I think you should go then, Charles, I believe Kenya is a beautiful country. You have no ties as a single man, it's an opportunity to see beyond Belfast and Lisburn." Thomas knew Charles had had numerous liaisons with beautiful girls, but he had never seemed to be serious about any of them. But girls just seemed to gravitate towards his brother wherever he went. He was without doubt the most handsome in the family. Tall and lean with dark hair and brows, vivid blue eyes which seemed to mesmerize anyone he might be talking to, and gleaming white teeth in a wide sensuous mouth added up to a perfect specimen of a young man.

"I just wish I could go with you."

"That's the only part I don't relish, Thomas, I am going on my own. They tell me I will have a couple of scouts with me and a couple of helpers but no one from here."

"When do you go? You must tell Mum and Dad straight away. Give them time to get used to the idea."

"I'll be going in three months' time, that will be November but yes, I intend to tell them straight away."

The boys had gone to bed later than usual, Charles had talked at length to both his parents about his transfer. He was relieved they were so encouraging and interested in what was happening.

"I don't believe Pop will ever touch a drink again, Charles, how long is it do you think?"

"I know exactly. It's since Matthew came home from Palestine. Seven years ago."

"Sometimes I feel guilty about how we treated him in those days; we were a bit rough I think." This bothered Thomas many times when he watched his father now, a hard working, youthful-looking man.

"Thomas we were only ever doing it to help Mum, never forget that." Charles continued, "Besides we didn't know what else to do. So put it behind you, Thomas, don't dwell on it. It's all in the past."

"I know – and actually he is so stable now, that I think I'll have a word with Matthew, see what he thinks my chances of getting work out in Kenya might be. I really fancy going with you."

"That would be fantastic, Thomas, but are you serious?" Charles couldn't believe his ears; this idea had come out of the blue. "How could Matthew help?" He was dubious.

"I know he takes great interest in other countries since he was in Palestine. I'll call with him tomorrow evening. Just for a chat and see what he says."

"Don't be too disappointed if he can't help you. That is if you're even serious about such a move. You have a good steady job where you are and with good pay, Thomas, so think carefully."

"My job is so steady; it's just boring now, to be honest. But it is good money and I don't intended to do anything rash. Now let's try and get some sleep, it's been a kind of exciting evening for everyone."

It was the following weekend before Thomas had an opportunity to visit Matthew. His older brother lived on the opposite side of town in a quiet suburban area in an enchanting two up two down cottage set in beautiful grounds. Matthew lovingly tended the garden himself in his off duty. Thomas knew the bank had very generously given him a loan to buy the place with few questions asked. But then Matthew had a very secure job with a pension at the end of it, so he was a safe bet. Yes Matthew, in Thomas's eyes had done alright for himself, he was happily married and had a gorgeous son who was adored by his parents, grandparents and aunts and uncles.

Thomas had decided to cycle over this Saturday evening as the bus service was so infrequent and it was just a bit far to walk. He was glad to see Matthew's car parked in the driveway, because he had just taken a chance that he would be home. He was pushing his bicycle through the front gate, when Matthew appeared in the doorway.

"I thought it was you I spotted cycling along the lane. Come in and sit down, you look very warm after your travels. Would you like a beer?"

"I'd love one, cycling is warm work you know." Thomas placed his bicycle carefully against the wall, careful to avoid the beautiful flowering plant leaning there.

"I know Julie and you usually call on Sunday afternoon if you're not on duty but there is something I would like to talk to you about before then."

Matthew was intrigued. "It's not Dad, I hope?"

"Oh no, Father's great, working away diligently." Thomas followed his brother into the cool hall. "It's about myself."

"Go on into the sitting room, I'll get the beers and tell Julie where we are, she's putting Jason to bed at the minute."

Two hours later after having two or three of Matthew's cold beers, and a very detailed discussion, Thomas began his journey home, his mind scurrying with Matthew's suggestions. He wondered what Charles would make of it all; he wasn't too sure he would approve but he would find out later tonight, when he put's Matthew's proposal to him.

"Join the Kenya police. Well, I certainly never thought of such a thing. In fact, it never entered my head." Charles was astonished at Matthews's suggestion, Thomas of all people, who had never shown any interest in any uniformed services, and secretly Charles thought he was too meek, maybe even lacking in courage, for such a career. But discreetly he kept his thoughts to himself.

"Well you're the right height for a policeman, that's for sure," was all he could think of. "What about training, surely you need training and experience to go out there?"

"Matthew tells me I would go for an interview and training here first. He also says he knows a couple of men in charge of this recruiting and he intends to speak for me, they might be able to help." Thomas was keen to have Charles's approval, it was important to him, especially if they were going to be working and living in the same country.

"I think you'll find it hard work, the training, I mean, but I've no doubt you'll make it. You are a very fit man, Thomas."

"I hope so. Matthew says I just write a letter of application and wait to hear from them. I'll be out there with you, Charles, wait and see."

Thomas sounded so enthusiastic about it all and the idea of his brother being in the same country and probably sharing accommodation would be wonderful, really wonderful, Charles thought. But even so, he was worried about this venture of Thomas's. His inoffensive, diffident brother joining the Kenya Police was a rather daunting thought.

Chapter 43

"It will certainly be a different Christmas this year," Lucie thought regretfully as she sat at the back of the bus looking out at the grey skies and relentless rain. It was a typical dark November morning. She never liked the month, and this morning, with its grey, low clouds and swirling fog, added to her feeling of melancholy. She was going to miss Charles, they had always done so much together, gone to the cinema, even played ball games together and frequented their favourite cafe which served such delicious pork pies and peas. Now she felt she had taken it all for granted.

When Charles had first told her he was being transferred to Kenya in November, it had seemed something that would happen in the distant future. Then suddenly he was away last week and she was devastated at his going. She would miss him so much – his wisdom, his strength of character, but mostly his companionship. To add to her sense of loneliness and isolation Thomas would be going to join him in three weeks time. That left her the only one at home with their parents. She knew they would feel the separation more than she did. She had a fortnight's leave from university for the Christmas recess and she intended to spend as much time with them as she could. She was sure too that Matthew, Julie and young Jason would call and join whatever celebrations they might be having. Jason's winning ways would be bound to cheer them all.

Perhaps she might even surprise her parents by asking Paul if he would like to join them for Christmas dinner if his parents were agreeable. She had become friendly with Paul shortly after starting university. They were both studying medicine and in the same year, so it seemed very natural to go to the library together and to the canteen for lunch. Then it seemed a natural step for them to occasionally have a meal together in the evening or go to the cinema.

When she told her father of her first meeting with Paul Greenlees and that he was Tom Greenlees' son, he was delighted to learn that his daughter was up there with people he considered to be the most highly respected members of the community. Since then he had, on numerous occasions, asked her when she was bringing him home. She could see that her father's mind was racing to her marrying and having a family to Paul in the near future.

So Lucie was cautious about asking Paul to dinner, it might prove to be embarrassing for everyone. Besides she had no intention of marrying anyone for a long time. She wanted to be well established in her career before she even thought of such a thing. But somehow Christmas was different, people did have friends round and there needn't be any connotations to such an invitation. So she would ask Paul today when she met him. They had arranged to meet for lunch in the canteen at one o'clock.

"I'd love to come, Lucie," Paul looked disappointed, "but Grandma was admitted to hospital at the weekend, so I'll have to see how everything goes for her. She's ninety-three now and so very frail."

"Oh I'm so sorry, Paul." Lucie regarded her friend, he looked tired today, his tall frame seemed thinner and more fragile and his vivid grey eyes were sunken in his face.

"Of course, you wouldn't know or, even be interested in anything about Christmas." Lucie felt guilty now, she should have noticed he had something on his mind when he sat down.

"I'm so sorry about your grandma. Is there anything I can do?" She rose from her seat. "I'll get the coffees and ham rolls as usual, is that alright? It would be better than rambling on about Christmas."

"Lucie thanks. Yes – a ham roll is just fine." He managed to smile at her as she left him to join the queue for coffee.

Three days later, Paul was waiting at the gates to Queen's to inform Lucie that his grandma was dead. She had died in her sleep and his father was devastated at the loss of his mother. Paul felt he should spend a few days at home with his parents, but he would be in touch.

Lucie's father attended the funeral of Mrs Greenlees, he had very fond memories of her kindness to him as a young boy. When he returned he informed Ellen and Lucie that Tom Greenlees and his wife, and Paul of course, had accepted his invitation to join them for Christmas dinner, Paul's brother would not be coming, as he was going to his girlfriend's home.

"Rob, that's a good idea. It will give me someone special to cook a good Christmas meal for. Somehow without Charles and Thomas it didn't seem worth while getting a turkey and all the trimmings. Now I'll feel more justified in splashing out and spending a bit of money." Ellen had had no incentive to do anything much about Christmas, with the boys away and Matthew secure in his own home. She had felt guilty about Lucie and Rob, but couldn't shake off the lethargy that clung to her. Now she simply had to knuckle down and prepare for her guests.

"How did you manage to persuade them, Dad? They must feel Mrs Greenlees loss so much." Lucie paused in her note-taking from her medical book.

"When Tom told me his partner had insisted he would do surgery duties over Christmas, I said how much we would miss Charles and Thomas and would appreciate their company. Paul did say you had invited him but he did not wish to leave his parents. Now the invitation was extended to them that changed everything and he encouraged his parents to accept." Rob smiled happily at Lucie. "As simple as that," he added.

"Please, Dad, no match making now, Paul and I are just friends," Lucie pleaded, "and I want it to stay that way."

"Me – match make – I wouldn't dream of it," Rob assured her. "We'll just have a good old-fashioned Christmas with them. That's all. I promise." Lucie breathed a sigh of relief and settled down to another hour of intense study.

Christmas proved to be a huge success, Ellen excelled herself with her cooking and baking. She had made succulent stuffing for the turkey, baked a beautiful Christmas cake and steamed a moist fruity pudding for hours. On Christmas Eve, Lucie cleaned all the cutlery and glasses and set the table for six with a pristine white tablecloth and napkins. Rob brought home the Christmas tree on Christmas Eve morning and decorated it all himself. He shopped for the wine, whiskey and brandy without a word of complaint and when Ellen remarked how brave he was to do that without wanting to drink it, he remarked quite seriously, "I just love to look at it – no harm in that."

On Christmas Day the Greenlees arrived promptly at two o'clock in the afternoon with presents for Rob, Ellen and Lucie.

"Oh, Tom – you actually thought to go shopping for presents at such a time in your life, it is so kind of you." Ellen was touched by their generosity.

"We were determined to enter into the spirit of Christmas. It is how Mother would have wanted it," Tom answered earnestly.

"How are your parents, Ellen? I know they too must be elderly, are they in good health?"

"Father is now 84 and my mother 82," Ellen replied. "Father becomes increasingly frail and slow I'm afraid – and as you know, Mother has been frail for many years now." Ellen didn't add that her mother had been like this since Hugh's death but she was anxious that no dark clouds would spoil the Greenlees' day. They must have found it difficult enough to try to have some sort of Christmas. "But she is still quite active about the house and does a little of her own cooking and shopping, I'm glad to say. My sisters all call on Christmas Day and then Rob and I visit at the New Year. That has been the routine for some time now."

"Please give them my regards, Ellen, when you next visit." Turning to Rob then, Tom enquired about his stepmother.

"Jane is very well. She's in England as you know. We had a letter just recently to say she was contemplating getting married again," Rob answered. "She is young enough still, I suppose. She must be in her early sixties, I think. We wrote back immediately of course, to congratulate her."

"Now let's move out of the hall and in here – much more comfortable than standing around." Rob led the way into the sitting room where a blazing coal fire cheered them all immediately. Rob had thoughtfully placed the sofas and chairs around it and the whole room looked very welcoming and festive.

During the afternoon Rob confidently took charge of the drinks for everyone, something he was now able to do without craving one himself. It was seven years since he had touched the stuff. That horrendous time in his life was well and truly behind him. As Ellen watched him, she too marvelled at how he had finally overcome his addiction.

Tom encouraged them to open their presents before dinner and presented Rob with a blue and white striped shirt and a beautiful grey cardigan for Ellen, presents which Ellen knew must have cost a good deal of money. Impulsively she went over to Tom and his wife and hugged and kissed them both.

Paul had bought Lucie a beautiful pink silk blouse, and Lucie thought she had never owned anything so exquisite or so expensive. "Oh, Paul – this is so lovely I will treasure it and I intend keeping it for special occasions only." She too leaned over and hugged and kissed Paul with unexpected ardour.

Paul seemed taken aback at such a gesture of affection from Lucie, but quickly and passionately returned the gesture, when he unfolded the cream cashmere scarf she had purchased for him.

Rob had been quick to notice Lucie's warm embrace and Paul's eager response and secretly was delighted things seemed to be going well for them. He could sense a romance in the air – he was sure of it. His daughter's happiness was so important to him. She was a sensitive, compassionate girl who had always seemed to understand, perhaps better than any of his children, the difficult struggle he had with his alcohol addiction. He felt Paul Greenlees was a decent, honourable sort of chap who would always treat Lucie with the utmost respect. He just hoped everything would turn out for them.

Chapter 44

1957

Thomas glanced anxiously at the clock on the mantelpiece again – it was seven o'clock in the evening and Charles was late as usual. He did have a long arduous trip to make from Mount Kenya where he was surveying at present and Thomas tried to curb his impatience. In spite of his anxiety and need to confide in his brother as soon as possible, he had managed to cook an evening meal and had drinks ready for them both. Since coming to Kenya they always tried to meet up with one another every weekend, but that depended very much on Charles and where his surveying expeditions took him. Of course, there was no way of getting in touch with him once he left his base camp. It was now two weeks since they had been together and for Thomas, it had been a long two weeks, he was so anxious to talk to him.

Now willing himself not to look at the clock again, he went over to the cabinet that housed his drinks and poured a good stiff brandy. He needed it, if he was going to be able to tell his brother what had happened without breaking down. He should never have come here, never have joined the Kenya police. He knew that now. He abhorred the violence – both that inflicted on the white farmers by the Mau-Mau and the cruelty from his supervisors towards the Mau-Mau. The whole situation had become more terrifying by the day, and when his work colleague had persuaded him to leave and join him in a motor servicing business he had jumped at the chance. When he thought about it now he had scarcely known the fellow – he should never have trusted him, but had naively assumed that anyone in the police could be trusted. Now he knew that was not the case, there were dishonest people in every walk of life. Because of one man, Nigel Pollard, he was in serious trouble and whether Charles would have any idea of how to help he simply didn't know.

He was just finishing his drink when he heard the welcome sound of Charles' jeep pull into the driveway. As he opened the door of his ground floor apartment, he was relieved to see Charles, with his overnight bag slung over his shoulder and his keys dangling from his hand, appeared to be his usual calm placid self, even after his long trek. Somehow his brother's whole appearance reassured him and he felt calmer than he had done for the past fortnight.

"Charles, it's good to see you." Relief washed over Thomas.

"You too, mate – I hope dinner's ready, I'm starving. I have been driving most of the day. I decided to forego stopping off for any food along the way."

"Put your bag in your bedroom. I've everything ready, what about your favourite drink first perhaps?"

"Oh definitely." Charles proceeded down the short hallway to his room where he deposited his holdall on the bed, then on his return to the lounge gratefully accepted his whiskey Thomas had prepared then sat down eagerly at the table, where an enticing dinner of lamb chops, potatoes and peas was placed in front of him.

Thomas watched his brother eat heartily for a few moments then, without preamble he said, "I'm in serious trouble, Charles, really serious trouble."

"Oh dear, oh, dear," Charles replied, still placidly continuing to relish his meal. "You better tell me about it."

"Nigel Pollard," Thomas said the name now with bitter disgust in his voice, "he has been embezzling the loan companies it seems," he hurried on, "putting in false customers' names, obtaining thousands of pounds by deception, even pocketing customers' deposits, instead of forwarding them to the loan companies."

"How does that affect you, Thomas?" Charles looked up from his dinner and waited patiently.

"I'm his partner, for God's sake and that it seems makes me equally liable. We were both arrested for fraud eleven days ago and at present we're out on bail."

"I see." Charles was obviously now deep in thought. "Have you any chance of making any recompense? Is this man Nigel going to replace the money?"

"I certainly haven't any, and now it's in police hands anyway, so it's a criminal offence. I never suspected anything." Thomas was desperate. "You must believe me, Charles."

"Of course I believe you, Thomas, I'm not that daft." Charles knew Thomas could never have thought up such a devious scheme or taken anything to do with it. He had simply been naive, going into business with someone he scarcely knew. But then he had been desperate to get out of the Kenyan Police. It was a career Charles would never have recommended for Thomas and had always firmly believed Matthew had talked Thomas into joining. Thomas was so easily led and now this man Pollard had no doubt convinced him that the car sales was a sound business venture and Thomas had let himself be led into it.

Charles was silent for so long, Thomas began to think he had lost interest in what might happen to him. Then he spoke quietly and firmly. "We have to get you out of here, Thomas. You must go home."

"Home, Charles? Well that would be just wonderful. But the question is how? They confiscated our passports so I've no chance."

"I know they would take your passport before they let you out on bail, but," he emphasized, "we have to get you home. Leave it to me, we'll sort something out, rest assured. Now let's go and sit in the easy chairs and have another drink." And then changing the subject, went on, "I have some news from home. I don't know what you'll make of it, but let's have that drink first. And don't worry, in two or three days' time we'll have you on your way home."

Charles' whole attitude was one of total confidence and Thomas felt there and then he could put his total trust in him. His brother was, after all, the genius in the family. Relaxed now, he sat down beside him. "Well what's the latest from home?"

"I've had a letter from Lucie this week and – wait for it – she's getting married."

"Lucie is getting married! I always understood she was in no hurry, at least that's what she always maintained." Thomas was shocked at this news. "The last I heard was, Paul was away to London to specialise in surgery. Is he back home?"

"I'm afraid it's not Paul she intends to marry, it's some young man by the name of Patrick Mullan. It seems she was introduced to him by Matthew, he is a police constable and she says in her letter she was simply bowled over by him. She can't wait to marry him." Charles regarded his brother. "You look as shocked as I did when I read the letter. I must admit I thought Paul and her hit it off very well." Charles was his old cautious self. "I hope she knows what she's doing. She says she met him three months ago, it's not very long is it?"

"It certainly isn't," Thomas had briefly forgotten his own predicament, "but Lucie's a smart girl, unlikely to make a mistake such as marriage."

"I'll answer her letter tomorrow morning and you can add your good wishes, Thomas. I wonder how Pop's taken this news, he was set on her marrying Paul."

"According to Mum, he seemed delighted about Lucie and Paul, but no doubt, he'll go along with Lucie and soon get used to the idea. Please don't say a word about my predicament in the meantime, Charles, until we see how everything goes."

"Of course I won't, you know me better than that." Charles was annoyed at Thomas, to even consider the idea he might not keep his confidence. "That problem is strictly between you and I and it must remain so – at all costs."

Reassured, Thomas fetched two more drinks and the remainder of the evening past uneventfully with Charles describing his week's trekking through Mount Kenya with his two ever faithful scouts and servants for company.

It was Charles who did not sleep well that night, Thomas and he had gone to bed around midnight and Charles had come to realise sometime during the evening that the responsibility of getting Thomas safely out of Kenya now rested on his shoulders. Thomas had stated emphatically several times during the evening how much he trusted Charles to help him. As he lay now, wide awake, in the small compact bedroom he had always slept so soundly in on his visits to his brother, he thought a lot of their time together since coming here almost two years ago. He had known soon after Thomas's arrival that his brother was unhappy in the police here. Certainly his position was fraught with danger. Being called out in the middle of the night to isolated farmhouses, not knowing what he might find when he got there – not knowing at what corner the Mau-Mau lurked, ready to annihilate any British that crossed their path.

No, it had not been easy for Thomas, and when he had told Charles of the opportunity in the car industry Charles had paid little heed to the venture, just thankful that his brother was getting out of the police. But now this, Charles just hoped he would be able to pull something off to get him home. And if he did manage that, Charles would be advising him to look for his old job as sales manager back again. That would be the safest thing for Thomas to do, and in future not go along with other people's ideas.

For himself, he loved Kenya and he loved his work, he felt totally safe with his scouts and his servants. He knew this was mostly because he treated them as his own, they drank together and ate together, and they knew he very much respected their knowledge of the country. He did often wonder if any of them did liaise with the Mau-Mau but because of their relationship with him, he was left in peace. He had heard that some of the property owners who treated their servants well escaped the violence, but he was not prepared to ask any questions on the matter.

He must have fallen asleep in the early hours of the morning; when he woke he felt groggy and weary and he was aware of Thomas telling him breakfast was ready. Recollections of the evening before came back to him and, aware he had a job to do, he pulled on his dressing gown and pushing his feet into his slippers went into the kitchen where Thomas was frying bacon and egg for breakfast.

"That looks good and smells delicious, Thomas. I'm hungry again, must have been all that whiskey last night, always does give me quite an appetite."

"Glad to hear it, as I'm hungry too, Charles." Thomas set the plates on the table and as Charles sat down he added, "Have you thought much more about my predicament?"

"I've thought about nothing else. This is Saturday and we need to have things sorted by the middle of the week. Luckily enough I have booked three days leave. First thing, I'm going to need a few potatoes, a good sharp knife and some good ink. I'll need to practice my printing. You must think of a name for yourself and book a flight from the airport in Tanganyika as soon as you can."

Chapter 45

1957

Lucie opened the drawer in her desk and withdrew the letter she had received earlier in the post. She had decided she would wait until after her morning's surgery was over before opening it. She knew by the London postmark that it was from Paul, besides she would recognise his familiar writing anywhere, she had seen it often enough on the evenings they had studied together for their graduation. This letter from him must be his reply to hers telling him of her intention to marry.

As she slit the letter open her thoughts went back to their last evening together six months before. She had rung him early that morning to tell him that she was accepted as a junior partner in a general practice in Lisburn and he had been so delighted for her, insisting they meet in their favourite restaurant on the Lisburn Road that same evening. He told her excitedly that he had news for her too but it would keep until he saw her.

His much battered Morris Minor was already there when she drew into the car park. She found herself hoping his news was as good as hers. She could scarcely believe she had managed to get a post as a junior doctor so quickly. General practice really appealed to her and she was determined to work hard and make a success of it. As for Paul she knew he would be delighted for her. She would be equally delighted for him if he had been successful in getting into some of the hospitals to specialise in surgery. She knew it was what he really wanted.

When she entered the restaurant she spied him almost immediately seated at his favourite table in one corner of the dining room. He rose immediately when he saw her walking towards him.

"I've ordered you a glass of your favourite wine," he remarked as he pulled out a seat for her.

"Thank you, Paul, this is nice." She smiled then went on impatiently, "Now let's hear your news."

"Let's order first, Lucie. Have a look at the menu. This is a joint celebration, hard to believe, isn't it?"

Lucie decided she would just have some chicken salad and some chips. Paul opted for steak and chips. And when the waiter had taken their order and left the table he withdrew an official looking letter from his pocket and handed it to her. "I'll let you read this yourself, Lucie."

Lucie took the letter and saw that it was from the Neurological Department in University College Hospital in London, accepting Paul as a graduate there. "Paul, this is exciting news for you, I'm really happy for you." Lucie leaned forward and kissed him affectionately. "I'm delighted – Neurology – that will be tough, won't it?"

"I imagine so, Lucie and it's for two years you know, and I'll be in London." This statement seemed more like a question and it hung in the air between them.

Lucie broke the silence. "That's alright, Paul. You are going to accept this, aren't you?"

"Yes, I am." Paul hesitated then added quickly, "You must know how I feel about you, Lucie, but this is something I really need to do, you do understand don't you?" His voice held a pleading tone.

"Of course I do, Paul, you must do it and two years is nothing. Just think it is four years since we started medical school."

"Lucie, you too, are just setting out on a new career, as I am. I want to say that I won't hold you to any promises while I'm away. I don't expect you to sit around waiting for me."

"Paul let's not look too far ahead but just try and write regularly to one another. Besides you aren't so very far away."

No, I'm just across the Irish Sea and we will keep in touch regularly Lucie."

They had corresponded regularly for the first three months when Paul had been in London and then she had met Patrick.

Now as was she reading this brief letter congratulating her on her forthcoming marriage and wishing her many years of happiness she was suddenly overcome with an acute sense of loss. Loss of his much valued friendship, his understanding and quiet, steady companionship. But she knew she could not ignore this passion she felt for Patrick, it seemed to consume her. Her every thought was of him, and the emotion she felt each time she saw him raced through every fibre of her being. She knew she had to be with him.

She had met Patrick one evening when she arrived home from work. Matthew had called in to see everyone while still on duty and had a young police constable with him, who Matthew introduced to her as Patrick Mullan. He explained Patrick had just been assigned to his department and Matthew was showing him "the ropes". As Lucie shook hands with Patrick Mullan and looked into his blue eyes and felt the hot burning sensation race through her, she was lost.

Theirs had been a whirlwind, passionate romance in every sense of the word, meeting almost every spare evening they had, hungry for each other's arms and kisses. So much so that Lucie felt it was only a matter of time before they became lovers, something she still believed – because of her upbringing and her church's influence – was terribly wrong. So they had set a wedding date and now it was only six weeks away. The 20th of October it was to be, and they had both decided it would be a simple affair in a registry office. This was mainly because of Patrick being a Roman Catholic and he had stated quite categorically that his parents would never tolerate the idea of him marrying in a Protestant church. As for Lucie, her father was in despair at the thought of her marrying Patrick and had flatly refused to attend. He informed her he could not bear to see his daughter marry in a registry office. But Lucie secretly wondered if her father was so disappointed she was not going to marry Paul and that was the real reason for his awkwardness. The whole situation between them was making her totally miserable, but did nothing to influence her decision. Yes she would marry Patrick in six weeks time and surely her father would, by then, have got used to the idea. Even if he still did not want to go to the registry office, perhaps he could be persuaded to join the family for the celebratory meal they had organised in the Garvey hotel on the edge of town.

Now she reassembled her thoughts away from her father and his obvious misery and began to clear the files from her desk, at the same time mentally noting what she had to do this afternoon. It was half day in the practice and she wasn't on call. She had planned to confirm the arrangements for the wedding meal at the hotel, and then call for a fitting for her outfit. She was just pulling on her jacket and checking her handbag for the car keys, when her private phone rang. Expecting to hear Patrick's voice greeting her lovingly she was surprised to realise the call was from a phone kiosk – she could hear the pips – then money being slotted in.

"Hello, Lucie." The caller's voice was a familiar one, instantly so recognisable.

"Thomas, is that you? My goodness, where are you ringing from? I didn't think to hear from you. How did you get this number?"

"I'm at Belfast docks, Lucie. Charles gave me this number, but," Thomas sounded impatient, nervous even, "never mind all that. Can you possibly collect me here, I need a lift home."

"Does Mum or Dad know you're here – back in Belfast?" Lucie was astonished. The last news she had heard was about Thomas going into business. Almost immediately Lucie sensed something was wrong.

"No, no one knows. You're the only one I thought to ring."

"I'll be there shortly, Thomas – but first I'll have to call and tell Mum and Dad you're here and prepare them a little, don't you think?"

"If you think that's best – how long will you be?"

Lucie glanced at her watch, it was showing 12.45pm, "I'll be there by one thirty, just outside the main entrance?"

"Good, Lucie, thank you so much."

Lucie locked her office door, checked for her car keys once again, then deep in thought, made her way to the car. Why on earth had Thomas returned to Northern Ireland without letting anyone know? Was he ill? Was he in financial trouble? Had he been attacked or threatened by the Mau-Mau? Her mind raced on thinking of possible reasons for his sudden return, but as she drew up outside her parents' house she made a conscious effort to control her emotions. She needed to let her parents know, somehow without alarming or distressing them. There was, after all, quite possibly a simple explanation. No point in letting her imagination run riot.

She need not have worried about either of her parents' reaction. Her mother was simply delighted that Thomas was back safely, and her father, who had not spoken to her in weeks, was smiling happily at her.

"Right, go on, Lucie, go and bring Thomas home safely." Relieved, Lucie left her parents talking excitedly about preparing Thomas's room for him and what Ellen should have for dinner. Meantime her own plans – going to the hotel and her dress fitting – would more than likely have to be postponed.

Chapter 46

Ellen's initial euphoria on seeing Thomas safely back home from Kenya and looking so tanned and fit soon evaporated when he confided to Rob and her, how he had had to leave there under a cloud. She sat listening with a sense of disbelief – as he told them about his initial enthusiasm for the new venture, how his hopes for success there had been cruelly dashed and the realization that he was in serious trouble. He was reluctant to say much about his journey back home, only stressing that without Charles he would have been lost. But Ellen, watching him as he talked, was well aware the journey home must have been a fearful, horrific nightmare for him.

"Son, you're home safely now, that's all that matters." Ellen's heart was heavy with sadness for what Thomas must have been through. "You'll soon get a job again, but don't think of anything in the meantime."

Thomas nodded sombrely. "I'll be fine, Mum."

He turned to his father. "Don't be thinking anyone is likely to come looking for me, Dad, Nigel Pollard is the one responsible, the police will soon realise that when they investigate the whole thing. Besides he's sure to say I knew nothing about it. We were friends you know."

"I should think the Kenyan Police have enough on their minds trying to control the Mau-Mau, without trying to trace you. Anyway, you were one of them so they will remember all that – you're safe enough." Rob still followed the news avidly and he had taken great interest in the events unfolding in Kenya.

Within a few days Thomas had shaken off his mood of despondency and had started to help in his father's new jute business. This business involved collecting the empty meal bags from farmers, paying them an agreed price and then Rob sold them on to a sack mill where they were cleaned and sold on to meal companies. The farmers knew Rob so well, they rarely quibbled about price and had all the bags neatly folded and counted for him when he arrived. Ellen was delighted when Thomas set off with his father each morning; he seemed enthusiastic and more than happy to help. He seemed determined to put the past behind him...

"Thomas, speak to your father one last time about Lucie's wedding?" Ellen was in the kitchen with Thomas who was just finishing his breakfast of poached eggs and toast before joining Rob in the van outside. "It is next week, and he really ought to be there you know – she is his only daughter."

"I know he should go, Mum, but I've tried to talk to him – it's like talking to a brick wall. He says he is just not going."

"Do you think it's because Patrick's a Catholic? Or is it because of Paul Greenlees?"

"I've discussed all that with him and he assures me it's none of those things. He says he just doesn't like the man." For his mother's sake Thomas had tried several times to get his father to change his mind about going to the wedding but he simply maintained he wasn't going.

"So I've to go without him – to our only daughter's wedding. Well. I think it's a disgrace." Of all the annoyances and worries Rob had given Ellen over the years she was finding this estrangement between father and daughter the most difficult. She had been hopeful they were going to be friends again the day Thomas came home, but their antagonism towards one another resurfaced and she was at loss as to what to do. She wasn't entirely happy about Lucie being married in a registry office, but there was no way she intended to let it influence her presence at her daughter's wedding. And although Patrick Mullan might not have been her choice for her daughter, he seemed nice enough and had a good steady job with excellent prospects.

"Please, Thomas just try one last time – for my sake."

"I will, Mum," Thomas said resignedly. Privately he thought he was wasting his time. His father wasn't going to give way. "At least Matthew and Julie intend going and I wouldn't miss it for the world."

Ellen brightened up at that and reaching Thomas the lunches she had packed for them both, smiled. "You better get out to the van; your dad will wonder what the delay is."

Ellen went to the living room window and watched as Thomas climbed in beside his father and she stood quietly until the van disappeared from view. She desperately needed Rob at her side when Lucie married Patrick Mullan and somehow, someone had to make him see that. She too was disappointed that her daughter was not marrying Paul or getting married in a church with God's blessing. But Lucie was a good, intelligent girl who must know what she was doing and Ellen felt she needed both her parents' blessing for her forthcoming marriage.

Throughout the day Ellen went about her chores automatically, her thoughts dwelling on the hope that Thomas could make Rob see sense. After all the whole service was only an hour long, and most importantly, Patrick was Lucie's choice of husband. Somehow her day dragged – time was heavy on her hands and when she finally heard the van pull up outside the front door, she was in a most despondent frame of mind. When Thomas opened the back door and greeted her, she saw his wide smile and when he nodded his head emphatically she knew everything was alright. She threw her arms around her son.

"Oh, Thomas thank you – you're wonderful." She was close to tears, Thomas hugged her back. "I think Dad was beginning to see for himself he had to be there. So everything's alright."

Just then Rob entered the kitchen. "Oh, Rob, I'm so glad you're going to go." Her voice was shaking; she didn't know how she would have gone through it happily without him.

"I'm going because of you, love. No other reason." He hugged her tightly. "I still think Lucie's making a terrible mistake. I just don't like the man, there's something about him."

"I know you feel like that, Rob, but try to make the most of it. Next thing is though we have to get you a decent suit for it."

Ellen was back to her practical self. "You really need a new one anyway."

"I suppose so. I have had that other one about twenty years now I think."

Ellen could scarcely believe that Rob was now showing some interest and agreeing to get a new suit but thought it best to say nothing more.

Ellen thought her daughter had never looked more beautiful than on her wedding day; she had chosen a cream dress in sheer silk which clung to her slim waist and hips and flattered her slim figure. Her dark hair was swept up from her face and forehead, highlighting her cheekbones and dark luminous eyes. Any doubts she had of her daughter's happiness were dispelled now as she watched her walk down the steps of the registry office with her new husband. And certainly Patrick Mullan was a very handsome man, tall and lean with jet black hair and dark eyes, he looked every inch the rugged Irishman.

As for Rob, he had held his wife's hand tightly during the entire ceremony, only relaxing his grip as they made their way out of the registry office. Since the evening Rob had declared his intention to attend Lucie's wedding, he had insisted on making a substantial contribution to the celebration meal in the Garvey hotel. Lucie had shown her appreciation of her father's change of heart by declaring him to be the best father in the world. At the reception Rob was in top form, spending time with Dorrie and Eve and their husbands and talking at length to Ethel who had suffered the loss of Billy from cancer the year before. Ellen was delighted that Ethel had insisted she would be there and Gladys would accompany her. Rob was very gracious to Ellen's parents and all past animosity seemed forgotten about. They were both very frail now, but being anxious to see who this man was their granddaughter was marrying in a registry office had decided to travel with Sara and her husband As the evening wore on and the newlyweds prepared to leave for their honeymoon in Dublin, no one noticed Rob go to the bar on a couple of occasions to buy drink.

Chapter 47

Normally Ellen rose around 6.30 a.m. every morning, but after the buzz and activity of Lucie's wedding, talking to all the guests and trying to ensure everyone was happy and felt included in the celebrations, she had overslept. The clock showed 7.30 and she realised Rob was up and moving about downstairs. She lay quietly for a moment or two reflecting on the events of Lucie's marriage. Everything had gone well, the food was delicious, and everyone had seemed in harmony with one another. The compliments about the bride and groom had flowed throughout the entire day, and when they were leaving for their honeymoon, Ellen was thrilled to see her daughter glowing with happiness. Now dragging herself out of bed, she slipped on her dressing gown and headed downstairs to join Rob in the kitchen.

"I've tea ready here, love. Are you ready for some?" Rob reached into the cupboard for another cup as he spoke. "It's not like you to have a lie in; you're usually up and about before this."

"I'm tired after yesterday – it has all caught up on me, I think." Ellen took the tea gratefully and sat down at the kitchen table.

"I think I'll give Thomas the day off, he is bound to be tired too and I'm only doing local calls today, so I don't really need him. It'll give him a break." Rob put his cup in the sink and taking his keys for the van from their hook, proceeded to put on his coat which he had earlier placed on the back of the chair in readiness to go to work.

"Are you going now, Rob? It's still only eight o'clock" Ellen was eager to find out what he thought of the wedding, he had never passed any comment about anything throughout the day. "What did you think of everything yesterday?"

"It all went well, love, Lucie was beautiful – no doubt about that and Patrick seemed to be on his best behaviour, no one could say otherwise." Rob proceeded to put on his coat. "You take it easy today, I'll see you later," and with that Rob made his way out of the kitchen and Ellen waited until she heard the sound of his van starting up before she rose from her chair and prepared some toast for herself. She was glad Thomas was off today, he would be good company for her. After the rollercoaster of excitement and anxiety of the last few weeks, the worry about Lucie and Rob's coldness to one another, she felt strangely deflated and depressed.

Rob's mood was one of excitement and resolve as he drove through Lisburn and on to the Antrim Road which would lead him to Co. Tyrone. There he would be able to talk openly to his friends, about how he really felt about his daughter and her marriage. He was determined to have a drink – he desperately needed to – just today. Then he would forget about alcohol again. He could do it, he knew he could. He did not need to contact any buddy in the AA, this would be a one off occasion for him. It was what he needed more than anything. He should be in Aughnacloy by ten-thirty, he would call with his good friends, Fred and Betty Speers, have a cup of tea with them, collect any jute sacks they had and then park his van there. "The Three Bells" in the main street would be opening their doors at eleven-thirty, and the Speers' farm was just a short walk from the pub, and he was fairly certain some of his friends would already be there by that time.

He was looking forward to it, unlike yesterday when he had had to act the part of the proud happy father as he watched his daughter marry a man he did not like and certainly did not trust. Not that he regretted his decision to be there. It had been the right thing to do, and he had done it all for his beloved Ellen's sake, because he knew deep down, she too was uneasy, mainly because Patrick had insisted on a registry office wedding. That's what worried Rob – Patrick Mullan had done it simply to placate his Catholic parents. He had not considered, for one moment, as to what Lucie, or her parents, had wanted.

The very thought of his new son-in-law's arrogance was

enough to make Rob's blood boil. Was it not the bride's prerogative to get married in the church she belonged to? He felt it didn't bode well for Lucie if Patrick had got his wish here, was that going to set a pattern for their married life? He had never shared these doubts with Ellen, he knew she still thought he had only wanted Lucie to marry Paul Greenlees, and although initially he had been disappointed, he had come to terms with the knowledge that that was not going to happen. But he knew Ellen still had doubts about the real reason for his objections.

Ellen and Thomas had a leisurely peaceful day together, they reflected about the wedding, both agreeing the bride and groom looked a happy, beautiful couple. They discussed the guests at length, how good an opportunity it had been to get all their relatives together and get up to date with what was happening in their lives. Ellen expressed her surprise that her own parents had seemed to enjoy it all, even though they both looked frail and old. Thomas was quick to reassure her they seemed to have reasonably good health and had both eaten a hearty meal.

"It was wonderful to see Eve and Harry, it has always intrigued me how things worked out so well for them," Thomas remarked. "I always enjoyed hearing their story from you, Mum. I know it was sad young Amy was lost in the shelter in Belfast, but of course, I never really knew her, but it is strange how fate seems to take a hand in our destiny, don't you think? But then, I have a very soft spot for Eve and I'm so glad she is happy. As for Aunt Ethel, she looked great, and she, in particular, was always so kind to us when we needed help most."

"We all have a soft spot for both my sister and sister-in-law, I think, Thomas. And they have both suffered, especially Ethel, losing her darling son and in such a cruel way. It's good to see they have been capable of overcoming so much."

The conversation flowed on between mother and son, until Thomas realised the time, remarking, "I did promise to clean the windows for you, Mum so I'll start now. It will be dark in no time. It's almost four o'clock."

"I'll start and make dinner. Rob should soon be home, he did say he was only doing local calls today."

By nine o'clock that evening Ellen was beginning to suspect the worst – that Rob would not be coming home that evening, and that could only mean one thing – he was drinking again. Thomas had cleaned all the windows as he had promised, they had waited for a time and then decided to have dinner without him and both of them had become strangely silent as the evening had worn on. Finally at eleven o'clock Ellen locked the back door and turning to Thomas said in bewilderment, "I can't believe this is happening again, your dad hasn't touched drink for years. He couldn't possibly start again. But if he has, he'll be ill, he's not as young as he was." She was close to despair.

"I know, Mum, I know." Thomas decided to be honest and realistic. "The truth is, Mum, I thought I smelt it off him last night, but there were so many people enjoying a glass or two that the smell was everywhere, I thought I was just imagining it. But I must have been right. We'll just have to hope it's a one off episode for him. But you and I really should go on to bed."

Torn between anger and worry for Rob's safety, reluctantly Ellen had to agree and after rechecking the house was locked up and the lights off, they made their way upstairs to bed. In spite of her worry and annoyance over Rob, Ellen was soon fast asleep and slept soundly until 6 a.m. the following morning. She knew Thomas's presence in the house made a difference to her. He was so thoughtful and considerate towards her, always calm and never critical of anything or anybody. In fact he was a tower of strength. With Lucie being away on her honeymoon, Matthew married and working such unsocial hours she felt she needed her second son as never before.

The next day slipped by with the usual routine of food shopping and cleaning. Thomas had gone for the shopping.

Ellen had thought it best she stayed in, in case Rob came home and needed assistance. That evening before they retired to bed, Thomas said he would go to the phone booth in the morning and make a few calls to try and establish his father's whereabouts. Thomas had become familiar with his father's clients over the last few weeks.

Next morning Ellen rose at her usual time and after preparing breakfast for Thomas and her she decided to take coins out of the money box – Thomas would need them for the phone. She was beginning to count them out when Thomas appeared in the kitchen.

"Oh, Mum, a cooked breakfast; bacon and egg is so good." Ellen was just placing the plate in front of Thomas when the front door bell rang.

"I'll get it, Thomas, it's probably the postman."

Ellen opened the door and two well dressed men stood there, gazing sombrely at her.

"Mrs Hampton?"

"Yes."

"We are detectives from the CID." The elder one proceeded to show Ellen his identification.

"Oh, God – it's Rob my husband, isn't it? What has happened?" The man facing her looked puzzled.

"No, ma'am, we need to speak to Thomas Hampton, age 26 years. Is he your son? Is he here?"

Ellen nodded dumbly and indicated that they follow her into the lounge. This could not be happening, this was some horrific nightmare. They must be here to arrest Thomas and send him back to Kenya.

She opened the lounge door and turned towards them.

"Wait here please. I'll fetch him now." Wearily Ellen went to where Thomas was sitting, enjoying his breakfast.

"Thomas, the police are here, for you." Her voice was barely a whisper, but she grasped her son's hand, Thomas's colour drained from his face and he sat so quietly for a moment that Ellen thought he hadn't heard her.

Then his face cleared and he returned her grip tightly. "It's alright, Mum, it'll be fine – I'll speak to them."

When he entered the lounge, the two detectives rose from their seats.

"Thomas Hampton?" The elder one spoke quietly.

"Yes that is me."

"We are here to arrest you on suspicion of abetting fraud in Kenya – if there is anything you wish to say..."

Thomas broke in. "I know I know, you want to read me my rights. Let's get it over with and I'll go and collect my coat and things."

The detective nodded and Thomas left the room quietly.

"Mrs Hampton, would you please tell your son we must be going, he has had fifteen minutes to collect his belongings." Detective Brown looked knowingly at his watch. Ellen turned and left them, hoping against hope that what she was beginning to suspect was true. Her heart leapt when she entered Thomas's room and it was empty, as was the bathroom and other rooms. Thomas had gone and she knew exactly how. God bless the builders who had decided to install such a beautiful landing window. She made her way downstairs to rejoin the detectives. It was with much regret she said, she had to inform them that Thomas seemed to have disappeared.

Chapter 48

When Thomas left the two detectives in the lounge with his mother, he opened the landing window as quietly as he could before going to his room to get some money. He was glad he had left his father's radio on; he had automatically put it on while having breakfast, something he thought was merciful for him now. Shaking with fear, he retrieved his wallet from the drawer in the bedside cabinet, pulled on his coat and carefully placed his wallet in the inside pocket. He went into the bathroom and turned on the water tap, then as calmly as he could tip toed down the first flight of stairs and stepped out of the landing window onto the ground. He knew he must try to remain calm but he was really terror-stricken, expecting the two men to appear at his side at any minute. Gingerly he stepped over the low fences which separated the back gardens and then ran as fast as he could until he reached the railway line which lay at the extreme end of the estate. Keeping as close to the bank as he could he hurried on until he spied the Lisburn train station ahead of him. As unobtrusively as he could he climbed the bank which led him to the platform. From a safe distance he studied the time table displayed there and when he realised there was a train to Newry in five minutes time, a definite plan began to form in his mind. He went to the ticket desk and bought a ticket just as the train pulled in, then nervously handed it to the ticket collector. All the time his heart beat heavily in his chest, his hands shaking and clammy with sweat.

They were bound to come here, he thought wildly. He must have been mad to think to come to the train station at all. But he had just thought of escape and nothing else. Deliberately he sought out a carriage thronged with commuters. He reckoned he would be safer in a crowded area – in an empty compartment he would be spotted much easier. Somewhat relieved that he had got so far safely, he sat down in a small corner beside a plump, middle-aged woman who obligingly moved over ever so slightly to make room for him.

As the train rattled along the line, Thomas found he was able to begin to consolidate the plan which had been forming in his mind. Once the train arrived at Newry station and providing no R.U.C. had been alerted and were waiting for him, he would try to get a lift over the border to Drogheda. Every station the train pulled into he was expecting some policeman or other to come on board and find him. But none did and when the train pulled into Newry station, he quickly hopped out, wrapped his jacket closely round him and proceeded out of the station.

He headed towards the main road to Drogheda and began to wave to passing cars and lorries in the hope that someone would eventually stop. He must have walked well over a mile and was giving up hope when a builder's lorry pulled in beside him. "Need a lift, mate?" The driver leaned over to open the passenger door.

"Where do you want to go?"

"I'm heading for Drogheda." Thomas was already on the step of the lorry and hauling himself up and into the seat.

"Right ye be, that's where I'm heading – you're in luck." He grinned cheerily at Thomas. "Not too many stop to lift strangers these days, you know, but you looked a bit weary to me."

Thomas turned to look at the man behind the steering wheel. He was around fifty years of age, he reckoned, dressed in working clothes, but with a friendly face and who spoke so sympathetically that Thomas felt tears welling up. Struggling to contain himself he said, "I am tired – very tired – I need to get to a friend's house in Drogheda."

Even when Thomas had decided to try to get across the border he hadn't thought of what he might do. Then he had remembered about Albert Lyness. They had worked together for a time, in the furniture trade. When Albert's grandmother had died and left him a house in Drogheda, he and his wife had moved down there. Albert would help him – he knew he would – and now, luckily for Thomas – he even remembered the name of the street. He had very been interested at the time – happy for Albert who had been fortunate enough to be left a grand terrace house by a relative. And now, well that's just where Thomas was going to go tonight if he was fortunate enough to be able to find his way.

Once they were safely over the border the lorry driver noticed his companion seemed to relax and he felt certain he was in some kind of trouble. But he looked a respectable hard working young man and he didn't intend to ask any questions. He would simply take him to Drogheda and even to the street where he said his friend lived.

The journey was done in companionable silence and Thomas found his thoughts going back to the events of the whole morning and he wondered and worried how his mother was. She must have been so shocked when the CID arrived but had remained very calm. How did she feel when she realised he was gone? Relieved he had got away or angry about being put in such a position? He had no way of knowing.

After the detectives had left the house, Ellen had sat quietly in the lounge with a cup of tea scarcely able to comprehend all that had happened. She was full of mixed emotions, but her overriding feeling of relief was that she hadn't had to witness Thomas getting into a police car. How she longed for Rob's presence, the house felt so lonely and desolate, after all it had witnessed that morning. But Rob did not appear and later that evening she went to the phone booth and rang Matthew and asked him to call around, stressing it was fairly urgent. Fifteen minutes later Ellen heard Matthew's car draw up and then his key in the front door. She was so relieved to see him after all the fear and trauma of the whole day, the emotions she had held in control welled up and she burst into tears. In a couple of strides Matthew was beside her, and sitting down he held her tightly in his arms until her sobs subsided.

"What it is, Mum? Has Dad never returned home?" Matthew had never seen his mother like this before. In all their experiences she had always managed to hold everything together very well.

Making an effort to speak Ellen muttered, "No – No – it's Thomas."

"Where is Thomas?" He had just realized his mother was alone in the house.

In an uncertain voice, interrupted by sobs, Ellen related the day's events to her eldest son.

Matthew sat stunned as he listened, so the Kenya police had pursued Thomas. They weren't going to let it lie unresolved on their files. No doubt because Thomas had been one of them – that in their estimation – made it even more important to catch him.

"Mum, I'm going to stay the night here with you – I won't leave you, and if it is any reassurance to you, I have heard nothing about Thomas. I think if they had arrested him it would have leaked through to our barracks. So take comfort from that." Matthew paused, considering for a moment, "Who did you say the inspector was?"

"There were two of them – one of them said his name was Brown". Tomorrow I'll make a few enquiries and find out, if I can, what's happening."

"I'll go out now to the phone booth and ring Julie, let her know I'm staying with you. While I'm out at the phone, do you think you're up to making a good strong cup of tea with some of your fruit cake? I'll be as quick as I can."

Nodding her head and drying her eyes, Ellen made a conscious effort to pull herself together.

"Oh, Matthew it's so good of you to stay – and I hope Julie won't mind. Tell her I would appreciate it so much. I think I might sleep knowing you are here."

"Right, have that tea ready and then you're going to bed. In the meantime I have to believe Thomas is lying low somewhere, very safe indeed."

Matthew slept little that night, he thought of his father, probably lying drunk somewhere, oblivious to what was happening to his family and what Ellen had been through today. He must have been desperate, Matthew reckoned, to go back to alcohol after all this time. No doubt it was all to do with Lucie's marriage – he just hadn't been able to cope. He thought of Lucie and Patrick on honeymoon, unaware too of the day's trauma. But mostly he thought of Thomas, and worried and wondered if the CID were still searching the town and countryside for him.

Neither of the two C.I.D. men spoke until Detective Inspector Brown had driven clear of the housing estate. Then he turned to Alan Turner his detective.

"How did he manage it do you think?"

"Well, sir, when you sent me upstairs to check I didn't have to look far, the landing window is only a few steps up the stairs and it opens out like a door. He literally just had to step out of it. That must have been his intention when he left us in the lounge."

Detective Turner felt foolish, foolish not to have accompanied the suspect up the stairs – but then, his boss had not told him to do so.

"He can't have got far, sir – I thought we might do a house to house search."

"Thomas Hampton, you must remember, was a policeman himself. He would never be stupid enough to go to any of the neighbours. No, believe me, he is well away from our clutches."

"What are we going to do, sir? It looks bad, we had him right there and we let him go."

"Turner, we are going to do nothing," Inspector Brown added authoritatively. We have to say he wasn't at home and as far as we know he never was. Is that understood, Turner? Otherwise we look like total fools."

"That's good, sir." Turner heard a sigh of relief. "Will you be filing a report along those lines then, sir?"

"Of course I will. Wouldn't you think the Police in Kenya would have more to worry about? They must have known their chances of getting Thomas Hampton back were remote." Kenneth Brown could hardly believe Thomas Hampton was actually sitting at home when they arrived. After all the trouble and stress he must have suffered to get out of Kenya in the first place, he would have thought he would have been over the border long ago. He would love to know how he had managed to get out of Kenya at all. The fellow was resourceful, no doubt about that. And some part of Kenneth Brown's conscience was glad that they had returned to the barracks without him. Besides, he was the brother of Sergeant Matthew Hampton and he hadn't relished the idea of having to arrest his brother.

Chapter 49

Lucie had been to Patrick's apartment on several occasions before their marriage and although disappointed with the austere look of some of the rooms, she liked the large airy sitting room with its picture window and the dining area leading directly off it. There was an adequate kitchen, two spacious bedrooms and a quite functional bathroom with its walk in shower. The apartment was on the ground floor, so they were fortunate enough to have a small garden to the rear which caught the evening sun. Lucie was looking forward to a home with Patrick and she knew that by adding a few feminine touches of her own, the apartment would be much cosier. They were starting their married life together here, but they both had aspirations to buy their own home when they managed to save enough money.

Patrick inserted the key in the door, then turning to Lucie, lifted her bodily, at the same time thrusting the door open with his foot. He kissed her roughly and passionately and his arms tightened around her so much, her breath caught in her chest. But that was Patrick, impatient and passionate. During the first few nights of their honeymoon, Lucie had longed to tell him to take things slowly and calmly, but instinctively she felt he might see her words as criticism. Their love making, so far, always left her feeling disappointed and dissatisfied but no doubt they could sort it out. They had their whole lives together after all.

Struggling to disentangle herself from his grip she merely said, "We need to get the groceries in from the car, then I'll make dinner. We have a lovely long evening to look forward to." Slipping from his arms she proceeded to make her way back to the car to unload the provisions they had brought on their way back from their honeymoon. Patrick joined her and quickly carried meat pies, milk, bread, butter and potatoes and a bottle of gin to the kitchen.

"I'll put these away and make us dinner – there's the evening paper – you have a sit down and a read, Patrick, I can manage here." Lucie proceeded to turn the oven on and taking some potatoes from the basket, began to peel them at the sink.

"I'm more than happy to do as you say. I know nothing about cooking you know, that'll be your role, I think, darling." And smiling at his wife, Patrick lifted the paper and proceeded into the lounge. He returned a few minutes later with a couple of glasses and lifting the gin began to pour some out.

"I thought we should celebrate our home coming. Are you going to join me, darling?"

"Not just now, Patrick. I will later, when I have the meal ready and on the table. It won't be much of a meal tonight though – just pie and potatoes. But we will soon get ourselves more organised." Lucie placed the saucepan of potatoes on the plate and the pie in the oven. Just then the phone rang.

"You answer that, Patrick, my hands are wet. No doubt some of our family checking we're safely home"

"It'll be some of your ones." Patrick sounded disgruntled as he went to answer it. He just said a brief hello and then he handed the phone to Lucie. "It's for you. It's Matthew."

Lucie quickly dried her hands and went into the lounge and lifted the phone from where Patrick had set it on the table. She spoke to Matthew and then listened silently to what he was telling her. Quietly she replaced the receiver and turned to her husband.

"Pop's ill and Matthew would like me to come over and check him out. Mum's worried about him."

"We are only just home, for God's sake, Lucie, surely you don't intend to go straight out again?" Patrick sounded aggrieved.

"We'll have our dinner first, love, then I'll drive over." Lucie felt she had to placate her husband; he suddenly seemed in such foul form.

"I should think so indeed. What's wrong with him anyway?" Patrick hadn't much time for Rob Hampton, he knew the man hadn't looked favourably on him as Lucie's future husband and that suited him just fine, he had never warmed to the man.

"I don't know what's wrong – Matthew didn't say."

"I didn't mean to be so abrupt with Matthew, it's just, we are only just home." Patrick knew he had been short with Matthew and he shouldn't have been. They had to work together after all and it was important their relationship was a stable one.

Lucie and Patrick's apartment, being situated at the other end of Lisburn from her parents' house, meant Lucie had a twenty minute drive to get there. She parked her car and was about to put her key in the door when it was opened by Matthew. He hugged and kissed her warmly. "I'm glad you're here, Lucie."

Matthew went on to explain their father's disappearance and his return to alcohol.

"I rang different places – his old haunts – where I thought he was most likely to be. I traced him to Aughnacloy and went for him earlier today." He paused for a moment and then went on. "I had to leave his van. I had no one to come with me to bring it home."

"But where is Thomas? Could he not have gone with you?" Lucie was mystified. Thomas was always at home if he was not out helping his father – he never went anywhere.

"I'll explain about Thomas afterwards. First come upstairs and have a look at Pop, see what you think. Mum just made him some tea and took it up to him."

When Lucie entered her parents' bedroom and saw her father lying, so pale and shrivelled looking, she was shocked and alarmed. Her mother set the teacup on the bedside table as Lucie approached the bed. "I don't know why I bother making him anything. He has taken nothing since he came home."

After a thorough examination Lucie turned to her mother. "We have to get him into hospital. He is seriously dehydrated, has a chest infection and I suspect he has not eaten anything since he left home a few days ago. I'm glad you went for him when you did, Matthew."

Matthew nodded in agreement. "How do we arrange his admission, sis?"

"I'll have to go to the phone booth on the corner and arrange for an ambulance." Lucie was busy writing a note to the admissions officer as she spoke.

"Matthew, I'll go in the ambulance with him, you follow in your car, then I'll have a lift back with you." She turned to her mother.

"Don't worry, Mum, he'll be alright, but it is vital he is admitted straight away."

"Shame you have to go out and phone – I've been meaning to get Mum a phone for some time now." It was something Matthew had been meaning to do, but just kept putting it off.

"I'll give that priority tomorrow – Mum needs a phone if Pop's going to be in hospital for a time."

"When I come back from the phone booth – and while we're waiting for the ambulance – I want to know about Thomas." Since entering her parents' house and realising Thomas wasn't there, she had been worried about him. But she had had to put her worries to the back of her mind and concentrate on her father. Now her feelings of unease resurfaced when she thought of her brother and the traumatic time he had had in Kenya.

The ambulance arrived some twenty minutes later and during that time Lucie learned the reason for Thomas's disappearance. As simply as he could, Matthew related all that had happened.

"But I have made a few discreet enquiries, Lucie and certainly he has not been arrested. As to his whereabouts, we just don't know. We have no idea."

Later that night Lucie and Matthew remained at the hospital until Rob was examined by the house doctor and an intravenous infusion was erected through which antibiotics were being administered. When Matthew eventually led Lucie back to her car three hours had passed since she had left Patrick alone. Now, anxious to get back to him, she turned to Matthew,

"Explain to mum I needed to go home. I'll call tomorrow, but reassure her about Dad, won't you?"

"I'll tell her they have already started treatment." Matthew leaned in towards Lucie as he sat in the driver's seat. "I'm sure Thomas will be in touch with you, sis – sooner rather than later. It was you he rang the last time. He daren't ring me, I know that." Matthew lowered his voice.

"If and when he does contact you, Lucie, please be careful and tell Thomas to do the same." Matthew leaned over and kissed her on the cheek. "As I've said, I'm just glad you're back – it's been quite a strange couple of days."

The light was still lit in their lounge as Lucie pulled the car into the parking space outside their apartment. She was glad Patrick had waited up for her. After all, it was only ten-thirty. They could have a pleasant hour together before going to bed.

She entered the lounge smiling, in anticipation of Patrick's welcome, but the expression on his face when he turned towards her shocked her to the core and her breath caught in her throat.

"Is this how it's going to be then? Going back home to your mum and dad, every time they ring you?" His voice was dripping with sarcasm.

Lucie stood stock still – stunned into silence. This wasn't Patrick speaking, not her darling Patrick. Her eyes flew to the bottle of gin sitting on the table and she saw it was almost empty. He must have been drinking steadily since she left him. As calmly as she could – although she knew she was shaking all over, she answered, "You've been drinking all evening, Patrick. We will talk in the morning when you are sober." Turning on her heel to make her way out of the room, she added, "My Father is ill – I had to have him admitted into hospital – that's why I've been quite a while." And wearily, Lucie made her way upstairs and began undressing for bed. She wouldn't tell Patrick tonight about the underlying cause for her father's illness, she would tell him tomorrow when he was sober, more himself and perhaps more rational. As for telling him about Thomas, perhaps it would be best if she said nothing at all about his disappearance. She would prefer to wait and see if they had any news. She hated having secrets from Patrick and knew she shouldn't be doing it. But just at the moment, she felt sure it was all for the best.

Sometime later, Lucie heard Patrick stumble up the stairs to bed. Quickly she turned on her side and feigned sleep when he entered the room. She didn't want a quarrel erupting between them. She realized he was probably very disappointed they hadn't been together on their first evening home. She knew she should have been with him tonight, but what else could she have done when Matthew rang her? Thinking about it, perhaps she should have told Matthew to ring Rob's own doctor but she could never have done that. She only wanted to do her best for her father.

In the morning when Patrick was sober, she would apologise to him for her neglect. If she and Patrick had been spending the evening together, Patrick would not have drunk so much. It was unlike him, he had never shown much interest in alcohol in the time she had known him. It was simply because she hadn't been there. Lucie eventually fell asleep promising herself she would make sure Patrick and she spent most of their free time together.

Chapter 50

A couple of days passed before Patrick seemed to lose his sullenness and return to his former cheery self. During that time Lucie had apologised on a number of occasions and told him repeatedly how much she loved him. This morning when he came down to breakfast he hugged and kissed her as passionately as he had done when they were courting and Lucie heaved a huge sigh of relief. The storm was over, and she could go into her work with a much lighter heart, she hated to see Patrick so obviously unhappy. As they were parting to go to work – him to the police station and she to her surgery – he suggested they would go for a meal to the Garvey hotel that evening.

Delighted their differences had been forgotten about Lucie hugged and kissed him. "That would be lovely, Patrick – I'll be home around five-thirty and we'll have time to get ready and have a quiet drink together before we set off." And with a fond wave she made her way to her car, looking forward later to a quiet uneventful evening with her husband.

The surgery was particularly busy that morning, influenza and chest infections were prevalent but it was November and it had proven to be a damp and miserable one so far – the perfect breeding ground for germs.

She had had two significant phone calls to her private phone during the morning. The first one from Matthew with the good news that their father was responding well to his treatment. "Oh, Matthew, thanks for letting me know, I won't be able to visit him this evening, Patrick and I are going out for a meal."

"Well there's something more, Lucie," Matthew's voice sounded hesitant over the phone, "they want to transfer Pop to the alcoholics department in Holywell Hospital for a few days. See if they can prevent him from going on another binge."

"Oh, Matthew, what does Pop say to that?" Lucie was shocked; she certainly had not been expecting this.

"He doesn't want to go – in fact he says he isn't going to." Matthew went on, "Would you have a word both with him and with the ward sister?"

"I'll ring them, Matthew, but I can't do anything until tomorrow. I don't want to disappoint Patrick."

"Ok, Lucie, I'll ring the ward sister and tell her you'll be round tomorrow."

"Thanks, Matthew, I'll let you know how I get on."

Lucie's second phone call was from a call booth and when she heard money being inserted and then the dear, familiar voice of Thomas, all her anxieties of the last few days quickly dissipated.

"Oh, Thomas," was all she could say – she was so close to tears, "Oh, Thomas."

"Sis, I'm fine – just fine, sis." He sounded so cheery and optimistic. "I want you to let Mum know I'm staying with Albert – down in Drogheda and I've got a job working as a labourer in a building company."

"Thomas, is it safe for you down there?"

"Oh they can't touch me here. Tell Mum I'll write soon and tell her everything. How I got here and where I'm living – I'll bring you all up to date." Thomas hesitated then went on, "I'm sorry for all the worry and annoyance I've caused but it was the only way, Lucie. There was no way I was going to go back there."

"I know that, Thomas, we all do." Lucie could hear the pips going.

"I've no more money, but I'll write, very soon."

The phone went dead and Lucie replaced it slowly. Thank God Thomas was safe; he was out of harm's way. She would go to her mum during her lunch hour and tell her the good news.

As she drove to her mother's home, Lucie thought about the upheaval and annoyance of the last few days and was relieved that everything was beginning to settle down. Her mother was in the kitchen when Lucie let herself in; she was just pouring boiling water from the kettle into the teapot.

"Oh, Mum, this is good. I'm just in time." And Lucie reached into the cupboard for another cup and saucer, which she set down facing her mother's.

"Lucie I'm glad to see you, let me make you a ham sandwich."

Lucie thought her mother looked weary, but simply said, "Sit down a moment before you do anything, I've some good news for you."

Her mother brightened visibly and pulled her chair out and sat down opposite her daughter, an expectant look on her face. Quietly and calmly Lucie told her about the phone call she had had from Thomas adding, "He is safe and well, Mum."

Ellen just nodded dumbly for a second then broke into floods of tears.

"Oh my God, he's safe then, Lucie. You've no idea of the torment." Her mother's chest heaved and great gulping sobs punctuated what she was saying.

"I thought the worst you know. But they can't touch him now he's over the border, oh, Lucie."

Lucie held her mother tightly in her arms, until her sobbing ceased and she became her old composed self again.

"Imagine, silly me, crying at such good news, would you believe it?"

"It's the relief, Mum, you're crying with relief." And soon the two women were chatting and laughing together, trying to imagine Thomas labouring in the building industry, after years of working as a sales man. Then, while her mother sipped her tea Lucie made ham sandwiches for them both, which they ate in companionable silence. Lucie noticed her mother ate three of them quickly and suspected she had eaten very little over the last few days; preparing food was probably the last thing she had been thinking of. She did not raise the subject of Rob and Holywell Hospital, she knew her mother would be ignorant of the implications and the stigma attached to such a move. She would speak to Pop and the ward sister before she said anything.

Later that evening she was tempted to confide in Patrick over dinner, both about Thomas and her father. Patrick was still in the dark that Thomas was no longer at home, simply because, Lucie reminded herself, the subject had never come up. In the early days of their relationship she had told Patrick of her father's past history, but always stressing he had been dry for years. Now she realised Patrick would suspect straight away it was because of alcohol her father had been so ill that evening. So she said nothing, she was so anxious to have a romantic, perfect time with her husband. She did not want anything to spoil that.

The evening proved to be a relaxing, loving evening for them both and Lucie felt happy and invigorated by it. She believed she could deal with anything life might have in store for her, as long as she had Patrick's love and affection.

The next day when Lucie visited her father and spoke to the ward sister, it proved a harrowing experience for her. Her father was in such a distressed state when told what the consultant's plans were, that Lucie just wanted to pack his clothes and bring him home with her.

"Dad please try this, they will be able to help you – I know they will, they do have a good success record." Her father broke down in floods of tears.

"Lucie I just want to go home – home to Ellen." He was scarcely able to speak, he was in such a state. "Holywell's a mental hospital, that's what it is. People can be kept there for life."

Lucie was heartbroken as she watched him and putting her arms around him and holding him tightly she tried her best to reassure him, yet she knew she had to be honest with him too,

"Dad you won't be near the psychiatric unit but in the alcohol unit – and I promise you this, if you don't like it in a couple of days, I'll come straight for you." She held him tightly and his sobbing lessened as he clung to her.

"You could have died this time, Dad, if Matthew hadn't gone for you. You were in some state you know, and none of us want to lose you."

279

"Well, I'll try it for a couple of days, love. I'm only going because you want me to and you think it will help."

Lucie kissed her father lovingly. "Some of us will be up to visit you later this evening. We'll see then what it is really like. Now I'll tell sister that you have agreed to go and do take care, Dad."

"You too, love." Her father looked much cheerier as he said goodbye.

Lucie felt torn apart as she went in search of Sister to make arrangements for his transfer. She hoped she had done the right thing by persuading him to go, but the knowledge that he could have died simply because of alcohol appeased her doubts. Later that evening she told Patrick where her father had been transferred to. Although she knew Patrick had little time for him, she was stunned when, after listening to all she told him about her day, he remarked with contempt in his voice, "So he's gone into a psychiatric hospital, that's it in a nutshell – a mental asylum – that's where he is." His voice was dripping with scorn, "But then I always knew he was an unstable character – carrying on the way he did about us getting married in a registry office."

At first Lucie tried to reason with her husband that it was the alcoholics' department he was in but Patrick was having none of it. Rob Hampton was in a psychiatric unit, where he should have been before this. Probably Patrick was quite justified regarding his attitude to Rob. Lucie knew her father had been very dramatic and unreasonable around the time of their wedding but still, his words had been very hurtful and cruel. Wearily, Lucie left her husband sitting in the lounge and went to their bedroom in the knowledge that the wonderful time they had had might as well never have happened.

Three days later, after her afternoon surgery had ended Lucie drove to Holywell and brought her father back home to Ellen, who welcomed him with open arms and the utmost relief. The very next day Rob returned to an alcoholics anonymous meeting and was soon assigned a new buddy to help him fight his addiction.

Chapter 51

Rob missed Thomas terribly on his travels around the country. The two of them had established a good rapport and Rob knew that his son's quiet, serious manner had impressed the farmers. He had noticed recently they seemed intent on keeping the jute sacks exclusively for him and Thomas. He had been stunned when Ellen had told him when he came home from Holywell, about the visit by the C.I.D., Thomas's means of escape and then his subsequent contact with Lucie. At least he was safe and well, had managed to get a job and hopefully they would be able to visit him soon.

Now, thinking of that awful morning when the detectives called, he knew Ellen and Thomas must have been so traumatised by their visit – their shock and panic would have been dreadful. To think he had been lying somewhere comatose with drink, when his wife had needed him more than she had ever done. But obviously Thomas and she had kept their heads in the crisis and Thomas was now safely down South and Ellen seemed fairly well recovered from the trauma of it all, but it was no thanks to him. In fact he knew he had simply compounded her misery and worry. That was why he had gone to the A.A. meeting so promptly. He could not live with himself if he did not get back on the straight and narrow. And to add to his sense of shame and guilt he regretted his behaviour when Lucie had first announced her intention of marrying Patrick. He really ought to have gone along with it all – instead he had got himself in a right state, and could only think of drink as a way out of his misery.

Somehow Lucie and Patrick's marriage and his dislike of the man had paled into insignificance, beside the injustice that had been done to Thomas. Lucie would be alright, she loved the man, they both had excellent careers and no doubt their marriage would be a success.

Well, Christmas was coming in three weeks time, and surely Patrick and he could try and bridge the gap between them in the season of goodwill. He would talk to Ellen this very evening about having Lucie and him over for Christmas dinner and no doubt Matthew and Julie and young Jason would be there – they hadn't missed a Christmas yet. Unfortunately there was no way Thomas would be able to join them, but he would suggest to Ellen they should travel to Drogheda before Christmas to see him. Now that Thomas had written and sent his address, they would book into a hotel and spend some time with him.

"One thing I'm sure of – I don't intend sitting having Christmas dinner with your parents, I've already accepted my own parents' invitation."

"Well I didn't know that, Patrick, you didn't tell me that was where we would be going." Lucie's heart sank at the prospect of dinner with the Mullans and Patrick's two brothers. She knew only too well from the previous experiences at their house, the drink would be flowing and they would all end up plastered and having heated arguments with one another.

"Surely we can make some sort of a compromise about this – have dinner with your parents, then spend the evening with mine – that seems fair enough to me." Lucie was anxious to resolve this without any discord between them. "I would have to spend some part of the day with Mum and Dad. Dad's doing his best here to make amends for his past behaviour, even calling personally this evening to invite us."

"Well, that's as maybe, but he should have thought of that before our marriage."

"Please, Patrick, for both our sakes, try and forget about all that – any time Dad's name is mentioned we end up arguing."

"O.K. O.K. I'll try to do my best." Patrick put up his hands in mock surrender. "Tell them we'll call with them on Christmas night."

Secretly Patrick hoped that as Christmas evening wore on and they all had a few drinks they would not get round to calling with Rob Hampton, although he too, was getting tired of the disagreements between Lucie and himself. He was going to have to try and overcome some of his resentment for Lucie's family, best to go along with it in the meantime.

"You've been very quiet since we got back from Lucie's, love, what's on your mind?" Rob had made tea and biscuits on their return from their visit to Lucie and Patrick. Now he carried the tea into the lounge where Ellen sat obviously preoccupied with her thoughts.

"Nothing much, Rob. I just sensed Lucie seemed uneasy somehow – I don't know. Probably I imagined it. Besides they weren't expecting us."

"I thought I was doing the honourable, decent thing by calling to ask them personally, but we're as far on as ever. He certainly didn't commit himself, did he?"

"Oh, Rob. Certainly you did the right thing – but look if they come, they come. They must sort it out for themselves. It's not up to us to put any pressure on them." Ellen, always the peacemaker, didn't think a Christmas dinner invitation was a valid reason to widen the gulf which still seemed to exist between Rob and Patrick. She only wanted Lucie to be happy, that's all that mattered.

Lucie called two days later to see her mother. It was lunch time and she had brought sandwiches to share over a cup of tea. She explained Patrick was anxious this year to have dinner with his parents, but they would call on Christmas night, adding she hoped Rob would understand. Ellen hugged her daughter tightly.

"You must both do what suits you best. Rob won't mind, as long as he sees you sometime that day."

Lucie kissed her mother warmly.

"I knew you would understand. Now what about coming with me on Wednesday afternoon – that's my half day – and we'll get some Christmas shopping done." Lucie knew her mother just adored window-shopping, and most especially, around Christmas time.

"I'll certainly look forward to that, love."

"I'll pick you up around one-thirty and we'll go to Belfast. I have so much shopping to do and Christmas is only ten days away."

"I'll be ready and waiting, Lucie."

Lucie and her mother had a wonderful time together that afternoon. Belfast was so festive, with its magnificent tree and all its decorations taking pride of place in front of the city hall. The shops were so enticing with their array of merchandise, all displayed so attractively that the two women were initially at a loss as to what to buy anyone. Lucie finally settled on a fine woollen sweater for Patrick, an expensive shirt for Rob and pyjamas and dressing gown for Matthew's boy. Ellen purchased heavy socks and underwear for Rob, a shirt for Patrick to tone with Lucie's sweater. Biscuits and chocolates, Lucie thought, would be acceptable to Patrick's parents. They also bought a heavy knit sweater and warm socks for Thomas, which Ellen and Rob would take down to Drogheda that very weekend.

It was six o'clock by the time they were trudging back to the car and Lucie was thankful Ellen and she had gone for tea in one of the many cafes thronged with people. Patrick had told her he would eat in the canteen and not worry about rushing back for dinner. Ellen had left a shepherd's pie for Rob to heat for himself.

Lucie was relieved to see that Patrick had not arrived home before her. It meant she could have all the presents she had bought, wrapped and under the tree in the lounge. She loved Christmas and as a young girl she remembered her mother had always made great excitement of the whole atmosphere. She and her brothers had always enjoyed the anticipation of what they might get from Santa rather than the actual presents themselves. Now as she placed her carefully wrapped presents around the tree she felt a satisfaction in her purchases. Patrick especially would be sure to love his sweater, it was an expensive one and he did like good clothes.

She made hot chocolate for herself before retiring to bed early. There was no sign of Patrick, but he probably was having a couple of drinks in the local bar with his colleagues. She was wakened much later to the sound of her husband trailing himself up the stairs to bed. She lay as quiet as she could – he must have had a few drinks and she didn't want to do anything to upset him when he was like this. He plumped himself down on the bed and began taking his shoes off, but thwarted by his laces, he switched on the bedside light and Lucie noticed the time on the clock showing five forty-five. Where had Patrick been until this time? But she did not intend to ask any questions now. She would have to get up for work in an hour's time and if he was awake she would ask him then.

But when Lucie rose an hour later Patrick was snoring loudly and then she remembered he had a late shift today, he would be able to sleep to midday if he wanted to. It also meant he would not be home early this evening as his shift did not finish until nine-thirty p.m. She would see very little of Patrick for the next four days, as usually he did four late shifts in a row. But at least, they both had leave at Christmas and she was really looking forward to that – to spending some time together, instead of perfunctory exchanges as they both went to work.

Chapter 52

"Mum, we have had a lovely time, but we must get this young man home to bed." Matthew indicated his son, lying curled up, fast asleep on the sofa. "He has had a very exciting day. Your dinner was marvellous as always. You always excel yourself."

"I'm sorry we can't stay to see Lucie and Patrick." Julie was wrapping young Jason in his thick blue rug. "I would love to have waited for them – I haven't seen them since their wedding. Hopefully we'll catch up with them over the holidays."

Rob and Ellen both got to their feet to bid their son and daughter-in-law goodnight.

"It's gone nine o'clock, Matthew, I doubt if Lucie and Patrick will get here at all." Rob was bitterly disappointed. He had so wanted to spend an hour or so with his daughter. He enjoyed her company and was proud of her and what she had achieved. He was disappointed too, that his attempts to befriend Patrick Mullan had been so blatantly rejected, but he had to accept it and keep trying.

Christmas dinner at Patrick's parents' house was a rather grand affair. The dining room table had been set with Mrs Mullan's best glasses, cutlery and china and the house was tastefully adorned with berried holly and ivy picked from their own back garden. Mrs Mullan loved Christmas and this year she had been looking forward to it more than ever. Lucie would be coming – Patrick's new wife – and she wanted to create a good impression. She thought highly of her new daughter-in-law. She seemed a quiet, confident girl and clever too. She had been worried about him for quite some time – there had always seemed to be a restless energy about him and a real liking for a good time. Few girls had been able to resist Patrick's charms and obviously Lucie Hampton had succumbed to them too. But now they were married they seemed very settled and happy, and Patrick seemed to have left those days far behind him. The fact they had chosen to join her and her husband on their first Christmas had delighted Mrs Mullan.

Lucie had become reconciled to having Christmas dinner at the Mullans' place. She liked Patrick's parents a lot, his father was a quiet inoffensive man and his mother was rather sweet and effusive. When Lucie had rung to confirm that Patrick and she would be coming on Christmas Day, her mother-in-law had sounded so delighted Lucie was glad she had gone along with Patrick. Besides, she would be seeing her parents and Matthew and family later that evening. She would have to make sure Patrick didn't have too much to drink even though she knew it wouldn't be easy with his younger brothers there. They seemed quite hardened drinkers in spite of their youth. Lucie had made it clear to Mrs Mullan that she wished to call with her parents later. Mrs Mullan had told her she would be serving dinner around 4 p.m. and to come round at three in order to enjoy a couple of pre-dinner appetisers.

The Mullans' home was aglow with Christmas lights around the door and a huge holly wreath tied to the knocker. When they walked in Lucie noticed the hall had been converted into a bar with all sorts of drink and glasses assembled on the hall table. Mrs Mullan greeted them warmly.

"Come through to the lounge, Lucie. Patrick, you get drinks for Lucie and yourself." Gratefully Lucie sat down in the chair beside the glowing fire and greeted Patrick's father and brothers who raised their glasses jovially and wished her a Happy Christmas. Lucie could see for herself the two boys had already over indulged and felt the first stirrings of unease, even though Patrick was totally sober.

The meal of turkey and ham with Mrs Mullan's homemade stuffing was delectable and when the Christmas pudding appeared Lucie could only manage a token tablespoon but noticed the men – even after their huge dinner – still managed huge helpings of Mrs Mullan's pudding. After everyone had declared they could not eat another bite, the men returned to the sitting room and Lucie began to help her mother-in-law to clear the table and do the dishes.

"Now, you don't need to be standing here helping me, Lucie." Mrs Mullan glanced at the clock above the cooker. "It's gone seven o'clock. You really need to think about calling with your parents. You have three quarters of an hour's drive from here."

"I'm going to help you finish off here, but I'll speak to Patrick and tell him we'll go soon."

Patrick seemed at his most affable. "Make Mother and you a cup of tea while I finish this drink, love," indicating the glass in his hand.

"Just that one, Patrick, don't have any more please." Patrick's expression quickly changed and he glowered at her. "It is Christmas, loosen up a bit. We're alright, we have plenty of time."

Quietly Lucie closed the living room door and rejoined her mother-in-law – made some tea – contemplating as she drank it how best to appeal to Patrick to hurry up. Well she would give him plenty of time to finish his drink. She didn't want him thinking she couldn't wait to get away. So she waited twenty minutes before returning to the room where she had left him.

"Patrick, I think we really ought to go. Time is getting on."

Patrick either didn't hear her or chose not to, and instinctively her eyes went to the glass in his hand.

"Oh, Patrick, that's another drink you've started, you promised we'd go after your last one." Immediately her husband was on his feet and, in despair, Lucie realised he was now very drunk indeed.

"So, I'm having another drink – it is Christmas, you know."

"Patrick, that'll do – Lucie wants to call with her parents." Patrick's mother had come in to the room. "You get your coat, Lucie, while I make him some coffee."

"Look, I'm fine, Mother." Patrick seemed somewhat subdued at his mother's words. "I'll knock this back." And with that he raised his glass and quickly drained it.

"Right, Lucie, let's go." And he began to make his way unsteadily towards the door. Quietly Lucie thanked her mother and father-in-law for a lovely day, then followed Patrick, who was now out on the footpath making his way to the car. In silence Lucie unlocked the door, got in the driver's seat and switched the ignition on.

"Right, Rob Hampton here we come to celebrate Christmas with you." His voice was dripping with sarcasm.

"No, Patrick, we'll just go straight home. It's much too late, we'll leave it and call tomorrow." There was no way Lucie was going to go to her parents with her husband so drunk and in such foul form. She knew she would be simply asking for trouble.

"Well, don't blame me for not getting to visit them, I'm willing to go."

Lucie did not answer, but drove on in silence until they reached their apartment. As soon as they entered their living room Patrick grabbed her roughly and swinging her round, shouted into her face, "Don't ever say it was because of me you didn't get to your Mum and Dad's, I'm willing to go."

"Actually, Patrick I don't think it's a good idea."

Lucie strove to keep calm, although the pressure of his hands on her arms was hurting her. "It's just, you've had a bit much to drink tonight."

"Oh so that's it – ashamed of me, are you? Your own father is an alcoholic you know, and you're ashamed of me. Indeed." And with that he hit Lucie a stinging blow across her face. The force of the blow made her stagger against the wall and she felt her shoulders impacting with it as she hit it. She let out a cry of pain and the next thing she felt Patrick's arms around her and he was sobbing into her sweater.

"Oh, darling, I'm so sorry – I don't know what came over me – I really don't." He hugged her tightly. "I love you so much."

"There, there, Patrick, it's alright. It's alright." Lucie was so relieved at her husband's change of heart and touched by his remorse, she was only too anxious to forget the incident. Hopefully by morning there would be no sign of any injury.

Now she hugged Patrick back. "Let's just go to bed, love, and try to forget this ever happened, but one thing's for sure, you must promise never ever to raise your hand to me again."

"Oh, darling, of course I won't," and Patrick kissed her passionately.

Chapter 53

1960

Two years had passed since Thomas had left Kenya so quickly and so daringly, to try to make it back home without being arrested somewhere along the way. Many times since, Charles had thanked God his brother had made it safely back, it was more than either of them had dared hope for. But perhaps the very audacity of the plan had ensured its success. When Charles thought of the whole day spent practicing stamping "British Colonial services" with the slightly moist potato on to waste paper before he perfected it and then stamped the false passport, he had to congratulate himself on his patience. No doubt his necessity for meticulousness when drawing ordnance survey maps had stood him in good stead that day. Then it was just a matter of driving into Moshi then on to the airport.

After that he had heard nothing more for three whole months, but that had been the agreement between them, they both knew Thomas could not do anything which might alert the authorities. Then the letter had arrived from the South of Ireland and Charles was shocked to learn that the C.I.D. had so determinedly tracked Thomas down but he had eluded them and gone to live and work in Drogheda. Now it looked as if he would soon be able to return to the North. The manager in the car showroom, at his trial two months previously, had accepted full responsibility for the fraud. Nigel Pollard had only been given a suspended sentence because he had pleaded guilty and on condition the money was paid back to the credit companies. Thomas Hampton had been exonerated from any involvement.

Charles had followed the court case with interest and when it was over was convinced there was a total lack of interest in the courts with any of these cases. An utter apathy seemed to be creeping into several aspects of the British government, which was hardly surprising considering they were withdrawing from Kenya and the country was to be decolonised.

So Charles too, was going home, back to his family and his own country after five interesting years and at times highly dangerous work. He would be leaving his apartment, his jeep, his faithful servants, but saddest of all he was leaving his beloved dog, Rover, behind.

His faithful, loving companion, through day and night, had never left his side and in his loneliest moments out there in Mount Kenya it was Rover who had kept him sane. His grief at their parting was lessened by the knowledge that Greg, his comrade in the office where they met to discuss their work every month, had promised to give Rover a home and Rover had always taken well to Greg. Greg intended to stay in Kenya as a lot of settlers had decided to do, with the hope that the country would settle down under Yuma Kenyatta's rule, but that still remained to be seen. Charles had no intention of remaining here, he already had his flight booked and in three weeks time he would be home.

Lucie was delighted when her mother told her Charles would soon be home. She had missed her brother dreadfully in the years he had been away. They had been so close as children and through their school years she had found Charles' calm, efficient way of dealing with homeworks and study a source of inspiration for her. And she prayed they would quickly regain that shared empathy they had had, for during the last year of her marriage Lucie had desperately needed someone to confide in. She could not confide in her parents, they worried about her enough already, she could see it in their eyes and their caring manner towards her. Matthew she knew, she would put in an awkward situation if she told him anything about Patrick. After all they worked together and she would never want anything she might say to influence Matthew's decision making in his working environment.

It was Sheila Morrow she had gone to on a few occasions after Patrick had returned home drunk and was violent towards her. She knew she could not stay in their apartment to endure his endless verbal and physical abuse, and Sheila had always been such a good friend to her, she had driven to her home on many occasions since her marriage. When Sheila had seen the distraught state Lucie had been in she had been so kind and understanding, as had her parents. They insisted she stay the night with them, after they had bathed the cut on her cheek and made sure she had painkillers and hot tea before going to bed. But always the next morning when she arrived in the practice car park Patrick would be there, begging her forgiveness and telling her how much he loved her and always, because she loved him, she returned to their apartment. The truth was, she didn't know what else to do, she wanted to save her marriage at all costs, but Patrick's episodes of drunkenness and violence were becoming more alarming and her excuses to her parents and colleagues for her bruises were beginning to wear thin. Yet she always felt her happiness with Patrick was just within her grasp, if only she knew how to behave when he was drunk, so that she might not provoke him. She was confident that Charles with his wisdom and patience would be able to advise her about her dilemma, that is, if she herself could pick up the courage to tell him.

It was a late Friday evening four weeks after Charles' return from Kenya when he answered his parents' phone in the hall, his parents had just gone to bed. "May I speak to Mr Charles Hampton please?" a polite but quite officious voice enquired.

"Yes, speaking." He was momentarily mystified, so few people knew he was back home, then the voice continued and his heart constricted in his chest as he listened. "It is Staff Nurse Greer from accident and emergency here in Lagan Valley Hospital. Your sister has asked me to contact you."

"Lucie, my goodness, is she alright? What has happened?"

"She is fine, Mr Hampton. She had a slight accident and would like to talk to you." Nurse Greer had dropped her officious tone and now she sounded warm and friendly. "Shall I say you will be along shortly?"

"Yes of course, give me fifteen minutes. Can you tell me what happened?"

"We can't give out information over the phone, but your sister is well and we will give you the details later." And with that Nurse Greer said goodbye and replaced the receiver.

As Charles gathered up his coat and retrieved his father's car keys from their hook in the kitchen his mind was racing. What on earth had happened to Lucie? Had she had a car accident? And where was Patrick? Why did Lucie want him there and why not her husband? Perhaps he was already there. He felt very uneasy as he let himself out of the house but he was thankful his parents had not been disturbed by the phone call, obviously they were both fast asleep.

When Charles entered the Accident and Emergency Unit, the nurse indicated the cubicle where Lucie was. When he pulled back the curtain to enter the room, he was shocked at his sister's appearance. Her left cheek was swollen grotesquely and her left arm was in plaster and a sling. As he approached her bed, he was struck by her frailty and some overwhelming sadness about her. Just as he was about to speak she looked at him lovingly and then burst into tears, great gulping sobs which shook her whole body. He gathered her into his arms and she clung to him with her free right arm, whispering between her sobs, "It's Patrick, it's Patrick."

And the implications of those words made Charles blood run cold and he clung to her even more desperately.

Chapter 54

"Lucie can't possibly go back there – Mum, Dad." Charles had returned from hospital in the early hours of the morning, after taking Lucie to the Royal Victoria Hospital. When the consultant had come to look at her X-rays, he had informed her she needed an anaesthetic because the bones in her wrist needed to be reduced. As there was no anaesthetist in the Valley Hospital, she must be transferred to the Royal for surgery in the morning.

On returning to his parents' home, Charles discovered that his mother had heard the car leave and she had been waiting and worrying as to what was wrong. Now, both his parents listened intently as Charles told them what had been really been going on in Lucie's marriage since shortly after their return from their honeymoon.

White faced and shocked to the core, Ellen's voice was a mere whisper. "But they are only married a year, Charles, just a year. How could any husband beat his wife and why?"

Charles looked over at his father, who seemed to be shocked into total silence, simply shaking his head as he held tightly to Ellen's hand.

"Lucie has this bizarre notion that she keeps saying the wrong thing or doing the wrong thing. She feels if she could only put that right, everything would be fine and they could be happy again. But to my mind that's utter nonsense of course. He's simply a thug and a man who likes to batter his wife into submission."

"What will she do? What can we do to help her?"

"Somehow, Mum, we have to find her a place to stay where Patrick Mullan can't find her, to tell her how sorry he is one more time, simply get her back home and do the same thing all over again. That seems to have been the pattern, pretty much anyway, in their marriage. But..." Charles stressed,

"...she can't come here, it will be the first place he will think of."

"Let's take first things first. We need to go and see Lucie. See what she wants to do." Rob's voice was slow and ponderous, he was trying to come to terms with what all this might mean for Lucie. Was she terrified? Did she still love this man? Did she want her marriage to survive, even with the ever constant threat of violence in it?

"What does she intend to tell her partner in the practice how she sustained her injury? By the sound of it she won't be in a fit state to work for a day or two, so he'll have to be told something. What did she tell the hospital, do you know that, Charles?"

"She told them she tripped on a rug in her lounge, whether they believe her or not is another story, because she rang for a taxi and made her own way to the hospital. The staff must think it very odd. They know she is married, but where is her husband in all of this?"

"Look, Ellen, let's get some sleep." Rob had just noticed that Ellen might faint at any moment. He put his arms round her shoulders. "It's four o'clock in the morning. We can catch a few hours, then go to the hospital and see Lucie."

"Good idea, I'm whacked." Charles made his way upstairs. "See you later – we'll sort something out, Mum, so please don't worry."

Lucie wakened from her anaesthetic as the nurses were transferring her from the trolley to her bed and for several minutes she was confused as to what was happening. Then the reassuring words of the Anaesthetist and Consultant in theatre came back to her. She looked down at her arm and the memory of the last few hours came flooding back to her. Patrick's initial verbal abuse of her, the physical violence, then her phone call for a taxi when she realised that this time she had at least one broken limb. This injury, she feared, might illustrate to everyone how unhappily married she was.

What had she said or done to annoy Patrick on this occasion? She had no idea – if she said something, it was sure to be the wrong thing. If she said nothing, that seemed to provoke him even more. This time there had been no signs of remorse from him. Instead, he had stumbled out of the house and gone to God knows where and she had not seen him since.

She had been so thankful it had been Charles' familiar figure that had entered the cubicle she was in – not her husband's. And that profound sense of relief had released all the terrible pent up emotions of the last few months and she had wept openly, telling him everything between her sobs.

Now she realised the staff had moved her bed into a private ward, probably because they were aware she was a doctor. Well, she was glad to have privacy and could look forward to Charles' return visit. He had promised her he would come back later that day and bring their parents with him.

"I've brought some tea and toast for you, Mrs Mullan." At the sound of the nurse's voice Lucie opened her eyes realizing she must have dozed off again. After her fast, she was very hungry, and the toast smelt delicious.

"After you've had this I've been instructed to take you for an X-ray just to make sure the bones are set properly, before we let you go home."

Lucie nodded in response as she ate her toast, but all the time thinking, "Home... where was home?" Home was with Patrick but even the prospect of seeing him was too fearful at the moment and Charles was adamant that she could not go back near him. As for Patrick – he probably thought she had gone to stay with some of her friends, unaware she had a broken arm and had ended up in hospital. No doubt he would be waiting in the G.P. car park as he always did after any of their rows, but he would be disappointed this morning when she did not appear.

She was relieved when the Radiologist informed her that the bone alignment was very good, at least she had been spared any complications there. Her life however was much more complex and was not going to be so easy to sort out. Preoccupied by these thoughts, she did not see the man approaching from the opposite end of the corridor as the nurse wheeled her back to her ward. Only when he stopped in front of her and took her hand did realization dawn. "Lucie, what has happened to you?"

The rich mellow voice was unmistakable. "Paul – what are you doing here?" Lucie took in the white coat and the stethoscope at a glance; obviously he was working here in the R.V.H.

"I took up my new post in Neurology last week and I was just on my way to X-ray but..." Paul Greenlees studied Lucie as he spoke. He thought her greatly changed – she seemed so subdued and fearful almost. Not at all the serene, confident Lucie he had known. A mix of emotions swept over him, feelings of love and loss for this girl he had worshipped, but had made no attempt to fight for. He had simply let her go. Now here she was facing him as he had always dreamt and longed for so much in the last two years. But she was married now of course and out of his reach.

"What happened to you, Lucie? Did you have a fall?"

"I tripped on a mat – at home, Paul." Her voice was so low he could scarcely hear her and had to bend close to her. He looked over at the staff nurse accompanying her, and something about her stance, her expression, suggested disbelief at Lucie's statement and a terrible suspicion presented itself to him. Was this a domestic incident? He prayed that was not so. He could not bear to think of such a horrible situation. Quickly he changed the subject.

"Are you getting home today, Lucie? Is your plaster satisfactory?"

Lucie nodded and smiled at him, relieved that the awkward moment had past.

"Yes to both questions, Paul."

"Tell your dad I intend to visit him soon, now I'm back in Belfast. I owe him a game of draughts."

"Of course, Paul, I'll probably see you around at their house soon."

The staff nurse, taking her cue from Lucie's words, began their journey along the corridor and towards the ward, after they had said a hurried goodbye to one another. As they entered the room they had left a short time before, it struck

Lucie forcibly that Paul had suspected she was lying. And somehow the thought of such a valued friend knowing that, made her humiliation over her disastrous marriage complete.

Chapter 55

Paul stopped the car at the beginning of the avenue that led to Lucie Hampton's old home. Some impulse had brought him here this evening, some urgent need to visit the Hamptons to talk to them and renew their acquaintance. He had tried to tell himself Lucie's welfare was none of his business and if he called with any of them they might just accuse him of being nosy and interfering. His surgery had finished early today and since four o'clock he had grappled with his emotions, trying to dissuade himself from doing anything. But the urge to at least talk to someone was overwhelming, and here he was, and he would pay the visit he so longed to do and trust he would be made as welcome as he had always been.

"Oh, Paul, my goodness, you're a stranger." It was Charles who opened the door to him. "Please come in, Mum and Dad will be so pleased to see you." And with that Charles stepped back to allow Paul to enter the hallway.

"I've just returned to Northern Ireland recently and I thought I'd call and say hello to Mr and Mrs Hampton." Paul turned to Charles as he spoke. "I certainly wasn't expecting to see you – I thought you were still in Kenya."

"I'm home a couple of months now. Mum, Dad... here's a visitor." And he ushered Paul through to the living room.

Mr and Mrs Hampton sat side by side on the couch at the window but of Lucie there was no sign. Why had he thought she might be here? She would be home with her husband of course. He had let his imagination run riot. No doubt she had had a simple accident and that was all that had happened to her.

"Oh, Paul, it's so good to see you." Rob Hampton shook his hand heartily and as Ellen approached him the air of sombreness he had noticed seemed to lift and she too came forward and welcomed him with a kiss.

"Please sit down, Paul, we are so glad to see you – would you like a drink? Perhaps tea or coffee?"

"Coffee would be lovely, Mrs Hampton."

"I'll get some for us all, Mum. Give you a chance to catch up on everything with each other."

While they waited for Charles to return with the coffee, conversation flowed easily between them. Paul told them about his new post in the R.V.H. and Rob brought him up to date about Thomas and his work in the South and that now Charles was home from Kenya he intended to ask him to think about joining him in the jute business. Lucie's name was not mentioned by either of them and he was just about to enquire about her when Charles reappeared with the tray laden with sandwiches and coffee which he sat on a table at the window.

Everyone was silent as they enjoyed the hot fresh coffee and delicious cheese and ham sandwiches, then Paul, needing to know now more than ever, ventured to say, "I met Lucie in the X-ray corridor coming from having a Colles fracture confirmed I think. Did she say I might be calling with you?"

"No she didn't, Paul, but she was just discharged yesterday you know," Charles countered. "She has a lot on her mind at the moment, she must have forgotten." This remark of Charles was followed by an uncomfortable silence and Paul felt his uneasiness about Lucie's welfare return.

"Well, six weeks should see her fracture well healed." He addressed the words as reassuringly as he could to Ellen, who was sitting still and silent in her chair.

"She should be fine." He was anxious to dispel the awkwardness which seemed suddenly to pervade the room.

"I see she told you the same story as she told the staff on the ward, Paul." Charles had made the decision to confide in this man; he was after all, of the medical world and would keep their confidentiality. "That she tripped and fell. Well it wasn't quite like that, Paul, our Lucie is the victim of repeated domestic violence, I'm afraid."

Paul looked round bleakly at each of Lucie's family. He was numb with shock and shaken to the core; to hear the truth told so starkly and forcefully was heart wrenching. It was true, he had suspected it but hoped against hope it wasn't true. Now he knew this awful truth he had been told accounted for the look of apathy and despair he had seen in Lucie two days before. Gathering his wits, Paul asked, "But where is Lucie now? She hasn't gone home surely? Has she?"

"Oh no, no, Paul, she's with a friend at present. You probably remember her – Sheila Morrow. I went to see Sheila and arranged for Lucie to go there. I brought her there myself yesterday afternoon. She has had to stay with Sheila before, you know. In fact I gather she has stayed quite a few times. This violence wasn't new, Paul, but this seems to have been the most serious."

"Has her husband been in touch with anyone?"

"Not to our knowledge, he usually waits for her coming in to work and begs for forgiveness."

Paul could think of no suitable reply to this, he knew Lucie had a very forgiving nature – she would be prepared to overlook a lot.

Impulsively he went over to Ellen Hampton and putting his arms around her, pulled her close. "I'm so sorry for your worry, Mrs Hampton. I'm sure Lucie will be able to sort this all out. I'll go now, but I'll call again soon, and I'll bring Father with me next time." He addressed this last remark to Rob.

"Good idea, Paul, we do try to catch up with each other from time to time, but it's been a few weeks now."

"Perhaps, Paul, you would consider coming with me when I go to see Lucie," Charles remarked.

"Of course, Charles, but only if Lucie is agreeable to me coming, and," he added, "that she knows I know that truth."

"I don't think she'll have any objections, Paul – she'll be glad to see you – after all, you and she were very close friends."

Paul had to agree they had been close but he wasn't as convinced as Charles appeared to be that she would be happy for him to know her marriage was in trouble. Lucie's dignity and self-respect would always be important to her and they were at stake here. He would never ever want to deprive her of either. And if her pride stood in the way of them meeting again, difficult though it would be, he would have to respect it.

A deep sense of fear woke Lucie, she had been dreaming again. She was running, and then she was falling, falling into space, a huge bottomless pit. A scream rose in her throat, which she attempted to squash and instead a low pitched groan escaped. A door opened somewhere over from her, then a light was switched on and a voice spoke. "Lucie, you're alright. You're safe here."

Disorientated, Lucie slowly realised the voice was that of Sheila and she was not at home, not with Patrick. Slowly and gratefully her fear eased and her heartbeat returned to something approaching normal. She held Sheila's hand tightly.

"I know, Sheila, I know I'm safe here – Patrick doesn't know about our friendship and I'm so grateful for that and for you and all you have done."

"Shush, shush, Lucie, lie over a little and I'll lie beside you, keep you company for a bit, you're still hurting I know." And with that Sheila climbed in beside her friend, adding as she did, "And we've something to look forward to tomorrow. Charles said he would call to see us."

And as the two women faded into sleep, Sheila found she was really looking forward to seeing Charles Hampton again. He was so attractive, with those vivid blue eyes and his quiet dignified manner. Those were Sheila's last thoughts as she went into a deep sleep, snuggled down beside her best friend.

Chapter 56

"Lucie I called with your partner – Dr Sands – this morning, just to bring him up to date with what's happening. He has managed to arrange a locum to come during your absence. He stresses you mustn't worry, your job will be there for you when you feel up to returning."

"Charles, thank you once again. And thank you for telling him about my circumstances, in the first place. I just didn't feel up to it and I must admit I was worried how he might react, but he has been most understanding. I'm so relieved to know he's got a locum – that will ease things considerably for him." Lucie had been concerned as to how her partner might view this latest injury of hers, and how he viewed her private life. The fact he had got a locum so quickly indicated to her he was happy to have someone in on a temporary basis only. Her job seemed safe enough.

"He did tell me Patrick called with him demanding to know where you were and why you weren't at work." Charles had decided to call at Lucie's practice again in order to keep Dr Sands informed about her welfare. He was shocked to hear Patrick had been there looking for her. Did the man really think his wife had just taken off in a taxi to spend the night where she usually did – and expecting her to be at her work the next day.

"Oh no, Charles, he didn't call and annoy anyone did he?" A sense of disgrace swept over Lucie and her eyes filled up with tears. Sheila, who had been listening quietly to brother and sister, went over to her and held her tightly.

"It's quite natural. I suppose, he should be looking for you and," turning to Charles, "I think some of the family, should let him know the extent of Lucie's injuries and that she won't be at work for a few weeks. Then he won't be calling in the practice to see if she's there."

"You're right, Sheila – I think Matthew thought to do that – but he mustn't have got around to it. I'll remind him again. Lucie you did mention getting some of your clothes from your apartment – but we don't want you going there – not at the moment."

"I know," Lucie nodded dumbly, "but I can't stay here with Sheila for long. Her parents are due back from their holiday in three days time – I don't know what to do – where to go."

"As it happens, Lucie, Paul Greenlees called the other evening. I told him what actually happened, he had guessed anyway. He would like to come and see you – as an old valued friend – he says his parents have a cottage at Helen's Bay which you could stay in while you recuperate and think about your future."

"Oh, poor Paul, I feel so bad about him. Telling him downright lies about what happened to me. I'm surprised he still wants anything to do with me. It is really kind of him to offer somewhere for me to stay – and I'd love to go to Helen's Bay. But I couldn't go there alone, Charles, I can't drive – I can hardly dress myself – so how could I cope?" Lucie was near to tears.

Sheila intervened in the conversation. "For some time now Mum and Dad have been anxious for me to take a holiday – away from the farm. When they come back, the two of us can pack our bags and go off for a break. How would that do, Charles? That is, if Paul has no objections to me being there too."

"I'm sure Paul will be more than happy with that arrangement." Charles was quick to reassure Sheila and he himself thought it a wonderful idea.

And so it was settled, Matthew informed Patrick Mullan exactly how Lucie was and that she would not be returning to work for six weeks. On no account was he to try and find out where she was, as Matthew would quickly get a restraining order on him.

At a time when Charles knew Patrick was at work, he took Sheila to Lucie's apartment where she packed a suitcase with some of Lucie's clothes. The following day Paul called to confirm the cottage was theirs as long as they wished. He would travel down to show them where they would be staying, where the switches for heating and gas were, the nearest shopping centre and anything else which might spring to mind.

Lucie loved Helen's Bay – she had been there once before as a child with Auntie Dorrie and Uncle John and her cousins. John and Dorrie had told her about their romance and how Helen's Bay had been their favourite spot. As a child she had not understood the significance of the beauty of the bay and the azure blue sea and its effect on a young couple in love. But now as an adult she could see its impact so clearly and she thought of Patrick and their uncertain future. And she knew that sometime soon she must make a decision about her marriage. But not here, not now, where everything seemed so calm and peaceful and where Sheila and she were enjoying the solitude. Never mind the beautiful June sunshine which soothed her body and mind so that she slept soundly at night, untroubled by any unhappy thoughts. On the occasions Charles drove down to see them both, sometimes Lucie accompanied Sheila and her brother on their outings in the car and on other times, sensing how things were developing between Sheila and Charles she pleaded tiredness and the desire to rest that afternoon. She was so happy to see how her dear brother and her best friend were when they were together. It gave her great consolation to think that her plight had brought them together. Her mother always said every cloud had a silver lining.

Paul Greenlees had proven himself to be as good a friend to her as he had always been. On the few occasions he drove down to the cottage his quiet support and lack of condemnation of her plight was just what she needed and she found herself looking forward to him coming. She always felt comforted and more able to face the future after his visits.

Sheila and Lucie had been at the cottage in Helen's Bay for almost four weeks when Lucie's parents drove down one

Saturday afternoon to see their daughter but with sad news that Ellen's mother had been found dead in her kitchen by Sarah that morning. She had been living alone since Jack had died from kidney failure six months before. Lucie hugged her mother tightly, deeply saddened at the news and keenly aware that although her mother and grandmother had not always seen eye to eye, they had become so much closer in the later years. Lucie realised this was no doubt due to her grandmother's acceptance of Ellen's love for Rob, no matter what and also the fact that the old lady herself had mellowed over the years.

"Mum and Dad, I do want to come home for Grandma's funeral, so if it suits, Charles could collect Sheila and I tomorrow. I'm sure Sheila would like a couple of days with her parents and that would suit everybody, don't you think?"

Sheila had gone into the kitchen to make tea and butter the scones she had made earlier that morning and was just coming into the living room with the tray as Lucie was speaking to her parents.

"Did I hear my name mentioned just now?" She smiled at Lucie as she spoke. Lucie quickly explained that she wished to go to Granny's funeral on Monday and did Sheila wish to visit her parents?

"I could do that, if Charles is able to collect us tomorrow and also let Paul know no one will be here for a couple of days."

"Also, Mum..." Lucie addressed her mother very hesitantly and in a soft voice, "I want Matthew to let Patrick know of Grandmother's death – he is family after all."

Rob sat quietly regarding his daughter, the plaster of Paris still on her arm, a constant reminder of what had happened.

It was Ellen who spoke in her quiet, reassuring voice. "Yes of course, Lucie, if that is what you want, I'll see Patrick is informed."

"Lucie, are you prepared for the fact that Patrick may attend the funeral? If so, are you up to meeting him?" Sheila paused in the act of buttering another scone, and regarded Lucie with an anxious look.

"Yes, Sheila, I'm aware of that, but I will be alright. I'll have family around me for support. Actually it may be better if I meet him in these circumstances than having to meet up with him alone." Lucie sighed deeply then resolutely added, "I do know I have to meet him sooner or later you know, that's how it is for me. We can't drift on like this."

And for Rob and Ellen listening to their daughter their hearts were filled with dread. Was Lucie actually contemplating returning to her husband? They sincerely hoped not, but the signs from Lucie were not good and they knew they were powerless to do anything about it.

Chapter 57

1964

Sheila and Lucie made their way excitedly through the main car park, heading towards the shopping centre and to Cleaver's coffee shop. It was only nine-thirty on a beautiful Saturday morning in April but they had a lot of shopping to do. First, they were meeting Thomas's fiancée Jenny and her sister Joan for refreshments before planning the most important details of Sheila and Charles and Thomas and Jenny's double wedding.

When Sheila and Charles first announced their engagement, they were so caught up in the joy of the event, that their actual wedding date had been vaguely thought about but nothing concrete discussed. But when Thomas and Jenny had announced their intention to get married the idea of a double wedding had just seemed to evolve naturally, especially now that Thomas had established a successful, modest building business in the North, and was back living at home with Charles and his parents.

The beautiful traditional church in Garvey had been booked for September 20th and both Sheila's minister and Jenny's minister would be in attendance. Garvey hotel had been reserved and the guest list was currently in the hands of the brides' parents. Today the prospective brides and their bridesmaids were getting down to the business of shopping for wedding outfits. Today was theirs and they intended to make the most of their time together.

Jenny and Joan were already seated at a table in a corner of Cleavers when Sheila and Lucie arrived, and they waved excitedly to them, indicating the empty seats beside them. When Lucie looked at the two girls they were going shopping with, she felt they had a mammoth task on their hands, shopping for dresses which would have to ultimately suit all four of them. Where Sheila and she were dark haired with olive complexions, Jenny's hair was a deep auburn colour, she had a peaches and cream complexion and deep brown eyes, whereas Joan's hair was a bright carrot colour and she had pale porcelain skin and vivid blue eyes. Yes, Lucie thought, as she approached their table, even though Sheila and Jenny just had to choose something white, it would be a test of endurance to get a style and colour which would suit herself and Joan. But they had the most of the day, no one was expecting them back anytime soon, and she had stressed to Patrick in particular that it might be tea time before she was home.

"We've just ordered coffee and scones for four," Jenny was in very bubbly form, "then while we're having it we'll plan our route – probably start with the bridal department upstairs here." She turned to Sheila. "What do you think, Sheila?"

"Good idea – by the way, the men are supposed to be coming into town this morning too, to be measured up for their suits. I personally don't want to bump into them, as I think we would get nothing done if we did."

"Well, as soon as we get our coffee we'll make a move," Lucie responded.

"Lucie, just thinking of the men reminds me that I've been wondering – I meant to mention it before, but we have all been so busy – how Patrick feels about not being best man. Charles and I hope he's not too disappointed but Charles and Paul have become so close in the last couple of years, Charles wanted to have him." Secretly Sheila knew that under no circumstances did either she or Charles want Patrick Mullan as best man. In fact, even having to have him as a guest was more than they wished for, but Lucie had chosen to return to him and try to mend her marriage. If she could do that, they were duty bound to welcome him as one of the family.

"Patrick's fine about everything, Sheila, why shouldn't he be? After all, Julie isn't a bridesmaid even though Matthew is Thomas's best man."

Lucie thought back to the last few days when she had discussed the wedding with Patrick – who the attendants would be and what the seating arrangements were. She knew it was important he would feel included. Sometime during their conversation she thought she witnessed a brief flare of annoyance in Patrick but then he turned, smiled and assured her everything sounded just fine.

Lucie was very aware how her family had felt towards Patrick when she had made her decision to return to him. She would never forget the look on Charles and Sheila's faces when she had told them, in Helen's Bay, of her intention to try to mend her marriage. She knew she had shocked everyone by her decision, but thankfully not one of them had tried to talk her round to changing her mind.

The Saturday that Lucie told Sheila and Charles of her intention to return home, had shown promise of being a bright clear day and Sheila and she were having a leisurely breakfast when Charles arrived accompanied by Paul. At the sight of Paul, striding purposely to the front door, his hair glinting blond in the sunshine, it came to Lucie how much this man had come to mean to her in the last few weeks and knew without a doubt that he felt the same about her. But now the knowledge of their love only saddened her, because she knew she could never wish to involve this lovely man in her sordid affairs. Bad enough that her reputation would be in tatters, but the thought that Paul's standing in the medical profession would be threatened was more than she could bear. Instead she must turn her back on her only chance of happiness and return to her husband. She knew now she never should have married Patrick. It had been nothing; only some animal magnetism and sexual attraction which had brought them together, an attraction which had quickly burned itself out.

She had returned to their apartment and her marriage – even though her feelings for her husband were dead. But she had returned with a different attitude. Her fear for him had gone, to be replaced by a determination to stand up to him. Since her stay in hospital she had carried a sad secret in her heart and had spoken to no one about it, but on her return to Patrick she had told him. Told him that on the same evening she had acquired her broken arm she had suffered a miscarriage. She had been eight weeks pregnant when Patrick had been violent towards her. On her return to the marital home she made it clear if he ever touched her again, she would tell his parents about their lost grandchild and who, without a doubt, was to blame for their loss.

"Right, Lucie are you with us at all? You seem miles away." Jenny's voice brought Lucie back to the present.

"Oh sorry, girls – I was just wondering what colour of dresses Joan and I will wear – we're such different colouring, it's going to be quite a challenge, I think."

"Well let's get this bill paid and make a start at looking for outfits which will dazzle everyone on the day." With that Jenny signalled to the waitress and then ignoring everyone's protests, paid for them all and gave the young waitress a healthy tip.

Three hours later the four women were back in the restaurant for lunch. They were exhausted but jubilant shoppers – unbelievably all dresses, shoes and head dresses had been purchased in that time – in one very select bridal shop.

The bride's dresses, though white, were very different; Sheila had chosen a halter type, beautifully sequinned with shoestring straps decorating a low back which swept down to form a short train. It suited Sheila's olive skin to perfection. Jenny had chosen a more modest style with a mandarin collar and pearl buttons decorating the front with fine long sleeves. Both brides had chosen simple tiaras with short veils.

The bridesmaids had had little hesitation in deciding on the beautiful aquamarine dresses with their off the shoulder design and narrow skirts. The soft green colour flattered both girls' complexions very well. Their headdresses were simple bands of artificial flowers in blues, greens and white.

After all the incessant chatter in the bridal shop, the women were quiet as they ate their lunch, but all of them agreed everything had gone smoothly. They would soon be home, and able to take a hard earned rest.

When Lucie arrived home around 3 p.m., it was to find Patrick entertaining his mother in the living room. Lucie never minded Mrs Mullan's frequent visits to their home; she knew she was discreetly checking on Patrick's behaviour and his level of drinking.

Lucie kissed her mother-in-law warmly. "Have you had tea, Mrs Mullan? We've just been shopping for the wedding – and with great success I might add."

Mrs Mullan said Patrick had made her tea when she arrived, but perhaps he would give her a, "wee warm cup" before she headed for home. Patrick Mullan's mother loved Lucie and could scarcely believe she had forgiven him and come back to mend their marriage. It was more than she had dared hope for. But then of course, she had said her, "Hail Marys" every night and prayed to all the saints on a regular basis, that Patrick would catch himself on and learn to control that temper of his. Did he appreciate the chance he had been given with this lovely girl – a chance which sometimes Teresa Mullan wondered did he even deserve?

Chapter 58

The day of the weddings promised to be a brilliant sunny one. The sun had been shining brightly since 6 a.m. and Lucie – conscious of her duty as bridesmaid – had risen early in order to prepare the bride and herself to look their very best. Lucie had arrived at Sheila's house around nine o'clock last evening and would travel to the church with Sheila's mother where they would then meet with Jenny's mother.

Now, as Lucie prepared scrambled eggs on toast and fresh coffee for Sheila and herself, her mind was on Patrick and how he had been yesterday evening when she had been preparing to go to Sheila's place. He had seemed quite morose and withdrawn – a side to him she hadn't seen for some time. She had been glad when his mother had called and insisted Lucie go on over to Sheila's. She and Patrick, she insisted, would have a quiet hour and a small whiskey together before she made her way home. Lucie left their apartment in a much happier frame of mind, knowing her mother-in-law had a way of cheering her son up.

Hopefully when she caught up with him later he would be more amicable than he had been yesterday evening. It was up to Patrick to try to enter into the spirit of things. It was going to be a long day for everyone, but she really wanted it to be a happy one. In the meantime she must concentrate on helping Sheila arrive at the church looking her most beautiful and very importantly, on good time.

"Joan and Jenny's mother haven't arrived as yet." Eric, Sheila's younger brother, one of the ushers, was waiting in the hall and seemed to be taking his role very seriously.

"We'll wait here." Lucie indicated a corner of the main hall to Mrs Morrow as she spoke. "There is still plenty of room for other guests who arrive and wish to loiter for a bit, before being shown to their seats."

"I've just shown your husband Patrick to his place beside Matthew's wife and boy – wasn't that right?"

"Perfect, Eric. Thank you." Lucie was relieved to know Patrick was here and had been given his rightful seat beside her family, even if she couldn't be beside him until much later.

Patrick had made sure he was looking his very best – his good suit was just out of the cleaners the day before. He had treated himself to a new pale blue shirt and matching tie, and when he looked in the mirror before leaving the house, he was very pleased with what he saw. When he saw the two bridegrooms and the best men seated at the front of the church he was glad he had gone to so much trouble with his appearance. Even so, when he saw Paul Greenlees seated there beside his three brothers-in-law, he had to make a conscious effort to control his jealousy and his sense of injustice. He should have been sitting there, waiting with his wife's brothers for the arrival of the brides and bridesmaids. But no, Paul Greenlees occupied that space.

The arrival of the brides' mothers and Eric Morrow ushering them into the seats in front of him momentarily distracted him, and then he realised the bridesmaids too must be here. Before he had time to think anything further, the organist began to play the wedding march and he was aware the bridal procession was making its way up the aisle. As he watched the four girls slowly making their way towards the men at the top of the church, he had to admit it was a spectacular, awesome sight. The beauty and elegance of the four women was totally breathtaking.

As Lucie, walking slowly behind Sheila and her father, passed the pew where Patrick stood, he willed her to look towards him. But Lucie's eyes seemed resolutely fixed on the minister and the four young men who waited so patiently for the women to join them.

Lucie was aware of Patrick's eyes on her as she passed him, but conscious of her unfailing duty to Sheila and Charles today, she knew she needed to focus on making sure everything went right for them. Any distraction might well

315

throw her, and she was anxious there would be no hitches on her part. At the same time she could not afford to do or say anything which might upset Patrick today, above all days. So she intended to join her husband as soon as she could and spend the evening with him. Since their reunion two years ago she always seemed to have to work hard at making their union – if not happy – comparatively peaceful and secure. And today it was vitally important that that peace was maintained.

In order to give her marriage any hope of recovery it had been vital she locked all feelings and thoughts of Paul Greenlees in a private corner of her heart. A corner which must never be disturbed until, she hoped, some day her love for him would be just a distant, wonderful memory.

She prided herself she had achieved a measure of success. Each time Paul and she met, as they sometimes did at her mother's house and more recently, at rehearsals for the weddings, she found she could conduct herself in a friendly amicable manner. Hopefully today would be no different as – out of necessity – they would be spending a good deal of time together, but they would be surrounded by all their family and friends. And as soon as she could she would seek Patrick out, share a drink with him before the evening's dancing began.

"We would like Thomas and Jenny, Charles and Sheila followed by the best men and bridesmaids to lead off in the first dance of the evening. Then everyone else can make their way on to the dance floor," the D.J. announced over the microphone as everyone assembled into their groups for the evening's entertainment.

"Patrick, once this dance is over most of my duties as bridesmaid should be over – apart from helping Sheila change into her going away outfit, so we'll have that promised drink together and relax for the rest of the evening." Lucie was aware Patrick was tense and irritable as she spoke to him, He made no attempt to answer her, and then Paul was at her side offering to lead her on to the dance floor. As she took Paul's hand and stepped forward to join him, she was acutely aware of Patrick's steady unwavering gaze on them both, a look which seemed to bore into her. As she and Paul followed the bridal party around the floor she began to feel more and more uneasy. Patrick seemed to be totally obsessed with watching her. And his whole frame seemed tense and angry. Even so, she was totally unprepared for her husband's actions as Paul and she followed Charles and Sheila round the floor. Nothing could have prepared her or Paul for the violent push her husband delivered to her chest and stomach. Lucie staggered, tried to keep her balance as Paul attempted to steady her, then he too was pushed. She staggered again and then felt an overwhelming pain in her temple as it came in contact with one of the drinks tables. She fell to the floor as blackness enveloped her.

Paul looked at the clock on the wall for about the tenth time as he sat silently in intensive care. It was 2 a.m. and Lucie had returned from theatre an hour and a half ago. She had awakened from the anaesthetic, and then gone back into a peaceful sleep, with the nurse beside her bed monitoring her progress. He knew all was well. He knew too, that he needed to get home to rest, to shut out the traumatic events of the last few hours. But each time he contemplated leaving the quiet, still ward, he seemed consumed by fear. Fear of what could have happened here today. The outcome could have been so very different to the one he was witnessing right this moment in intensive care, before his very eyes.

His thoughts went back over the events of the last few hours and he knew he was only now suffering from the shock and horror of what he had witnessed in the hotel. He had known immediately Lucie had been knocked unconscious by the force of her fall. The angle of her body told him all he needed to know. In the space of a few seconds he needed to call on all his professional experience as never before. He could not, must not dwell on the fact that it was Lucie lying there. If he did he would be lost and totally unable to help her. And now he was so grateful he had decided, some time ago, to become a teetotaller. His mind was totally clear and focused and he was able to assess the gravity of the situation. He had never had much desire for alcohol; he had tried it once or twice after he had met Lucie, but he just did not like the taste.

He was probably the only man at the wedding who had not been celebrating with alcohol. Calmly he heard himself issuing orders for an ambulance, for help to turn Lucie on her side and for a blanket to keep her warm. Somewhere he was aware of Patrick being led away by some of the family, but that did not concern him. There was only Lucie there, lying on the floor, critically injured. He was scarcely aware of climbing into the ambulance which would take Lucie and him both to the Royal, then Lucie straight to the X-ray department and without a doubt into theatre, where he himself intended to operate on her.

"Sir, Mr Greenlees." He was conscious of the nurse's hand on his shoulder, shaking him gently. Struggling to stand he smiled at her.

"I see you have brought tea, thank you."

"No problem, sir." Nurse Graham hesitated. "If you don't mind me saying, sir, you look all in."

Everyone knew Mr Greenlees was a dedicated surgeon, but she had never known him to stay with a patient quite so long, even though she understood this girl was a close family friend.

"Mrs Mullan is sleeping peacefully, sir. Her vital signs are very stable. If you want to go home and I notice any change at all I will ring you immediately, sir."

"I know you will, nurse." Paul rose stiffly out of his chair. "I have no reason to worry, no time was wasted in getting Lucie – Mrs Mullan – to theatre and the blood clot in her temple was small. There were no complications whatsoever during surgery, nurse. I will take your advice and go and get some rest, I assured her family that all was well and they have gone home a short time ago. But I will just go over to the doctors' quarters and find a bed there. That's where I'll be if you need me." As he spoke Paul approached Lucie's bed one more time, checked her chart and then placed his hand on her pulse himself. Before leaving her, he gripped her hand tightly and spoke softly to her, telling her that all was well. He was delighted when she responded by straightening her fingers within his grip. Satisfied, he left her there and made his way to the doctors' quarters and soon found an empty bed and more or less collapsed onto it, fully dressed.

"I brought Patrick Mullan upstairs to the room Lucie and he had been allocated. I made him coffee but I never left him until his father arrived to take him away." This was the first time during the long dark night that Lucie's husband had been referred to. There was no need for talk or explanation; everyone had witnessed the violent scene on the dance floor and what had happened to Lucie.

The whole family were back in Rob and Ellen's house after being reassured by Paul that Lucie would be alright – the surgery had been successful.

During the endless, frightening hours she was in theatre, the family had sat huddled together, too overcome and shocked for any conversation. Honeymoons had been postponed, the evening dance cancelled, and the guests advised to go home. All the family's thoughts and prayers were firstly for Lucie and her welfare. But there was concern too, for Ellen and Rob, but with Paul's latest report on Lucie they could relax a little and Matthew knew he needed to tell them of his intentions.

"I told Patrick's father I would be in touch in the morning, but I said this time I would report it to my superiors, even without Lucie's say so. She is too ill at the moment to make that decision."

"I think we would all support you in that, Matthew." Rob had been listening intently as his son spoke and now he looked at his other two sons and their wives where they sat side by side on the sofa.

"Do we all agree he has to be reported?" Rob's question had been unnecessary. The expression on everyone's face, when Patrick Mullan's name was mentioned, told Matthew and Rob that the family were in agreement. Now Matthew looked at his son sound asleep beside Julie.

"Julie and I will go over home, Thomas and Charles and the girls, you stay here with Mum and Dad. There's room enough upstairs – I'll be in touch first thing in the morning."

Quietly Ellen went upstairs and returned with a blanket for her sleeping grandson. She kissed him gently, then Julie her daughter-in-law. Turning to Matthew she hugged him fiercely. "Thank you for everything tonight, Matthew. You must do what you feel is best and God be with you."

The next morning when Paul returned to intensive care it was to find Lucie sleepy and quite lucid but not asking anything about what had happened to her. She made no reference to her husband, where he was, why he had not been to see her. And Paul decided it would be best if she was unaware, in the meantime, that Patrick Mullan was responsible for her condition and that, drastic as it might seem, arrangements were being made to transfer him to duty in Crossmaglen in Co. Armagh. Clearly she had no memory of the events of the previous evening and Paul knew from past experiences with head injuries, that Lucie might never recall much.

On the third morning after the incident, when she had just returned from being X-Rayed, and Paul was studying the result, Lucie asked to speak to him in private. Turning to the ward staff, Paul discreetly asked if Mrs Mullan and he could have five minutes privacy.

"Paul, I need you to find me a good solicitor, I want to discuss how I go about filing for divorce proceedings."

"Lucie..." although Paul's heart lifted at the very thought of Lucie ever being free and he felt like reaching for her and hugging her closely, he had to remember he was still the professional surgeon. Instead he just asked, "Lucie, what has triggered this?"

"I have remembered what happened, Paul – well perhaps not everything, but enough to realise there is no going back this time." Her voice was steady as she looked at him.

"Will you get me a solicitor, Paul? That is all I ask. I would love to ask so very much more from you. I would love to hear you tell me you love me. But I could never expect you to hang around and be involved in this horrid mess. So if you can get me a good solicitor that will have to do."

Lucie's tongue seemed to be running away with her and Paul began to suspect that the shot she had received earlier that morning had not worn off completely. Now she was telling him how much she loved him, something he had always longed to hear. But he could not cope with hearing it here. She was still his patient, and any discussions about their feelings would have to wait. Besides, if she was serious about divorcing Patrick she would have to be very careful.

He took her hand gently in his and simply said, "We'll sort this all out together, Lucie, but we have to get you well first. Now I'll let Sister and Doctor Welsh back in." As he did so he addressed them both. "Mrs Mullan's memory is improving rapidly – a very good sign indeed."

After her initial outburst, which Lucie herself suspected was due to her being high on Morphine, she quickly realised, that while she was in hospital, she must control her emotions and try to be as professional as Paul was being. She found this extremely difficult to do. In her present emotional state she just wanted to tell him again and again how much she loved him. Loved him with a strong, ardent passion, not the fleeting animal magnetism she had felt for Patrick.

She wanted too, to tell Paul how sorry she was for everything – for having messed up both theirs and Patrick's lives – and that she was sincere in her wish to get a divorce. Patrick, too, deserved freedom from this unhappy marriage and destructive relationship. He too, needed to have a chance of meeting someone else to love instead of hate, as he obviously did her.

She had managed to be the soul of discretion during the remaining two weeks she was in hospital, addressing Paul as respectfully as she knew how. He, in turn, was the consummate professional consultant at all times.

On the day of her discharge Lucie's father collected her and took her to his home, where Lucie was to stay to convalesce. Here Paul could visit quite openly, as, thanks to his good friendship with Charles and Rob and Ellen, he had been doing for some time. It was here – in her parents' house that

Paul and Lucie were able to weave a routine of suppers at her mother's hearth, listening to the radio and between many kisses and innumerable caresses – declare their love for one another. Here they agonised over their future and their uncertainty if the law would ever allow Lucie a divorce from a Roman Catholic, and if they would ever be free to marry.

Chapter 59

Many times Patrick Mullan wondered how he had survived the last five years in this God forsaken location, the routine of the job was so boring. Then of course, there were the countless other times when he was highly motivated and totally intrigued when they were assigned to patrol the countryside and told to keep their senses alerted for signs of subversive IRA activities. Just recently, he had noticed the patrols had increased and they were informed they should be on high alert at all times.

This shift in the pattern of the work at the police station was due to the latest intelligence reports indicating South Armagh was a great training base for young men who wished to enlist in the IRA. There seemed little doubt that that particular army were now resorting to using violence as a means of getting what they wanted. Indeed, they had officially announced that anyone who worked for the "Crown" and in particular, the Security Forces was considered a legitimate target. Patrick was well aware the Police Force constituted a very high risk and the whole of the Police Force in South Armagh were in no doubt the Republicans had the profile of each one of them on their files. Yet strangely, he felt comparatively safe here. He was, after all, a Roman Catholic, with the same religious beliefs as the IRA themselves had. Of course he understood political beliefs and religious beliefs were not the same thing. While he had an interest in, and some love for his religion, Politics held no appeal for him. The fact he was the only Catholic in the depot and that he had once been married to a Protestant but now divorced, must have been well documented by them. He believed his marital history gave him some immunity against their strong arm tactics.

That morning five years ago when he had been called for interview with his sergeant and other supervisors and informed he was being transferred to Crossmaglen, he had known immediately Lucie's family were responsible. This was how it was to be for him then. Instead of charging him with assault and grievous bodily harm, or worse, attempted murder, he was to be removed quietly. No stigma must threaten the police force or Lucie Mullan. That would never be acceptable, either for the Hampton family or the security services.

Patrick appreciated he had got off lightly, but still he felt oddly cheated. No one had given him a chance to explain how jealous and isolated he had felt that day. A jealousy that just invaded his whole mind and body and he didn't know what he was doing. But no one – not even his own parents – wanted to hear anything about how he had felt at the wedding, so he had had no choice only to bury his feelings. The "up" side to the whole sorry mess was that he still had his job and his freedom. He might as readily have been languishing in some prison cell with no hope of getting a decent job at the end of it all. But even so, sometimes the bitterness he felt towards the Hamptons, and towards Matthew in particular, threatened to engulf him. He knew without a doubt it was Matthew Hampton who had reported him and had him transferred here.

As for Lucie, he had known the moment he attacked her on the dance floor the evening of her brothers' weddings that he had just ended his marriage. It was such a public act of humiliation and display of violence that reconciliation was impossible. Besides he had, for some considerable time, become reconciled to the fact that Lucie only tolerated him because she believed in the sanctity of marriage. He had been well aware that, during the last three years, she had lived in fear of his violence resurfacing. He knew their marriage was fated to end but, even so, he was shocked to the core when three months after Lucie's discharge from hospital, he was served divorce papers.

Initially he contemplated fighting her in court on the grounds he was a Roman Catholic and he believed marriage was for life. But in his heart he knew the hospital records would easily show his repeated acts of violence towards her and he would only run the risk of exposing himself very publicly and the Police would have no choice only to arrest him. So he resigned himself to the fact that the divorce must go ahead and he dare not contemplate contesting it.

Shortly after his transfer to Crossmaglen he had acquired a rented flat, within walking distance of the police barracks. A police barracks he now believed he would serve in as a Constable until his retirement.

For some time now he had accepted the fact that any promotion was beyond his reach. He had applied a couple of times for a Sergeant's post without success. But when he heard how Matthew Hampton was moving up through the ranks, he was now a Detective, Patrick's sense of injustice, jealousy and resentment towards his brother-in-law became a deep and malevolent feeling. His hatred for him deepened over time, far more than any adverse feelings he had for Lucie. Even Lucie's wedding to Paul Greenlees three years before had surprisingly, not troubled him greatly. In his heart he knew his behaviour towards her had been intolerable. He had, however, believed that Matthew and he had a reasonably good working relationship, but when it came down to it, that relationship had counted for nothing, And he now despised Matthew Hampton so much that he hoped that their paths would never cross – if that ever happened he believed he would find it difficult to refrain from harming the man. That thought terrified him because that would certainly bring an end to his police career.

It was seven-thirty in the morning, the clock informed Lucie, as she climbed as quietly as she could out of bed and over to the cot where her five-month-old daughter was beginning to sound annoyed that she had not been lifted and fed sooner. It was a bright Sunday morning in May and Lucie quickly pulled on her dressing gown and lifted her daughter before her cries awakened Paul. He had had an emergency to deal with during the early hours of the morning and she would like him to get a few hours sleep before the children made their demands on him. As she made her way along the landing and towards the stairs with the somewhat quietened Louise in her arms, she opened the door of the nursery and was thankful that Robert, her three-year-old son, was still asleep in his bed.

Lucie had just finished changing Louise's nappy and after placing her in her high chair with a bottle of milk, was making porridge on the Aga cooker when the kitchen door opened and Paul appeared with a smiling Robert in his arms.

"Paul, did Robbie waken you?" As she spoke Lucie reached for her son and sat him in a chair at the kitchen table. "I did want you to get some sleep. You were back so late."

"Darling – I have had enough sleep to manage. It is Sunday and we like to spend the day as a family. I don't want to miss it and I love our visit to your mum and dad and everyone being there at the family home. So please don't worry, besides this young man here," hugging his son tightly, "was determined I was getting up with him, I hadn't really much choice in the matter."

"Well let's have breakfast. I've some porridge made and then we'll have poached eggs to follow." Lucie always liked to make sure her family had a hearty breakfast in the morning. She treasured her family and the fact she had been given a second chance of happiness, in spite of her first impulsive, disastrous marriage and the traumatic divorce. She had never expected to experience such bliss and passion as she did with Paul, and lived with the knowledge that she would appreciate it until her dying day. And then, to be doubly blessed with two beautiful children when she had often wondered after her miscarriage while married to Patrick, if she would ever be able to carry a child to full term.

The only dark cloud in their four years of marriage had been the sudden death of Paul's mother from a heart attack. They and Paul's father had been plunged into a dark pit of shock and grief and a huge sense of loss for a much loved wife and mother. But if Paul and she had been devastated by Mrs Greenlees' sudden death, Paul's father had been truly felled by it and they were both aware that he moved in a place of unbearable loss and pain. He was consumed with quite irrational guilt, believing there had to be some sign that Norma had been ill. Some symptom that as a doctor he should have picked up on but did not. Nothing consoled him, neither Paul's or his grandchildren's company and more and more Lucie worried for his sanity. It was she who insisted he join them on a Sunday afternoon when they went to visit her parents. This was something which was a family ritual now with Thomas, Matthew, and Charles, accompanied by their wives and children, anxious to keep up the traditions of family visiting which seemed to have just evolved.

To Paul and Lucie's relief, Tom Greenlees' Sunday visit to Rob and Ellen's house seemed to bring some life back to him. Rob's tales of their childhood together, the dances they attended and the memories of Tom's expert driving behind the wheel of his father's car, seemed to interest him more than anything either Paul or Lucie had tried to involve him in. So they never minded the extra drive from Malone Road, where they now lived, to Poyntzpass to collect Tom and then drive to Lisburn in time to join all the others for tea. But although Paul and Lucie were more than happy with the present arrangement, their long term plans were to try and persuade Tom to come and live with them. They had plenty of rooms – some of which would be suitable to convert into an annex for him. But first they would have to persuade him to sell his large, rambling house in Poyntzpass and make him see that moving to be with them would be beneficial for everyone. Paul felt his father would be unwilling to move, which was why today, if he got a chance, he intended to ask Rob to broach the subject. He felt if anyone could talk to his father and encourage him to come to Lucie and him, Rob could.

Chapter 60

Rob looked forward to Sunday afternoon with his family. There was Matthew, now promoted to Detective Superintendent and so modest about it all and his wife Julie and young Jason, both obviously very proud of him. Thomas was now a successful furniture shop owner, happy with his exuberant wife Jenny, and their son Colin – named after Thomas's hero, Colin Wilson, who had died so soon after Dunkirk, and their daughter Jayne – named after his own stepmother who had died in England two years before. He often thought of Thomas's time in Kenya, and wondered what his son had actually witnessed and had had to go through with the Mau Mau. That particular period in his life was something Thomas never referred to and Rob felt it must have been a horrendous experience and probably one which was best laid to rest. When he thought of his son's daring and resourcefulness – with Charles' help and ingenuity – in getting safely out of Kenya, he was always amazed at their success. And Thomas's quick thinking in escaping through the landing window. Who would have thought Thomas could think on his feet so quickly? And of course the family's relief when they learned he had been completely exonerated.

Charles was happy in his job as Ordnance Surveyor and also very happy in his marriage. Sheila and he now had two daughters. Evelyn, after Rob's mother and then Ethel, for Ellen's dear sister, frail now, but delighted to have a namesake. Then lastly, his precious daughter who had come through so much but had made his happiness complete when she had married his old friend Tom Greenlees' son, Paul.

They had survived so much and Rob believed they were all much closer as a result. Certainly he felt he belonged to them and hoped they felt the same about him, in spite of his neglect of them in their earlier years. He appreciated them, and no less did he appreciate the fact that alcohol no longer held any threat for him, and he could enjoy his family and make a contribution to their contentment. He had finally earned their love and respect and he could hold his head high.

Ellen, he knew, appreciated this serene happy family circle they now had more than any of them, after having endured much trauma over the years. The worry she had had during Matthew's time in Palestine, and Thomas and Charles in Kenya. The anger and feeling of helplessness she had endured during Lucie's first disastrous marriage. They had been hard times for her – and Rob knew so well his own addiction and seemingly endless times of helplessness and despair, had contributed to a lot of her worry and unhappiness. But now he knew she looked forward to Sundays as much as he did when they would be swamped by the whole family for several hours. And now there was the added bonus of Tom Greenlees, his old friend, visiting too. Paul and Lucie had brought him with them initially, as Paul confided in Rob, because Lucie and he were so worried about him being on his own so much. But last Sunday Lucie had told him Tom had actually said he would like to accompany them. This was good news for everyone and hopefully a sign Tom was beginning to come to terms with the loss of his wife.

"Rob, I think we should start and peel some potatoes, you know how it is when everyone arrives – we get nothing done and then we've a mad rush to get all the food sorted and children fed."

"Well I'll start straight away – I've the large table set for the adults and a small one for the children." Rob joined Ellen in the kitchen and began peeling the potatoes she had set out on the draining board. "I think Sheila's idea of feeding the grandchildren first worked well last Sunday. Hopefully, we can do the same today. Then we can give Matthews's boy the job of amusing the others while we have ours."

"It was rather nice for us to sit down with our own ones and their spouses, and Tom of course," Ellen agreed. "We were able to catch up on the latest with them, but," she went on, "you never know with children, we'll have to wait and see."

"Mother, could you leave these dishes for a moment?" Matthew appeared in the kitchen doorway, smiling as he watched his mother trying to make some order of the dishes from the meal they had just partaken of.

"Lucie and Sheila have made tea. It's in the dining room, and we need you back in there to join us."

Ellen turned from the sink and began to dry her hands on the towel hanging beside the cooker. "Am I being summoned?"

She looked at her eldest son's face and wondered briefly what she was going to hear. None of her family ever called her Mother unless it was something serious – it was always Mum. She followed Matthew back into the dining room, the chores in the kitchen temporarily forgotten as she wondered what news might be forthcoming. She took her seat beside Rob who was looking as puzzled as she was.

Without any preamble Matthew proceeded to voice his concerns. "We are beginning to worry about our safety here, in this housing estate. Intelligence sources indicate that there is an IRA recruitment drive around here." Matthew looked directly at his parents and indicating the rest of the family, sitting quietly and soberly, Matthew continued, "We – as a family – feel the time has come for you to move to safer accommodation."

"Oh, Matthew, Rob and I do know there has been a bit of a shift in the residents here recently. Some men who have moved in do look very threatening. Rumours abound that they are IRA. We aren't worried about ourselves, it's you we worry about, we think visiting us here is becoming more and more risky for you."

"I've been thinking about that aspect of things too, and although I'm not uniformed, you never know what information some of them have, nor do we know how they come by it."

"Matthew, it is all very well to talk but we have little chance of another house. The Housing Executive will never see us as priority." Rob had been listening quietly to Matthew. He too had been aware of the risk his son was taking. The whole estate had deteriorated so much over the past year, with strange people visiting houses late at night, and lights burning until the early hours of the morning. He reckoned the presence of the army in Northern Ireland over the last year had increased the tension and led to even more riots in several towns. Now he looked round the table at his family and wondered if any of them had any solutions to offer.

"Actually, Dad, I wasn't thinking of approaching the executive. I was thinking in terms of buying a small property. Lucie and I have been to see one, it's not too far from Lucie and Paul's house, it's at the corner end of the Malone Road." Matthew went on enthusiastically, "I would be putting up the money for it. You and Mum would have no expense. So what do you think?" Matthew had never forgotten how his father had repaid every penny he had taken from his account when he was in Palestine. He had never touched that money, but indeed had managed to add to it every month. He now had a very tidy sum, enough for a substantial deposit ensuring the mortgage would be a minimal amount each month which he intended to pay himself.

And before this evening was over, he would make sure arrangements were made for them to view it in the next day or two. Then he would move things on quickly from there.

Meanwhile, Rob was reflecting on the audacity of him trying earlier that day to persuade his old pal Tom to move house and then before the day was over, he had discovered his family had the very same idea for Ellen and him.

Chapter 61

Although Patrick Mullan had been aware since he was a teenager that his father was a staunch Republican, he himself had no interest in politics and was appalled at the bigotry and sectarianism which was so deep seated in Northern Ireland. He had always considered himself to be moderate in his views and had, in fact, been keen from an early age to join the police force. The fact there was a British crown on the helmet and that they were actually called the "Royal Ulster Constabulary" bothered him not one bit. He was more interested in the work, the money and the pension he would one day be entitled to.

But one singular incident which occurred in Belfast made him question where his loyalties should lie. The incident transpired on a Saturday in June 1970, when groups of so called Loyalists made incursions into the Catholic Short Strand area of East Belfast threatening to burn the Catholics out. The IRA had taken up position in the Catholic Church and engaged in a gun battle with the Loyalists. This was done to protect the Catholics in the area but seven people were killed during this confrontation.

Patrick had listened avidly to the news, fearful for some of his old school friends who lived in the Short Strand area and he grew increasingly angry at the Loyalist treatment of the Catholics.

On impulse, around 10 p.m., he decided to walk to the nearby pub, something he rarely did, preferring to drink at home. He knew it was a predominantly Catholic pub and no doubt this incident would be the main topic of conversation. As Patrick walked the short distance from his flat to the pub he had no way of knowing that this visit would colour and change his whole life.

After ordering a whiskey and soda at the bar, Patrick became aware of two young men – he reckoned they were around 22 or 23 years of age, watching him intently. On seeing

Patrick had spotted them watching him, they raised their glasses in salute and Patrick, out of courtesy, acknowledged the two men. He recognised them as two locals; he had seen them around the village. As he was sipping his drink, one of the men indicated a table in the corner and walking towards him suggested they join up for a quiet social drink, away from the bustle of the bar. Patrick was very willing to join them, he could do with a bit of local gossip, it would make a nice change from sitting alone, night after night, watching television and drinking in solitude.

The three men's attention was drawn primarily to the large television screen which dominated the pub, and as they watched, the news was highlighting the trouble in the Short Strand area, showing vivid images of the gun battle and the police's attempt to contain it all.

"What do you make of this latest attempt by the Prods to kill our fellow men?" The elder man spoke directly to Patrick.

"I was concerned for some of my friends in the area, I must admit," Patrick replied.

"So you too, have friends in the area. So have we. Isn't that right, Seamus?"

"Several of our mates live there but our Army were well able to defend them, we're glad to say. I daresay no one thought our men would actually take up position in a Chapel – but sure it had to be done." The young Seamus's voice held a deep note of pride.

"But more needs to be done for the cause, you do know that, Patrick Mullan, don't you?" The elder brother spoke firmly, as he looked at Patrick directly.

Patrick realised these two men were obviously volunteers in the IRA and that they already knew who he was, and probably everything about him. Now, as they insisted on buying him another drink, their jovial attitude seemed to have gone, to be replaced by a more threatening one. He began to wonder what exactly he had let himself in for by coming here and by joining their company.

Bernard Caughey and his younger brother Seamus were new, enthusiastic volunteers and anxious to please but also wishing to avoid the wrath of their superiors. Tonight's work had not been easy – in truth it had proved to be much tougher than they had anticipated. They had had to make it quite clear to their new friend that physical violence would be used if the goods were not delivered to them within the next few days. But they had left their new companion reasonably confident that he could come up trumps. The Caugheys knew if that were to happen, they would be in a good position to be looked on more favourably by their superiors. So far, they knew they had not produced much useful information that interested them. In fact, they knew that when they met their superiors every week, they were being looked upon, more and more, as a liability to the cause.

As tonight was scheduled for such a meeting Bernard knew he would have to relate last night's introduction to their "friend" and what their hopes were of achieving results. He realised that by doing this, increased pressure would be put on his brother and him to succeed. So they in turn would be forced to achieve results no matter how. He was hopeful of success, and if this was so, he and his brother would be looked at in a new light by the organisation.

Four days later when Bernard received the phone call, he was rather surprised to realise his new companion was now more than happy to supply any information he might need and some of this had been easier to acquire than he had first thought. His friend's only concern seemed to be that his name must never, under any circumstances, be mentioned to anyone. Here Bernard was only too happy to reassure him everyone involved in supplying information were anonymous and would always remain so. He would be referred to by code only.

Chapter 62

From the first moment Rob and Ellen saw the gate lodge that Matthew was in the process of buying for them, they were enamoured with it. It had such character. Situated at the beginning of a large, wide avenue of beautiful houses, the house was surrounded all around by a hedge of rhododendrons, with a small wooden gate guarding the path which led directly to the front door. At the side of the garden and lying back off the road was a compact garage with its up and over door, the perfect place for Rob's van. The house and garage were both built in traditional red brick style and the house itself had beautiful Georgian windows and a front door with its fan-shaped window above.

Inside there was a sitting room and dining room both with beautiful marble fireplaces. They were generous sized rooms as were the two bedrooms at the back of the house. A good square kitchen with an Aga cooker delighted Ellen as did the bathroom, with its beautiful white bath.

There was no doubt Matthew had done a wonderful job acquiring the property and the added bonus was that it was a stone's throw from Lucie and Paul's home and not far from Matthew either.

They had been surprised when Matthew informed them the estate agent had offered them the key to move in, even though the transaction had not been quite completed. The completion was something Rob and Matthew would be doing through Matthew's solicitor in the next few days. In the meantime some of the family had been helping to paint walls, hang curtains and put down carpets. Then Rob, Thomas and Charles would move the furniture in Rob's van and Rob and Ellen would soon spend their first night in a home of their very own. It was hard to believe, that this house would be their first private property since their marriage more than forty years ago. Ellen could only watch Rob with a measure of disbelief as he enthused about colours for walls, painted everything so carefully and discussed where their somewhat shabby furniture should be placed when they managed to transport it from their previous home.

Ellen had worried her furniture would look unsuitable and dowdy in their new home but she was pleased when it seemed to fit the decor and style of the house really well. The evening after it had all been installed, the family gathered together to see for themselves how comfortable and secure Rob and Ellen now were.

They were installed in their new home three weeks before Matthew managed to pin his solicitor down to a time and day when his father and he might come and have everything finalised. The solicitor had been closed for a full week during the "Twelfth of July" celebration so the 20th July was the earliest anything could be arranged and the time for their meeting was scheduled for 11 a.m.

"Oh, Matthew, this is so generous of you – I know I keep repeating myself, but I truly can scarcely believe we are here, and this is ours." Rob had been watching for Matthews's car to arrive. He had showered, shaved and dressed in his good suit to accompany his son. He had done so very early that morning, and had paced about from room to room in a high state of excitement.

"Dad, I can well afford it. Besides, it is a wonderful place for you both, close to Lucie and me, and so much safer than the estate you were in." Turning to Ellen he added, "We have time for coffee before we go, Mum, have you the kettle on?"

"I've all set out on the kitchen table, I know you like your coffee."

"I'll have my usual strong cup of tea. Ellen, I don't know how you can drink that stuff it's so bitter." Rob proceeded to put a heaped teaspoon of tea into a teapot and set it on the cooker, where it almost immediately began to splutter and boil over.

"And I don't know how you drink your tea like that, it's so strong." Ellen remarked as she watched him pour some into a cup.

"Just the way I like it, my love."

"Right drink up, Dad, we need to go shortly."

The solicitor's office was housed in a very old bank building with several other offices. It was approached by a flight of broad steps with gracious Georgian type pillars placed at intervals on either side of the steps.

"It's certainly an imposing looking building," Rob remarked as he and Matthew entered through the heavy swing doors, "I suppose it's very suitable for a man of the law."

Matthew smiled and nodded in response as he guided his father along the corridor towards the office. He was anxious to have everything settled today because he was beginning to lose patience with his solicitor who had certainly taken his time over it all. But from what Matthew's experience was of solicitors, it was more or less typical of them. They seemed to move through their work at a snail's pace.

"Well that didn't take too long, did it, Dad?" They were making their way back along the corridor. Matthew had made sure the deeds and remaining mortgage was in his father's name but he was paying the mortgage by direct debit every month.

"I can only say, son, I am indebted to you for the rest of my life." Rob's voice shook as he spoke and Matthew knew he was close to tears. So he just gave him a friendly hug as they made their way towards the exit.

The sun was shining when they came outside and for a split second Rob was blinded by it. Then he saw the figure move out from behind the pillar, he saw the glint of metal in his hand. He knew in that instant it was pointed at his son and he knew what it meant. Without thinking, he flung himself with all the force he could muster at the tall figure of Matthew. Instantly, he felt an agonising pain in his head, which concentrated his whole mind and body and encircled and clamped his whole being. Mercifully an awful blackness began to envelop him and he knew he was sinking into it and it was a darkness he welcomed, it was bringing such relief. Suddenly there was a bright light in front of him and he could see her so clearly – his mother. She was here, and she looked just as she had always looked when she was waiting for him at the school gates. She was smiling, her arms outstretched towards him and she was saying, "Rob, my Rob – we are so proud of you. Come with me. I have been waiting for you for so long."

Matthew, as he crouched down beside the deathly still body of his father, could hear someone screaming; agonising screams which went on and on. How he wished they would stop. He only realised it was himself who was uttering these awful noises and cries when someone tried to release his arms from his father, where he held him in a vice-like grip.

Chapter 63

Rob's funeral was held on the 24th July at two o'clock in the afternoon. It had rained continually throughout the day, heavy bursts of rain which beat off roofs and windows incessantly. To Ellen, sitting in the front pew of the Methodist church with her family beside her, the weather seemed in keeping with the awful tragedy that had engulfed them over the last four days. The black clouds, looming low in the sky and the black dress of the mourners matched the dark sombre atmosphere of the occasion.

A vast number of people attended the ceremony, publicans who had ensured Rob was safely home on many occasions, farmers who had bartered many times with him over disinfectant and then later jute bags. Friends and neighbours too, came from near and far and then Rob's own dear relatives, all profoundly shocked by what had happened to Rob Hampton, a quiet inoffensive man, shot dead while out on business with his son. Shot by the IRA who had – according to the media – claimed responsibility for the shooting. Bewilderment pervaded the whole ceremony, how could such a monstrous thing be? How could anyone do something so barbaric to another human being?

Ellen was unaware how many mourners were present, who they were or what they might be speculating about. She was only aware of Rob's coffin sitting ahead of her and she was so conscious too, of Matthew, her dear son, sitting so still and silent beside her. She could not bear to think of what he alone must have witnessed in that awful moment when Rob was shot. She was totally enveloped in her own selfish grief and had no way of reaching him. He was in a world she could not bear to inhabit, to contemplate those awful moments would, she knew, bring her to the very edge of insanity. Instead, she must try to blank those last moments of Rob's life from her mind.

Fleetingly, as she listened to the strains of the last hymn "Abide with Me" being played she prayed that Julie, Matthew's wife, and indeed his brothers would be able to reach him, console and sustain him in some way. She only knew she was powerless to help him in his awful hour of need.

Later, as food and drink was offered to those mourners who had come to the hotel looking for sustenance, Dorrie and Eve, themselves devastated by the death of their beloved brother, kept close to Ellen, in an effort to comfort her. They were concerned for her well being, she seemed so frail and shrunken and totally unable to function. Meanwhile, their husbands, John and Harry, felt compelled to stay with Matthew. It was the pain and anguish in their nephew's face which was so difficult to look upon, that, and the bewildered expression in his eyes. Almost as if everything was now beyond his comprehension. The two older men could only hope that simply their presence beside him might have some impact and give him a feeling of familiar solidarity. It was family, only family, that was – in their opinion – what Matthew needed. Not all those people, milling about eating and drinking, as if it were some kind of celebration. Charles and Thomas, too, tried to set aside their own grief in order to give a measure of consolation to their brother. But Matthew remained unresponsive to anything any of them said. He seemed deaf to their words of consolation. He simply gazed at them with that black hopeless expression on his face and then despondently turned away.

So for now all Charles and Thomas could do was to stay close by and maintain a silent dignity. Lucie, meanwhile, clung to Paul throughout the entire day; during the service, the burial and the time during refreshments. She was totally overcome with shock and grief and Paul was frantic with worry. He had never left her side since he had entered the house four days ago to break the news that her father had been murdered. Murdered – her father? Oh God, it couldn't be so, there was some mistake, but as Paul held her tightly in his arms and went on to tell her two eyewitnesses had seen Rob throw himself at Matthew and push him out of the target range of the bullet, she knew it must be the truth. And the bullet which had entered Rob's temple had killed him instantly. Lucie knew then it was Matthew they had meant to kill. Instead it was her father who now lay in the morgue, lifeless and gone from them forever.

Paul had insisted his father come and stay with Lucie and him. He knew his father was distraught and deeply shocked at Rob's death and Paul felt he needed company and some solace. Not hiding away in solitude in Poyntzpass, grieving so deeply for his lifelong friend. Paul was surprised and greatly relieved when his father had very willingly agreed to come and stay, leading Paul to believe his father secretly yearned for some company and solace at this time in his life. He was delighted too, when he had turned out to be a great help with the children, feeding and amusing them and taking them into the garden. No doubt the children's presence eased his father's grief, too.

And now today, Paul was glad to see his father make his way over to Ellen, he had begun to think Tom was going to shirk that particular duty and not offer any condolences to Rob's widow. But he had made the effort, and surely if anyone in this crowd of people here today had any insight as to what Ellen was coming through, it was Paul's father, after the shock of his own wife's sudden death.

Through his own misery and grief at the loss of his father-in-law, Paul noticed that Thomas and Charles had scarcely left Matthew's side since entering the hotel. They seemed intent on protecting him from well meaning but inquisitive sympathizers and they were right of course; Matthew was in no fit state to talk to anyone. His brother-in-law's face had a sickening pallor which was frightening and Paul realised that whatever any of the family were coming through, it was nothing compared to Matthew's despair and anguish.

Chapter 64

Julie switched on the light on the bedside table and glancing at the clock realised it was almost seven am. For the first time in six months she felt a glimmer of optimism as she climbed silently out of bed, anxious not to waken Matthew lying so still beside her. Was it really only six months since that awful tragedy that had taken Rob from them and taken her husband's interest in anything from him? It seemed forever that Matthew had been like this, unable to work, unable to show interest in any of the family, even his son. Only in the quiet and comfort of their bedroom and in their bed was Matthew able to show any of his feelings. Here he held Julie night after night with a passion and emotion so alien to him. It was a wild, uncontrollable passion he released in the darkness of their bedroom, a room which they had always looked on as their sanctuary. Here he told Julie over and over, how much he loved her. How much he wanted her – to make love to her. And always Julie responded with her own ardour and with the deep love she felt for this broken man, her husband. Always she hoped, after a night of passionate love making, that the next day would see an improvement in his mental state. But each day he retreated into his own tortured hell, where neither she, nor anyone else, could reach him. He had simply withdrawn from them all and lived in his own private world of grief and quiet and horror. Where no one could comfort him.

Now after so many years of yearning and hoping for another baby, and the dashing of those hopes, Julie realised, she was pregnant again. At forty-one years of age. She could scarcely believe it, but had thought she was having an early menopause. Just this week her doctor had confirmed her baby would be due in six month's time.

Their family doctor had been very attentive to Matthew since the loss of Rob. Within a month of his father's death his GP had felt he must prescribe antidepressant pills. They had

had very limited value, but at least gave him an appetite for food and brought some sleep towards the early hours of the mornings. Their doctor had also advised Julie it would be best not to mention anything about the baby at present, as Matthew might not deal with it well emotionally. So Julie had gone about her duties and responsibilities as best she could, hoping that by maintaining the normal pattern of their lives Matthew would come back to her and Jason.

But after a miserable Christmas and New Year looming she had decided Matthew needed something much more than she could give. And she was putting all her hopes on the two men who were coming to see him this afternoon.

It was Paul and Lucie who had suggested some of Matthew's supervisors might be able to make him see he could still be of use to them. They would be able to remind him how clever he was, the excellent detective he had been, and how more than ever, he really was needed. When the phone call from the Chief Inspector came, Julie was taken by surprise, as she herself had taken no action to be in touch. The Inspector explained it was her brother-in-law who had spoken to him and went on to say he and his Superintendent would come and visit on a day and time suitable to Matthew and her. Today was the day and Julie was surprised how much she was looking forward to their arrival. Even Matthew, when she had told him, had not objected and Julie thought she had even seen a glimmer of interest from her husband – an animation she had not seen for some time.

Now, she crept downstairs as quietly as she could and made her way into the kitchen and switched on the light. As the room lit up, she thought again, as she often had over the last six months, how quickly Matthew and her, in spite of everything, had adjusted after the sudden move from their original home. Once Matthew's supervisors realised an attempt had been made on his life, they were moved, under cover of darkness, to this, their new home. It was a beautiful detached house, but not as isolated as their last one had been. This was a built up area, where assailants would be more easily spotted, so were much less likely to risk being caught red handed. The same evening they moved house, their car too, was taken away and a different model with different registration plates provided. Matthew had been totally indifferent to any of the changes they had endured. But now today, Julie vowed, she was going to beg him to listen to what the Chief Inspector had to say. She herself felt at times she was losing patience with this man who meant so much to her, but each time she felt her tolerance threatened by Matthew's apathy, guilt overwhelmed her, when she thought about everything he had been through.

Later that afternoon, sitting in the cafe with Jason, having collected him from school, Julie felt apprehensive about returning home. Would the Inspector's visit have done Matthew any good? Would they have been able to help him, when all his own family's efforts seemed to have been in vain?

Now looking across at her son, obviously enjoying the rare treat of an enormous chocolate éclair, she thought how much he too must miss the old Matthew who had been such an inspiration and help to him with his college studies. But Jason never complained and if Julie talked to him about Matthew's depression, he would simply hug his mother and tell her his daddy would be alright soon, he knew he would.

"Let's finish off here and head home, love," Julie suggested. "The visitors will have gone, I'm sure, by the time we get back. I left them with your dad, after serving them coffee and some of my best sponge cake." Julie moved her chair back as she spoke. "Let's see how Matthew is when we get back."

Julie's anxiety increased when she entered the living room. Matthew was pacing up and down the living room and an air of impatience hung over him as he momentarily stopped when he saw his wife. But miraculously when he spoke his voice was more animated than Julie had heard in months.

"I'm glad you're home, darling." He stopped his pacing and there was an excitement about him, a tension, as he spoke. "I'm going back to work, I'm going back next Monday."

Before he managed to say anything more Julie crossed the room, her arms embracing him and kissing him passionately as all her anxiety evaporated. "Oh, Matthew, I'm so glad, so very glad."

"Superintendent Hirst thinks there might be an informer in our police force and he wants me to be the one to investigate it. That's about all I can tell you, obviously it's all very top secret. So the Superintendent

isn't telling anything much." Matthew returned Julie's embrace holding her tightly in his arms. "But today he really helped me realise that I must try and get justice for Dad and they made me see too, how awful this has been for you and Jason. I've been so selfish, I know, but it was the guilt I felt that it should have been me lying there, not my father. But I am beginning to see there was nothing I could do that awful day to change things. But at least I can do my best to bring whoever was responsible to justice. In the meantime," and Matthew managed a glimmer of his old smile, "let's go and interrupt Jason at his homework and tell him his father is going back to work. I have neglected him so much – and you, darling – but I will try to make it up to you."

Julie, overcome with emotion, could not answer, but silently thanked God that Matthew was possibly on the road to recovery at last.

Chapter 65

Lucie had risen earlier than usual, it was Sunday morning and normally Paul and she tried to get a little extra rest in bed, even if it meant bringing the kids in beside them. But today Lucie was anxious to have everything prepared for dinner well in advance. Matthew, Julie and Jason were going to join them later on in the day. When Matthew had rung to tell her the news that he had returned to work a week ago Lucie was hopeful that, somehow, Matthew was beginning to climb out of that black pit of despair he had been in. Eagerly she had invited him for dinner and then, as an afterthought, decided to include Thomas and Charles and their families. Her mother would be here as usual, occupying herself playing with the children or taking them for walks and invariably she was accompanied on these walks by Tom, Lucie's father-in-law. Lucie had found Tom's support and friendship for her mother a true blessing, and she knew that he alone, had helped her mother enormously in those dark days following Rob's murder. After Rob's death, Paul and she had managed to persuade Paul's father to move in to live with them. Initially Tom had insisted he would only stay for a few days, but then a farmer in Poyntzpass had offered him a very attractive sum of money for his house. After some discussion with Paul, the decision was made to sell and Tom had moved in lock, stock and barrel in the space of a few days. He had his own sitting room, bedroom and bathroom, and patio doors from his bedroom led out to a secluded area of the garden. This way he maintained a good measure of independence.

Secretly Lucie wished her mother would decide to come and live with them too. But she insisted on staying in her new home, even though Lucie had begged her to come to her.

"Mum, this house is large enough for us all, and I do worry about you all by yourself. We can do a bit of conversion and make another annex for you – like Tom has."

"Lucie, the gate lodge was bought for Rob and I. We had just finished decorating it the way we wanted it, all my memories are there. Besides, love, I'm only sixty-two, I consider that too young to move in with relatives, besides, I'm only a stone's throw from you. We visit each other often, even Tom, bless him, pops in regularly and it can't be that enjoyable for him at times, because we usually end up talking about our losses and sharing our grief."

Lucie was always ready to reassure her mother that Tom's and her time together seemed to help Tom as much as it helped Ellen. He returned home with a lighter step and a brighter expression on his face.

By three o'clock that afternoon Lucie had everything prepared for her family's arrival. Paul and Tom had taken the children for a walk over to her mother's house and intended to return around 4 p.m. with Ellen, who insisted she would help with the children's meal in the kitchen before the adults were served theirs in the dining room.

Now Lucie regretted agreeing to Paul and the children going out. She was alone in the house – alone with her grief and sorrow – and the awful emptiness and silence brought the realisation starkly to her that her father would be absent from this, her first semblance of a family get together since his death, and he would never ever be present again. The finality of his absence from all their lives was truly brought home to her, as she sat weeping uncontrollably for his absence in her life. Yet, in spite of her despair and tears, Lucie knew today was important. For their sakes, they must remain constant to one another, and even more importantly for their children's sake, Most especially, Lucie felt they must welcome Matthew and Julie's wonderful news of a baby on the way. Matthew and Julie had told them all last week of her pregnancy, and everyone was hopeful this new life would bring Matthew the comfort and peace he so desperately needed in his life.

Now with sheer determination and will Lucie forced herself to go upstairs and make herself presentable for her brothers and their families. She hoped that today would somehow help them to take courage from one another to be strong and try to bear what was so unbearable.

"Sheila, Jenny and I are going to do all the washing up," Julie stated firmly as she moved her chair back from the table. "After such a beautiful meal it's the least we can do, and..." she nodded over to Paul and Tom seated facing her, "...what say you entertain the children for a while in the playroom – it would give Ellen and her family a little while to spend with one another."

Instinctively Ellen rose from her seat and putting her arm around her daughter-in-law said, "It is thoughtful of you, Julie, but this precious pregnancy, are you sure it isn't too much for you? Oughtn't you to rest more?"

"I never felt better and the exercise is good for me." Julie was anxious to reassure her mother-in-law.

"If that's the case we'll move into the drawing room. But please join us as soon as you've everything cleared up."

Lucie's drawing room was her favourite room in the house. It was quite a formal, spacious room with French doors leading onto the patio and arbour at one end. At the other side a Georgian window looked out over the green lawn sweeping down to the box hedgerow beyond. Today Paul had lit a log fire which glittered and sparkled against the marble surround of the fireplace, making the ambiance relaxing and restful.

Two pale turquoise velvet settees and two armchairs were placed in a semi circle around the fire and now as Lucie led the way into the room, she was glad she had decided to invite everyone here today. Surely the company of one another would help sustain them and find comfort and solace.

After everyone had been seated – Ellen and Lucie together on one sofa, Thomas and Charles on the other and Matthew in the comfortable armchair, there was a long silence. Matthew was the first to speak and he addressed his mother.

"Mum, Lucie told me last week that you have written to the parents of the two RUC officers blown up by the IRA bomb in Crossmaglen a couple of weeks ago."

"Was that the right thing to do, Matthew?" Ellen sounded unsure. "I felt I should show some empathy for them. I wanted to let them know I am thinking of them and what they must be coming through."

"I think it was a wonderful and very brave thing for you to do." Matthew's voice was warm as he spoke. "I would never have thought of it. Of such a compassionate gesture – I must say. I just thought in terms of getting back to work and finding out who is responsible for these, horrific cowardly attacks – and now," Matthew hesitated as he looked at his brothers, then Lucie and his mother – as they sat listening to him, "we think we might be on to something. I am doing a bit of undercover work. It is early days – and I can't say anything about it. But I will do anything to get justice for Dad. It's the least I can do." He added, "I am just sorry it took me so long to realise this is what I want to do above anything. Get justice for Dad."

"Be careful, son." Ellen was anxious about what exactly the undercover work might entail. "Don't, please, take any risks. They are so ruthless."

"I promise. I will be on the alert at all times. Please don't worry, Mum."

"Whether the terrorist responsible for your father's death is ever brought to justice or not, it must never be allowed to interfere with our memories and before the others join us," Ellen went on, "I need to emphasize to you all how much your father really loved you. As you very well know, I'm not one for long emotional speeches, but this is so important to me, to say this. It was because of his love for us all he fought his drink addiction so hard. He succumbed often but in the end he mastered it. And it is because of his love for us we have lost him. I want you all to remember that and that we must forever be proud of him."

Chapter 66

1972 June

Matthew glanced at the clock on the dashboard for the umpteenth time as the car inched along the Malone Road. It was now six-thirty p.m. and he was anxious to return home to his own house – to Julie, Jason and their week old baby girl; a baby girl as yet unnamed by either of her parents. Julie, for some reason or other, had only considered boys' names for this surprise, but oh, so welcome, baby.

But first he must see his sister, it was imperative he talked to her. He had decided to call with her after his shift was finished, but because of the events that had unfolded he had been much later leaving headquarters. That delay meant he had hit the rush hour traffic and the journey to Lucie's now seemed endless. He only hoped Paul and she would be at home. He reckoned they should be because Lucie always liked to get her children to bed early. As he drove towards Malone Park where Lucie and his mother lived, he was able to make better headway and as he turned into Lucie's drive the clock told him it was a quarter to seven. He was relieved to see both Paul's Mercedes and Lucie's Volkswagen parked ahead of him in the driveway. After locking his car, he proceeded to walk to the front door, but before he could ring the bell, it was opened by his sister.

"Matthew, this is a surprise. Come in, the children have gone to bed, and Paul should be down from them in a moment or two." Lucie ushered Matthew into their hall as she continued. "He likes to see them before they go to sleep. I'm just clearing up the kitchen – will we sit in there? I'll make some tea, would you like something to eat? Cake – or perhaps a sandwich?"

"Tea would be fine, Lucie, but nothing to eat. Julie will have dinner ready, I'm sure." And Matthew pulled out a chair and sat down at the long, pine table Lucie used daily for her family's meals.

"Matthew, apart from when I called with Julie and you last week to celebrate the birth of your beautiful new daughter we haven't seen very much of you recently. Your work load must be very heavy at the moment, I presume. Mum was here earlier and was saying the same thing."

"I know. I had some important work to do, but I think I'll be having a bit of a break at the beginning of next week. I'll call to see Mother then, how is she by the way?"

"She keeps herself busy, walks down here and helps with the children and she seems to enjoy Tom's company. She sometimes calls in in the evening to his annex and plays cards with him or he walks down the drive to visit her." Lucie set down steaming mugs of tea for them both. "I must say, they have helped one another cope with their grief. You know what Tom was like after Paul's mother's death. We were in despair about him."

Matthew, while he drank his tea, was listening to Lucie, but he was anxious to hear Paul's step on the stairs. He was just about to ask after him, when he appeared in the kitchen in his dressing gown and slippers, which explained why Matthew had not heard him approach. He greeted Matthew warmly.

"Excuse the dressing gown and slippers, I have to pretend I too, am going to bed, otherwise my son would be very disappointed."

Matthew waited until Paul was seated at the table beside them with a cup of tea, then decided quickly he must let them know, before the conversation drifted on, the real reason for his visit. "I needed to call with both of you, tonight, Lucie," he began, "I have some news for you. It's very serious and I know it will come as a great shock to you."

"What is it, Matthew?" Lucie had gone quite pale and Matthew cursed himself that he was the one who had to tell his sister this.

"We arrested Patrick Mullan today – for being an informer for the IRA."

For a second, Lucie looked stunned. Then she cried out in shock and horror and her hands flew to her face in an attempt to steady herself. Immediately Paul moved close to her and encircled her in his arms, nodding at Matthew to continue.

"He has been remanded in custody and will appear in court on charges of having relayed information likely to be of use to terrorists and of collusion with an illegal organisation." Matthew looked across at his sister – she was deathly pale – did she understand so quickly the implications of her ex-husband's arrest and the possible implications with their father's death?

"I'm very sorry, Lucie – Paul – but I had to tell you. I didn't want you hearing it on the news as I'm sure it will be." Even as Matthew spoke Lucie made a visible effort to pull herself together. And although when she spoke her voice was low, it was resolute.

"Thank you, Matthew for coming to tell us." She took a deep breath and went on. "I want to know everything. Please, Paul," as her husband made to interrupt, "Don't you see I must know everything, every last detail. And I'm fine now really, it was just such a shock, that's all."

"Are you sure you're ready for it all, Lucie – Paul, what do you think?"

"If Lucie wants to know that's fine by me. She may regret not hearing everything you know, Matthew."

"I'll try to tell it as it happened then, right from the beginning."

Matthew had only been back at work a few days when his Superintendent asked to see him in his private office. Here he informed Matthew he must change his appearance as he needed him to visit places where the IRA were thought to meet for drinks and to plan their atrocities. Because of the publicity around his father's death, and although Matthew's link or any photographs of him were never published, they needed to be extra careful. With this latest investigation he would be taking serious risks.

One of the places Matthew was detailed to go to was Crossmaglen, thought to be an IRA stronghold and although he was aware his former brother-in-law worked there, he thought very little about it. But just the same, he would prefer Patrick Mullan did not recognise him. He was reasonably satisfied with his changed appearance after Julie had dyed his hair and eyebrows a deep auburn colour and bought him rimless spectacles. Indeed he doubted if any of his former colleagues would know him. Besides, during his time on sick leave he had lost almost two stone in weight; this alone had drastically altered his appearance.

He had been instructed to visit one of the public houses in Crossmaglen, which had been under surveillance for some time. It was frequented by men who were known by the police to be in the IRA.

On his second visit to the pub, when he was standing at the bar, having ordered himself a beer, he was shocked to see Patrick Mullan enter and go straight over to two young men seated at a table in the corner. They pulled out a chair for him and as he sat down his eyes swept over to the bar and barman. Matthew froze as he watched him, but he showed not the least sign of recognition of him, and Matthew realised then his disguise was most effective.

Later, on reporting back and looking at profiles of IRA suspects, he quickly identified the two men to his superiors. After that evening, Matthew was convinced they had found their informer. The next step was to find access to Patrick Mullan's flat and telephone and have them bugged when Patrick was known to be safely at work.

It was some time before they gathered sufficient evidence, during which Matthew often wondered if perhaps his ex brother-in-law had been tipped off. But then he realised that – with his police training – Patrick would know to be ultra careful. Then, one evening, they struck lucky, when one of the bugged devices relayed Patrick's voice repeating police constables' car registration numbers and addresses to other acquaintances when they visited him and again on his phone. Four armed police had gone to his house and arrested him at six o'clock the very next morning.

Lucie and Paul had been listening intently to Matthew's narrative and when he had finished he looked at them both. "That's about it. That's all I can tell you at present. There will be lots more when he's charged, no doubt." He rose from his seat, then hugging Lucie and shaking Paul's hand, quietly said he would let himself out. He knew they needed time together after the news he had brought.

"I'll stop with Mum on the way past and let her know and I'll ask her to let Thomas and Charles know. It's for the best they hear it from me. Not through the media."

"Tom has just gone up to her, Matthew. He talked about going to play a game of cards with her. He will be able to offer her some support. It will come as a shock to her as well."

"Good." Matthew was relieved to hear his mother had company, it meant he wouldn't have to stay long. He was exhausted and had found relaying such news to his sister soul destroying. Now he just wanted to get home to Julie and his family.

Chapter 67

After Matthew left, Lucie and Paul sat together at the kitchen table in silence. Paul – conscious of the shock such news had given and the implications of everything Matthew had told them – enveloped his wife in his arms in an effort to ease the impact. But Lucie, usually so pliant and relaxed in his arms remained still and unresponsive.

"Lucie darling, if you want to talk, to talk about Patrick Mullan, I'm here, darling. I don't mind what you want to talk about. Patrick Mullan can do us no harm, he is in custody." And Paul began to caress his wife's hands and shoulders in an effort to bring some heat to her body – she felt so cold. Then she began to speak, in such a low voice, Paul had to bend down to hear her, and the words she spoke filled him with despair.

"It's all my fault my dad is dead. I know it in my heart. Before there's any court case I know that my ex-husband was involved in some way in everything." Her voice began to rise and Paul felt she was on the verge of hysteria.

"All these years we thought he had accepted the divorce, but deep down he must have been harbouring resentment and spite ever since."

"Lucie, please," Paul interrupted her flow, "we don't known that, besides there is no way you must blame yourself. When you married him you trusted him and believed in him. He, and he alone, broke that trust."

"But if I'd never met him, I believe Dad would still be alive." Lucie had withdrawn her hands from Paul and was now wringing them in a pathetic, distracted way, which tore at Paul's heart.

"Lucie, darling, it was the IRA who did the shooting, please don't lose sight of that." Again Paul pulled her close to him and seemingly worn out by her outburst she leaned her head against his chest.

"Shall I make tea or perhaps we should have something stronger. How about a brandy? It would steady us both I think."

Lucie nodded and even attempted a half smile. Encouraged by this, Paul rose and went over to the drinks cabinet. Just as he was pouring the brandy into glasses he heard a step in the hall and was relieved when the kitchen door opened and his father and his mother-in-law appeared. Ellen went straight over to her daughter and wrapping her arms around her, held her in a tight embrace.

"Matthew called and told us, love, and we came straight over. I do know it is going to be very hard for you, Lucie. It will be hard for us all, but so much more for you – he was your husband. It will take all our reserves to deal with this grim bit of news. But we must remember we have survived Rob's death and this latest information is nothing besides that. You must not let this monster divide you and your family and you must not let your past relationship with him and his behaviour define you."

"Oh, Mum, you are wonderful, you really are and you're right of course. I just feel contaminated in some way by my association with him."

"Lucie, you were innocent, little more than a child when you met him. Look at you now – the mother of two perfect children," Ellen moved to fetch the glasses from Paul, "so come on, we'll have a drink. Tom and I arrived in such good time." And Ellen began distributing the drinks before joining Tom at the kitchen table.

"I don't think we will be going to bed for a time, Lucie, so I propose we go into the drawing room and sit in comfort," Paul suggested, then added, "You probably want to watch the news later, anyway." Taking Lucie's arm he led the way to the drawing room, with Ellen and Tom carrying the four glasses.

Ellen had been surprised to see Matthew at that time of the evening and was deeply shaken and horrified at the news he brought them. Her thoughts quickly turned to Lucie and she realised her daughter would blame herself for having brought Patrick into the family. She knew she needed to be with her at

356

this time. After Matthew had left them and she had told Tom she intended to go to Lucie's at once, he was in total agreement. Dear Tom, he had proved himself to be such a support to her in the agonising months since Rob's death. Many times she had felt she could not go on, she missed Rob's presence so very much, she missed the sound of his key in the door, his step in the hall and his voice as he called out her name. But most of all she missed his warm lean body in bed. The long desolate nights had been unbearable and then Tom had suggested they go for a walk in the evenings, or play a game of cards, followed by a quiet drink and a chat together. Gradually, some of the sharpness of her grief and pain had eased over the last couple of months, and Ellen felt stronger, more able to cope. But now, more than ever, she knew she was going to have to be strong in the days that lay ahead. God alone knew what news would unfold about Patrick Mullan during his court case.

Now, sitting in her daughter's house with Lucie and her husband and Tom she felt prepared to deal with anything unsavoury they might learn.

Just before the news came on, Thomas rang and then five minutes later Charles. Both boys were anxious that Lucie knew their thoughts were with her. At 9 p.m. the Northern Ireland news stated that a man had been arrested in Crossmaglen on charges of being in collusion with an illegal organisation and of passing information likely to be of use to them. No name was given, but he was arraigned to appear in court on the following morning and quietly Ellen decided to prepare herself and Lucie for what might be ahead.

Chapter 68

"Patrick, when you do wrong you must confess your sins before God. It is the only way you have any chance of ever getting to Heaven. Do you really want to go to hell?" Mrs Mullan's voice was desperate. Tomorrow her darling son would be brought to the high court and charged with conspiracy with the IRA and aiding and abetting murder. Over the past four weeks she had appealed to him relentlessly to think of his soul and to repent of his sins. She knew the evidence against him was overwhelming, he had told her that himself. So why he was not prepared to plead guilty and face the consequences she had no idea. Now, facing him at the small table in the prison's visitors' room she gripped his hand tightly.

"I beg you, Patrick, give God a chance to forgive you. Who knows – then the Hamptons might find it in their hearts to forgive you too. You certainly owe it to that family, especially Lucie. Don't put them through the torture of a long arduous trial, having to listen to gruesome evidence. Please don't do it, Patrick." Theresa rose from her seat. "I'm going straight to the chapel now to pray for you, son, and I intend to be in court tomorrow." Giving her son's hands a final tight grasp, she turned and left just as a prison officer arrived to take him back to his cell.

The court was already packed to capacity when Charles and Thomas arrived to witness the trial of their ex brother-in-law. Much discussion had gone on in the family in an effort to decide who, if any of them ought to go. Matthew would be there as a witness for the prosecution and in his professional role, but Thomas and Charles both felt they wanted to be there too, to see justice for their father. Lucie, Paul and Ellen seemed quite happy with this decision, as the women felt it would be too traumatic to hear what the judge would have to say.

With great difficulty Thomas and Charles finally made their way to the back of the visitors' gallery where they had spotted two seats and very gratefully they sank into them, thankful they had decided to arrive when they did. They would either have had to stand or worse, not have gained any access at all.

The noise had been incredible as the men made their way to their seats, but suddenly an awesome silence had ensued, the judge had arrived. Lawyers and police moved back from the front of the court to allow the judge proper access. Then the jury took their seats. This was quickly followed by the prisoner being brought to the dock by two uniformed officers. The deadly silence that had ensued as the prisoner was led in was suddenly broken in the most unexpected manner, when the lawyer for the defence stood up and addressed the judge. "My Lord, my client wishes to change his plea to guilty. Guilty on all charges, My Lord."

Then pandemonium broke out, and a lawyer, whom Thomas thought must be for the prosecution – stood up and began to speak, "My Lord."

Firmly the judge interrupted him. "This court is adjourned – we will reconvene at 2 p.m. this afternoon." He brought his hammer down. "Court dismissed."

Thomas and Charles looked at one another in total wonder. "Thank God. Charles, thank God. Hopefully now, we are going to be spared a lot of trauma."

"Aye, Thomas." Charles nodded over towards the lawyer who had attempted to address the Judge. "I think he's pretty disappointed though and who could blame him. I'm sure there are many here today who would have liked to see Patrick Mullan brought low in that dock over there. Let's hope, just because he has changed his plea, he won't get off too lightly."

"Charles, I see Mrs Mullan over there, in the front row, she has her rosary in her hands. It must be such a nightmare for her. She didn't deserve any of this."

"Well if we get a chance to speak to her on the way out we will."

And the two brothers were able to convey their sympathy to Mrs Mullan in her time of trouble. Patrick Mullan was sentenced to ten years in prison, the judge stating that because of his guilty plea he had not given him a life sentence. As Patrick was led from the dock, he was resigned to his fate, and thanks to his mother's influence felt he deserved just such a punishment.

When Ellen learned later from Charles and Thomas that Patrick Mullan had pleaded guilty to the charges she was relieved Lucie would not have to listen to and read much about the depths to which her ex-husband had sunk in his pursuit of revenge.

Lucie stood, still and quiet in the hall, the letter in her hands. She wanted on one hand to go into the living room and put it in the fire, but something stopped her, a sense of fatality, of finality of everything that had gone before.

When one of Matthew's colleagues, an Inspector Jackson, had arrived at her door earlier she had greeted him with fear and trepidation. But then, since her father's murder, anxiety was her constant companion, especially if she had to have dealings with anyone in uniform. The Inspector had hastened to explain he was covering for Matthew while he was off on leave. Inspector Jackson had informed her in a very matter of fact manner that a prisoner by the name of Patrick Mullan had tried to commit suicide by slashing his wrists. Thanks to the lightning fast actions of a prison officer who had found him and expertly administered First Aid, his life had been saved and he was recovering well in Lagan hospital. Inspector Jackson went on to tell her that a letter addressed to Lucie had been found in Patrick's locker. The prison officer who had found the letter had duly handed it into his superiors, who confirmed the letter was genuine and instructed it to be delivered to Lucie.

"Are you alright, Mrs Greenlees?" Matthew Hampton's sister had gone so pale and still when he had handed her the letter that John Jackson secretly berated himself for his thoughtlessness and lack of tact. He knew this beautiful girl had once been married to Patrick but it was some time ago. He had thought approaching the matter in a cool detached way was more respectful, but now her pallor and awful stillness alarmed him. "Will you be alright, Mrs Greenlees? Do you want to sit down? Have a glass of water perhaps?"

Lucie, aware she was alarming this young man, made a visible effort to pull herself together, assured him she'd be fine. With that he had to be content and saying his goodbyes made his way down the drive, aware the front door had closed immediately he had left her. Obviously she wished to be alone.

Lucie made her way into the kitchen and sitting down at the table determinedly tore the envelope open and unfolded the letter. The old but still familiar hand writing leapt out at her, evoking a sad mixture of memories of time past.

Dear Lucie,

You will no doubt be shocked, when you hear the news of my suicide. Me – I'm such a coward – to have the courage to actually kill myself. Ironic isn't it? The stark truth is that I cannot live with the enormity of what happened to your father, and my part, however unwittingly, I played in it. When they told me no one would be killed, just cars and houses wrecked, I foolishly believed them. Now I know how evil they are – as am I. I want you to know, dear Lucie, that I have never held any bitterness towards you. You were quite justified in divorcing me and I need you more than anything to believe that. I deserved it when you left me just as I deserved the sentence I received last month. No, Lucie, I was jealous and resentful of Matthew, how well he had done. And I knew that because of my record of violence towards you, I would never be anything more than a constable. I blamed him for everything, when I only had myself to blame. You were absolutely right to divorce me. I was prepared to accept my punishment like a man, but the consequences of my actions on your family and how it has savaged them is too much. When you receive this letter I shall be dead. I only wish for your happiness, Lucie and if you can find it in your heart to visit my mother from time to time – she has suffered so much – it would be wonderful. And perhaps someday you will be able to forgive me.

Patrick.

Chapter 69

From the window of his sitting room Matthew looked out at his well tended garden. He was gazing at it, but not seeing the green lawn with its rose bushes and neat hedges. He was instead, reflecting on the phone call he had had from Lucie some fifteen minutes ago. The phone call, her tone of voice, her insistence that her mother and Tom remain with him until she arrived was troubling him. She was already on her way, she informed him and she had contacted Paul, Charles and Thomas to come to Matthew's house as well.

He could only guess it was something to do with Patrick Mullan's attempted suicide. His supervisor had telephoned him earlier that morning to let him know and had assured Matthew the prisoner would make a full recovery. Perhaps it had nothing to do with her ex-husband's suicide attempt, because Lucie, thankfully, did not sound unduly distressed. Rather she sounded much calmer than she had been since her father's death.

The sound of Thomas's car in the drive, followed almost immediately by Charles was so reassuring to him. At least all the family would be together when their sister arrived – he instinctively felt they were going to need one another, although as to why they would, he had no idea.

From the sitting room he heard Julie open the front door for his brothers and their families and as he made to go and welcome them, he spotted Paul walking up the drive. His brother-in-law must have left his car at home, but where was Lucie?

"Charles, Thomas – everyone – Paul, we may go into the sitting room and wait for Lucie. I gather none of you have any idea what this is all about." The men looked at one another and slowly shook their heads. Matthew put an arm around Paul's shoulder as he led the way back into the room he had just vacated.

"Was Lucie not at home when you arrived in from work?" Matthew realised Paul was as much in the dark as any of them when with a puzzled look on his face, Paul just shook his head again.

"Would anyone like a drink while we're waiting? Tea or coffee?"

"Coffee would be good," Thomas said and Paul and Charles agreed.

"I'll get it." Julie proceeded into the kitchen, where Sheila, Jenny and the children were all trying to gather around baby Emily fast asleep in Ellen's arms. Julie was relieved to see the women and children were not nearly as concerned as the men were as to Lucie's reason for everyone's presence here.

Julie was just carrying the coffee into the men, when they heard the sound of Lucie's car and then her step in the drive. Matthew hurried to open the door for her, and looking questionably into her face, gave her an endearing hug by way of reassurance and support.

"Matthew, it's so good to see you. I have so much to tell you."

Lucie, setting her keys on the hall table, went on, "I need everyone in the living room, Matthew, to hear what I have to say. Perhaps the youngest children don't need to be there, but certainly Jason. He's old enough and strong enough to hear what I have to say to you all."

"Right, I'll fetch them from the kitchen."

Lucie, on entering the room went straight to Paul and embraced him tightly. When everyone was seated comfortably Lucie looked round at all the family and her eyes came to rest on her mother where she sat, Tom by her side and her new granddaughter on her knee. Then she proceeded, in a strong, warm voice to speak.

"I have a letter here which I received this morning and I want you all to hear what it says."

Lucie began reading the letter from Patrick, slowly and deliberately, and the words she spoke seemed to reverberate around the room and fill the air with pain and despair. And the silence that followed when Lucie set the letter down on the table beside her was both agonizing and expectant. Someone must respond, but the family seemed incapable of any response. And then Lucie spoke again in a more uncertain tone, not sure of how the rest of her words would be received.

"I have just come from the hospital – I visited Patrick there this afternoon."

There was an audible gasp from Ellen and when Lucie glanced at her mother, she saw her mother had gone deadly pale, and Lucie felt a moment of panic. Was it all too much to expect her mother to cope? But she felt bound to continue, to let the family know what exactly she had done. She would have to accept the consequences of her actions.

"I had to go, you see. I felt another man's death wouldn't solve anything. It is true, I wanted him punished but I don't want him dead. There have been too many deaths. Our father, other fathers, brothers, husbands. It is all so futile. And what of Patrick's parents, haven't they suffered too?" Lucie knew she was rambling on now, anxious her family, especially Paul, would try to understand her reasons for going to the hospital.

It was Paul who spoke next, he moved closer to his wife and taking her hands in his said, "Tell us about it, it must have been so very difficult for you."

Lucie nodded and giving Paul a half smile continued. "When I was shown into the ward I had difficulty finding Patrick. He is a mere shell of what he used to be. It was in fact his bandaged wrists which identified him. When he saw me, he tried to sit up, but fell back on the pillows and began to weep. It was an agonizing sight, to see him brought so low, and perhaps I was wrong to have any pity for him, but pity I had."

Lucie stopped and looked at her brothers and her mother.

"I'm sorry if you think I did wrong but I had to do it. He begged me to forgive him and I promised him I would, if he promised he would not attempt suicide again. In turn I begged him to think of his parents, what they have been through, and stressed he must confide in his parents, talk to them. Talk to his parish priest and beg God to forgive him."

Lucie looked earnestly at her husband standing beside her and addressed her next words directly at him.

"Since I visited him, I feel absolved from the guilt I have been harbouring. It was the best thing I have done since my dear father died, it was so cathartic." Still holding Paul's hand she made her way to the nearest seat in the room and sat down.

Charles was the first to move from his seat and coming over to Lucie hugged her closely. "I, for one, am glad you have found some peace, Lucie, because I know you have been torturing yourself and blaming yourself. Patrick Mullan's letter has shown us all his attitude was mostly to do with his feelings of inadequacy in a competitive world, and less to do with his marriage." Then Charles added in an uncertain voice, "Whether I can ever find it in my heart to forgive him for his role in terrorism and his betrayal of our family, remains to be seen, Lucie, but I don't resent you for what you have done, rather I admire your courage."

Matthew, who had been sitting pale and still, spoke harshly. "Personally I think you have let your pity for the shell that is Patrick Mullan cloud your judgment, Lucie and I feel it demeans our father and everyone else who has suffered at the hands of the terrorists. I certainly will never forget their actions and atrocities." His voice was cold and distant towards Lucie as he spoke.

Thomas seemed overcome with all the emotion of the last couple of hours and in a voice fraught with feeling tried to defend his sister's actions. "I'm sure Lucie feels, as I do, Matthew, that Father would be proud of her and what she has done today and the last thing he would wish is that any of us would become estranged over this tragedy. Lucie was very brave today as Father was on that other, fateful one and he has left a wonderful legacy for his grandchildren and we will always ensure he is remembered by them with pride and devotion."

Meanwhile Ellen, overcome with this latest development and deeply thankful Lucie had found peace, sat quietly contemplating her family's future. She prayed Matthew would not estrange himself from his sister because of her actions, even though she understood all he had suffered on that awful day and was still suffering. She prayed Matthew would become reconciled to Lucie's all forgiving manner to the atrocity. She was prepared to accept feelings ran very deep and some legacy might be left as a result of their tragedy. Sitting quietly now with Tom, she prayed he would remain constant to her, she needed him in her life, but it was too soon to contemplate any future with anyone because she had loved Rob unconditionally.

For now, Thomas's words had had such a profound effect on her she knew all the generations in the future must know the sacrifice Rob had made. She knew she wanted to add some additional words to his headstone. She felt "Rob Hampton 1908 – 1972, shot by the IRA while shielding his son" was not enough. She needed to see the words, "Greater love hath no father than this" added. Those words would be, she believed, the ultimate legacy of Rob's love.